Acclaim for Christina Courtenay's enth

'Seals Christina Courtenay's crown as the Q
Catherine Miller

'This epic romance is sure to sweep you off your feet!'
Take A Break

'A love story and an adventure, all rolled up inside a huge amount of intricately detailed, well-researched history. Thoroughly enjoyable'
Kathleen McGurl

'Christina Courtenay is guaranteed to carry me off to another place and time in a way that no other author succeeds in doing'
Sue Moorcroft

'The Queen of Time Slip Romance has done it again! A romantic and compelling read – a total page-turner'
Sandy Barker

'A brilliantly written time slip that combines mystery and romance into a compelling and vividly imagined story'
Nicola Cornick

'A wonderful dual timeline story with captivating characters and full of vivid historical detail bringing the Viking world alive, I didn't want it to end!'
Clare Marchant

'An absorbing story, fast-paced and vividly imagined, which really brought the Viking world to life'
Pamela Hartshorne

'Prepare to be swept along in this treasure of an adventure! With a smart, courageous heroine and hunky, honourable hero at the helm, what's not to like?'
Kate Ryder

'Christina Courtenay's particular talent is to entice you into her world and capture you'
Alison Morton

'I was totally captivated by this story of love and adventure which had me racing through the pages . . . I was drawn into the Viking world so easily which felt authentic and real'
Sue Fortin

Christina Courtenay is an award-winning author of historical romance and time slip (dual time) stories. She started writing so that she could be a stay-at-home mum to her two daughters, but didn't get published until daughter number one left home aged twenty-one, so that didn't quite go to plan! Since then, however, she's made up for it by having sixteen novels published and winning the RNA's Romantic Novel of the Year Award for Best Historical Romantic Novel twice with *Highland Storms* (2012) and *The Gilded Fan* (2014), and once for Best Fantasy Romantic Novel with *Echoes of the Runes* (2021).

Christina is half Swedish and grew up in that country. She has also lived in Japan and Switzerland, but is now based in Herefordshire, close to the Welsh border. She's a keen amateur genealogist and loves history and archaeology (the armchair variety).

To find out more, visit **christinacourtenay.com**, find her on Facebook **/Christinacourtenayauthor** or follow her on Twitter **@PiaCCourtenay**, and Instagram **@christinacourtenayauthor**.

By Christina Courtenay

Standalones
Trade Winds
Highland Storms
Monsoon Mists
The Scarlet Kimono
The Gilded Fan
The Jade Lioness
The Silent Touch of Shadows
The Secret Kiss of Darkness
The Soft Whisper of Dreams
The Velvet Cloak of Moonlight
Hidden in the Mists

The Runes novels
Echoes of the Runes
The Runes of Destiny
Whispers of the Runes
Tempted by the Runes
Promises of the Runes

Promises *of the* Runes

CHRISTINA COURTENAY

First published in 2023
by HEADLINE REVIEW
An imprint of HEADLINE PUBLISHING GROUP

1

Cataloguing in Publication Data is available from the British Library

ISBN 978 1 4722 9319 0

Typeset in Minion Pro by Avon DataSet Ltd, Alcester, Warwickshire

Printed and bound in Great Britain by Clays Ltd, Elcograf S.p.A.

Headline's policy is to use papers that are natural, renewable and recyclable products and made from wood grown in well-managed forests and other controlled sources. The logging and manufacturing processes are expected to conform to the environmental regulations of the country of origin.

HEADLINE PUBLISHING GROUP
An Hachette UK Company
Carmelite House
50 Victoria Embankment
London EC4Y 0DZ

www.headline.co.uk
www.hachette.co.uk

To Sue Moorcroft and Maggie Sullivan (aka Myra Kersner),
extraordinary friends and fellow authors, huge thanks
for your support, encouragement and friendship!

Prologue

The dream was always the same – they were coming for her.

She could hear them, sense them, smell them, their excitement an almost tangible current in the air. Like hunting dogs scenting prey, their shouts were high-pitched and increasing in volume. The heavy footsteps drew closer, making the ground shudder. And when they caught her, she'd never be able to escape again . . .

As she waited to be discovered, her heart was racing, her chest heaving. The fear inside coalesced into a hard knot in her stomach and paralysed her limbs. A scream was building in her throat, but she swallowed it down. Even if she hadn't been tangled up in the blanket she'd hidden under, she would have been unable to move. She was a prisoner of her own terror.

But then someone lay down behind her; a human shield against those who would harm her. She was acutely aware of every part of him pressed against her, one muscular arm coming round to encircle her waist. It should have petrified her more, but it had the opposite effect. Although she couldn't see this stranger's face, she began to relax, sinking into his embrace.

'Shh, don't fret,' he murmured. His voice soothed her, the low timbre vibrating through her, spreading a calm and sensation of safety she hadn't experienced in years.

She let him pull her tighter towards him, and when he whispered, 'Trust me,' she did.

If only he'd never let her go . . .

Chapter One

Stockholm, 24 September 2021

'What are you doing?'

The question startled Ivar Thoresson and made him bang his head on the shelf above the drawer he'd been examining. 'Ouch! Er . . . nothing. I mean . . . Jeez, you scared the crap out of me! I didn't hear you come in.' Rubbing the top of his head, he glared at his foster-father, Haakon Berger.

The older man had appeared at the entrance to the aisle Ivar was standing in, which was part of a secure storage room belonging to the Historical Museum in Stockholm. They both worked there: Haakon as head archaeologist in charge of Viking items, and Ivar as a curator. Mostly it was great that they got to see so much of each other, but there were times when Ivar could have wished for slightly less supervision. Like now, for instance.

'You're in the *vōlva*'s section. I thought you were working on the warrior exhibit?' Haakon crossed his arms over his chest and leaned on a shelf post. His blue eyes were slightly narrowed, as if he suspected foul play.

He was right to do so, but Ivar couldn't allow him to find that out.

'I was. I am. I was just . . . um, returning some shears. They had been wrongly placed in the warrior section. These.' Ivar held up a small pair of iron shears decorated with an intricate pattern of inlaid silver. 'Someone must have thought they were for clipping beards or whatever, but I happened to know they were missing from the seeress's items.' He shrugged and busied himself with tidying the stuff in the drawer unnecessarily, avoiding his foster-father's sharp gaze.

'I see.' Haakon didn't sound convinced, but he let it go without making any further comment. 'You're coming over for dinner tonight, right?'

Although it had been many years since Ivar had lived with Haakon and his wife Mia, they were still close and he saw them at least once a week after work. The couple had more or less adopted him when he was orphaned at the age of fourteen, and Mia still mothered him, despite him having reached the grand old age of thirty-five. As his only blood relative, an aunt, had died recently, Haakon and Mia, together with their three children, were the only family he had. There had never been any distinctions made between him and his foster-siblings, and he loved them all the more for that. And yet . . . sometimes he itched to be left alone, though at the same time he felt immensely lonely and longed for a family of his own.

It didn't really make sense, even to him.

'Sure. I'll be there at six as usual.' He did his best to sound upbeat and as if he was looking forward to it, and Haakon seemed to buy it.

'OK, great. See you later, then.'

Ivar waited while Haakon made his way back out, shutting the storeroom door behind him, then let out a sigh of relief. The tiny shears were still in his hand, gripped so tightly they were branding a pattern into his palm. Slowly he unfurled his fingers and stared at the little object, his heart beating a rapid tattoo. This was it. The thing he'd been looking for during the last year. The holy grail. Well, sort of.

'*Yesss!*' he whispered, turning the shears over to study the runic inscription he'd found mere moments before Haakon's untimely appearance. He read it out loud. '*Með blōð skaltu ferðast.*' It meant 'With blood you shall travel' and it wasn't just a random inscription. It was magical, and Ivar knew exactly what it could do. 'Oh yeah. You can bet your boots I will,' he muttered. 'I'm going to travel through time – at last it's my turn! It has to be.'

It sounded insane when you said it out loud, but he knew it was possible. His foster-sister Linnea had done exactly that a few years ago, and so had a friend of hers. Ever since then, Ivar had been itching to follow them. They had both gone back to the Viking age, fallen in love with men from that time, and were now living there with their husbands and children. Linnea and Sara had different magical objects to transport them back and forth, but each seemed to only work specifically for them and their immediate families.

'Can't you take me with you?' he'd begged Linnea last time she came to visit her parents, but when they'd tried, it hadn't worked. They had expected it to, because she'd brought other people with her before without any problems, but only she had disappeared, while Ivar was left behind. Neither of them knew why. It was hugely frustrating.

That was when he had started looking for a magical item of his own. Because who was to say the ones Linnea and Sara had were the only time-travel devices in existence? And now he'd proved that they weren't. Or he would, as soon as he had a chance to try it out, of course. With any luck, this one would work for him.

Recently, his younger foster-sister Madison had gone missing during a trip to Ireland, and Ivar had a suspicion she too had ended up in the ninth century. The Irish garda, or police, hadn't found any trace of her, apart from a few grainy images from a CCTV camera that had captured her walking along the River Liffey. After that, it was as though she'd disappeared off the face of the earth. It couldn't be coincidence; he didn't believe in that.

The girls had all seemingly ended up in the ninth century by mistake, but Ivar intended to be more organised about it and plan everything meticulously. He'd been studying Old Norse intensively, had been buying up silver and gold items at auctions to melt down into little ingots and crude bracelets, and had taken extra lessons in self-defence, swordsmanship and a whole host of other possibly useful skills. There was no knowing what awaited him if and when he managed to travel back in time.

The only problem was keeping it all secret from Haakon and Mia, because they would try to stop him. It was dangerous – he wasn't deluding himself otherwise – and they cared about him. Even so, he was his own man and made his own decisions. This was something he was determined to do, and no one was going to get in his way.

No one.

He pushed the drawer shut, but something prevented it from sliding all the way in. Pulling it out again, he checked the items that had belonged to the Viking-age *vísindakona* – wise woman or seeress. There was the most important object, her *galdrastafr* – a staff made of iron with a sort of basket shape at the top. It must have been used as part of the magical rituals she'd practised called *seiðr*. Then there was a string of glass beads, a linked belt hung with charms, a buckle that must have formed part of a leather purse, a selection of tiny bones from birds and animals, a jar of henbane seeds, and some silver amulets. As he studied them, he had the impression that the air around him vibrated slightly, close to humming, as if it was charged with electricity. It made the hairs on his arms and the back of his neck stand up.

He shook his head. 'Now I'm getting too fanciful for words,' he muttered. They were merely inanimate objects. *No, ancient magical items.* He pushed that thought away.

The staff stuck up a little too much, and he repositioned it on its bed of soft unspun wool. That dislodged one of the charms, which looked like the foot of a swan made out of silver. Ivar had no idea of its significance, but he picked it up to return it to its proper place. The moment he touched it, however, his head started spinning and dizziness made him grab the nearest shelf. He closed his eyes and sank to the floor as his mind suddenly flooded with images of a young woman . . .

She was being manhandled towards a ship, a surly man gripping her upper arm fiercely through the cloak she had wrapped around her. Shrugging out of his grasp, she held her head high and climbed on board by herself, making her way to the stern. A pair of bronze tortoise brooches flashed in the sunlight, but were soon hidden from sight when, with a graceful sweep, she gathered the cloak more tightly around her. She sank on to a wooden chest and turned her face away. But Ivar had already seen the anger and frustration burning in her gaze, as well as the tears she was holding at bay.

The woman wasn't conventionally beautiful, but she was lovely in an other-worldly way, like a fairy-tale creature. Long, straight red-gold hair had been literally tied in a knot at the nape of her neck and hung down her back past her waist. It shone brightly in the pale sunlight, in stark contrast to the dull brown of her garments. A heart-shaped face, pale and a trifle gaunt, with high cheekbones and a straight nose that was slightly pointy at the tip, added to the fey impression. A lush mouth and clear green eyes completed the picture and made Ivar's lungs constrict.

He wanted her.

But as that thought assailed him, she turned to look straight at him, her eyes glistening with unshed tears. 'Help me,' she whispered. 'Please, help me . . .'

Ivar would have promised her anything in that moment, but he didn't get the chance. In the next instant, the vision was gone and he found himself slumped on the floor of the stockroom, more confused than he'd ever been in his life.

'What on earth . . . ?'

He stumbled to his feet, wondering exactly how hard he'd hit his head earlier, but his questing fingers didn't find so much as a small bump. The dizziness had disappeared as well, leaving him frowning at the seeress's items.

The amulet was still in the palm of his hand, hot to the touch. Was it some sort of conduit to the past? A different kind of magic to that of the time-travel device? The image of the anguished woman in his vision was seared into his mind, and he closed his fingers around the little swan's foot. Perhaps it could help him find her? If there was any chance he'd see her again, he had to keep it. Without hesitation, he slipped it into his pocket together with the shears.

If that made him a thief twice over, so be it.

'Are you OK, Ivar? You seem preoccupied.' Mia passed him the bowl of pasta bolognese and urged him to have seconds.

'I'm fine. Just, you know, been busy.'

More like totally dissatisfied with his life. In a rut, unfulfilled and seriously bored. Not to mention yearning for adventure before he got too old to enjoy the experience. But Mia didn't need to know any of that. She had a mother's keen eye and she loved him as if he was her own. He knew that she longed for him to meet the perfect woman and settle down to marriage and children, but it hadn't happened for him yet. Although he'd had a couple of serious long-term relationships, in the end they'd both fizzled out. Neither woman had been right for him and he didn't regret ending things. That didn't mean he hadn't wished to find someone else, but so far, no luck. Instead, he'd watched with growing sadness, and a certain amount of envy, as all his friends settled into domestic bliss while he was left behind, alone. Still, that meant this was the perfect time to do something reckless, as there was no one who depended on him or who'd be hurt by him leaving. Well, apart from Mia and Haakon, of course, but he hoped they would understand.

Keeping his expression neutral, he helped himself to another large portion. Pasta was good fuel for his workouts, and Mia's cooking was superb. He said as much after taking another mouthful, which made her smile, although her gaze continued to be sharper than he'd like. She didn't miss much.

'Still training at that gym?' she asked. 'You're not overdoing it, are you? It's important to relax sometimes too, and—'

'Mu-um! Give it a rest. He's an adult.' Ivar's foster-brother, Storm, interrupted her with a scowl. 'He can decide for himself.'

'I know that. I'm just concerned for his health.' Mia sent her son an irritated glance. 'I'm allowed to worry about you both. It's what mothers do.'

Ever since that trip to Ireland, there had been friction between Storm and his parents, although the comment just now was probably meant to be brotherly solidarity. It was hard to tell these days. From what Ivar could gather, Storm was supposed to have been hanging out with Madison the evening she went missing, but instead he'd gone on a pub crawl with some mates. To be fair, Maddie had been nineteen at the time and didn't need a baby-sitter, but Haakon and Mia still appeared to blame Storm for her disappearance. Ivar disagreed, but he didn't voice an opinion, as he knew that wouldn't help. He wished they'd all put it behind them, but the grief and anxiety of not knowing whether Maddie was even alive set everyone on edge. The unanswered questions hovered in the background like a malevolent thunder cloud.

He shook his head at Storm with a small smile to take the sting out of his words. 'Stop trying to stir up trouble, little bro.'

'Little? I'm growing almost daily. Officer training isn't a walk in the park, I'll have you know.'

Storm was in the Swedish army, and after a year of national service, he'd signed up for three terms of officer training, specialising in hand-to-hand combat. Like Ivar and Madison, he'd been doing martial arts since he was a kid, and the brothers had also been part of re-enactment groups for years. These honed their skills with Viking-style weapons and fighting techniques, and Ivar assumed this training came in handy in the regular army too.

'You sure?' he teased, then ducked as a punch was aimed in his direction. 'Maybe you should come to the gym with me. Looks like you need to work on your technique.'

'Sod off.'

He didn't want Storm to come, though. If he did, he'd discover that Ivar wasn't going to a normal gym at all, but was having special training sessions with historical re-enactors. Even though he had already grasped the most common sword-fighting techniques, and how to swing a battleaxe to best effect while using a shield for protection, he'd wanted to hone his skills to as near perfection as possible. That wasn't something he wished anyone to find out. It would be a dead giveaway of his intention to leave soon. As long as the magic worked this time, of course. There were no guarantees, but he had a good feeling about it.

'Speaking of mothers, I'm hoping Linnea will come for a visit this month.' Mia's expression brightened at the thought. 'She promised to bring little Estrid as soon as she's old enough to repeat the magic words. I can't wait to see her again! Our oldest grandchild . . .' She smiled at the thought.

Linnea had two children: Estrid, who was now three, and a one-year-old boy called Eskil. She'd been unable to bring them until they were old enough to say the special sentence necessary for time travel, but Mia had visited them twice. Ivar clenched his fist under the table, annoyed that his foster-mother had been able to go back in time when it hadn't worked for him. He assumed it had to be because he wasn't really a member of the Berger family, no matter how inclusive they'd always been. What other explanation could there be?

It made him feel like an outsider, despite everything.

Ever since his failed attempt, he'd watched with barely suppressed envy as the others came and went. It wasn't fair that they all seemed able to move between time periods when he was more prepared than anyone for taking a leap back to the Viking age. He'd done his homework in every way, and yet he was the only one who wasn't allowed to have such an adventure. But hopefully now he would, with the help of the magical shears he'd just found. He was so ready to experience something new, just for a while. He needed some excitement in his life, something to stir things up a bit. The years were slipping by and he'd become restless and dissatisfied. His work as a curator was no longer enough, and who knew when – or even if – he'd ever find the perfect woman? Either way, he was sure that once he'd had some adventures, he would be more ready to settle for ordinary routines. He wouldn't feel as if he'd lost out.

Chewing his pasta slowly, he glanced around the table, memorising the scene and storing it up in his mind for the future. There was no denying he'd miss these people. Haakon, a big, quiet man with a shock of white-blond hair, who'd been a rock in Ivar's life ever since his real father died. Mia, small and lithe, her curly chestnut hair in a messy bun on top of her head, always ready to smother all four children with love, including Linnea, who was Haakon's daughter by his first wife. She'd comforted Ivar, supported him, given him the confidence to believe he could do anything in life. He appreciated it more than he could ever say.

Next to his mother sat Storm, so like her in appearance but taking after his father in height and build. At only twenty-one, he was already a force to be reckoned with. Impulsive and reckless, he was nevertheless easy-going and could charm anyone when he put his mind to it. To Storm, everything in life was exciting and new, something he couldn't wait to experience. Or at least it had been until he'd lost his sister. Lately there was a new, more sombre side to him that Ivar wasn't sure he liked. Especially since he didn't think Storm was to blame and that therefore he was feeling needlessly guilty.

He suppressed a sigh. It would be hard to leave them all, but he had to. If he didn't at least try, he would regret it for the rest of his life. Now was the time. His turn.

And hopefully, one day soon, he would be sitting at this table with them all again.

Chapter Two

Thorsholm, Lake Mälaren, 25 September 2021

The following day, Ivar was in his big house overlooking Lake Mälaren when the doorbell rang. Swearing under his breath, he went to open it and found Storm outside, his expression unusually glum.

'Hello? Weren't you expected back at the academy today?' He frowned at his foster-brother, who was standing on the porch with his hands in the pockets of his jeans. Storm didn't get much time off from officer training, so it was unusual to see him two days in a row.

'No, tomorrow. Can I come in?'

'Sure.' Ivar waved him inside, hoping he hadn't left any clues lying around that would alert Storm to the fact that he'd been busy packing. 'What's up?'

His brother threw him a glance from under lowered brows. 'You do know what day it is, right?'

Ivar swallowed hard before nodding. 'Yes.'

It should have been Maddie's twentieth birthday. No, it *was* her birthday, damn it. He wouldn't give up on her so easily. She was alive somewhere. She had to be.

'I just couldn't stand to be around my parents,' Storm muttered. 'They're pretending everything is fine but walking around with long faces.'

'Well, it's understandable in the circumstances.'

Of course Mia and Haakon were upset. Birthdays and other special occasions were always the worst when you were missing someone. In this case, they had the added burden of not knowing whether Maddie was well or being mistreated, if she was even still alive. That she had ended up somewhere in the Viking age was something they all tacitly agreed on. No one had said it outright, but it was implied in most of their discussions about her disappearance. It couldn't be a coincidence that two people in their circle had already time-travelled to the same era – virtually the same year even – and Ivar knew that Haakon and Mia clung to the hope that Madison had done the same thing.

Linnea had told them she'd been a slave – a Viking's thrall – for a while, and the mere word sent shivers down his spine. That could have happened to Maddie as well, but Ivar preferred to think that she had fared better than her sister.

He led the way into the kitchen, which faced the lake and had far-reaching views across the water. It was a lovely day, the sun sparkling on the small waves, and several boats of various shapes and sizes could be seen skimming along – some with sails, others with outboard motors or oars. Ivar knew he was lucky to own this place, which he'd inherited from his father, Rolf, who'd been very well off. The house and money had been held in trust for him until he turned eighteen, but he hadn't moved in to live here by himself until he had finished his university studies. The house held mostly sad memories, but these days he considered the past over and done with. And he'd made some changes to the decor, so that the place felt more like his own.

'They still blame me.' Storm accepted the cold beer Ivar handed him, having shielded his brother's view of the fridge as he retrieved two cans. There wasn't anything else in there, since he was planning to leave this afternoon, and seeing the empty shelves would be a dead giveaway.

He didn't pretend to misunderstand. 'For Maddie vanishing? Come on, you know that's bullshit. She's not a little kid, and she's a black belt in karate. No one could have abducted her without a major fight, and someone would have noticed that and reported it to the police. I think we both know what's happened to her, and we can only hope she'll be OK there.'

Storm regarded him with green eyes that held deep sadness. It was a long way from his normally carefree expression. 'Yeah, but I was being a selfish arse, I can't dispute that. She didn't want me to go out that night. I should have listened. At least then we would have been together.'

'You weren't her keeper. If you'd been here in Stockholm, no one would have expected you to hang out with her the whole time, would they? Please stop torturing yourself. It won't do any good. Like Linnea and Sara, I'm sure she'll turn up eventually.'

He only hoped she wasn't completely traumatised by that time. Anything could happen to a woman alone in the Viking age. The other two had been lucky, but would Maddie be too?

With a sigh, Storm acquiesced. 'I suppose you're right, but I feel like I should go after her, you know?'

'What, time-travel?'

Ivar had vaguely toyed with the idea of asking Storm to go with him, but he'd decided he couldn't do that to Mia and Haakon. They'd already lost two children, and now he was about to leave as well. The least he could do was leave one behind.

'Mm-hmm. I don't know where to find a magical artefact,

though. Any ideas? You haven't by any chance come across anything in the museum's archives, have you?'

For a moment, Ivar wondered if Storm had seen through him and guessed his secret. They'd always been close, despite the big age gap between them. They might not be related by blood, but they were true brothers nonetheless. He schooled his features into a mask of innocence. 'I don't think there's anything there,' he replied, which wasn't what Storm had asked but was the truth. *Not any longer, at least, because it's in my pocket.*

'Right.' Storm looked like he was about to say something else, but changed his mind. 'Well, I guess I'd better get going then. Thanks for . . . you know, not judging me like they do. It means a lot.'

Ivar went over to his brother and gave him a bear hug. He had the fleeting thought that it might be the last time, and the poignancy weighed heavily on him, but he couldn't let it influence his decision.

'It probably makes them feel better to have someone to blame. If you think about it, it was as much their fault as yours, if anyone's. They didn't have to attend some fancy dinner and leave her behind at the hotel, did they?'

That made Storm's mouth tilt up in a small smile. 'True. And if anyone can kick Viking butt, it'd be Mads.' He sighed, growing serious again. 'I just hope she's all right and celebrating her birthday in style somewhere. She'll know we're thinking of her.'

'She is, I'm sure of it.' Ivar walked Storm to the door. 'How much longer have you got to go before you're fully trained?'

'A few more months. Then I'll have to try and find a permanent post – apparently not the easiest thing at the moment. Anyway, I'll worry about that later. See you, bro.'

Another quick hug and Storm was gone, leaving Ivar feeling

guilty in his turn. But with any luck, he wasn't going to be away for ever, and he'd see his brother again one day. At least Storm wouldn't have to wonder where Ivar had gone, as he was planning on leaving a note to explain it all. His foster-family would worry, but they'd know he had disappeared of his own free will.

Skiringssal, Vestfold, Haustmánuðr AD *875*

'You will wed Kári Knutsson in two weeks' time. I expect you to be ready to travel to Rogaland with him the following day. I need trustworthy men in position, ready to defend my realm from that *niðingr* Haraldr Hálfdanarsson. I've had reports that he's planning to usurp my domains and is turning his greedy gaze eastwards. It's intolerable!'

Ellisif Birgirsdóttír clenched her fists in the folds of her *smokkr* and blinked away the sting of tears. She refused to show any emotion in front of the king. It would only reinforce his belief that she was a weak, defenceless woman whom he could gift to a stranger at will. Exactly as he'd done ten years ago.

'You should be thanking me. Kári will make you an excellent husband – better than you could hope for. He is a warrior of some renown, and with silver aplenty. He brought back much tribute from Frakkland last time he went there.' From his elevated position sitting in an intricately carved chair on a dais at one end of his huge feasting hall, King Hjorr fixed her with a stern gaze. 'Now go, prepare yourself, and do try to summon up a less hangdog expression on the day of your nuptials.'

'Is there no one younger I could wed?' she ground out through gritted teeth. It went against the grain to beg him for any favours, but she had to at least ask.

Hjorr's eyebrows rose almost to his hairline. 'You have a yearning for a young lover to warm your bed, eh? But they wouldn't want you, old and barren as you are, because they'd need heirs. Kári already has grown-up sons, so he's not bothered. No, it's the perfect match for both of you. Now be off with you, and stop wasting my time. It is every woman's duty to make an advantageous marriage, and you must accept that I know best in this matter. Why, take my queen, for instance – sent far away to cement my alliance with her father, but never a word of protest. She's always acted with dignity, and I honour her for that. You should strive to be more like her.'

It was true that Queen Ljufvina was meek and obedient. In fact, Ellisif had never heard the woman say a word. She apparently came from Bjarmeland, a place past the end of Norðvegr – the sea route to the far north – and her looks were exotic. She stood out with her long, straight black hair, eyes like polished charcoal, and skin that was darker than that of anyone else at court. King Hjorr had married her to gain access to an endless supply of the much-sought-after walrus teeth and hides her people hunted. They had become harder to find along his own coastline, and his marriage had therefore been eminently practical. However, people whispered that he'd fallen in love with his foreign princess, as he never took other women to his bed. He also doted on their twin sons, Hámundr and Geirmundr, both of whom had the nickname *Heljarskinn* – 'the Black-Skinned'. Ellisif had seen the little boys and thought that epithet was rather an exaggeration, as their complexions were just darkly tanned rather than black, but who was she to judge? They were adorable either way.

The king clearly considered their discussion finished and waved her away. Still frustrated, but recognising the futility of trying to change his mind, she turned and stalked out of the hall without a word.

She'd wanted to scream 'I'm not old!', but having seen six and twenty winters, it was undoubtedly true. As was also, unfortunately, the fact that she was barren. She didn't feel old, though, and most people would say she still had the appearance of a much younger woman. That was the only advantage of not having had children. And compared to her own age, her future husband was positively ancient.

But if the king thought he'd won, he was mistaken. This time she wasn't a naïve sixteen-year-old; she was a woman grown. And anything would be better than being tied to another old man with the right to do whatever he wished with her person and her property. Let Kári have her domains if he must, but he'd never have *her*. She'd rather die.

'Men. The Miðgarðr serpent take them all!' she muttered under her breath.

She knew, as an orphaned heiress, that it was the king's prerogative to arrange a marriage for her, but she had expected to be consulted this time. Having been married to that disgusting goat Þjódólfr for so long, she felt she'd earned the right to choose her next husband, or at least have a say. She wasn't expecting a prince among men, but someone who wasn't too old and distasteful would have been an improvement. Or at the very least, a man who didn't seek to belittle her at every turn. But Kári was cut from exactly the same cloth as Þjódólfr, more was the pity.

Swallowing down a sob, she barged into the sleeping hut she shared with a group of other women, all in more or less the same position as herself. One of them, the kindest by far, came forward and put a hand on her arm.

'I take it the meeting didn't go well? Come, sit down for a moment. I will fetch you some ale.'

'Thank you, but no. I couldn't force down a single swallow. I . . . I'm sick to my stomach.' Ellisif wrapped her arms around her middle to try and stem the nausea.

Ingibjorg sent her a look of compassion. 'As bad as that?'

'Yes. Kári Knutsson is to be my husband in a fortnight's time.' She closed her eyes and swallowed hard. 'I can't bear it. He'll be worse than Þjódólfr, if that is possible.'

She'd told Ingibjorg a little about her life so far. Married young to a man thirty years her senior who disgusted her, she'd nevertheless managed to force herself to endure his attentions at night. There had been no other option, as the few times she'd tried to resist had resulted in harsh punishments; thereafter, self-preservation had made her stoical. During the day, he'd found fault with everything she did and had constantly belittled her in front of the entire household.

Mostly the criticism centred around the fact that she'd been unable to bear him children, but he had also discovered that her eyesight wasn't very good. This meant she'd been unable to take part in any of the more refined womanly pursuits, such as embroidery and band-weaving, as she couldn't see anything that close. Ordinary household chores were fine, but nothing else. Although it shouldn't have been important – there were lots of other women in the hall who could perform these tasks after all – Þjódólfr had pounced on her weakness. It became a never-ending source of torment, with him reviling her at every turn.

She simply couldn't go through that again.

'Oh, my dear,' Ingibjorg sighed now. 'None of us have any say, you know that. The king has heard rumours that Haraldr Hálfdanarsson is preparing to attack his kingdom, and he wants every heiress married off to a man who can help defend his lands.'

'I am aware of that, but surely there must be younger men than Kári around. Someone more capable and better at fighting. He has seen at least forty-five winters, and I cannot imagine he'd last long in a battle, although perhaps that is what I should be hoping for.' She shook her head. 'No, I never want to marry again.'

'I'm sorry. I don't see that there is anything to be done, other than accept our fate.'

There probably wasn't, but Ellisif hadn't given up yet. She had two weeks to come up with a solution, and she was willing to try anything. Anything at all.

Chapter Three

Birkiþorp, 25 September/Haustmánuðr AD *875*

When Ivar came to, he found himself face down in a mound of springy moss, his cheek slightly damp from its inherent moisture. The nausea and dizziness still roiling inside him slowly died down, and he pushed himself on to his knees.

'Jesus! That was horrible,' he muttered. *But it had worked!* At least, he thought so. He'd travelled through time, and now that he was here, he could barely believe it.

Linnea had warned him about the side-effects that day when they'd attempted to time-travel together, but he hadn't realised it would be quite this bad. He'd never felt anything like it; it was like being inside a tornado and unable to escape. Or one of those weird fairground rides where you stood against the wall of a rotating cylinder until it spun so fast you were plastered to the sides without your feet touching the ground. And much worse than when he'd had that strange vision in the museum storeroom.

'Yuck!'

Taking a few steadying breaths, he clambered to his feet and picked up the sack that contained his spare clothing. He'd brought three extra shirts, two woollen tunics, a spare pair each of linen and woollen trousers, several pairs of socks, and some mittens and a hat. Right now he was wearing more of the same, covered by a cloak fastened on one shoulder with a small bronze brooch. At his belt hung a vicious knife honed to perfect sharpness, a pouch full of silver and gold, and another with things like a sewing kit and a crude razor. A hone stone was also attached to the belt, as well as an axe, hanging heavily on his hip. In addition, his fingers were covered in gold and silver rings, and he wore quite a collection of silver armbands, mostly concealed by the sleeves of his tunic. It felt weird – he wasn't normally a jewellery kind of guy – but needs must, as they were the local currency. He hoped he'd come prepared for everything.

He took in his surroundings. It would seem he'd ended up at the edge of a forest, and before him lay a settlement. It was prosperous, judging by the size of the main hall and the large number of outbuildings. He admired the slightly curved outline of the hall's roof and the carvings around the doorway. The craftsmanship was exquisite and aesthetically pleasing, the patterns typically Viking in style. The sight of them sent a thrill through him, as they proved that he'd ended up in roughly the right time period. He would have liked to study them in detail, but now was not the time.

There were people going about their daily business, dressed in what he considered the right type of clothing for this era. Another sign that his time-travelling had been a success. As he emerged from the shade of the trees, a few of them threw him surprised glances. He supposed most visitors arrived by boat rather than on foot. There was one medium-sized ship – again, the correct shape and build for this period – and several smaller boats tied up by a jetty to his right. It would appear the ship was being readied for a journey, as there was a steady stream of items being loaded.

Ivar hesitated, then headed up the hill towards the main hall. He figured that would be the best place to start, as he could confirm that he'd ended up in the right era, and announce his presence in the least suspicious manner possible.

Just as he reached the large double doors, which stood open, a man emerged. He was huge; taller than Ivar by several inches, and broad across the shoulders. He had a shock of white-blond hair, reminiscent of Haakon's but much longer, and his piercing blue gaze immediately fastened on Ivar with a frown.

'Greetings,' he said politely. 'I am Haukr *inn hvíti* and this is my domain. Who might you be?'

A little thrill raced through Ivar as he recognised the name – Haukr the White. It was one he was very familiar with from his youth. Back when he was only fourteen, Haakon and Mia had done an archaeological dig in this area, and they'd found a rune stone with the names of the Viking occupants of the site, including Haukr. Ivar couldn't believe he'd been fortunate enough to run into this particular man first. *What amazing good luck!*

He had decided not to embrace the Viking tradition of taking on his father's name as a surname, as he'd hated the man. Instead of Hrolfsson – his father had been Rolf in Swedish, which would have been Hrolf in Old Norse – he'd keep the name he had grown up with. He therefore replied, 'I am Ivar Thoresson, of no particular abode. I seek a kinsman, Thorald. I believe he resides here.'

His Old Norse was pretty good, if not perfect, and this was a sentence he'd rehearsed many times. He hoped it didn't sound too demanding or impolite. He didn't know this Thorald's surname, which was a shame, as the name could be a common one, but Linnea hadn't told him what it might be. She'd probably never asked.

Ivar had spent years listening to speculation about the man.

His father had been obsessed with what he was convinced was their family's Viking heritage, and had spent ages trying to learn more about this supposed ancestor. All he really had to go on was a sword that had been handed down from father to son through the generations, as well as a handful of stories that had been passed down as well. The sword had an inscription that read: *I am Man-Slayer. Thorald carries me*, but there were no further clues. Despite the fact that Ivar had generally avoided his father like the plague, the stories about Thorald had caught his imagination. He'd found himself listening in spite of himself, fascinated by a man who could inspire such tales. He must have been exceptional, and the desire to meet him had grown.

When he had first realised that time travel was possible, the idea of meeting Thorald had taken shape. Then Linnea had mentioned someone of that name in passing; a neighbour of hers in the past. It had seemed like too much of a coincidence. Ivar wanted to grab the chance to confirm the man's existence, and perhaps to see for himself what had made him worthy of remembrance. Of course, it could all be a pack of lies, or tall tales, but now he'd know for sure.

Haukr brought his musings to a halt with what sounded like a snort of disbelief.

'As far as I know, Thorald has no kin.' The giant crossed his arms over a massive chest and narrowed his eyes at Ivar, tilting his head to one side and regarding him for what seemed like ages. Those blue orbs bored into Ivar's as if the man was trying to look into his very soul. Finally he said, 'Come, let us go for a walk.'

'Er . . . why?' Ivar wasn't sure he wanted to go anywhere with this man. If he didn't believe him to be Thorald's kin, he might simply beat him to a pulp, or even kill him. And fit though Ivar was, he very much doubted he could best Haukr in a fight, no matter what he tried.

'We need to talk in private,' the Viking hissed.

Without waiting for a reply, he strode off towards a meadow at the back of the hall, where a herd of cows were grazing contentedly in the early autumn sunshine. They were smaller than the breeds Ivar was used to, and seemed to come in varying colours, but they looked healthy and well fed.

Once they were out of earshot of the other people in the settlement, Haukr rounded on him. 'You're . . . from the future, aren't you? Your speech is slightly strange and you've appeared out of nowhere. If you'd arrived by ship, someone would have informed me.'

Ivar blinked. 'What? How . . . ?' The man's words were totally unexpected and rendered him more or less speechless. He hadn't thought that anyone other than Linnea and Sara's husbands would be aware that time travel existed. The shock of Haukr's accusation reverberated through him. How the hell was he supposed to answer him without knowing what his thoughts on the matter were?

'Listen, I assume you know Hrafn Eskilsson,' Haukr continued. 'He is one of my closest friends, so he entrusted his secret to me. I have, in fact, seen him vanish with my own eyes. I do not pretend to understand how it is done, and I am not much in favour of *trolldomr*. Magic, or rather the people who practise it, are not to be trusted, in my opinion. But I am aware that it exists and I need to know why you are here before I can allow you to see Thorald. He is my right-hand man and my foster-brother, and I value him highly.' There was no let-up in the big man's frown.

'I mean him no harm, I swear.' Ivar held up his hands in the universal gesture of peace. 'Yes, I am from the future. I am a descendant of his. I have a foster-family too. Hrafn's wife Linnea is my foster-sister, but I am the last of my own line and no longer have any blood relatives in my time. Therefore I wished to meet Thorald. He . . . he is all I have left.'

That was technically true, but he would never be without family as long as Haakon and Mia and their children were around. Haukr didn't need to know that, though. Nor would Ivar tell him that the idea of finding Thorald had taken root and grown until he'd been compelled to act on it. It had become an obsession, and he would never have any peace of mind until he'd at least tried.

Haukr regarded him in silence, as if trying to judge what manner of man he might be. 'You're Linnea's brother? Hmm. I assume you wouldn't claim as much unless you were sure she would confirm it.'

'She would, and Hrafn will vouch for me too, I promise you. If you wish to ask them before taking my word, I will understand.'

'No, no, I believe you, but how will you explain your presence here? As far as Thorald knows, he has no family.' He gave Ivar another piercing look. 'I will admit you are strikingly similar in appearance. He might accept the possibility.'

Ivar shrugged. 'A very distant connection?' He'd rehearsed this part as well. 'A cousin on his mother's side who told me on her deathbed that Thorald was my kin?'

'Very well. You will have to prove yourself somehow. Show him you're someone he can depend on. It will take time and patience. I warn you, he's not one to trust easily. Do you still wish to try?'

Ivar nodded. The way he saw it, he had no choice. He'd come this far and he wasn't backing down now. This was something he needed to do, and if Thorald never accepted him, so be it. At least he would have made an attempt. And he would be able to observe and learn about everyday Viking life at the same time, which was his other reason for wanting to come here. It was a chance no archaeologist could possibly turn down.

Haukr studied him for a moment, as if assessing him and weighing up his options. 'You are sure you have no purpose here other than to become acquainted with your kinsman?'

The image of a young woman with red-gold hair rose up inside Ivar's mind, as it had done frequently in the last few days, but he suppressed it. He had no way of knowing what the vision had meant, or even if she was of this time. Judging by her clothing, she could be – those tortoise brooches were distinctly Viking age. If he was supposed to be part of her life in any way, only time would tell. It wasn't his priority right now.

'No, you have my oath on it. If anything, I would do my utmost to protect Thorald, because if he should die without issue, I assume I will not exist.' He hoped the man already had children, but if not, Ivar would need to make sure Thorald stayed alive long enough to father some.

Haukr nodded curtly. 'Very well. I believe you to be sincere. But rest assured that if any harm were to come to Thorald, I will hunt you down to the ends of Miðgarðr and beyond, and you'll rue the day.'

'Understood.'

'Good, then let us go back.'

Skiringssal, Vestfold, Haustmánuðr AD 875

The king's main hall was noisy and crowded, the fug of smoke, cooking smells and damp wool like a tangible wall as Ellisif entered with Ingibjorg and the other heiresses. She recoiled slightly and tried to take shallow breaths in order to avoid breathing it in. Her stomach was already queasy with nerves; she didn't need anything else to add to that. They went to take their places at a table halfway down the length of one wall, but before she'd had a chance to sit down, her arm was snagged and she was pulled roughly round to bounce against a hard chest.

'You're to come with me. Father wants you next to him.'

She looked up into the face of one of Kári's sons – which one, she had no idea. The man had at least five of them, so she'd been told, all by different wives and concubines. She'd seen them loitering around the place. This one had his father's rather prominent nose and cold stare, but otherwise was nothing like the older man in appearance. He took a step back, as if he didn't want to stand too close to her, but he didn't let go of her arm. She shook herself loose.

'Why?' She glared at him. Could she not be left in peace at least until after the wedding?

He raised an eyebrow at her. 'Why do you think? It is customary for betrothed couples to sit together, is it not?'

'I haven't agreed to any such thing, no matter what the king might have said.'

There was a flicker of something in the depths of his eyes – pity, and a grudging respect perhaps – but he shook his head as if she was deluded.

'We both know that makes no difference. Come.'

He walked off without checking to see if she was following, as if he trusted her not to be stupid enough to resist. That, more than anything, made her do as he said. He was right, after all, and refusing to play along now would only raise suspicion. Perhaps get her punished or – the gods forbid – locked up. Then she would never be able to escape.

As they reached a table much closer to the king's, Kári's son stopped. 'Here she is, Father,' he grunted, nodding at her.

'Good. Sit, woman.'

Kári gestured with a half-eaten roast rib and indicated a place on the bench next to him. Ellisif sank down, trying her best to keep some distance between them. It was almost impossible, however, with so many people crammed into the hall. A young man squeezed in on her other side and seemed to have no compunction about pushing her closer to her intended. Gritting her teeth, she swallowed down her revulsion.

The man made her skin crawl.

It wasn't merely the fact that Kári was so much older than her, with a face that had been ravaged by time. Jowly, with ruddy cheeks criss-crossed with visible veins and a nose that was red with large pores, he had the visage of someone who had lived a hard life. Much worse, though, was the look in his eyes as he glanced at her. A strange mixture of disapproval and lust that made her want to shudder, especially as his gaze lingered over the swell of her breasts. He leaned closer and his foul breath hit her, making her want to shrink away from him.

'You'll do,' he told her with a smirk. 'And I'll soon have you tamed, so you can take that haughty expression off your face right now.'

His large hand landed on her thigh under the table, and he gripped it hard, squeezing her flesh until it burned. She hissed in a breath but didn't cry out. She wouldn't give him the satisfaction, but her defiance served merely to amuse him, judging by the chuckle she heard.

'Eat,' he ordered. 'I prefer women with a bit of flesh on their bones. You're too thin by half.'

She didn't care what his preferences were, but helped herself to some food in order to have something to do. In truth, she wasn't hungry and only managed to swallow a small amount. When his hand returned to fondle her leg, moving dangerously close to the junction between her thighs, she froze and stopped eating altogether.

'What's the matter? Not a shy maiden, are you?' Kári guffawed and pawed at her some more, his stubby fingers digging into her. 'I would have thought Þjódólfr had broken you in by now.'

As if I'm a brood mare to be tamed! Bile rose in her throat, and she had visions of stabbing his hand with her eating knife, but she held still. She'd learned early on in her previous marriage that resistance only made things worse. And it wasn't as though the man could bed her right now in the middle of the king's hall. He was only trying to provoke her.

She pretended indifference and took a sip of her ale, swallowing past the lump of misery that was rising in her throat. Kári might think he had the upper hand, but if anything, his actions this evening had only strengthened her resolve. One way or another, she'd escape. Nothing would make her marry the hateful man. Thankfully, he soon tired of the game and removed his hand as he focused on chatting to the man seated on his left. Ellisif drew a sigh of relief and took a bite of flatbread, chewing slowly.

The young man on her other side nudged her with his shoulder to gain her attention. 'I'm Ketill, the youngest of Father's offspring. Most people call me Kell. You're Ellisif, his new wife-to-be?'

'Yes.' She was surprised that he had the manners to introduce himself, and regarded him out of the corner of her eye. Perhaps she had been wrong to think Kári had raised all his sons to be oafs like himself. Now that she studied him properly, Kell seemed rather young – eighteen or nineteen winters at the most – although he was big for his age. He was peering at her intently, but there was nothing except curiosity in the blue depths of his eyes.

He refilled her ale mug from a nearby pitcher. 'So where exactly are your holdings?'

'Rogaland. Not far from Hafrsfjordr. I thought your father would have told you.'

Kell snorted and lowered his voice. 'He doesn't tell me anything. I'm the runt. I merely do as I'm bid.'

'I see.' She had the feeling he imagined they were both in the same boat here, as she would soon be at his father's beck and call as well. Or so he thought.

'Should I call you Mother?' he asked.

'What? No!' The thought of being this boy's stepmother was ridiculous. When she turned to him to say as much, she caught the twinkle in his eyes and realised he was joking.

He chuckled, a much nicer sound than the one his father had made earlier. 'Do not worry, I wouldn't presume. And you have my oath that I will try to help you in any way I can. Not that anyone really pays attention to me, but still . . .'

'Thank you.' Ellisif was touched at his offer and almost sorry that she wouldn't be getting to know him better. From what she could tell, he was sincere, and she didn't doubt he would have tried to assist her if she asked. A shame that the only thing she really wanted wasn't something he could be part of – running as far away from his father as possible.

Kári left her alone for the rest of the meal and Kell didn't say anything else either. When it was over, the younger man stood up and escorted her back to the other women, leaving her with Ingibjorg.

'I will see you soon,' he said, before melting into the throng of people making their way outside.

'Sadly not,' she muttered, but so quietly he didn't hear her.

A pity she hadn't been asked to marry Kell. Young though he was, he would have made a much better husband than his father ever would, of that she was sure.

Chapter Four

Birkiþorp, 25 September/Haustmánuðr AD *875*

Haukr had been right. Meeting Thorald for the first time was a bit like staring at himself in a wonky mirror. There was more than a passing resemblance between them, and people might have assumed the two of them were brothers. From what Ivar had gathered, his ancestor was actually younger than himself at this point in time – eight and twenty winters, Haukr had told him – but because life was tougher in Viking times, he imagined they looked about the same age.

'A kinsman, you say?' Thorald's scowl was not encouraging as the introductions were made, but with Haukr backing him up, Ivar felt relatively safe as he launched into his lies.

'That's what I was told, and your jarl here seems to think we resemble each other.' He shrugged. 'My mother's cousin could have been wrong, but as I have no one else, I thought it worth my while to come and seek you out.'

Thorald glanced at his chieftain and rubbed his chin as if he was mulling it over. 'I suppose it could be true. I never knew anyone on my mother's side of the family. She died birthing me. My father brought me to Birkiþorp before I could walk and left me with Haukr's parents. He died soon afterwards as well. I have been here ever since.' He fixed Ivar with a penetrating gaze. 'And you are just passing by?'

'Well, actually I was hoping there might be a more permanent place for me here, at least for a while. I have nowhere else to live right now and I'm willing to do almost anything.' Secretly he hoped that wouldn't mean shovelling manure or some such lowly task. He added, 'I could go a-viking, of course, but thought I would visit you first.'

'You sound as though you've already been abroad,' Thorald commented. 'There's something about your speech . . .'

Ivar had anticipated this and Haukr had already noticed it as well. He knew that despite all his Old Norse lessons, there were bound to be words he didn't know or grammar he got wrong. 'I was raised mainly by foreign thrall women.' He tried to make light of the matter by smiling and holding out his hands in a 'what can you do?' type of gesture. 'I think their way of speaking rubbed off on me, but I'll try to do better.'

'Hmm.' His kinsman's expression told him he wasn't convinced, but it was the only explanation Ivar could come up with for now.

'You can train with us tomorrow and we shall see how well you handle yourself in a fight,' Haukr decreed, clapping Ivar on the back. 'Now let us all go and have our *nattverðr*. Ceri won't want to be kept waiting.'

Ceri was clearly his wife, and Ivar had to hide a smile of triumph. He'd already known that before he arrived here as well, and not because Linnea had told him. The rune stone that Mia and Haakon had found mentioned both Haukr and Ceri along with a daughter called Jorun, and it was extraordinary to think that he was now meeting them. He took a moment to allow the unreality of it all to wash over him. This was the ninth century and he was here actually talking to people whose bones he'd seen in a grave back in his own time. That was nigh-on impossible to get your head round.

'Come, sit next to me this evening. I want to hear what training you've done.' Haukr pointed to the other end of the large hall, where a petite woman with dark chestnut-coloured curls waited in one of the two carved chairs set out in the place of honour. Ivar did a double-take. For a moment there, he'd thought Mia had also travelled back through time. Blinking, he realised this had to be Ceri. Her features were not really the same as Mia's, merely vaguely similar at a distance. The hair and colouring were a close match, though.

'Thank you,' he said, following the jarl. Thorald walked behind them, and Ivar was sure the man's gaze was boring into him, but he pretended to be calm.

So far, so good. He'd arrived safely, he hadn't been killed on sight, and now it was up to him to make this work. Thank goodness for Haukr's support; that certainly helped.

As he took a seat between the jarl and Thorald, a little girl who had to be around ten or eleven peered round Ceri with blatant curiosity. Haukr noticed and smiled. 'That's my daughter, Jorun,' he told Ivar. 'She is mostly deaf, but if you look at her and speak slowly, she'll understand you, and you will soon become used to her speech.' He pointed to a child of about four sitting next to her. 'And that is our son, Cadoc. We also have a daughter, Aase, and a two-month-old baby boy, Bryn. They're both asleep already. At least, we hope so.' He glanced fondly at his wife, who returned his gaze with a warm one of her own.

Ivar smiled and waved at the children. 'I am Ivar,' he said, making sure he exaggerated his pronunciation so that Jorun could catch his words. When he winked at her, she giggled, while the boy simply stared at him with big, solemn eyes.

'You like children?' Haukr held out a wooden mug for a servant to fill with ale, and Ivar followed suit.

'Yes, very much so.'

'You should marry, then, like my friend here has recently done.' The man grinned at Thorald, a teasing glint in his eyes. 'And here comes his beloved, Askhild Ásbjornsdóttir. Evening, cousin.' He turned back to Ivar. 'She's a relative of mine, although I forget how, exactly, as is her brother, Álrik.'

A woman who seemed to be a few years younger than Thorald took her place next to her husband. If they'd not been married for long, they obviously didn't have children yet. That gave Ivar a twinge of unease but strengthened his determination to stick around and make sure the man lived long enough to father a whole brood of them. The way he was looking at Askhild, that shouldn't be a problem. As soon as she'd appeared, it was clear he had eyes for no one else. Still, life was a lot more precarious in Viking times and anything could happen to either of them.

Introductions were made, reluctantly on Thorald's part, but Askhild didn't question Ivar's story. It was clear his ancestor wasn't so easily persuaded, but the man couldn't be blamed for that. Had he accepted it too readily, that would have been strange.

The food arrived. Despite the fact that it was plentiful, it wasn't the sort of fare Ivar was used to. Never a fusspot, he ate whatever was put in front of him with gratitude. His mother had died young, and for years he'd had to survive on microwave dinners or takeaways, as his father had never been interested in cooking. He'd mostly been out attending business dinners and Ivar was left to fend for himself, which was why, even many years later, he appreciated it very much whenever someone cooked for him.

While eating and trying to keep up his end of the conversation, he let his gaze roam the hall. It was an impressive building and fairly new, judging by the colour of the beams and upright posts, which weren't blackened by age or soot. He remembered that Haakon and Mia's dig had uncovered the fact that the original hall had burned down and a new one had been erected in its place. Presumably this was the second one. He'd have to try and find out what had happened to the older version.

Benches lined the room on two sides, all covered with furs and cushions to sit and sleep on. Woven and embroidered hangings covered the walls, colourful to the point of being garish, and on the end wall behind them hung an assortment of circular shields. In the centre of the room was a huge hearth built of stone, with several cauldrons suspended above it. The smoke from the fire permeated the atmosphere, but as it mostly rose towards the rafters, it didn't make it difficult to breathe. He caught lots of other scents too – wool, damp soil and cooking, as well as the odour of animals and humans in close proximity. It was an assault on his senses, but his nose adjusted gradually and he grew used to it.

I'm here! I'm really here, in the ninth century!

He wanted to jump up and down like a little kid, shouting with joy. It was unreal, magical, but he'd been dreaming of this for ages now. Joy bubbled up inside him. He'd succeeded and the adventure had begun. But when he noticed his kinsman's pensive gaze on him, he knew this wasn't going to be easy. The man was clearly suspicious, and rightly so. It would take a huge effort to win him over, but Ivar was determined to try. He'd do anything to be allowed to stay here for a while, which was why his ears pricked up at the mention of travel.

'You are going somewhere?' he asked Thorald, leaning forward slightly so that he could see the man's expression.

'Yes. We are going to Hörðaland to take back Álrik's domains.'

Thorald pointed to a teenager sitting on the other side of his wife. 'Their uncle has usurped them, thinking the boy too weak to fight him, but he has new kin now and I will not let the matter rest until justice has been served.'

Hörðaland – or Hordaland as Ivar was used to calling it – was a part of Norway on the west coast, around the modern-day city of Bergen. That was a long way to go for revenge, but he merely nodded. 'I see.'

'You could come with us,' Thorald bit out, although judging by his expression, he wasn't sure he wanted to make the offer. 'If you prove any good at fighting, that is. I need all the men I can find, and you said you were looking for something to do.'

The offer was so unexpected, Ivar blinked at him, then beamed. 'Thank you! I would like that above all things.'

If it meant he could stick around and get to know the man better, he was all for it. And he'd been training to fight for ages now. No point letting his skills go to waste, even if a small voice inside his head told him this wouldn't be pretend warfare. It would be all too real.

Well, he'd wanted an authentic experience, and here was his chance. He simply had to take it.

'*Help me, please! Help me . . .*'

Ivar woke with his fist curled around the little swan's-foot amulet that he'd stolen from the museum. He still felt bad about that, but after what had happened, there was no way he could have left it behind. He'd taken it out of his pouch the previous evening and must have fallen asleep clutching it. There had been no vision, but he'd definitely dreamed of the woman. He'd had her in his arms this time, stretched out beside him and curling into his body. The remembered sensation of holding her sent a shiver through him. Who was she? And how could he find her? It seemed an impossible task, especially as he had no way of knowing if she was even real.

Having spent the night on a wooden bench with only a couple of sheepskins as a mattress, he was stiff as a poker. He was a light sleeper and woke when others began to stir around him. It was barely dawn, judging by the faint light spilling in through the door and the smoke holes up near the roof of each gable end, but that didn't bother him. He'd always been a morning person and loved watching the sun rise over the lake outside his house. It made him smile to think that he could do the same here. It was still Lake Mälaren even if he was looking at it over a thousand years earlier than usual.

He stretched and tried to ease the knots out of his limbs. Hopefully he'd get used to the hard surface, but it was a far cry from his memory-foam mattress, soft pillow and duvet. There was no point being fussy, though – life in Viking times was tough and he'd chosen to come here. He couldn't complain when the experience was too authentic for his liking.

'Ah, good, you are awake.' Haukr had emerged from a room at the end of the hall and stopped before Ivar. He guessed the jarl had the privilege of a sleeping chamber and some privacy – lucky man. Others here didn't seem to have the same. 'Come outside and join us for some early-morning sparring. We'll stop for *dagverðr* a bit later.'

'Coming.' Ivar dry-washed his face and rubbed the sleep out of his eyes. He could murder a cup of strong coffee, but that wasn't going to happen. 'Deal with it,' he muttered to himself in English. There was probably some water outside, and that would have to do for now. He hoped breakfast wouldn't be too long in coming, though. If these Vikings were going to put him through his paces, he'd need sustenance.

They stopped to wait for Thorald, who came out of some sort

of hut that was half dug into the ground. Obviously he too had separate sleeping quarters, and as a newly-wed, he probably needed them.

'Let's away to the training ground. I wish to see how your kinsman fares.' Haukr gestured for Thorald to hurry.

The latter's mouth turned into a thin line at this reminder of Ivar's supposed status. It was clear he had yet to have any faith in the claim.

Two hours later, Ivar's stomach was growling, but that was the least of his problems. He'd been through a gruelling, and rather violent, session of pretend sword-fighting, where he'd received several nicks and bruises. That had been followed by archery, and then training in how to wield an axe to best advantage. Finally he'd been urged to take part in some type of wrestling – *glima*, the others called it. The rules were simple: you had to unbalance your opponent and throw him to the ground left-handed while holding on to his trouser waistband with your right. Legs were allowed to be used and Ivar had taken full advantage of that, managing to trip his adversary. The whole experience reminded him of judo. So far he'd resisted using his modern self-defence techniques, but he'd come close a couple of times when the men he was training with got a bit too vicious. Still, he figured it was better to take it on the chin for now. If he wanted to win their trust, he had to show himself to be a man.

Apparently he'd passed muster, but it wasn't over yet.

'Now for a swim. Let us see who can be the first man to the island and back,' Haukr shouted.

Ivar had often swum out to the small island that faced his and Mia and Haakon's property. It was where Haukr and his wife would be buried one day, but he kept that thought to himself. At the moment, the man was very much alive, and although Ivar gave it his all, he couldn't beat him back to shore. But he came a respectable joint second with Thorald, which made the jarl's face split into a huge grin.

'Not bad, Thoresson. Not bad at all.'

The big Viking gave him a playful shove between the shoulder blades. If Ivar hadn't seen it coming, it would have pitched him face first into the grass, as the jarl was so strong. 'I think you'll do. What say you, Thorald?'

They both turned to regard Ivar's kinsman, who hadn't smiled once since they began their training. He nodded, somewhat grudgingly. 'Aye, he'll do. You still want to come to Hörðaland?'

'Yes. If you'll have me.' No point showing how eager he was, so Ivar toned down his enthusiasm while keeping his expression serious so that Thorald would know he meant it.

'Very well then. We leave tomorrow at first light.'

Relief coursed through him. He'd successfully inveigled himself into his ancestor's life, at least for the moment. On the long journey to Norway, it should be possible to get to know him better, despite the fact that he seemed enigmatic and taciturn to a fault. Except when he was with his wife, that was. Ivar almost smiled. Perhaps if he were to make friends with Askhild and her brother, Thorald would open up a bit more. It was worth a shot, anyway.

And he looked forward to learning more about them as well.

Skiringssal, Vestfold, 9 October/Haustmánuðr AD 875

'Shh, don't fret. Trust me, I'll protect you . . .'

Ellisif jerked awake, the voice of the man in her dream still whispering inside her brain. She sat up and tried to block him out. Welcome though a protector would be, he wasn't real, and she had only herself to rely on. She shouldn't have dozed off in the first place. Tonight she was putting her plans in motion and there was no time to lose.

The hut was in complete darkness, but she was used to not seeing very well and she'd memorised every part of it during her days cooped up with the other heiresses. She tried not to make a sound as she pushed herself off the straw-filled mattress she'd been lying on, but it was impossible not to make it rustle. Her only hope was that the other women would think the noise was being made by vermin or someone stirring in their sleep.

Once off the bench, she knelt beside it and pulled out the small bundle she'd stowed underneath. She had had to be very careful when putting it together, only adding one thing at a time when no one was looking. The majority of her possessions were in a kist, also under the bench, but she wouldn't take more than she could carry. Some extra clothing, the few pieces of jewellery she owned, the silver she'd managed to scrounge from Þjódólfr before his death and religiously hoarded in secret, and a few other things. There was a fire iron and flint, a horn spoon and a wooden bowl, as well as her winter shoes. At her belt hung her sewing kit and a knife.

It would have to be enough.

If anyone heard her moving stealthily towards the door, they didn't give her away. The others appeared to have resigned themselves to their fate, but they still appreciated the fact that she wasn't happy about hers and understood her need to rebel. No one had said it outright, but she'd sensed their support and was grateful for it. If she'd asked Ingibjorg for help, the woman probably would have given it to her, but it seemed best not to involve anyone else in case it caused trouble for them. That was the last thing she wanted to do.

Hiding the bundle under her skirts, she opened the door as quietly as possible and slipped outside. There was a guard sitting on a stool, his bleary eyes blinking at her in the light of a torch. But he didn't say anything when she moved towards a small withy-enclosed space on the outskirts of the courtyard. For the past few nights, she'd made a point of using the privy, claiming she had an upset stomach. He'd gone with her the first couple of times, but after that he'd just waved her off. Thankfully, tonight he seemed barely interested, his eyelids half lowered.

The air outside was fresh, but the shiver that coursed through her was mostly one of nerves. She had no idea how she was going to slip out of the king's compound, but she had to try. She'd never be able to live with herself otherwise. It was situated on a low hill, surrounded by a wooden palisade and guarded at all times. Keeping to the shadowy parts next to the walls of the buildings, she stopped to watch the gate. There was only one guard at this time of night and he didn't look massively alert. Still, she couldn't simply walk past him without an explanation.

She bit her lip. Now that she had got this far, she refused to turn back. If she did, no doubt she'd be under constant surveillance. Perhaps they'd even lock her up until the wedding ceremony. She couldn't bear it.

As she waited in the darkness, she was aware of time passing. That guard outside the women's hut would become suspicious if she didn't return soon. She had to do something, but what? She contemplated throwing a rock in order to cause a distraction, and bent to search the ground with her fingers. Just then, footsteps approached and a man ambled towards the guard by the gate. He called out to him and they moved to one side for a quiet conversation.

This was it – her chance. Ellisif grabbed it and moved as quickly as she could, whisking through the gap behind the men's backs before they had time to react. They must have seen or heard something, however, as one of them cried out.

'*Hei!* You there, stop! Where do you think you're going?'

But she paid him no heed. Instead she picked up her skirts and ran as fast as she could, straight into the darkness of the night outside. If she had any say in the matter, she never wanted to set foot in the king's compound again.

Chapter Five

Birkiþorp, 27 September, to Skiringssal, Vestfold, 10 October/ Haustmánuðr AD *875*

Ivar was having the time of his life. They had set off at the crack of dawn two days after his arrival at Birkiþorp, and although he'd been on a reconstructed Viking ship in his own time, travelling on an authentic vessel was far superior. The sights and sounds of the Norsemen – and one woman – who surrounded him were exhilarating, and he studied them surreptitiously while listening to their conversations. He still had the urge to pinch himself from time to time, not quite able to fathom that this was real. But he couldn't doubt the movement of the ship gliding smoothly through the water, the cool breeze caressing his cheeks, and the smells of wool, tar and brine all around him.

Sitting on a kist that Haukr had lent him, he did his fair share of rowing until they were out at sea and the sail could be raised. Once out of what he thought of as the Stockholm archipelago, they journeyed south, following the east coast of Sweden. He tried to spot familiar landmarks, but it wasn't until they sailed between the coast and the island of Öland that he recognised anything. Mostly, all he could see was forest, with the occasional settlement dotted in between. It was clear why travelling by ship or boat was the most common way in this era – there simply weren't any roads to use on land.

He was fascinated by the ship and paid attention to how the sail was raised and lowered and the steering oar operated. Occasionally they had to row again, but it wasn't a hardship, as everyone did it together, making it easier. He never complained – he was strong and fit and had no trouble keeping up, which earned him a glance of approval from his kinsman. And he loved the sensation of the oar in his hand, the wood smooth from long use.

'What would you call this type of ship?' he asked Thorald on the afternoon of the first day. The man was steering, and appeared at ease holding the long oar that acted as a rudder.

His question elicited a sideways glance, and Ivar realised he ought to know the answer to this. He hastened to add, 'I grew up inland and haven't seen many vessels of this size.'

'Ah. Well, it's actually a blend of *snekkja* and *knarr*. Haukr had it built and he wanted both speed and enough room for storing a possible cargo.'

'I see.' Ivar knew that a *snekkja* was a small warship, usually long and thin, while a *knarr* was larger and wider, built to transport goods. It seemed a good compromise to incorporate features of each. Haukr's ship, which he'd happily lent Thorald, wasn't huge, but the group of ten people fitted comfortably on board, together with all the supplies they'd brought.

As his ancestor seemed to be in a talkative mood – or perhaps communicative was more accurate, as each word had to be prised out of him – Ivar continued his questioning. 'So how do you navigate? You've sailed this way before?'

'A few times, yes.' Thorald shrugged. 'I check the sun's position, but mostly I stay close to the coast. I remember the way. If not, there's usually someone to ask who's been there before.'

There was no sign of any navigational tools. Some modern archaeologists believed the Vikings had used something called a sunstone for this purpose. Ivar could see no evidence of that. Instead, directions were memorised, and the sun or stars observed. How that would work out on the open sea, he had no idea. It wouldn't be an issue when going to Norway, though, as it was possible to keep land in sight all the way.

Whenever they stopped – which they did each evening, as it was too dangerous to sail at night this close to the coastline – he tried to memorise every detail of what was happening. He observed the way they made campfires, how their meals were cooked, what type of food they'd brought, the various utensils and eating implements used, and much more. It was all invaluable information for when he returned to his own century and carried on working at the museum.

He learned to construct a simple tent using a wooden frame and canvas made out of what looked like felted and greased woollen material.

'You've never put up a tent before?' Thorald blinked at him in astonishment the first evening when Ivar had to confess to his lack of skill. The ones he'd used for re-enactment camps were different, and possibly not as authentic as they should have been.

'No. Never had cause to sleep in one. I told you, I haven't travelled much.' He shrugged as if it was no big deal, and his kinsman seemed to buy it, grudgingly showing him what to do.

Haukr had given him a bundle of sheepskin furs to sleep on, and Ceri had added a couple of blankets, for which he was very grateful. Lying on the ground each night on various beaches wasn't much more comfortable than the hard benches in the jarl's hall had been, but he was so tired, he fell asleep within seconds of his head hitting the makeshift pillow – his sack of clothing.

By the third night, he was becoming used to the daily routine and didn't feel as weary. After he'd crept into his tent, he rummaged around in one of the pouches hanging off his belt. His fingers closed on the silver swan's-foot amulet. For some reason, it had been on his mind again this evening. Perhaps because he was becoming more used to being in the ninth century and had time to relax and think of other things. Taking the charm out, he held it up. It flashed in a beam of moonlight that seeped in through the tent opening. Almost immediately, the dizziness began to swirl inside him and he swallowed hard, closing his eyes . . .

The woman was sitting on a bench, a desperately sad expression on her lovely face but with a determined set to her mouth. There were tears sliding down her cheeks, but she brushed at them with an impatient swipe of her fingers. She glanced around furtively, then bent to quickly place something underneath the bench before lying down on top of the bed furs. Turning her face towards him, she stared him straight in the eyes, and mouthed, 'Help me! Please . . .'

Ivar sucked in a huge breath and blinked his eyes open. What was going on? Who on earth was this woman? And why was she somehow connecting with him?

He glanced at the amulet in his hand and frowned. Haukr might not believe in *trolldomr*, but Ivar certainly did. What choice did he have? He'd travelled through time, and if that wasn't magic, he didn't know what was. Now the *võlva*'s charm was trying to tell him something. What that was remained to be seen. So far he hadn't come across any women with that distinctive hair colour, and therefore the only thing he could do was wait. If the Norns had some fate in store for him, they'd let him know when they were good and ready.

He hoped that would be soon.

* * *

Eventually they turned west, past the most southerly point of Sweden, then north up through the Öresund Strait – with Denmark visible on the left-hand side – and on towards Norway. Thorald kept the Swedish west coast in sight on their right, and Ivar remembered that in this period it was called Ranrike and belonged to a Danish king. He lost count of the days, but relished every moment. It was the kind of journey he could only ever have imagined, and as an archaeologist specialising in the Viking era, it was a dream come true.

After crossing the wide opening of a fjord, which Ivar guessed was the Oslo fjord – called Viken at this time – they entered the mouth of another. Islands and islets of various sizes dotted the area, some merely rocky outcroppings while others were covered in forest.

'We are nearing the *kaupang* at Skiringssal,' Askhild told him. She happened to be sitting closest to him and must have seen him eagerly studying their surroundings.

'Oh, really? Excellent. I can't wait to see that. Are you hoping to buy anything special?'

Her cheeks turned slightly pink. 'Thorald has promised me some beads. The bead-makers here are unsurpassed, and they sometimes sell beads from faraway lands too. Oh, and a new eating knife. He . . . he said he wanted to spoil me.'

Ivar smiled at her. 'And why not? He clearly loves you very much.'

Askhild's face became even rosier at that. 'I can't believe how lucky I am. I never thought this would happen to me.' She turned to study him. 'What about you? Have you not considered marriage? You must be of an age with my husband.'

He shrugged and decided not to tell her that he was in fact seven years older. She might think him middle-aged. 'I haven't yet found a woman with whom I could imagine spending the rest of my life. I won't settle for less than what you and Thorald share.'

'That's very wise of you. Oh, look, there it is!' She pointed towards the shore. 'You'd better get back to your oar.'

As the sail was lowered, he sat down and slotted the oar into place while watching the shore approach. He had read about this town, and excitement fizzed inside him. A *kaupang* was a trading site or marketplace, an unusual thing in Viking times, when most people lived on isolated farmsteads rather than in towns or villages. There were only a handful of such sites known in Scandinavia during this period, the largest being Birka in Sweden and Hedeby – or Heiðabýr, as the Vikings called it – in Denmark, and he couldn't wait to see this one, situated on Norway's southern coast.

The ship rounded a large island, and the town abruptly came into view. There were lots of houses fairly close together, parallel with the shore, and several long quays or jetties with ships moored beside them. It wasn't a huge urban sprawl by any means, but there were quite a few buildings, perhaps as many as a hundred, and also numerous tents that presumably contained itinerant or seasonal traders.

Thorald steered them to a free space next to a jetty, and someone else jumped out with the mooring rope to tie it securely to a large pole. People were swarming around the area, but everyone was busy with their own concerns and paid little heed to the newcomers.

'This is . . .' Ivar tried to think of a word that would best describe the place, but came up blank. Bustling? Noisy? Dirty? It was all of the above.

'Smelly,' was Thorald's verdict, and as they shared a glance, the man actually smiled.

Ivar grinned back. 'I didn't want to offend anyone by mentioning that.'

'Pah, you can hardly miss it.'

It was true. The reek of humanity, excrement, rubbish and animals hung in the air and wafted towards them, mixed with smoke from numerous fires. It would be necessary to take shallow breaths for a while if he was to become used to the stench.

'We're going to stay here for a night,' Thorald told everyone as they huddled together on board, in order not to be overheard. 'I want to try to find out whether the king is here. It would be good to know what his movements are likely to be in the next few weeks. If he's busy down here in the south, he won't meddle when we go to take back Álrik's holdings. Once we have accomplished that, he will have no choice but to deal with us if he wants our support and allegiance.'

That made sense. Thorald and some of the other men melted into the crowds to try and glean information. Ivar stayed on the jetty, taking his turn to guard the ship during the afternoon, but after supper he was told he could go and stretch his legs.

'Just be careful who you speak to and what you say,' Thorald warned, as if he still didn't quite trust his new kinsman not to betray them.

'I will,' Ivar promised.

It stung to have to reassure the man, especially after the lighter moment they'd shared earlier, but Ivar understood that Thorald had cause to be mistrustful. They hadn't known each other for very long, and although they'd had a few short conversations during the journey, the man wasn't exactly a chatterbox. It would take time to befriend him, so Ivar had continued with his plan to reach him via his wife and brother-in-law instead.

Young Álrik was definitely more susceptible to friendly overtures, and Ivar had managed to get him to open up about the situation he and his sister had apparently fled from. Their uncle sounded like a complete bastard, and it would be a pleasure to thwart his plans. From what Álrik had let slip, the man had tried to force Askhild into marriage with him through attempted rape, which was extremely sick and twisted to Ivar's mind. After that, he'd hinted he was going to kill Álrik, thereby eliminating any other claim to the property.

It was despicable, and Ivar couldn't wait to play his part in putting an end to his schemes. But for now, he had a Viking town to explore.

Ellisif jolted awake and felt herself sway. Acting on pure instinct, she grabbed hold of the nearest thing, which proved to be a branch. That was when she remembered where she was – sitting high up in a tree, wedged in between two branches with her back against the trunk. She doubted she could fall, as she'd made sure she was securely anchored, but she didn't want to even contemplate such a thing. The mere thought of it made her dizzy.

The guards had hunted her last night as she ran into the darkness, and in her panic, she'd lost her bearings. She knew that the king's compound was situated on a hill overlooking the market town named after his enormous feasting hall, Skiringssal. The name meant 'the radiant hall' and was possibly on account of the fact that on sunny days it gleamed a dull gold from the pinewood planks it was made of. It was magnificent, she couldn't deny that, longer than any such building she'd ever seen before and with a beautifully decorated bowed roof line. Carvings graced the doorways as well as some of the walls, and its sheer size was overwhelming, so perhaps the epithet referred more to its splendour than its colour. Either way, it was a place she was keen never to return to.

The *kaupang* and its harbour were not visible from the hall, as they were hidden by a tree-covered ridge, but the islands outside it were. Occasionally it was possible to make out ships sailing between them, and Ellisif had been aiming to find passage on board one of them.

Until she'd lost her way.

Instead of heading south, she must have blundered west. After stumbling through muddy fields belonging to the king's farm, Huseby, she had ended up in a nearby forest. With the guards still in pursuit, and her lungs fit to burst, she'd had no choice but to climb a tree to try and escape them. It was lucky she remembered how to from when she was young, although it had been a struggle. She'd had to bunch her skirts up and loop them through her belt, then tie her bundle of belongings to her back before attempting to scale the trunk. Her palms and knees were scraped raw now – she could feel them stinging – and she longed for some salt water to clean the wounds. That would have to wait.

The guards had rushed past her and continued their search, eventually returning with more men to help. None of them had thought to look up, and she thanked the gods for that. She'd planned to make her way towards the harbour in daylight, but yet another search party had put a stop to that this morning. She had only left her hiding place a couple of times during the day to attend to calls of nature, and now that darkness was falling, she was cold and cramped. Her stomach growled, as she'd had nothing but an oatcake to eat all day, and her mouth was parched from thirst.

Glancing through the branches as dusk turned to proper night, she watched as campfires were lit along the shore. They appeared to be quite close, so it would seem she wasn't as far from the trading place as she'd thought. Finally she decided to risk venturing down. Surely the guards wouldn't still be searching for her? She hadn't seen or heard anyone for ages now.

Once on the outskirts of the town, she kept to the shadows. Some people had gone indoors and bedded down for the night, but there were still groups of men and women sitting around chatting, laughing and drinking ale. Her stomach groused again as the enticing scents of roasting meat reached her nose, but she ignored the hunger pangs. She couldn't afford to linger. As she passed one group, however, their campfire flared when someone added an extra log to it, and she was briefly illuminated. So were two men loitering nearby, whom she hadn't noticed before. Belatedly she registered their weapons and guessed them to be the king's men. *Skítr!*

'There she is! The wench with the red-gold hair. After her!'

Ellisif sprinted off without giving much thought to which direction would be safest. Anywhere away from them would do. She might be running straight into the arms of their fellow guards, but she hoped that wasn't the case. She cursed the distinctive colour of her hair as she wove in and out of houses, people and a couple of pigs snuffling around. Soon she found herself on the other side of the harbour. Clusters of tents showed that visitors were still coming to the marketplace and setting up camp here, despite the colder months of the year approaching. She ducked down behind one of them and prayed to all the gods that the guards wouldn't come this way. No deities appeared to be listening, though, and the men's shouts were growing ever closer. There was only one thing to do – find an unoccupied tent and hide in there.

Chapter Six

Skiringssal, Vestfold, 10 October/Haustmánuðr AD *875*

At first Ivar wandered aimlessly around, stopping every now and then to take in the details of his surroundings. If there was a king here, he didn't live in the *kaupang*, as all the houses were modest in size. They were laid out in rows following a grid pattern, each on a more or less equal-sized plot running along the shoreline. At a guess, they were around six or seven metres wide and ten long, so not very large at all. Narrow alleyways, ditches and wattle fences separated the properties, and although he couldn't see into the ditches in the dark, the stench emanating from them showed that they must be full of rubbish. There had to be cesspits and privies nearby as well, and he wrinkled his nose while trying to take shallow breaths.

'Bleurgh! How can they stand to live here?' he muttered.

From what he could see, the houses took up most of the space on the plots, and there were hardly any gardens or yards to speak of. Pigs, hens and other animals wandered at will, not confined to any one place. He assumed they must be marked in some way in order to be identified by their owners. The alleyways were covered in planking, presumably to avoid people having to walk through mud, and he tried to tread carefully in case there were animal droppings. Smoke emanated from little holes in the roofs of the buildings and wreathed the place in misty tendrils.

This late in the day, all the stalls and booths were closed, but there were still lots of people milling about or sitting around fires catching up on each other's news. Ivar listened to snatches of conversation and discerned many different languages. He didn't understand most of them, but could guess at their provenance – the guttural sounds of the Frisians; dialects possibly belonging to Wends and Obodrites, two West Slavic groups from the Baltic region; some Latin words mixed with what might be the tongue of the Frakkar – what he would call the Franks – and something he definitely recognised as Anglo-Saxon. He hadn't realised Skiringssal would be such a multicultural melting pot, but it was a nice surprise.

There was clearly a lot of trade going on here, and he'd heard the others in Thorald's group discussing the goods for sale. Norwegian soapstone, whetstones, furs, antlers and iron were exchanged for foreign luxuries like beautifully decorated swords, silk fabrics and glass objects. Local craftsmen produced textiles, wooden items, combs, shoes and jewellery, and Askhild had been right about the bead-makers.

'Look what Thorald bought me,' she'd said when she returned after a successful shopping expedition. Tipping the contents of a small leather pouch into her palm, she had shown Ivar an assortment of colourful beads.

Her husband hadn't exclusively bought her glass ones, although there were lots of those in blue, white and green, but also some made of amber, rock crystal, amethyst and carnelian. Ivar even spied a couple of black ones, which had to be jet from Whitby in England. Many of these little pieces had travelled a long way; the carnelian possibly from Byzantium and the amethyst perhaps as far as from India. Ivar was impressed at the extensive trade network this indicated. The only thing he didn't admire was the traffic in human beings. He'd seen some thralls for sale earlier and the sight had made his fists clench with anger and frustration.

Nothing he could do about that now, though.

He ended up joining a group of traders who were sharing ale and swapping tall tales around a campfire. Why they invited him to sit down, he had no idea, but most likely they'd already imbibed a large quantity of ale and were in an expansive mood. It provided him with another great opportunity to interact with real Vikings, so he stayed on until late, enjoying himself immensely.

Finally he stood up and stretched. 'I had better head back. Thank you for a convivial evening. I hope to meet you all again,' he told the man to his right, who seemed to be the leader of the group.

'The same. Good luck on your journey.'

'And you.' He had told them he was with a merchant bound for the west coast and the route north, Norðvegr, and they hadn't asked for any details. They were going in the opposite direction.

On his way back to his tent, he became aware of a commotion, with shouting and the sound of running feet coming from several directions. Two men materialised out of nowhere and hurried past him, shouldering him out of the way. He was about to protest, but they seemed oblivious to his irritation and didn't so much as spare him a glance. They were carrying flaming torches and their expressions were grim as they surveyed the immediate area.

'She has to be here somewhere,' the first one hissed. 'She cannot have gone far. We must find the little *bikkja*, or else the king will have our innards.'

'Yes, and with that red-gold hair, there is nowhere she can hide for long.' His companion snickered. 'You go left, I'll take the right. We'll search every dwelling and tent and meet up on the other side.'

'Very well.'

The mention of red-gold hair caught Ivar's attention and he froze. His thoughts turned to the woman he'd twice seen in visions. Could they be talking about her? Heart pounding with excitement, he wondered if he was finally about to meet her. But in that case, he'd first have to find her, and it would seem there were others looking for her as well. No, not looking – hunting her down. *Shit!* Then she really was in trouble.

Please, help me, she'd said, and he wanted nothing more than to do that.

'But where are you, lady?' he murmured.

Wondering why the men had called her a bitch and why they were after her, Ivar followed them while searching the darkness for a glimpse of someone in hiding. After a while, he brought out the swan's-foot amulet from his pouch. Could it be of use in guiding him to her? Sadly, no visions assailed him. He decided to fetch a weapon, in case he came upon her and needed to defend her. It was probably a foolish idea, as he couldn't be sure it was even the same woman, but if it was, she'd asked for his help and he intended to give it. Her anguish had seemed genuine, and whatever trouble she was in was not of her making, of that he was sure.

'Man, you're acting like a fool,' he muttered to himself. Chances were, he'd been dreaming and not had any magical visions at all. He was deluded if he thought he was actually about to meet the woman his mind had conjured up, yet he didn't stop walking or searching the shadows for a sign of her.

Back at the campsite, not far from the ship, he lifted his tent flap and ducked inside to grab his axe. This temporary canvas dwelling was nothing like the modern contraptions he'd used in the twenty-first century, but at least it kept the wind out, and he was lucky to have it to himself. Yet again, he owed this good fortune to Haukr, who'd lent it to him. He'd already placed his pile of sheepskins on the ground, and left the woollen blankets on top, neatly folded, so he knew he'd be warm enough.

There were several fires still going outside, partly lighting up the shadowy interior. As his eyes adjusted to the half-light, he noticed that the heap of blankets had been replaced by a bulky shape silhouetted against one side of the tent. A hastily indrawn breath reverberated around the tiny space. He stilled, his hand moving to grip the hilt of the knife at his belt.

'Who's there?' he whispered, although he had a fair idea already.

'P-please, I beg of you, don't give me away. Please! I meant no harm. I'll leave as soon as they've gone, if you just . . . if you could see your way to letting me . . . No, I'm asking too much, aren't I?' The voice was husky, but distinctly feminine, and there was a note of desperation, followed by defeat, that was impossible to miss. A head came up and he saw the glint of red-gold tresses despite the gloom.

Something stirred deep inside Ivar and that weird electrical charge he'd felt at the museum seemed to hum around them. Did she sense it too? He couldn't see her face and only had a brief impression of huge, wary eyes watching him. Sinking down on to the edge of the sheepskin pile, he sensed the woman scuttle backwards until she nudged the fabric wall. If she went any further, she'd topple the whole structure. The air fairly vibrated with tension and fear, and he had the impression he was dealing with a cornered animal. He'd always hated bullies and immediately decided to thwart them. Of course, he'd already been on the woman's side, the moment he overheard those men talking about her in such derogatory terms. It had made him bristle. And long before that, when she'd asked for his help . . .

She was the one he'd seen. The certainty was pure instinct, as he hadn't had a good look at her yet, but he was sure, the knowledge visceral. The little amulet briefly burned in the palm of his hand, as if it agreed, and he hastily stowed it in his pouch. She didn't seem to recognise him, however. The visions must have been one-sided, and she had no idea of their connection.

'Shh, don't fret,' he murmured soothingly. 'Trust me, I'll protect you.'

Her head came up. 'Wh-what did you say?'

'Just don't make a sound, and if anyone comes searching for you, follow my lead. Can you do that?'

'Y-yes. But . . . are you sure?'

'Mm-hmm.' He rooted around in the sack that contained his clothing and came up with a crocheted beanie. 'Here, put this on, quickly.' He fumbled in the darkness to find her hands and shoved the hat into them.

'What? Why?'

'I crossed paths with the men who are hunting you. I heard them mention that you have very . . .' he tried to think of the right word, but couldn't quite remember it, '. . . er, outstanding hair, so you need to cover it up. Stuff it inside the hat if you can.'

'Distinctive? Oh, I see.'

While she busied herself with this, he stretched out beside her and rearranged the blankets she'd been hiding under. 'Lie down,' he whispered, once her hair had been tamed and safely hidden. She did so, but scooted as far away from him as possible. That wouldn't do if they were to fool anyone.

'Come here,' he murmured, putting a hand at her waist and tugging her closer.

Her whole body stiffened, but he had to give her credit for immense courage, since she didn't try to resist for long. For all she knew, he could be a lot worse than the men who'd been sent to capture her, but she let him pull her towards him. He found her grudging acquiescence endearing, but there was no time to think about that now. The sound of footsteps approaching and voices raised in anger could be heard outside. Ivar guessed the men who were hunting her had made good their threat to check every tent and the respective owners were none too pleased.

Swiftly he covered both of them with the blankets, then moved so that he was more or less lying on top of her. Bracing himself, he took some of his weight on one elbow. She jerked back again instinctively and tried to put some distance between them, but he shushed her once more and didn't budge. Her heart was beating rapidly; he could feel it through their combined layers of clothing. If he hadn't been holding her down, he was sure she'd have bolted by now.

'Listen! They're coming.' She stilled and he tried to reassure her. 'Trust me. I promise I won't hurt you. This is merely for show, I swear.'

With one arm snaking underneath her, and the other cupping her cheek, he nudged her head into his shoulder. 'Bury your face in my clothing,' he instructed. 'And lift your knees up either side of my legs so it gives the impression that we're, um . . . joined under the blankets.'

She seemed to understand and followed his instructions, her legs shaking noticeably as they flanked his. It wasn't a moment too soon, as heavy steps thundered outside and the tent flap was suddenly pulled aside. The light from a torch shone in and a snarling face appeared.

'*Hei!* Get out! What do you mean by disturbing me and my wife at this hour, and in the middle of a good tupping too?' Ivar growled. He felt the woman quaking in his arms and tightened his grip on her. The light from the torch seemed too bright after the darkness of the tent, but he was glad to see that not a single strand of her hair was visible, and she kept her face hidden.

'Beg pardon. We're looking for a runaway female.'

'Well, you won't find her here. I keep my wife under control, as you can see. Now leave, or I'll challenge you to *einvigi*.'

The man backed away, muttering something under his breath. He let the tent flap drop and shouted something to his comrade, who replied. Ivar couldn't make out the words, but their frustration was clear, and he wondered whether he was harbouring a dangerous criminal. But surely someone who trembled like a leaf couldn't be that bad? And he'd seen her in his first vision being manhandled. She was the injured party here, he was convinced of it.

They waited in silence for a while until the commotion had died down and the search had appeared to move elsewhere.

'I think you're safe,' he breathed.

She didn't immediately wriggle away from him, which was intriguing, but perhaps she was simply so terrified her limbs had seized up. It was time for him to move, though, as his body was becoming all too aware of the sensual position they were in and the curves underneath him. Very soon she'd notice as well, and he didn't want to spook her.

He moved to one side but didn't let go of her completely. For some reason he couldn't bear to sever the contact between them yet, and she didn't protest when he lay beside her with one arm still holding her tight and one leg tangled with hers.

She took a deep breath and whispered, 'Thank you. From the bottom of my heart, I thank you.'

'You're welcome. I am Ivar. Ivar Thoresson from Birkiþorp in Svíaríki. May I know your name?'

She hesitated. 'Is that wise? I don't want to drag you into my business, and the less you know, the better. Probably.'

A huff of amusement escaped him. 'You think I'm not already entangled in it?'

'Oh, well . . . no, I suppose you're right.' A sigh whispered through her. 'I'm Ellisif Birgirsdóttír and I've run away from a marriage I want no part of.'

'I see.' Ivar took a moment to think this over. If he was harbouring another man's wife, he could be in deep trouble. 'So you're not a thief, and those were your husband's men chasing after you?'

'No, I haven't stolen a thing!' She sounded horrified at the mere notion. 'And they're the king's guards. I'm not married yet. I'm a widow, with extensive lands. King Hjorr is planning to wed me to one of his favourites, Kári Knutsson. I'm not willing, though, and I should have been consulted. I . . . I was brought here against my will and have been kept confined with a few other women for several weeks now. I simply had to escape. Unfortunately, although I managed to slip past them, the guards saw me and gave chase. They've been hunting me since last night.' A shiver went through her, and Ivar heard a small sob, which she tried to suppress.

Relief coursed through him. He didn't know her, but for some reason it seemed important that she should be single. Why, he had no idea, as a relationship with a woman of this era had been the furthest thing on his mind when he'd travelled back in time.

'Why weren't you asked for your consent? And do you not have anyone to speak for you? A father or brother?'

He knew a little about marriage customs during Viking times and was sure that usually male relatives arranged these things, even if they made sure the woman accepted the decision without too much protest. From what he'd gathered, it wasn't in anyone's interest for two people who detested each other to marry. That would never work.

'I have no one. That is why the king has the right to decide. He already forced me into one repugnant marriage when I was but sixteen winters. I'll do anything to avoid another. Anything!' A shudder racked her so violently, Ivar shook too.

This made them both realise simultaneously that they were still tightly entwined, and he loosened his hold on her a fraction yet didn't let go entirely. For one thing, he liked the feel of her against him, and for another, he wasn't sure she wouldn't bolt immediately. And now he'd found her, he wasn't letting her go until he had some more answers. Besides, the tent had been designed for only one person, which meant there wasn't a lot of room for the two of them. They'd have to stay close or one or other of them would crash out through the tent wall. That would never do.

No, for the moment, he was keeping her right here where she was safe.

Ellisif knew that she shouldn't linger in the stranger's arms. In Ivar's arms. But it felt so good after the fright she'd had – safe and comforting in a way she hadn't experienced since she was a child. She couldn't see him and had only had a quick glimpse when that guard had shoved his torch inside the tent. She'd noticed handsome features, dark-blond hair and a sharp jawline under a close-cropped beard. He was big and muscular, his legs much longer than hers, and she was aware of every lean inch of him as he pressed so tightly against her. *Like a lover*. But he wasn't holding her inappropriately – apart from the fact that they shouldn't be lying here together at all really – and he hadn't groped her. She'd never come across a man before who could keep his hands to himself, and found it hard to believe he was for real.

His size didn't intimidate her either; quite the opposite. Having his large body covering hers had been thrilling in a way she didn't quite comprehend. It also stirred memories of the dreams she'd had. As did his words earlier. A man had held her precisely like this, making her feel cared for and protected, telling her not to fret. Had it been a premonition? She'd never experienced such a thing before, but her grandmother had claimed to be related to a powerful *võlva*. It could be she'd inherited some of her gifts.

'I should go,' she mumbled. Where to, she didn't have a clue, but she'd have to decide. Those guards hadn't sounded as though they'd give up their search until they found her. How far could she escape on foot? Or would it be possible to sneak on board a ship before dawn? It all seemed so daunting, and she closed her eyes for a moment, battling the urge to simply break down and cry.

'Is that wise?' Ivar's deep voice broke through her misery and she blinked up at him, even though he couldn't see her.

'What? Well, yes, I've already put you to a lot of trouble. I can't stay. That would be asking too much.'

She felt him shaking his head. 'No, Ellisif, it wouldn't. I want you to stay.'

She drew in a sharp breath, suddenly more aware of him as a man. One who still had one leg across hers and whose face was only a hair's breadth away from her own. The sensation of having him so close didn't repulse her, the way Þjódólfr's nearness always had. In fact, his touch sent little sparks through her blood, and the air between them vibrated with awareness. That didn't mean she was ready to repay this complete stranger with her body. She needed to put some distance between them.

As if he'd come to the same conclusion, Ivar moved his leg and shuffled back a bit. 'I'm sorry. I didn't mean to imply anything improper. I . . . I would like to offer you my protection tonight.'

As she opened her mouth to protest, he added, 'Without any conditions, you have my oath on that.'

'Really? Why?'

What would he gain from this? In Ellisif's experience, no one did anything out of the goodness of their heart. Especially not for a person they'd only just met who meant nothing to them.

'To be perfectly honest, I don't know,' he admitted. 'It simply seems like the right thing to do. And . . . well, I didn't like the way those men spoke about you. If what you say is true, the king is doing you a grave injustice, and believe me, I am violently opposed to anyone having their free choice taken away from them. Or being coerced. Therefore, I want to help you.'

'I see.'

She had the impression there was something he wasn't telling her, but he sounded sincere, and some instinct told her she could trust him. It may be that she'd have to pay him at some point, but he clearly wasn't about to assault her right now. And what other option did she have? None, really. She needed to be pragmatic.

'Very well, I accept. And . . . thank you. Again.'

She heard the smile in his voice as he told her, 'Excellent. I promise you won't regret it. Now, how about we get some sleep? In the morning I'll find you some boy's clothing so that we can smuggle you away from here without anyone being the wiser. There is a youth among the group I'm travelling with. His garments should fit you.'

'Boy's clothing?' As far as Ellisif was aware, women wearing male apparel was frowned upon, but perhaps that was only where she came from.

'Yes. Everyone will be on the lookout for a woman with red-gold hair, won't they? Therefore, a youth wearing a hat won't be noticed much. It will only be until we have put this place behind us. What say you?'

She smiled into the darkness. 'I say you were sent to me by the gods.'

He chuckled at that, and muttered something that sounded like *You have no idea*, then told her to turn around. When she did, he gathered her close again, her back to his front, with his arm around her waist. They fitted together perfectly.

'Best if we sleep like this, in case those men return,' he murmured, and she didn't protest.

In truth, she wanted to stay like this for ever, exactly like in her dreams.

Chapter Seven

Skiringssal, Vestfold, 11 October/Haustmánuðr AD *875*

Ivar was woken soon after dawn by something tickling his nose. As he put up a hand and pushed it away, he realised it was a long strand of hair, glimmering reddish-gold in the light trickling through the tent covering. The happenings of the night before came rushing back. Ellisif and the men hunting her. Had they given up? Or were they still patrolling the area looking for her? No one had disturbed them again, but that didn't mean the king's men weren't still out searching for the fugitive.

A knot formed in his stomach. He had to protect her. Needed to spirit her away from this place and the threat from the king. It was an almost visceral urge that he couldn't have explained to anyone else. He simply knew he had to do it. As if he'd been sent here for this specific purpose. Was that what the swan's-foot visions had been about? It had to be. Good thing they were leaving today anyway, otherwise he would have had to try and persuade Thorald to set off early.

Thorald. What would he say about this? Ivar doubted he'd want to get mixed up in the king's affairs or rile the man unnecessarily by aiding a fugitive. On the other hand, the monarch hadn't done anything to stop Askhild and Álrik's uncle from usurping their domains, so perhaps Thorald wouldn't mind thwarting him somewhat. It was probably best not to get him involved, though, at least not quite yet.

Ivar knew he should move. Go and find Álrik to try and persuade him to lend Ellisif some of his clothes. But he was very comfortable, with a warm, pliant woman snuggled up against him. He was happy to do nothing more than hold her for now. Last night she'd seemed frightened when he'd told her he wanted her to stay. He didn't want her to be scared of him; he wanted to win her over.

That thought brought him up short. *Win her over?* As in courting her, as the Vikings would say? That was ridiculous. He hardly knew anything about her. Besides, this was the ninth century. You couldn't just have a casual relationship with a woman without marriage being involved. Not unless she was a whore, and he was quite sure Ellisif was far from that. It was obvious that she was high-born, if she was an heiress. Did he really want to start something with a woman like that? It would be madness, and yet . . .

No, he absolutely shouldn't.

She stirred, breaking into his thoughts. As she became aware of her surroundings and exactly where she was – no doubt registering every inch of him pressed up against her – her whole body went rigid. As his hand was near her ribcage, the sudden fluttering of her heart was very noticeable, and her chest rose and fell with an indrawn breath.

'Shh, it's only me, Ivar,' he whispered, keeping very still so as not to frighten her. 'You're safe for now. Remember?'

She turned within his arms and glanced up at him, her eyes large and luminous in the half-gloom, squinting slightly. 'I remember.'

They studied each other wordlessly. It *was* her! There was no mistaking it. Ivar's gaze travelled over the heart-shaped face he'd seen in his visions. It was still pale and drawn, but starkly beautiful to him in that fey way he'd glimpsed before. In the morning light, her eyes were the green of a mossy forest pool, surrounded by long dark-brown lashes and topped with bird's-wing eyebrows. Her nose and mouth weren't perfect, but they were eminently attractive nonetheless; the nose dotted with a few freckles and the mouth luscious with a pronounced Cupid's bow. The freckles continued across her cheeks and he found them enticing. But this was not the time to think about that.

'I should go.' She made a move as if to rise, but she was still trapped by his arm and didn't get anywhere.

'Please don't. I want to help you.' He waited for her reaction and watched her eyebrows lowering.

'You've already done enough. I must fend for myself now.'

'Ellisif.' He whispered her name and liked the feel of it on his tongue. It was a beautiful name and suited its owner. 'I'm offering you assistance. Refusing would be churlish, don't you think?'

'Are you sure about this?' she asked quietly, her eyes not leaving his, as if she was trying to discern what manner of man he was. She looked to be having trouble focusing, but he figured she was probably exhausted from everything that had happened.

He nodded. 'I am. Do you trust me to get you away from here?'

She didn't hesitate. 'Yes. I do.'

For some reason, he felt as though her words held a deeper meaning. There was a definite connection between them – chemistry unlike anything he'd ever experienced before – but it could wait. There would be time enough later to pursue that thought; for now, he needed to ensure her safety.

'Good. Then please stay here while I go in search of a disguise for you. I'll be back as soon as I can.'

With that, he reluctantly disentangled himself from her and ducked out of the tent. He was very much hoping he'd be allowed to wake up next to Ellisif again in the near future.

Sweet Freya, but that was some awakening!

Ellisif let out a long breath, relaxing under the warm blanket. When she'd first opened her eyes and found herself more or less caged in by a big male body, panic had slammed into her gut and made her freeze. She'd been completely disorientated and for a horrible moment she had thought herself back home, with Þjódólfr holding her prisoner in his bed. Until she remembered that he was dead and the man behind her spoke, his lovely voice resonating through her.

Ivar.

Relief had flooded her, but then she'd noticed how close their bodies were. Did she want to be snuggled up to a stranger like that? Perhaps take things a step further? She told herself she didn't, although she couldn't help a small dart of excitement from fizzing through her veins at the thought of what it might be like to lie with someone so much younger and fitter than her former husband. She'd heard other women whispering about the joys of such couplings and it had always made her jealous. But she shouldn't even contemplate such a thing.

Then she had turned around and gazed at perfection. Well, as far as she could see; at such close quarters his features were a bit blurred because of her bad eyesight. She couldn't describe him any other way, though. The dark-blond hair she'd glimpsed the night before surrounded a handsome face with intensely blue eyes. Despite his fair hair, his lashes and eyebrows were nearly black, the former as long as her own, from what she could make out. The effect was spellbinding. She vaguely noted a proud nose, firm mouth and jutting cheekbones, as well as a square jaw covered with a tidy dark-golden beard. It was a far cry from the horrible bushy thatch her former husband had sported, and she'd itched to touch it with her fingertips.

She knew Ivar was tall and muscular, and as he left the tent, he moved as smoothly as a lynx, so he was obviously well trained. It must have been sheer luck that brought her to his tent last night – if anyone could protect her, it was him. Still, she needed to stand on her own two feet now and not rely on anyone. She must learn to be strong, and letting Ivar help only delayed the moment when she had to strike out on her own.

But who was she fooling? It was a relief to let someone else handle matters, if only for a while.

After what seemed a long time but probably wasn't, he returned bearing a bundle of clothing and smiled at her, showing even white teeth. She could see him better from a distance and it confirmed her earlier impressions.

'Álrik was easily persuaded,' he told her. 'He's only sixteen and up for a bit of intrigue. We'll tell everyone you are a friend of his from home and that when you ran into each other, you begged a ride back on board our ship.'

She sat up and folded the blanket. 'Thank you.'

He grew serious. 'Where is your home? Perhaps you would prefer to go there rather than come with us?'

She shook her head. 'No, I cannot return without a husband. The king would merely come for me again. I . . . I hadn't planned to go back at all.'

He hunkered down next to her. 'Where *were* you heading then? Do you have somewhere safe to go? Someone who will hide you?'

'No, there is no one. I was going to look for work, perhaps become a thrall.'

'A thrall?' He frowned at her. 'You mean willingly?'

'Yes, if there is no other option.' She spread her hands in a helpless gesture. 'Anything is better than wedding Kári. Trust me on that.'

'Tell me about him.' That piercing blue gaze was fixed on her and Ellisif found herself wanting to confide everything, but she contented herself with the basics.

'He has seen at least forty-five winters and is uncouth and brutish. He has five grown-up sons, so he isn't bothered by the fact that I'm old and barren, and he's a loyal friend to the king. He'll fight for Hjorr against Haraldr Hálfdanarsson when the time comes, and for that reason he was to be rewarded. With me.'

'Old? You? May I ask exactly how many winters you have lived through?'

'Six and twenty. So I'm not exactly young, but my domains more than make up for my deficiencies, apparently.' She couldn't help the bitterness that crept into her tone.

Ivar smiled and leaned forward to gently kiss her cheek. 'I would have guessed twenty at the most, and from where I'm sitting, there are no deficiencies. None whatsoever.'

Ellisif blinked in surprise and had to restrain herself from raising her hand to touch the place where he'd kissed her. A friendly, reassuring sort of kiss only, but a kiss nonetheless. She felt her cheeks flood with heat and knew she was blushing; she couldn't remember the last time anyone had paid her a compliment. The blatant admiration in his eyes was a balm to her fragile ego, and she decided not to tell him right now about her terrible eyesight. He didn't appear to have registered her mention of being barren either, but she wasn't about to repeat it.

Before she could comment on his surprising action, he rose to his feet. 'Please get dressed and come and join me outside for some bread and cheese. I'll need to take down the tent and stow it on board. Oh, and don't forget to hide your hair under the hat.

Every last strand, mind. That man was right – it is extremely eye-catching, not to mention beautiful.'

With that admonition, he was gone again, and she was left staring at the tent flap.

What had just happened?

When Ellisif emerged, dressed in Álrik's clothing, Ivar had to smother a grin. The male outfit suited her, and it was a relief to see a woman with legs for a change, although he kept that thought to himself. Her lovely hair was well hidden and the woollen tunic was loose enough to hide any female curves. Nevertheless, he'd have to see about finding her some kind of binding for her breasts, or this deception wouldn't last long. It would do for now, though.

'Ah, there you are, Eli.' He beckoned her forward. 'Come and have some bread with me and Álrik.' He turned to the youth, who was waiting nearby, trying to hide a smile. It was clear he relished the idea of an adventure and was ready to play along. 'Álrik, here's your friend.'

Thankfully none of the other people in their group were nearby, and therefore there were no comments about the fact that a friend of Álrik's had emerged from Ivar's tent. He led Ellisif over to a couple of boulders and shared out flatbread, cheese and ale between the three of them. A little way away, Thorald and some of his men were readying the ship for the onward journey, loading victuals and other supplies. Askhild was close by as well, packing up her and Thorald's things. Ivar finished his food quickly and went to take down his tent and retrieve his belongings. Ellisif had her bundle by her feet already.

By this time, Álrik had discovered that Ellisif really did come from somewhere not too far from where he'd grown up, and they were soon discussing the area. If one didn't look too closely, they were no different from other teenagers around here, which was a blessing. Ivar went in search of Thorald to inform him of what was happening. The man might not like it, but Ivar didn't want to lie to his kinsman or keep secrets from him. He'd never establish any kind of rapport with him if he began by deceiving him.

'A runaway woman? From the king's hall?' Thorald scowled, but thankfully kept his voice down after Ivar had told him his story. 'Why do you want to bring her? It is not your concern.'

'I know, but she has no one else and it makes my blood boil the way she's been treated. It is no more right than the situation with Askhild and Álrik and their uncle. If she's discovered, I swear I'll take all the blame and you can pretend you knew nothing about it. Please, can she come with us?'

Thorald hesitated. 'Very well. I don't hold with women being forced into marriages that are repugnant to them, and if this is the second time . . .' He shook his head. 'We'd better leave as soon as possible, then.'

Ivar smiled. 'Thank you. I am in your debt.' He recalled that the man had already been kind in letting him come along on this journey, and added, 'Well, more than I am already, I mean.'

That made his kinsman's mouth twitch. 'That you are.'

Askhild seemed surprised to find that they had an extra passenger, especially when Álrik claimed Ellisif as his friend. Wisely, his sister didn't comment on this. Once they were away from Skiringssal, she could be told the truth.

As they were all jumping on board and settling down to take their places at the oars, a group of men made their way along the shore, scrutinising every ship. One of them shouted at Thorald to halt. He stopped with his hands on the gunwale, ready to push his vessel away from the jetty. Ivar was next to him, about to help.

'Yes? Is there something amiss?' Thorald threw the man, presumably one of the king's guardsmen, a cool glance and watched as the others came up behind their leader.

'We seek a runaway. A woman with red-gold hair, very distinctive. You can't really miss it. Have you seen her?' The man craned his neck to peer into the ship, as if he suspected that Ellisif was concealed behind a barrel or kist. There were no obvious hiding places, though, and luckily his gaze only skimmed over the youth sitting next to Álrik, gazing out to sea. Ivar forced himself not to look at her. He didn't want to draw any attention to her whatsoever.

'No, we've not seen any woman of that description,' Thorald bit out. 'My wife is the only female in our group.' He nodded towards Askhild. 'As you can see, her hair isn't red. Now if you don't mind, we need to be on our way.'

'You are sure? She ran away two nights ago and the king will pay handsomely for her return.'

'Quite certain. And surely she'll be far away by now after so long?' Thorald leaned into the ship's side, as if impatient to start pushing. Ivar followed suit.

The guardsman hesitated a moment longer. 'Very well, but if you come across her along the coast, you are to bring her back, is that clear?'

Thorald merely raised his eyebrows, and with a growl of annoyance the man stomped off towards the next ship. His cohorts trailed after him listlessly, their expressions uniformly bored.

'Odin's ravens, what a bunch of wretches,' Thorald muttered as he and Ivar finally scrambled on board. 'No wonder they lost her. I'd wager they couldn't find a cowpat in a field full of cattle.'

Ivar chuckled as he took his seat and grabbed an oar. It was good to know his kinsman had a sense of humour, even if he hadn't lightened up much around him yet. Perhaps there was hope.

Chapter Eight

South coast of Vestfold and Agder, 11 October/Haustmánuðr AD 875

Ellisif sat with Álrik in the bow. Neither of them was required to help with the rowing. The others only rowed until they were far enough out to sea to hoist the sail anyway. Just as well, as she doubted she would have been of much use right now. Her whole body was shaking again, the fear only slowly subsiding. She'd been so sure that man was going to recognise her and haul her out of the ship and back to the king. He was one of the two she'd seen by the gate the night she escaped, and he must have caught a glimpse of her face then.

Thankfully, he hadn't asked to inspect each and every passenger. She must remember to express her gratitude to Thorald – the leader of this group, Ivar had told her – for his superb lying. Come to think of it, he hadn't really told any falsehoods. He'd been asked if he had seen a woman with red-gold hair, and he hadn't, because she was currently hiding those accursed tresses under Ivar's big hat.

When she was very young, her mother had told her that her hair was pretty, but Þjódólfr had used it as yet another excuse to taunt her. 'You look like your head is on fire,' he'd told her on numerous occasions, and the way he said it was far from complimentary. She didn't think it was that vivid a shade of red, but she would still have wished it to be a pale blonde, as was the preferred choice for most men.

And yet Ivar had said he saw no deficiencies whatsoever when he regarded her. Did that mean he actually liked red-headed females? She wasn't sure whether to believe it.

As if conjured by her thoughts, he padded over on silent feet and sank down beside her. Álrik had just gone off to chat to his sister, who was at the other end of the ship – presumably to let her know who Ellisif really was, since the woman had been throwing her curious glances – and left room for Ivar. Well, more or less. The big man had to fold his long legs up like a knife in order to fit. Their shoulders touched, but she didn't mind. It was comforting and made her calm down instantly.

'How are you bearing up?' he asked, speaking quietly and looking around to make sure no one else was listening. With the sail flapping noisily in the wind and the waves slapping against the hull, it seemed safe to talk.

'Fine.' She bit her teeth together to stop herself from admitting quite how terrified she'd been, but he must have known, because he put a hand on her arm and gave it a quick squeeze.

'Hopefully you're safe now. We just need to get you as far away from the king as possible, then we'll see about finding a permanent solution.'

Ellisif turned towards him and squinted at him, trying to make out his expression. 'You know of someone who might take me on as a thrall?'

She definitely saw his eyebrows come down in a fierce scowl. 'No! That is not going to happen.'

'What? But that's the only—'

'No,' he interrupted her, seemingly battling to keep his voice down. 'You are not becoming anyone's thrall. Not if I have any say in the matter.'

'You don't,' she muttered.

That wasn't entirely true. He clearly did have a say, since she was dependent on his goodwill right now. That ought to have frightened her too, but it didn't.

'It can't be what you truly want. Is it?' He peered at her, and she turned away, blinking to stop the burn of tears wanting to spill on to her cheeks.

'Of course not, but I told you, I'd prefer that to being wed to Kári. He is of an age with my late husband, and from what I've observed, cut from the same cloth. Believe me, I am fairly certain he'd make an even worse spouse, and that's saying something. If only they'd let me wed his son instead. He seemed nice, but of course, he wouldn't want an older wife who can't give him children.'

Her insides clenched at the thought that she would never have the pleasure of holding a baby in her arms. She should have come to terms with it by now, but she hadn't.

Ivar must have sensed her anguish. No one was looking their way, and under cover of his tunic, he took her hand, plaiting his fingers with hers. It was curiously intimate, but also reassuring, and she drew strength from his touch as he tightened his hold.

'There has to be some other way. Together we will find it. Promise me you'll not do anything hasty, please? I am pledged to help my kinsman Thorald first with the quest we are on – I'll tell you all about that in a moment – but afterwards you have my oath that I will do my best to find a solution for you. One that doesn't involve being a thrall. Agreed?'

The warmth from his hand was giving her courage and hope,

something she hadn't had in a long time, so she nodded. 'Very well. Can I help in this quest?'

'That will be for Thorald to decide, but for now, here's why we are heading to Hörðaland . . .'

Ivar reluctantly let go of Ellisif's hand while he told her all about Askhild, Álrik and their evil uncle. He would have liked to keep touching her, but until the other men in the group had been apprised of her true identity, that seemed unwise. It probably wasn't wise in any case, but he'd think about that later. And although she hadn't pulled away from his grip, she had to be wondering why he'd taken hold of her fingers in the first place. This wasn't the twenty-first century – men and women had to keep their distance for the sake of propriety.

'I do hope Álrik can regain his domains,' Ellisif commented once he'd finished his tale. 'And at least now the uncle can't threaten to marry Askhild, as she's already wedded to Thorald.' She glanced at his kinsman, who was sitting in the stern, competently steering the ship. 'He seems a determined man.'

Ivar chuckled. 'Grumpy, you mean?'

That earned him a smile that almost had him gasping for breath. For a moment, her eyes shone and dimples appeared on either side of her mouth, lending her an impish appearance. He had to restrain the urge to grab her and kiss the hell out of her right then and there. Instead, he shook himself inwardly. What on earth was the matter with him? He'd reached the age of thirty-five without ever truly falling in love. Why was this woman affecting him so? He barely knew her. Had he gone all caveman by travelling back in time? His protective instincts were rushing to the fore in a virtual torrent. It was disconcerting, to say the least.

'Tell me how you are connected to these people.' Ellisif tilted her head to one side and squinted yet again before throwing another glance at Thorald. 'You resemble him. Are you related?'

'Distantly.' He trotted out the tale he'd fed everyone else and wished he could tell her the truth. It went against the grain to lie all the time. Also, it was hard work remembering what he'd said so he didn't give himself away. 'But I'm not sure Thorald is convinced we are kin. I suspect he's keeping me under observation and taking me along on this journey as some kind of test. That's partly why I'd like to help him with his endeavours first, if you don't mind.'

She shrugged. 'No, it seems eminently sensible. And my problems can wait, as long as I'm not a captive of the king. He might take my property by force, but if not, it will still be there in a few weeks' time.'

'I'm glad you see it that way. You are obviously a wise woman.' He grinned at her. 'And I don't mean a *vōlva*.'

She blushed at the compliment but grinned back. 'How I wish I was! Then perhaps I would have been taken seriously. And I do in fact have an ancestor who was a real *vísindakona*.'

He looked her in the eyes as he said, 'I will always take you seriously, you have my oath on that.'

'I . . . thank you.'

'Now then, are you going to tell me how long you've had difficulties with your eyesight?'

She gasped and stared at him in obvious horror. 'Wh-what? How . . . ?'

'How did I know? I've seen it before.' When her cheeks went so red he thought she'd combust, he added soothingly, 'It's not a crime. It happens to most people, you know, sooner or later.'

Ellisif hung her head and stared at the ship's planks. 'Yes, but not when you are young. I . . . I can't do even the most basic of stitching without making mistakes. My . . . my husband found me utterly lacking. A failure as a wife in every way. He—'

'*Hei!*' He interrupted her pity party. She had been brainwashed into thinking herself worthless, anyone could see that, and he needed to change her mindset as soon as possible. Such negativity would not help in the slightest. 'Surely you know better than that? He was obviously a complete *niðingr*.'

'What?' She blinked at him as if she didn't believe he'd just said that.

'From what you've told me so far, the man was an oaf and not deserving of either you or your property. He was probably well aware of that, which is why he tried to constantly demean you. It must have made him feel better about himself. Honestly, why would it be your fault that you can't see well? Surely there were others who could perform any tasks you couldn't?'

'Yes, but I should have been able to do them myself.'

'What utter rubbish.' Ivar was torn, wanting to give her some hope of seeing better. He could so easily do that if he took her to the future, but that would mean having to come clean about where he was really from. He compromised by saying, 'There might be a way to improve your eyesight, but I can't tell you about that now. Trust me when I say that it in no way diminishes who you are. Not to me, at any rate.'

He saw tears hovering on her lashes, but she dashed them away. 'Thank you. You are very kind, Ivar. In fact, I think you might be the kindest man I've ever met.'

'Not at all.'

For some reason he didn't want her to think of him as kind. Or at least not merely that. He wanted so much more. Kind was way too bland.

They made landfall towards dusk, while there was still enough light to see about finding wood for campfires and suitable places to pitch their tents. Thorald had steered the ship on to a small beach away from any habitation, which Ellisif was pleased about. The last thing she needed was to run into more people; strangers she'd have to hide her true identity from. It was bad enough to be deceiving this small group.

'You can have my tent to yourself tonight.' Ivar had come up behind her and his quiet voice made her jump.

'What? But where will you bed down?' He had already done so much for her, it felt wrong to deprive him of his tent on top of everything else. And a very tiny part of her regretted the fact that his big body wouldn't be warming hers tonight. Well, perhaps more than a tiny part, if she was honest.

'With Álrik and two of the others. Don't look so worried. I'll be fine.' He glanced around to make sure they were out of earshot of everyone else, and added in a whisper, 'I'd happily share with you again, but when these people find out you are a woman, that would make them assume things about you. I don't want that to happen.'

'Thank you.' She noticed he said 'about you', not about him. That warmed her, as it showed concern for her reputation and well-being. He really was a most unusual man.

'It might kill me, though.' At her sharp glance, he clarified, 'Not to lie next to you, I mean. I enjoyed it. Very much.'

'Oh.' Her traitorous cheeks once again became suffused with colour at his directness. She could feel them catching fire but could do nothing about it. It was ludicrous really – she was a widow well past her first youth, and not a blushing maiden. Not that she ought to encourage him to say such things to her, as it was too outrageous, but she couldn't help but delight in the fact that he so obviously liked her. She had no idea how to reply, though, so she kept quiet.

Ivar grinned. 'I'm sorry, I shouldn't tease. Forgive me?'

'I . . . Yes. Of course. I'd better . . .' She indicated the pieces of wood in her arms, which were destined for the nearest fire. She'd forgotten all about them while Ivar stood so close. Sweet Freya, what was the matter with her?

'I'll see you later.'

He sauntered off to put up his tent for her, and she shook herself mentally. There was no point mooning over this man. She didn't know anything about him and he was only in her life temporarily. Wishing for anything else was foolish, something she could ill afford to be. No, even if he was making eyes at her – and it definitely seemed that way – she had to ignore it.

Hard though that would be.

Precisely how hard she found out a short while later, when they all gathered around the fire to eat *nattverðr*. Ivar had sunk down to sit next to her at the last moment, and his arm brushed against hers as he folded his long legs and made himself comfortable. The brief contact made her stomach tingle. Her gaze strayed to his muscular thighs of its own accord. His tunic had ridden up because of the position he was in, and the woollen trousers he wore were stretched to the limit. She had a sudden urge to touch him, feel the solid warmth of him under her fingers. A memory of how his leg had felt slung over hers as they lay in his tent last night flitted through her mind. Butterflies started up a mad dance inside her stomach. She'd relished the weight of it, had wanted to snuggle closer . . .

No, what am I thinking? This was madness. She closed her eyes and tried to control her emotions, then bent to concentrate on her food. But as she took her first spoonful of stew, he leaned down to whisper in her ear, the brief contact sending a shiver through her.

'Thorald wants me to tell everyone who you really are, now that we are away from Skiringssal. Do I have your permission? Your secret will be safe with them, I promise.'

'Very well.' She trusted Ivar, and if he vouched for the others, that was good enough for her.

Ivar nodded at Thorald, who asked for silence, then said, 'My kinsman has something to tell you all, and I would appreciate it if you'd keep this to yourselves.'

She saw Ivar's eyes open wide with surprise, presumably because Thorald had referred to him as his kinsman. She remembered he'd told her the man was still suspicious, so this was a step forward. He gathered himself quickly, though, and launched into the tale of how he'd come across her and why. Everyone listened attentively, and when he was done talking, he pulled off her hat. Her hair spilled out in a long plait with messy strands sticking out everywhere. There was a collective intake of breath, and then one of the older men, who was called Holmstein, nodded.

'I recognise you, Mistress Ellisif,' he said. 'Your domains are not far from my uncle's and I visited once a few years ago. Thought there was something familiar about you.'

She swallowed hard, but tried not to let the panic rise to the surface. If he'd recognised her, chances were others would too. Ivar put a hand on her arm and gave it a gentle squeeze before addressing the man.

'But you didn't put two and two together until you saw her hair, am I right? Which means if she keeps it covered and continues to wear Álrik's clothing, she'll be safe enough for now.'

'Aye, that's true. Never fear, you make a convincing youth. And you have my oath I'll not say a word. That husband of yours was an *argr* and no mistake.' The man spat on the ground at the mention of Þjódólfr, and Ellisif couldn't help but smile.

'Thank you.' She glanced towards Thorald. 'And thank you most of all for allowing me to come along. I'll try not to be in the way.'

'It is nothing.' Thorald was being his usual gruff self, but she could tell he was a good man underneath his brusque exterior. His wife must have thought so too, as she smiled at him with love in her eyes, and took his hand before glancing at Ellisif.

'I'm very pleased to have another woman with us. I've been feeling rather outnumbered. Come, sit beside me and tell me more. We might have some acquaintances in common.'

Ellisif doubted that very much, as Þjódólfr had never taken her with him when he went anywhere. She hadn't left her home from the day she married until the king's messengers came to request her presence a couple of weeks ago. But she took her bowl and went to sit with Askhild. It was nice to be asked, and it felt as though she had an ally in the other woman. At the same time, she missed being next to Ivar. His steady presence had kept her grounded while he spilled her secrets, and she had the urge to always stay by his side. Safe. Protected.

But that was pathetic – she had to rely on herself, not lean on him for every little thing. She was stronger than that and she'd been through worse than the situation she found herself in right now. Soon he would be out of her life for good. He'd said he was going back to Svíaríki once he'd helped Álrik gain possession of his domains. And despite his assurances that he would assist her too, there wasn't much he could do in reality. She needed to figure out her future on her own.

With determination, she turned to Askhild and they started to talk about their respective homes.

Chapter Nine

South coast of Vestfold and Agder, 11 October/Haustmánuðr AD 875

'You could do worse, you know.'

Ivar turned as Thorald sat down beside him on the little beach. He'd been staring out to sea, watching the moonlight glimmering across the water and letting the peace soothe him. He hadn't been tired enough to go to sleep yet, and figured he'd let Álrik start snoring before he joined him and some of the other men in one of the bigger tents. The youth had a tendency to chatter, and that was the last thing he wanted right now. His brain was too full of thoughts of Ellisif.

'What do you mean?' He glanced at his kinsman. Well, ancestor really, but as the man was very much alive in the here and now, he couldn't think of him as such at the moment.

'If you marry Ellisif, you'll be set up for life. Holmstein knows of her domains. He tells me they are quite extensive. As her husband, they would be yours.'

'Husband?' Ivar shook his head. 'I'm not looking to marry anyone in . . . er, here.'

He'd almost said 'in this century' but caught himself in the nick of time. How could he explain to Thorald that he was only visiting for a short while in order to get to know him, and to gather information about the Viking age in general? Acquiring a wife was never part of thc plan, and neither was remaining here for good.

'Why not? You clearly like her.' Thorald's mouth turned up on one side and his eyes twinkled with amusement. He nudged Ivar with his shoulder. 'I'd say you more than like her, judging by the way you stare at her. If you hadn't told the others she was a woman, they would have started to worry about you.'

'*Jesus!*' Ivar dry-washed his face. 'Was I that obvious? I'm sorry . . .'

Thorald chuckled. 'Perhaps not to everyone, but I'm observant. It has always been my role to stay in the background and watch the people around me. That was one of my tasks on behalf of Haukr, and it kept him safe more than once.'

'You never minded?' Ivar turned to regard the other man.

'Minded? About what?'

'Not being the one in charge. Haukr having all the power, I mean. Did you not want that for yourself?' He was curious now, and extremely pleased that Thorald was finally being a bit more friendly and opening up to him. Joking with him.

Thorald shook his head. 'No, never. Haukr is a good man and deserving of everything he has. He and I grew up together. We were best friends and foster-brothers. We would die for each other and I've never coveted anything of his. I could have left at any time and set up my own hall somewhere. We went raiding – did you know that? – and I've been on trading ventures with his friend Hrafn too. I came back with more than enough riches to strike out on my own, but I didn't. I had no reason to, until I met Askhild.'

That made sense. 'But now you do?'

'Yes. As soon as we return to Svíaríki, I'll build a hall for us. Close to Haukr's but far away enough that we don't encroach upon each other's lands. If ever he needs my assistance, I'll still be nearby. Ever since he married Ceri, he hasn't needed me to the same extent anyway. Not like when he was wed to Ragnhild.'

By now, Ivar had heard about the woman Haukr had been married to before he met Ceri, and he knew she'd made him very unhappy. No wonder he'd needed the companionship and support Thorald had offered both before and after Ragnhild's death.

'I see. Well, I'm pleased for both of you, but as for myself, I'm really not planning to marry anyone. Even if she is tempting,' he added with a smile.

Thorald chuckled. 'It's early days and you've only just met. Don't dismiss the notion out of hand. It bears considering, at least. As I'm sure you are aware, power and standing come from a person's family connections and domains. Like me, you have no relatives to inherit from and have to make your own way in the world.'

'Yes, I suppose. I will give it some thought.' Seen from the point of view of someone in this century, Thorald was right, but he didn't know Ivar's true origins.

Ivar hadn't decided whether to tell him or not, but he'd like to. Not quite yet, though. It was too soon. They were starting to build a rapport and he'd like to get to know him better first. Gain his trust properly. After that, he'd see.

When the time was right, he was sure he'd know.

South coast of Agder, 12 October/Haustmánuðr AD *875*

'This land of yours is truly beautiful. May I sit with you for a while?'

Ellisif was in the bow of the ship again and had been lost in thought, trying to come up with an answer to her problems. She made room for Ivar, who was hunkered down in front of her while he waited for her reply, sensibly not standing up as they skimmed through the waves. 'Of course. And yes, I love this coastline.'

The ship was gliding along, hugging the coast but not entering any of the bays or inlets they passed. There were no deep fjords as yet. Instead, the bays were surrounded by low rounded hills covered in a mixture of evergreen and deciduous trees. Higher up, mist hung over the treetops as if trying to smother them, while down below, narrow, flat areas held settlements and farmland. There were plenty of islands that had to be passed, but Holmstein, who was steering now, appeared to know how to avoid any dangers.

Ivar made himself comfortable next to her, stretching his legs out and crossing them at the ankles. 'You had a very serious expression on your face. What were you thinking about?'

His blue eyes regarded her intently, as if he was trying to see into her very soul. He had beautiful eyes. Gentle. Kind, but with a touch of mischief lurking in their depths. She knew she was extremely lucky to have come across this man, of all the ones whose tent she could have hidden in. Without him, she was fairly certain she'd have been back with the king right now, as she had grossly underestimated the difficulties of escaping.

'My future,' she admitted. 'I've been wondering what would happen if I went home. Whether I have enough people to defend me, should the king's men come to try and take me or my domains again. They surprised us last time and I didn't have time to organise a defence.' She hesitated, then added, 'And also whether they are truly loyal to me. They might prefer to have a man at the helm. In fact, Kári could be there already.'

Ivar tilted his head slightly to one side as if he was considering this. 'The property was yours before you married?'

'Yes. I was my father's only child and he had no other relatives. He'd been dead for only a few weeks when the king arrived out of nowhere with Þjódólfr in tow and forced me to marry him.' She clenched her fists in her lap, remembering that awful time. 'He said that if I didn't, he'd evict me by force and I wouldn't have a home any longer. I was young and scared, used to a comfortable life. There was nothing I could do but submit.'

Ivar took her hand and meshed his fingers with hers like the last time, as if wanting to imbue her with his strength. It worked to a certain extent, as she calmed down more or less immediately.

'And now?' he asked. 'Are you going to be braver?'

'I think so. All I know is that I can never go through that again. I should have refused then too. Anything would have been better than marriage to Þjódólfr. I . . . He made me feel dirty somehow. Tainted.' She shuddered at the thought of him pawing her and taking her without any consideration for her feelings. Every time it had happened, she'd tried to scrub herself clean afterwards to rid herself of the stench of him, of his touch. It never worked.

Ivar's fingers tightened around hers. 'I wish I could take those memories away from you, but they will fade with time and you will have happier ones. For now, you need to concentrate on the future. Once Álrik's domains have been secured, I'd be happy to go with you to yours and we can see how matters stand. Thorald might be able to spare a few men too. Perhaps if you don't arrive alone, your people will take you more seriously.'

She bent her head, unable to look him in the eye. 'Thank you, but I can't ask you to do that. It is not your concern. Besides, that would make them think that I . . . that we . . .'

'That we are married?' he filled in. 'Not if I act deferentially towards you and allow you to do the talking. I can simply stand behind you wearing a menacing expression. Like this.' She peeked up to find him pretending to scowl for all he was worth, his eyes crossing in exaggerated fashion. Instead of making him seem fierce, it was merely ridiculous, and she couldn't help but laugh.

She swatted his arm. 'Stop it, *fifl*. That won't fool anyone.'

He smiled at her, his eyes twinkling in the sunlight. 'Very well, but I promise I can be intimidating if I want to. You'll just have to trust me on that. So will you let me help you?'

'I suppose. I mean, if you wish.' There was no way she could refuse his offer. Not only did it make her more hopeful of a positive outcome, but it meant she wouldn't be saying goodbye to him for quite a while. That was something she didn't even want to contemplate. In a short space of time, he'd become important to her. Sweet Freya, but how had that happened? She barely knew the man.

'Good.' He kept his fingers entwined with hers while his thumb stroked her hand in a soft caress.

She ought to pull it away, but for the life of her she couldn't. He didn't seem to want her to either. To distract herself from the sensations he was stirring up inside her, she asked, 'You do not consider it wrong for a woman to rule her own domain?'

His eyebrows rose. 'No. Why should I? Women do it all the time, don't they, when their husbands are away?'

'That is true, but it is not often that one is in charge permanently.'

'As far as I'm concerned, women are equal to men and as capable of doing anything they set their minds to.'

'Equal?' She gaped at him, doubting that she'd heard him right. He couldn't be serious.

'Yes, absolutely. You may be smaller in stature and not as strong physically, but that doesn't mean you can't be in a position of authority. If you want to rule your household, you should.

As a widow, you are entitled to do so, are you not? No one should be forced into marriage. It is an important decision, and I'm of the opinion that both parties ought to be in love before they contemplate such a thing.'

'In love?' She blinked at him. She'd never known a man to express such an opinion or so much as mention the word in connection with marriage. Of course, it helped if both spouses liked and respected each other, and desire might go a long way towards making a marriage a success, but love? She was equally astonished at his views on women in general. No man of her acquaintance had ever voiced the opinion that the sexes were equal. She didn't know whether to be shocked or astounded. Perhaps both.

Ivar's gaze turned teasing again. 'What, don't tell me you've never been in love, Ellisif. I won't believe you.'

She could feel her cheeks burning. Why did this man have that effect on her all the time? It was as though she was thirteen winters again, with no control over herself. 'No, I haven't,' she bit out through clenched teeth.

'No? Seriously? What was the matter with the men in your father's household?'

'Nothing. I mean, they weren't supposed to court me. Father was going to arrange a marriage for me and it wouldn't be to anyone in our settlement.' She had always known it would be his choice, but she'd hoped to have some say in the matter. He might not have been the most doting of fathers, but he would never have forced her to wed someone as repugnant as Þjódólfr.

Ivar nudged her with his shoulder and grinned. 'I'll wager there were at least one or two young men you couldn't stop peeking at, who threw you heated glances whenever your father wasn't around. I've never yet come across a young girl who didn't go swooning about some handsome swain. Even my younger foster-sister, Maddie, who swears she hates all boys. I've caught her staring a time or two.'

'Oh, very well, there was a boy. He tried to corner me one evening when he'd had too much ale. At the time, I thought it was exciting, but I knew it wouldn't come to anything.' Why she was confessing this to him, she had no idea.

'Aha! I knew it. Did he kiss you?'

'Ivar! That is none of your business.' She was sure her cheeks would spontaneously combust any moment now.

To her annoyance, he widened his grin. 'That means he did. And you liked it.'

'Did not. It was like putting my mouth on a wet fish.' She pulled her fingers out of his and thumped him on the arm. 'And now you're making me act like a stupid adolescent.'

Ivar chuckled. 'It's better than the serious expression you were wearing when I came over here. I like to see you smile.' He bent to add in a whisper, 'And blush. It suits you.'

She tried to send him an admonishing glare, but didn't quite succeed. Her mouth twitched. 'Oh, get away with you. You know you shouldn't be saying such things to me and talking about kissing and . . . suchlike.'

'Suchlike? Interesting word.'

'Enough, you provoking man! I am not discussing anything other than the weather with you from now on.'

'Hmm, that would be boring. I guess I'll have to find some other way of communicating with you. If only there weren't so many people around . . .'

His gaze turned distinctly smouldering and Ellisif looked away. No one had ever flirted with her before, and she didn't quite know how to react. He probably acted this way with all women and meant nothing by it. She shouldn't take him seriously, but a tiny voice inside her told her she wanted to. Very much so. But that way lay danger, because once he'd helped to settle her back into her domains, he would leave.

She felt him take her hand again and give it a squeeze. 'Forgive me. I'm behaving very inappropriately and making you uncomfortable. That was never my intention. Sometimes I forget myself.'

His expression was suitably contrite and serious when she dared a glance from under her lashes, and she nodded. 'Apology accepted, and I'm sorry too. You were merely jesting, were you not? At my age I should be able to take that in my stride. It's only that I've not had much practice at banter.'

'Then we'd better do it more often so that you get used to it. For now, I'll leave you to your musings, but please try not to worry. One way or another we will solve your problems. Together.'

She really liked the sound of that. Too much, perhaps.

South-west coast of Agder and Rogaland, 13 October/ Haustmánuðr AD *875*

The following day, they arrived at a larger settlement. Several farms that each had their own buildings but were situated close to each other as if clustering together for safety. Perhaps they contained different branches of the same family who all worked as a group. Ivar had been told they were somewhere between the regions of Agder and Rogaland, on the south-west coast of Norway. The landscape was distinctly agricultural, with fields stretching inland as far as the eye could see. It had to be a prosperous area, as land for cultivation was precious in such a mountainous country, and here there was an abundance.

Some sort of local market seemed to be happening. There were stalls and tents, people milling around, and campfires sending wisps of smoke into the air. Noise in the form of vendors crying their wares, animals bleating and braying and people chattering and laughing. Delicious cooking smells wafted on the breeze, mingled with the stench of animals and manure as well as the nicer scents of trampled grass and the briny wind coming off the sea.

'People come together from all around here to trade and barter,' Thorald confirmed when Ivar asked him about it. 'We should be safe enough here among so many.'

He wasn't just referring to Ellisif. The closer they came to Askhild and Álrik's home, the higher the risk of them being recognised, and they didn't want that. It was imperative that their uncle remained oblivious of their return if they were to take the man unawares. A surprise attack on the settlement was their best chance of regaining possession of it without too much trouble. Thorald was counting on it.

'I'll tell Ellisif to stay close to me or Askhild. And to make sure she keeps her hair well hidden.'

He found her helping the other woman with setting up a tripod for their cooking pot.

'Should I perhaps go and hide on board the ship?' she asked when he spoke to her quietly. 'If I stay down, I'll be out of sight. The last thing I want is to bring trouble to Thorald and the others.'

She bit her lip and Ivar momentarily lost his train of thought as he watched her teeth sink into that plump softness. He'd like to nibble on it himself, but that was not going to happen. He should never have flirted with her the way he had the previous day, since he had no intention of courting her for real. It wasn't fair of him, and besides, he'd had the distinct impression she wasn't used to such behaviour and had no idea how to handle it. She'd more or less confirmed it herself. To her, it wouldn't merely be a bit of fun; she'd probably take it seriously and could get hurt. No, from now on, he was determined to act like a gentleman even if it killed him.

To that end, he shook himself inwardly and focused on the matter they were discussing. 'No, I don't believe that will be necessary. You should be safe enough in your disguise. You make a fine youth, if a mite delicate-looking,' he added teasingly. At least he could joke about things like that without doing any harm.

She dug an elbow into his ribs and smiled at him. '*Fifl!*'

He turned away so as not to drown in her twinkling emerald gaze. 'Now how about we go for a walk and see what's for sale?'

He was curious to find out what sort of wares would be brought to a tiny provincial market like this. It was on a much smaller scale than the *kaupang* at Skiringssal, and presumably the goods on offer would be inferior. In his role as a historian and archaeologist, such insights were like gold dust. He was storing up every tiny detail for the future. It was fortunate that he had a good memory, as he couldn't take notes in writing.

'If you wish.'

Ellisif's reply sounded subdued, a contrast to their banter of a moment before, and he glanced at her. 'You do not like markets?'

That was strange. In his experience, most women loved shopping and he hadn't thought Viking females would be any different. But maybe he was being sexist. He quite enjoyed shopping himself.

'I love them, but I haven't the wherewithal to make any purchases, which makes it less enjoyable.' She shrugged. 'Not that I can remember the last time I was at a market. Þjódólfr always left me at home.'

Ivar's jaw clenched. The more he learned about the bastard she'd been married to, the angrier he became. If the man hadn't been dead already, he would have liked to beat the crap out of him. As it was, he could at least remedy matters in the present.

'I'll buy you something,' he promised. 'Whatever you wish – you have only to point.'

'What? No! I cannot allow you to do that. It wouldn't be seemly.'

'I don't care, and I'm not taking no for an answer. Now, come.' He put a hand on her shoulder and steered her towards the stalls. He didn't think anyone here would sell anything of great value, so he could afford whatever trinket she'd like. Because of the way Þjóðólfr had treated her, he wanted to spoil her. It was suddenly imperative to see those lovely eyes shining with joy again.

When she still hesitated, he whispered, 'If you do not come willingly, I'll have to take your hand to drag you along. Now that would cause quite a stir, don't you think?' With her dressed as a youth, everyone around them would think Ivar was gay. He assumed that was frowned upon in Viking times, although really he had no idea. But he couldn't imagine it was approved of in an era when men were so incredibly macho.

Ellisif's eyes opened wide as his meaning sank in, and she set off without a word. He chuckled and followed. 'So you don't want me to make a spectacle of myself, eh? That's good to know.'

'Of course not,' she hissed. 'But you are coercing me. I shouldn't accept gifts from a man I'm barely acquainted with. It's not right.'

'Barely acquainted? We're friends. And it would please me to buy you something. Truly, you'd be doing me a favour by accepting it.'

She sent him a glare over her shoulder. 'Now you're being ridiculous, but if you wish to spend your silver, so be it. You can buy me a leather cord. The one I tie my plait with is becoming old and frayed.'

He bought her two, as well as a new leather pouch to hang off her belt because he'd noticed that the one she had was very worn, with a hole in one corner. Then, because none of the vendors had anything else that caught her eye, he dug around in his own pouch and came up with a thick bracelet of twisted silver. He'd bought it at auction before leaving the twenty-first century. It was too small for him, and he'd intended to melt it down but had never got round to it. That was lucky, as it was exactly the right size for Ellisif's slim wrist.

'Here, I want you to have this. It's much nicer than anything sold around here.' He took hold of her hand and tried to thread it on. 'You'll need to squeeze your fingers together.'

'Ivar!' She tried to wriggle out of his grip, but he didn't let go. 'This is too much. Friends don't give each other such things. This is more of a . . .' She didn't finish the sentence, but he knew what she meant. It was something a lover or a man bent on courting would give a woman.

He kept hold of her hand and looked her in the eyes. 'Please, I want you to have it. If we should become separated for any reason, you can use it to barter with. I'd feel better knowing you have the means to do that.' He held her gaze, and after a slight hesitation, she nodded.

'Very well, but I still think you're being too generous. I have nothing to give you in return.' A wash of red flooded her cheeks. 'Unless you mean . . .'

'No. I am not asking you for anything you don't want to give me freely. You have my oath.' He meant it. He might desire her something fierce, but he'd never act on it without her express permission. In fact, he couldn't act on it at all in this era. Not unless he stayed and married her, and that was impossible. 'I just want to protect you. Please, humour me.'

She slid the bracelet on to her wrist. 'Then I thank you, Ivar.'

'My pleasure. Now, we'd better head back to the others. It must be time to eat.'

Chapter Ten

South-west coast of Agder and Rogaland, 13 October/ Haustmánuðr AD 875

They turned to walk towards the shore, but they hadn't taken more than ten steps when Ellisif stopped dead and gasped. She peered up at a man who had come to a halt in front of her.

'Kell!' she whispered, a note of horror in her voice that made Ivar's nerve endings prickle.

His hand automatically went to the knife at his belt as the two of them stared at each other with widening eyes. He gathered this was someone she knew but hadn't wanted to run into. One of the king's men, perhaps. Or Kári's.

The man broke the spell and swore under his breath. '*Skítr!* Go and hide somewhere this instant. I never saw you, understand?'

'What?' She seemed paralysed. 'But—'

'Father doesn't know you're here, and he won't hear it from me.' Kell glanced at Ivar and nodded slightly towards Ellisif. 'It's a good disguise, but make sure she doesn't look anyone in the face. She's too striking by half.'

'I will.' Ivar had no idea why the young man was helping her, but he'd take it if it kept her safe. 'Thank you.'

With a curt nod, Kell vanished into the crowd and Ivar grabbed Ellisif's elbow. 'Stare at the ground, I'll guide your steps.'

Soon they had reached their ship, and Ivar vaulted on board to grab his tent and their belongings. 'Here, catch.' He threw her sack over the side, and she caught it and hugged it to her chest, still keeping her face down and her back to everyone around them.

'We'll go further up the coast and camp there. It will be safer for tonight. Wait here one moment while I tell Thorald.'

He found his kinsman and gave him a quick account of what had happened. 'I'll take Ellisif away from here. Can you pick us up further along the shore tomorrow morning, please?'

'Will do.' Thorald was a man of few words, but he was intelligent and Ivar knew there was no need for further explanations. 'Take bread and ale with you, as you'll miss *nattverðr*.'

'Good point.'

Ivar grabbed some food supplies from Askhild after whispering a quick explanation, then set off with Ellisif in tow. As soon as they had left the marketplace behind and there was nothing but the sea on one side and fields on the other, he drew a silent sigh of relief and relaxed. There was a grove of trees ahead of them. That would give them better cover. In any case, he doubted Kári would search for them here, especially if Kell kept his word and didn't mention seeing them.

It took quite a while to reach the wooded area, but eventually he deemed it safe to stop. They chose a spot hidden from both the nearby fields and the sea by large bushes. In silence, Ellisif helped him set up the tent, and when they were finished, he ducked inside after her. She sank down on to the sheepskins, shaking visibly. At last she spoke, and her voice was trembling too.

'That was . . . He . . . Why?'

He knelt next to her. 'Who was that?' he asked, even though he had already guessed. 'Someone connected with Kári?'

She nodded. 'His youngest son, Kell.'

'No point questioning it. He is clearly on your side, trying to help. Do you trust him?'

He remembered her saying she wished she could have married the son instead of the older man. For a moment, the green-eyed monster rose up inside him, but he told himself he had no right to be jealous. Ellisif wasn't his, and he had no intention of staying in her century to claim her, should that even happen to be what she wanted. The way she and the young man had regarded each other made him wonder if there could be more between them, despite the fact that she was older than him. Either way, it was none of his business.

'I d-don't know,' she stammered. 'I mean, I've only met him once before and he was kind when all the others weren't. But I cannot fathom why he'd go against his father on my behalf. That is asking for trouble. Not to mention dishonourable.'

'Can you not?' Ivar couldn't resist brushing her cheek with his knuckles. 'As he said, you're a very striking woman, Ellisif. Beautiful, in fact. Perhaps the attraction you felt for him is mutual?'

She frowned. 'I never said I was attracted to him. Merely that I'd rather marry someone his age than his father's.'

'Well, you clearly made a huge impression on him. Shall we trust him, or do you want to carry on further?' He refused to analyse the sensation of relief that had coursed through him at her words of denial. That was neither here nor there.

Straightening her spine, she said, 'I trust him. If he'd wanted to capture me, he would have done so when I was standing right in front of him. It was the perfect opportunity. Or he could have shouted for one of his brothers or his father.'

'Yes, I agree.' As long as the young man didn't change his mind later, but for some reason Ivar didn't think he would. Kell had seemed genuinely concerned for her welfare. 'Now relax. No one will search for us here.'

'Very well.' With a big sigh, her shoulders sank. 'I'm sorry to be such a burden. You shouldn't have to rescue me all the time and—'

'Shh.' He put a finger on her mouth, then bent to replace it with his lips, giving her a quick kiss. It was intended to shock her out of her disconsolate mood, but he couldn't deny that he'd been unable to resist. 'Never consider yourself a burden. I am helping you because I want to, no other reason. Understand?'

The temptation to kiss her again was fierce, but he fought the urge. He shouldn't have done it even once, as evidenced by the wide-eyed gaze she was giving him. As soon as she nodded, he made himself concentrate on mundane things. 'I'm going to quickly check the area to make sure we're nowhere near a settlement, then we'll eat. Stay here, please. I won't be long.'

Ellisif sank down on to the sheepskin and pulled her knees up, looping her arms around them. 'Sweet Freya, but that was unexpected.'

Not just meeting Kell, and his assistance, which had come totally out of the blue, but the tender kiss Ivar had given her to stop her from talking. It had worked, too. That slight pressure of his lips on hers had rendered her speechless and sent tingling currents shooting through her veins. It had made her forget everything else.

She forced herself to think about Kell. The surprise in his eyes as he realised who he was looking at, the dawning concern and finally fierce determination. As she'd told Ivar, they had only met the once, but she had received the impression he was a good man. Or he could be, were he not obliged to do as his father bade him. For him to go against Kári in this way was incredible, and she wished now she'd had a chance to thank him herself. Ivar had done it for her, but it didn't feel like nearly enough.

She owed Kell, and she determined that if she was ever in a position to repay him, she would.

That almost made her laugh. Here she was, at the mercy of strangers, with no idea what the future held. But the gods had been with her so far. She'd have to hope they would continue to help her.

And then there was Ivar.

Her thoughts kept returning to that kiss. It had been fleeting, and she wanted so much more. Could she be that wanton? He'd sworn he wouldn't pressure her in any way, but unless her fuzzy vision was deceiving her, his eyes told her he desired her. If she gave any indication that she'd welcome his advances, she was sure he'd take her up on it.

She shouldn't. But she wanted to.

Confused thoughts were still scurrying around inside her brain when he returned and began to unpack the food and ale. She pushed them aside and tried to concentrate on the here and now.

'Did you see anyone?' she asked, accepting a couple of slices of dried smoked lamb and some flatbread. She wasn't particularly hungry, but she knew she needed to eat. It was vital that she keep her strength up in case she had to flee again.

'No, this is a complete wilderness. As long as the wolves leave us alone, we'll be fine.' He sank down next to her, sitting cross-legged, holding his own food.

She stopped chewing. 'Wolves?'

He smiled. 'I'm jesting. I doubt there are any here. They live further inland, do they not? In the forests? Besides, they don't normally bother us humans.'

'I suppose.' She had no idea, but wild animals didn't scare her anywhere near as much as Kári did. Hopefully he wasn't actively searching for her, and she was safe as long as Kell kept his promise not to say anything. 'It's strange that Kári and his men are travelling in the same direction as us. And how did he arrive here so quickly? Maybe they're going straight to my property, thinking that's where I'm heading. He probably believes I have nowhere else to go.'

'Mm, that makes sense. If he has a faster ship, they might have passed us along the way but further out to sea. As for why they are heading this way, I've no idea, but you may be right. At least they cannot know of your intention to become a thrall. I doubt that possibility would cross their minds.' He gave her a teasing smile. 'You have to admit it sounds rather foolish for a woman of your status.'

'Hmph. Not to me. Anyway, I never told anyone my plans. Not even Ingibjorg, my friend back at the king's hall. It was safer that way.' She shivered. 'But he must think I'm stupid if my home is the first place he'd look. I'd have to be exceedingly brainless to go there.'

Ivar's mouth quirked up slightly. 'Clearly you're not a fool, but he doesn't know that. In fact, presumably he knows nothing about you other than what the king has told him. That is to our advantage.'

'Yes, it's more likely he is going to claim my domains until such time as I am found. If I'm gone, I assume the king will simply allow him to keep possession of them.' That was a supremely depressing thought. 'He still needs warriors on his side in the fight against Haraldr Hálfdanarsson.'

Ivar nudged her with his shoulder. 'Nothing we can do about

it now. Eat up, then you can bed down for the night. I'll sit outside for a while, in case anyone decides to head this way during the evening.'

'Thank you. I really shouldn't ask it of you.'

'Of course you should. Friends, remember?'

He ducked outside soon afterwards while she lay down and tried to settle. She couldn't go to sleep, however, and found it impossible to relax without Ivar next to her. It seemed like forever before he crawled back inside and closed the tent flap, then stretched out beside her. She turned around to face him.

'All quiet?' she whispered.

'Yes. As should you be.' She heard amusement in his voice, which resonated inside her. His presence made her feel safe and secure, but unsettled at the same time.

'I couldn't sleep without you here. Ivar?'

'Yes?'

She hesitated, then blurted out, 'Will you hold me, please? I . . . felt safe when you did so back at Skiringssal.'

There was a slight pause before he replied. 'Yes, of course, if that is what you wish. Turn your back to me.'

She complied, and he aligned himself with her, pulling her close with one arm round her waist. Her body fitted his perfectly. The top of her head tucked under his chin and her backside was snug against him where his legs curled behind hers. The warmth from his skin permeated through their layers of clothing, and his hard muscles were a pleasant contrast to her softness. Because there was no space between them, she felt rather than heard him sigh. Although he had joked about sharing a tent last night, she gathered he wasn't comfortable sleeping like this. Doubt clouded her mind. He was a man, after all, no matter how many unusual views he held about women in general.

'If you'd rather not, I can—'

'Shh, it's fine. Go to sleep, *unnasta*. And please, keep still.'

His grip on her tightened and the steady thumping of his heart reverberated against her back, calming her down. Gratitude spread through her and a warm sensation squeezed her own heart. She'd never met anyone like Ivar, never had anyone who put her wishes first. She thanked the gods for bringing him to her.

As her breathing slowed down and she drifted off to sleep, her last thought was that she'd have to thank them properly as soon as she had a chance.

They rose not long after dawn and ate the leftover bread and smoked meat before packing up their belongings once more. The seashore proved to be only a stone's throw away, and they waited there among a dense stand of trees until they spotted Thorald's ship gliding along the water. When he was sure there was no one else around, Ivar made his way down to the small beach and called out, his hands cupped around his mouth to make the sound carry.

Thankfully Thorald spotted them straight away and changed course.

Soon they had jumped on board and the ship set off again. Ivar went to sit next to his kinsman, who was steering.

'Any trouble last night?' he asked. 'Did they come looking for her?'

'No, not as such. There was a man who briefly stopped by our campfire. He asked if we'd seen a woman with red-gold hair heading west, but he didn't sound as though he knew she was nearby. He was just making enquiries, as if trying to pick up her trail.'

'Good, then they're not sure where she is going. We speculated last night that Kári must think she is attempting to go back to her own domains so that is where he's headed too. It's best she stays away from there for the foreseeable future.'

It galled him that the man might take what was hers by force. Or perhaps tell her retainers that the king had declared him her future husband, and thereby make them do his bidding. There was nothing to be done about it right now, though.

'I agree. That would be asking for trouble. She is fine where she is at the moment. Askhild is enjoying her company too. I hadn't thought to bring another woman on the journey, but I see now that I should have done.' Thorald threw Ivar an amused glance. 'And something tells me you're not averse to her staying with us a bit longer either. Had a good night?'

'Not the way you're thinking, sadly.' Ivar narrowed his eyes at the man in mock frustration. 'She's not the type of woman I can just bed and leave.'

'True.' But the teasing glint was still there in Thorald's eyes. Ivar wanted to growl at him. At the same time, though, it warmed him that they were now at a stage where they could joke with one another. It was a huge step forward.

His thoughts spun back to Ellisif. Maybe he shouldn't have been a gentleman last night. It had been sheer torture to hold her again and nothing more. But if anything was going to happen between them, he sensed that he had to take things slowly, and he would never do anything to hurt her. By the sounds of things, she'd already put up with way too much in her life. But dear Lord, he'd wanted to turn her around and kiss her senseless, not to mention . . .

He shook his head. He had to stop thinking about it. About her. He couldn't have her; she wasn't for him. End of story.

Thorald distracted him by continuing the conversation. 'I picked up on a few other things last night,' he began. 'It's to do with the king.'

'Oh yes? Hjorr, was it?'

Ivar had read about the man in his own century. He was

famous for having married a woman from some sort of indigenous tribe based on the Russian Arctic coast. It had been purely a business arrangement that would have given him access to the walrus tusks and furs his queen's people were skilled at hunting. According to legend, however, he'd actually fallen in love with her and had forsaken all others for her. That was unusual enough that the tale had survived to be told through the centuries. They'd had twin sons, and there were some stories about them as well, but that was all he knew.

'No, not him. Haraldr Hálfdanarsson, son of Hálfdan Svarti – the Black – Gudrödarson. Originally from Rogaland, Haraldr is the ruler of some of the western and central parts of this land. At present, his domains are scattered, but he's ambitious. Rumour has it he wishes to consolidate his holdings and become king of everything. I heard tell he'd proposed marriage to a woman by the name of Gyda, the daughter of another king, Eiríkr of Hörðaland. Apparently she refused to entertain his suit until he was king of all the lands from here to Vestfold and beyond. Huh! As though he wasn't powerful enough for her already. That means he needs to vanquish King Hjorr and anyone else who stands between him and attaining this goal.'

'Interesting.'

It sounded like quite a love story, but Ivar wasn't sure his kinsman would see it that way. Perhaps Haraldr was merely annoyed that the lady had refused him and wanted to prove a point. If the story was even true. He'd read about that too, but historians in his time doubted it and saw it as a myth made up by skalds long after the king's death.

Ivar knew very well who Thorald was talking about, though. Most people in the twenty-first century knew the man as Harald Fairhair, but as an archaeologist and Viking specialist, Ivar was also aware that there was some doubt about this epithet. Although the king had been mentioned in some of the Icelandic sagas as Haraldr Hárfagri, which did indeed mean Fairhair, the authors might have confused him with the later Haraldr Hardrada – or Harðráði in Old Norse – whose hair really had been fair. Either way, the Haraldr that Thorald referred to would definitely be the winner in any coming conflict. It was yet another tale that was to be repeated for centuries to come. Ivar couldn't tell anyone this, for obvious reasons, but he could try to steer his kinsman in the right direction if it became necessary.

'Does this affect us in any way?' he asked casually.

'Not at present, though both kings are recruiting men to fight alongside them and pledge their allegiance.' Thorald shrugged. 'It matters not to me which king rules these lands unless it has a bearing on Álrik's claim to his domains. My first priority is to regain control of those, then we shall see. It may be that we have to show willing and help Haraldr out in order to prove Álrik's loyalty, and ours, if he is powerful in the west. Else we could be doing all this for naught.'

'You mean if Haraldr comes to power rather than Hjorr? How likely is that? One could argue the opposite to be true.' Ivar was playing devil's advocate now, but needed to see how seriously Thorald was taking this.

He hadn't really imagined he'd become embroiled in political upheaval in the ninth century. He should have realised he couldn't simply visit as an innocent bystander. If he truly wanted to be a part of his ancestor's life for a while, that meant entering into it wholeheartedly. Including possibly fighting in a war, it would seem. That was a chilling thought.

Thorald's expression was grave. 'From what I've heard, King Hjorr is not as strong as his opponent. He's been in league with one of the Danish royal houses for years, but currently they are fighting among themselves and have no forces to spare to help

Hjorr. Therefore, I would bet my last piece of hacksilver that Haraldr will be successful. That seemed to be the consensus of most of those I spoke to last night as well, although they weren't admitting it openly.'

'Hmm, well, that sounds reasonable. I suppose we'll see. For now, we're continuing on your quest?'

'Yes. Until I've accomplished what I set out to do, I care not about the petty squabbles of kings. My new brother-in-law is more important.'

Ivar couldn't fault him for that. He would have felt the same.

Chapter Eleven

West coast of Rogaland, 14–16 October/Gormánuðr AD *875*

Ellisif kept her distance from Ivar for the next two days, but she couldn't always stop her eyes from straying to him. Whether he was rowing, relaxing or chatting to the other men, he drew her gaze like a lodestone to the north. There was just something about him that appealed to her. She couldn't stop thinking about the light kiss he'd given her, or how good it had felt to sleep with him wrapped around her. It made the following nights alone seem very empty and cold.

She wished she'd been brave enough to ask him for more, but she couldn't quite bring herself to go that far. Acting wantonly simply wasn't done, at least not where she came from. And although she'd heard tell that congress between men and women could be pleasurable, she had a hard time imagining it. Everything Þjódólfr had ever done to her had been nauseating, humiliating or painful. Would it really be different with anyone else? She doubted it, but no man had ever attracted her the way Ivar did, and she wasn't sure why he in particular had this effect on her. The gods must be playing tricks on her.

They continued west until they had rounded the southernmost

point of the land, Lindesnes in the Agder province. From there on, they headed north-west, past the Jaðarr region of Rogaland. This was a large area of flat lowland, bigger than any other Ellisif had ever seen. Compared to most of the rest of the country, which was mountainous and not really suited to agriculture, this part was lush and fertile. There were long sandy beaches too, perfect for making landfall each evening. Before reaching Jaðarr, however, they had to pass one of the most dangerous stretches of the coast. This required the knowledge and fierce concentration of a good pilot, and Ellisif was pleased to find that they had one in Holmstein.

'I've sailed this way many a time,' he reassured everyone, but the atmosphere on board remained tense until they were past the most treacherous areas.

Eventually they passed the entry into Hafrsfjordr, where King Haraldr was rumoured to have a huge naval base. Thorald had made a point of stopping at a few settlements in order to glean information about the political situation in the region. This seemed eminently sensible to Ellisif. Still, she was glad that they didn't row into the fjord to check for themselves whether it was true about the king's forces there.

'To reach my home, Birgirsby, we would have turned inland after this point and as far into one branch of the next fjord as you can go,' she told Ivar, gesturing to the coastline. A pang of longing shot through her for all that was familiar at home, but she was fully aware that it wouldn't be safe for her right now. It was the last place she should be going.

Ivar seemed to understand her conflicted emotions. He threw her a sympathetic glance and gave her shoulder a brief squeeze. 'Patience. You'll be back there soon enough.'

And in that moment, she believed him.

They carried on north towards Hörðaland, where Álrik's domains were situated. This necessitated passage through

Karmtsund, a narrow strait between the mainland and the island of Körmt. There had been a strategically placed royal manor here for centuries, called Avaldsnes. Anyone wishing to travel from the south to the north, or vice versa, along the Norðvegr, had to pass through this strait. It was the only possible route unless you dared to go further out into the dangerous sea. That meant it was an ideal place for the local ruler to stop all travellers and demand that they pay a customs charge.

'Daylight robbery,' Thorald was heard to mutter, sounding grumpier than usual, but he paid up quickly so that they could be on their way. There was no point arguing in any case – you couldn't win against the king's men here.

Not long after that, they finally turned inland and sailed along a deep fjord. The water became still and mirror-like, reflecting the steep forest-covered mountainsides that surrounded them as the fjord grew ever narrower. It was a stunningly beautiful sight. A high peak, already covered in snow and ice, glistened in the distance, and there were several waterfalls tumbling down the sides. Some were broad and noisy, others like long, thin veils falling down a woman's back. The air had turned distinctly chilly. Ellisif shivered and drew her cloak tighter about herself. It wasn't merely the cold that had her trembling, but the thought of what might lie ahead as well.

That evening, as they made camp on an uninhabited stretch of land near the shore, tension seemed to be gripping everyone. Ellisif said nothing, merely went about her tasks with quiet efficiency, helping Askhild with the cooking. As they all gathered round the campfire, Thorald called for silence.

'We are nearly there,' he told them. 'My plan is for us to arrive under cover of darkness and disarm any guards. Egil, Álrik's uncle, won't be expecting us, as he doesn't know of my marriage to Askhild. And presumably he has no idea where she and Álrik disappeared off to when they fled in the night. They've been gone nearly three months now, and I'm hoping this has lulled him into a false sense of security. How many men do you reckon he has, *ást mín*?'

'A dozen,' Askhild replied. 'But some of them might not fight on his behalf if they see that Álrik and I are no longer helpless. They were caught in a dilemma – do Egil's bidding or lose their homes. Most have families and couldn't afford to be thrown out.'

'Well, there are eight of us – nine with Álrik – and if we put the guards out of action first, the numbers should be even, whether those men remain loyal to him or not. And we have the advantage of surprise. Not to mention the fact that we have justice on our side.' Thorald's expression was fierce – he clearly felt very strongly about this, as was only right.

'Do we kill them?' someone asked.

Thorald shook his head. 'Not unless we have to, and only if they're attacking us with intent to kill; otherwise we'll simply knock them out and tie them up. Everyone should be given a fair chance to swear allegiance to their true master. Egil will have coerced some of them, no doubt.'

'And what about him?' Álrik piped up. 'I want to kill him for what he planned. It's what he was going to do to me.'

Ellisif noticed that no one told the youth the obvious truth – that he wouldn't be a match for any grown man yet. At only sixteen winters, he still had a lot of growing and filling-out to do, no matter how fierce his determination.

Thorald's reply was measured. 'We all want to kill him for that very reason,' he told his brother-in-law, 'but no one wants to bear the taint of murder for the rest of his life. With your permission, I will challenge him to *einvigi* on your behalf, as we are now kin.

If he's been living well since you left, he won't be in any shape to best me. He is also considerably older.'

Álrik's expression was mutinous, but after his sister leaned over and whispered something in his ear, he nodded. 'Very well. I am grateful for your assistance and I promise to live up to your faith in me by being a good jarl.'

'What about us women?' Ellisif asked Askhild quietly, while the men continued to chat among themselves and sharpen their weapons. 'Can we help?'

'I plan to, but there is no need for you to risk yourself on our behalf.' Askhild smiled. 'My husband has been teaching me to wield a knife efficiently, and a few other things besides, like how to throw a small axe. I can't tell you how good it is not to feel so totally helpless as I did before.'

'Well, I have no such skills, but I'd be happy to do whatever you ask of me. You have all been so kind and welcoming. I owe you a huge debt.' She meant it. Without these people, she doubted she would still be free.

'That is mostly Ivar's doing, is it not?' Askhild's smile turned into a teasing grin. 'Without his insistence, I don't think Thorald would have shielded a fugitive. He can be very persuasive when he wants to be.'

'Who, Thorald?' Ellisif played dumb, but she knew she wasn't fooling anyone.

'No, *fifl*, Ivar, of course. I noticed you weren't averse to spending time alone with him in the forest the other night. And he keeps sending you heated glances whenever he thinks no one is noticing.'

'He does? I mean, no, I don't think so.' But Ellisif's cheeks were warming up and she couldn't stop that from happening.

Askhild elbowed her gently. 'You don't need to pretend with me. I won't tell. I married his kinsman, after all, so I am very partial to the men of that family. Anyway, back to our original topic of discussion. You won't be needed for the ambush, but if anyone is hurt, I'd be very grateful if you could help me dress wounds afterwards.'

'Yes, of course. I have some skill in such matters.'

'Good, then that's settled. Now why don't you go and talk to Ivar for a while? He looks lonely.'

'Stop it! I will do no such thing,' Ellisif hissed, but she laughed at the same time. The woman was irrepressible, and the truth was that she'd love nothing better. Talking to Ivar, being next to him, watching him – these were all becoming her favourite things to do.

And that was probably not good.

They crept through the forest like wraiths, taking care not to step on any twigs. There was close to a full moon to light their way, but it was still dark enough to shield them from view. Álrik's hall, Ulfstoft, was situated high on a slope overlooking a smaller branch of the main fjord, and they approached it from behind. There was a guard loitering by the back door, next to the midden, but he was half asleep and proved easy enough to get rid of. Thorald merely snuck up on him and hit him hard under the chin. The man's eyes rolled up, showing the whites, and he slumped to the ground, dead to the world.

'Tie him up,' Thorald ordered, and one of his men obeyed swiftly.

When he was done, they all lined up by the back wall of the hall and followed their leader to the corner. He signalled that the coast was clear and continued along the side wall, then stopped to peer out towards the front. As Askhild had told them, there was a porch closest to this end of the building. Thorald held up his hand to show that there were two men guarding this entrance. To Ivar's surprise, he was beckoned forward.

'We take one each, agreed? But put a hand over his mouth first so he doesn't make a sound.'

'Will do.' Ivar was absurdly pleased to be singled out to help in this manner. He wondered why, but it was something he'd have to ponder later. Right now, it was time for action.

After watching the guards for a while, Thorald picked a moment when they both had their backs turned, and then he and Ivar were sprinting as one. Grabbing his opponent from behind, Ivar put one hand firmly across his mouth, then punched him on the side of the head below his ear. He followed this up by spinning him around and hitting him with a solid upper-cut to the jaw, exactly like the one his kinsman had given the guard by the back door. It knocked the man out cold and he slithered to the ground.

Thorald had the other guard under control and had already started to tie his hands behind his back. Ivar did the same to the one he'd felled, and soon the pair lay trussed up beside the wall. The rest of the group were beckoned forward. At a sign from Thorald, a couple of them fanned out to check the outbuildings, while the rest burst into the hall.

'What the . . . ?'

'The gods help us! *Aaaiiiyyeehh!*'

'Wait . . . Álrik? It's *Álrik*!'

'The young jarl is back!'

There were cries of anger, fear and confusion from some, but also of welcome for the young master. One of Thorald's men stayed by the youth's side to protect him from harm, but for the most part the sight of him brought people up short. Thorald, Ivar and the others worked methodically to combat any resistance and disarm those of Egil's men who were grabbing their weapons. But there didn't seem to be as many of them as they'd thought, and Askhild's prediction that some were loyal to Álrik proved correct. Those men rushed to form a ring around the young jarl as soon as they saw that Egil's retainers were outnumbered.

Although he managed to avoid killing anyone, Ivar did his fair share of fighting. *Slash, parry, attack, dance out of the way of a deadly blade, slash again* . . . He used his sword to good effect, injuring a couple of people, but stopped short of inflicting any mortal wounds. The entire scene was surreal, as if he was in a dream going through the motions. But the tang of blood in the air, mingling with the stench of fear, was not something he could have imagined. The many hours he had spent training for just such combat had not prepared him for the way it would feel to actually watch a man being run through with a sword, or hacked about with a battleaxe. His stomach churned, but he swallowed down the bile. This was not the twenty-first century – this was an age where bloodshed was normal. Expected, even. He had to deal with it and keep his mouth shut.

A door at the far end of the hall banged open and a voice cut through the pandemonium. 'What is happening here? *Get out of my hall!*'

By now, any man not loyal to Álrik had been either killed or knocked out. The older man who stood framed in the doorway stopped to stare at the scene in front of him. His face went from ashen to bright red, his mouth tightening in fury when his gaze fell on Álrik, who stepped forward and raised his chin.

'I am here to take back what is mine, uncle. This is not your hall. You have no right to anything here and I want you gone.'

Egil sneered. 'You're too young to have charge of anything on your own. I've no idea why you ran away. You need me here to oversee matters on your behalf. Now, what is the meaning of this outrage?' He swept a hand to indicate the dead and wounded.

Thorald stepped forward. 'Ah, but you weren't planning on merely overseeing Álrik's domains, were you? Your plans to kill him and take his sister to wife were overheard. We have witnesses.'

'Lies!' Egil spluttered. 'I never said—'

'Yes, you did.' It was Askhild's turn to come into the light of the torches that had been hastily lit. She had hung back during the fighting but entered the hall when all was under control. 'I heard you with my own ears, which is why I persuaded my brother to leave with me. Your plans have failed, though, and you are not welcome here.'

Egil crossed his arms over his chest. 'You are deluded, girl, and I have every right to remain. You always were a meddlesome little creature. I shall enjoy teaching you a lesson.'

Thorald marched over to the man and peered down his nose at him. 'Do *not* speak to my wife in that fashion ever again, understand?'

'Your w-wife? But . . . who *are* you?' Egil was sounding more unsure with every moment, his bluster not quite as belligerent as his eyes darted round to check whether he had any allies left.

'I am Thorald Hrolfsson of Birkiþorp in Svíaríki, and Askhild and I were wed two months ago. That makes me Álrik's brother-in-law, and henceforth I will be overseeing his domains until he is old enough to take the reins himself. And unlike *you* . . .' he punctuated this last word with a poke in Egil's chest, 'I will be teaching him how to do it without defrauding him in the process.'

'Preposterous! I am clearly closer in kinship and it is my duty to—'

'You will leave or face me in *einvigi*,' Thorald cut in. 'Which is it to be?'

Even though he wasn't standing close to the two men, Ivar saw Egil's face lose all its colour once more.

'*Ei-einvigi*?' he stammered. 'On what grounds?'

'Planned murder and attempted rape of my wife.' His voice

colder than a hoar frost, Thorald stood his ground, while some of the onlookers gasped at this added accusation. 'And don't try to tell me that didn't happen either. There was a witness to that as well.' He looked around and nodded at an old woman Askhild indicated.

The crone shuffled forward and nodded. 'If I hadn't walked in on you, you would have succeeded,' she confirmed.

Clearly backed into a corner in every sense of the word, Egil clenched and unclenched his fists before finally giving in. 'Very well, a one-to-one fight it shall be. I will meet you tomorrow at—'

'No, we do this now. Fetch your weapons and a shield.'

'What? But—'

'*Now!*'

Almost as one, the occupants of the hall moved forward in an unconsciously menacing way. Egil scurried into his bedchamber, returning a few moments later dressed in an ostentatious tunic. He had a baldric slung across his chest and a knife at his belt, and was holding an axe and a shield. By this time Thorald had been handed a shield as well, and he led the way outside, where everyone formed a circle, some people holding up torches.

As he stepped into this makeshift ring, Thorald's demeanour was serenely calm and determined. When he walked past him, Ivar clapped his kinsman on the shoulder in encouragement. He was excited to get to watch him fight, although a tiny frisson of trepidation shimmered through him at the faint possibility that he might be killed. He shook it off. Thorald was supremely skilled and Ivar had faith in him. He had a feeling it would be a perfect example of all he had studied and learned. Only this time it was for real, and this bout of single combat would be to the death.

Chapter Twelve

Ulfstoft, 16 October/Gormánuðr AD 875

By the time the fight began, Ellisif had joined the crowd. She'd stayed behind in the forest with the oldest of Thorald's men while the others attacked, but as soon as the coast was clear, someone had come to fetch them.

'All is well. Thorald is about to kill the *niðingr* in a fair fight. You might want to watch.'

She wasn't particularly fond of bloodshed, but in this case she'd make an exception, as she believed it to be entirely justified. Askhild had told her how Egil had treated her and Álrik, and it fair made Ellisif's blood boil. She'd thought her own plight was bad, but at least her life had never been at risk. Planning to kill a youth of sixteen winters merely to gain his domains was despicable, and the man deserved a gruesome end.

Thorald seemed to agree. Being much younger than his opponent, and larger besides, he could probably have dispatched Egil in moments. Instead, he toyed with the man, like a cat with a particularly delectable mouse. While deflecting every one of Egil's thrusts, he harried the other man and pricked him with his sword every so often. Blood flowed, but never enough to kill, only to drive the villain to desperation.

'Be done with it, if you must!' Egil shouted, his cheeks mottled red with a combination of exhaustion and fury, while his chest heaved. 'Or are you not man enough to kill me?'

Thorald smiled, a wolfish grin that didn't reach his eyes. 'Oh, I will, but I'll take my time. I'm enjoying tormenting you, as you did my beloved wife and her brother. How many times did you slight them? How often did you belittle them to others? Deny them food and mistreat them through the years? And then you had the audacity to think Askhild would welcome you into her bed? You were deluded, old man.'

That final sentence produced a harder thrust, and Thorald's sword sank into Egil's side, eliciting a howl of pain. It still wasn't a killing blow, however, as the older man had plenty of extra fat around his middle and sides.

'She would have died rather than wed you, you worthless piece of *skítr*!' Another slash, this time to Egil's sword arm, drawing blood. 'And Álrik may be young, but he'll be a much better master of this settlement than you could ever be.' Slash. Feint. Slash.

Egil was panting hard by now, trying to jump out of the way of that relentless blade, his eyes bulging with the effort. The knowledge that he'd lost was written all over him, and the only thing that kept him going was anger, but that was fading fast too, along with any hope of survival.

'Askhild is a mousy little *bikkja* not worthy of any man,' he hissed, then yelped as another cut appeared on his hand as if by magic.

'She's beautiful, and she's worth a thousand of you,' Thorald shot back, but despite the deliberate slight to his wife, he didn't lose his calm. He carried right on with tormenting his opponent, slowly, viciously, without delivering that final *coup de grâce*. 'And she is carrying my child, which means my line will continue. Yours won't.'

Ellisif glanced quickly at her friend, who was standing next to her watching the fight with a blank expression. At her husband's words, Askhild's cheeks turned slightly pink, but the small smile that played over her mouth told its own story. Thorald was telling the truth, even if it was early days.

'Congratulations,' Ellisif whispered quickly. 'I'm so pleased for you.' And she was, despite the fact that it gave her a sharp pang of jealousy.

'Thank you.'

Their attention returned to the fight, and it was obvious that Egil was tiring fast. 'Enough!' he cried. 'If you mean to kill me, do it.'

'Very well, but I wish you to suffer, so a lingering death it shall be. You deserve no less.' Thorald's mouth curved into a snarl and he made one final slash across Egil's abdomen. This time it was deep, but not deep enough to kill instantly. Ellisif realised what he'd done. Men who were wounded thus could linger for quite a while as the life force ebbed out of them. And it would be painful to the end. This was Thorald's intention.

Good for him.

Ellisif only wished she could have done the same to her former husband. He'd deserved it too.

The fight over with, someone carried Egil into an outhouse, where he was left under guard. It would take him a while to die, but no one cared, and the curses he hissed were ignored.

'Everyone into the hall,' Thorald ordered, and all those gathered outside trooped after him through the doors, which were wide open. 'And fetch the men who've been tied up. They need to be present.'

Once inside, Álrik went to sit in the jarl's chair on a small dais at one end of the room, flanked by Thorald and Askhild, while everyone else came to stand facing them. To Ellisif's surprise, Thorald motioned for Ivar to join them on the dais, and the sight warmed her heart. This seemed like a clear sign that Ivar had been accepted by his kinsman. Besides, anyone present could see that they were related. Their features and colouring were as similar as those of brothers.

Holding up his hands, Thorald called for silence. 'You have all seen how traitors are dealt with. If any of you harbour any residual goodwill for Egil, I would have you leave right now. This hall and settlement belong to my brother-in-law, and I and my kinsman . . .' he indicated Ivar, 'will remain to protect him until he can do without our assistance. You are to come forward and swear an oath of allegiance to Álrik now, or leave Ulfstoft forthwith.'

'Will our past allegiance to Egil be forgiven?' someone called out.

'Yes, if you are sincere in asking for forgiveness,' Thorald confirmed. 'No lies will be tolerated – and rest assured, I'll see through you.'

Ellisif didn't doubt him. He had eyes as sharp as an eagle's and was a good judge of character, from what Askhild had told her. He kept his gaze trained on each and every man who stepped up to swear an oath, including those whose hands had now been freed from their restraints. A few of them squirmed and had trouble looking Álrik in the eye; Thorald allowed them to pass anyway. She assumed they were merely experiencing guilt for not supporting the rightful owner in the past.

She had just begun to relax, having seated herself on a bench to one side, when the calm was shattered. A young warrior was about to take his turn, but instead of sinking down on one knee in front of Álrik, he suddenly pulled a long knife out of his sleeve and lunged for the youth. A collective gasp of horror hissed around the room as the shiny weapon seemed to be on course to become embedded in Álrik's heart. Ellisif's own organ stopped pumping altogether, and she stilled, watching the tableau as if in a very bad dream.

'Noooo!' Her whisper was echoed by others, but she couldn't have moved if her life had depended on it.

As the point of the blade was about to reach its target, someone threw themselves in front of Álrik and shoved the attacker out of the way.

Ivar, no! Ellisif opened her mouth to shout, but her vocal cords refused to work and the words remained trapped inside her brain.

He'd been standing closest to Álrik on the youth's left, while Thorald and Askhild were on his other side exchanging a few whispered words. As she watched with mounting terror, Ivar now fought with the attacker using blows, kicks and his knife. She had never seen such strange fighting, but ultimately it proved effective, and he succeeded in flooring the man. His respite was short-lived, though, as his opponent raised his knife yet again, aiming for Ivar's gut. At the last moment, Ivar twisted away and struck out blindly with his own blade, which sank into the other man's heart as the attacker moved the wrong way. The warrior made a gurgling noise and stopped fighting. As his expression stilled and his eyes glazed over, Ivar froze as well. He was panting hard, kneeling next to his opponent, but the light of battle faded fast from his gaze, and he stared at the other man as if he'd never seen him before.

Thorald jumped off the dais and squatted next to the combatants. He clapped Ivar on the shoulder and squeezed hard. 'Thank you. You saved Álrik's life. We owe you a huge debt.'

Ivar shook his head. 'It was nothing,' he murmured, sounding dazed.

Ellisif rushed over. 'You are hurt. Come, let me tend to your wound before you bleed to death.' She tugged at him to make him stand up, but he remained motionless. It was like trying to move a huge boulder.

'What?' He peered at the stain spreading along the side of his tunic as if he hadn't registered that he'd been wounded.

'Now, Ivar. You're losing blood.' With Thorald's help, she got him on his feet at last, then took hold of his arm and led him through the hall to an adjoining room that seemed to be some sort of pantry.

Askhild came rushing after them, her hands visibly shaking as she searched the shelves for medical supplies. 'That was close,' she said. 'I should have seen it coming, but I'd forgotten about Erlendr. There were rumours that he was Egil's son by a thrall woman and I'm guessing he'd been told that. Maybe he imagined Egil would acknowledge him as such and he'd be next in line to inherit this place.' She shuddered. 'Like father, like son, obviously.'

'That would explain the animosity,' Ellisif acknowledged. 'And he must have been trying to avenge his father.' Still, it had been a futile endeavour.

'Yes.' Askhild found what was needed – needle and thread suitable for patching up human skin, and clean linens to bandage the wound. 'Here you go. Do you need my help?'

'No, thank you. I'll be fine.' It wasn't a job Ellisif relished, but for Ivar she would do what she had to.

She couldn't bear to see him hurt.

I killed a man. Sank the knife right into his heart. Jesus!

Ivar was barely aware of his surroundings, everything a blur as the images of the fight and the dying man played over and over in his brain. How could he not have realised that he might have to do something like that if he travelled back to the Viking world? It was a cut-throat society, based on survival of the fittest in every sense. You killed or were killed, and you used your weapons to protect what was yours.

But he hadn't meant to kill, only incapacitate the man. He'd struck out of pure instinct to deflect the slash aimed at his stomach. And that was all it took. If only the man hadn't twisted the opposite way to what Ivar had anticipated, his knife would have merely sunk into his arm . . .

Álrik would have died if I hadn't intervened. A sixteen-year-old boy who'd done nothing wrong. The man deserved it.

But even though his rational self knew this was true, he was finding it hard to reconcile his actions with his conscience. He should have tried harder to merely wound the man. And yet the outcome would have been the same, because Thorald would have killed him instead, whether in single combat or outright.

At least then it wouldn't have been me.

He shook his head at himself. He'd acted out of pure instinct and done what he had to do. What any man here would have done. It wasn't wrong if you killed someone in self-defence or in order to protect the innocent, was it? He had to keep telling himself that or he wouldn't be able to live with himself. If he was to stay on in the ninth century, he had to live exactly like a man of this era. Think like one of them. Become one of them. That included violence, whether he liked it or not.

Aarrgh!

'Ivar? Am I hurting you? I'll be done in a moment, I promise.'

'Huh?' He looked up to find Ellisif sitting next to him, frowning in concentration as she sewed up a large gash in his side. He'd barely noticed her taking his shirt and tunic off, but he shivered now as a cold draught swirled round him. There was blood everywhere – most of it his, he guessed – and she was valiantly trying to stop the flow. Strangely, he had gone completely numb and her ministrations didn't bother him. As if from far away, he heard himself say, 'You'll need to wash it with lye and then pour some wine over it if there is any to be had.'

'Wine?' She paused momentarily to blink at him. 'Why?'

'Old family remedy,' he muttered. 'And I'll need to dunk it in salt water too.'

These were the only forms of antiseptic he could come up with. He wished he'd been paying attention and had asked her to boil the needle and thread before using them on him, but at least he could make sure the wound was cleaned afterwards. With any luck, he wouldn't come down with a fever, but if the worst came to the worst, he'd have to disappear back to the twenty-first century for a while for some antibiotics. Hopefully without anyone noticing that he'd gone.

Or maybe he deserved to die for taking someone else's life. He swallowed hard, tamping down the emotions swirling inside him. What was done was done, and he had to somehow come to terms with it.

'If you say so.' Ellisif was speaking soothingly, like she was talking to a child, and it almost made him smile. 'I'll do anything as long as you promise not to bleed to death,' she added under her breath.

They were alone in the pantry now, Askhild having gone back to the dais to help oversee the rest of the oath-swearing. Ivar focused on the lovely woman in front of him, who was busy tying off a knot.

'Thank you.' He reached out and cupped her chin in the palm of his hand, drawing her face close. When she raised her eyes to his, he bent to drop a swift kiss on her luscious lips. He needed the contact between them as some sort of life-affirming gesture; to show him that what he'd done was necessary in order to protect people like her.

Or so he told himself.

'Ivar . . .' She pulled away slightly but didn't wriggle out of his hold. Instead she put her own hand over his and squeezed it tight. 'You did a good thing. Never doubt that. It was you or him, and I for one am heartily glad that you were the one to prevail. There was nothing else you could have done.'

'How did you . . . ?' He didn't know how to articulate his question. It was as though she'd read his mind, and he was afraid she would think less of him. To her, he might seem like a coward.

'I could see it in your eyes. You've never killed before, have you?' she asked gently.

'No. I am trained for it, but I have never had to put it into practice.' He swallowed hard. 'I'm sorry. You must think me very weak.'

'Never! Look at me, Ivar.' He gazed into her eyes. 'I honour you for it. You are a good man and you did what you had to do. Not wanting to kill for the sake of it is a trait I admire. I refuse to think less of you for that. And you have my word I'll never tell a soul.'

'Thank you.' Somehow sharing the burden with her made it easier, and if she thought he'd done the right thing, he couldn't regret it. Well, not as much anyway. 'Thank you, *unnasta*.'

To his surprise, she leaned forward and kissed him in return, hard but quick. 'Let us forget this and move forward. Come, I need to find some lye soap, wine and salt water. And don't you dare succumb to a fever, do you hear me?'

Her words were accompanied by a smile, and Ivar couldn't stop a faint smile of his own from peeping out. 'Yes, mistress,' he said, as if acknowledging an order from a general.

He hopped off the bench he'd been sitting on and followed her as she went in search of primitive antiseptics. The first shock of what he'd done had worn off. Now he needed to process it and put it behind him, if that was at all possible. Time would tell.

* * *

The man was an enigma – a trained warrior who had never killed anyone and who hadn't wanted to. She'd seen it in his eyes, the shock and horror at taking a life. Ellisif pondered this as she washed his wound the way he'd instructed her to. And what kind of strange remedy was this? Wine and salt water? She'd never heard of such a thing, but if it was what he wanted, she'd do it.

She couldn't help but sneak glances at his fine torso, broad shoulders and strong arms as she finished off her task. He was beautifully made, the ridges of muscle outlined by the light of the oil lamps standing on a nearby shelf. Although she was touching his skin, she longed to run her fingers over it in a caress instead of for healing purposes, especially the intriguing lines across his abdomen. But that way lay danger, and despite the kisses they had just exchanged, she knew she had to restrain herself. They'd done it in the heat of the moment and no one had seen them. Best if it didn't happen again.

By the time she'd bound his wound with strips of clean linen, the others had finished the oath-swearing and headed for their sleeping benches. It was close to dawn and some of the torches had gone out, but quite a few people were still awake.

'We'll take turns on guard duty,' Thorald decreed. 'I'll go first. Ivar, get some rest. We want that wound to heal quickly.'

'Very well.' Ivar turned to look at Ellisif. 'Where shall we bed down? I'm too tired to put up the tent right now, but I can't see any space for us here.'

It warmed her that he wanted her near him, and she didn't question it. The people around them had no idea that they weren't a couple, and they would be sleeping with all their clothes on in any case. She glanced around the hall, which did seem rather crowded.

'Perhaps there is a hay loft?' she suggested.

'Good idea.'

Outside, the world was a pearly grey colour and the birds had begun the morning chorus. It was cold, and winter was fast approaching. As they walked across the *tún* – a paved courtyard area in between the various buildings – they could see their breath in the air, and Ellisif huddled into her cloak. It felt strange to be going to bed at such an unusual time, but she knew they needed some sleep before tackling the rest of the day. There would be much to do over the coming weeks. She'd already noticed the neglected state of the hall itself, and some of the surrounding buildings were in even worse shape. Whatever Egil had been doing, he hadn't tended to the domains he'd usurped.

After checking a couple of buildings, they found the byre, with a hayloft at one end. They had to climb a ladder to reach it, and Ivar allowed her to go first.

'Don't worry, I'll catch you if you fall,' he assured her, following her up the rungs.

The hay was not as plentiful as it should have been for a settlement this size, but there was definitely enough for them to sleep on. Ivar took off his cloak and spread it out, then sank down on top of it.

'Here, lie beside me. We can use your cloak to go over us. That should keep us warm.'

She hesitated, as that indicated a rather intimate arrangement, but they'd slept like that before, so why was she debating the issue now? He must have noticed, as he sighed and rubbed at his face.

'Ellisif, I'm not in any state to ravish you. Please, just lie next to me. I need to feel your warmth, that is all. It's been a . . . difficult night. I swear, I'll not do anything you don't wish me to.'

In other words, he wasn't thinking of her as a woman, merely a fellow human being. He needed comfort, and that she could give him. And it wasn't as though she hadn't asked him for the same thing in the past. Taking off her own cloak, she lay down beside him and allowed him to drape it over them both. Then she wriggled closer and put an arm around him, leaning her cheek on his shoulder. 'Sleep then, Ivar. I'm here. I have you.'

'Yes, you do,' he murmured, kissing the top of her head.

His arms came round her and pulled her even closer, and she didn't mind at all. He needed her, and it was the least she could do for this complex man who had come to her rescue. It was her turn to give him something back.

Chapter Thirteen

Ulfstoft, 17 October/Gormánuðr AD *875*

'By all the gods, I wish I could kill the *argr* all over again!'

Ivar was standing with Thorald, surveying the sorry state of Álrik's domains, and could totally understand his kinsman's anger. They'd made an inventory of the cattle, grain and hay before deciding about the autumn slaughter, and things were dire. There were plenty of animals, but although Ivar had no experience of farming, even he could see that there wasn't enough fodder to keep many of them alive through a long Nordic winter. Not to mention all the people of the settlement, who would be in need of sustenance too.

He shook his head. 'What was he thinking? I can understand him neglecting things, but surely his own instinct for survival would have made him lay in stocks for the cold months ahead?'

'I have no idea. I doubt he thought much beyond the next mug of ale and willing wench.' Thorald's mouth was set in a grim line. 'We'll have to try to buy more supplies or no one will live to see the spring, human or beast.'

'I'd be happy to help. I have some silver.' Ivar jingled one of the pouches at his belt and also indicated the many silver armbands clinking on his wrist.

'You shouldn't have to. This isn't your problem,' Thorald bit out.

Ivar put a hand on his arm. 'I want to. We're kin. I'm sure you'd do the same for me.' And he really did believe that now. Thorald was still not the chattiest or friendliest of men, but he'd thawed considerably. And it hadn't escaped Ivar's notice what an honour it had been to be asked to stand on that dais with him the previous night. It showed that Thorald had accepted their kinship fully, which was wonderful.

With a sigh, Thorald capitulated. 'You're right, and I thank you. We'll go in search of extra provisions in a few days' time, after we've done some clearing up. I've ordered everyone to start cleaning the buildings and patching up those that are in need of repair. Winter will be freezing here by the fjord, and we can't afford any leaks or holes in the walls. I'm also sending away any hangers-on who have no right to be here, some of those aforementioned wenches included. A couple of my men will be transporting them to the nearest market later today.'

He glanced at a group of five women who were sitting by a jetty, their expressions supremely sulky. There were also two men who had refused to swear the oath to Álrik yet hadn't stood up for Egil either, merely laying down their weapons.

'How did you know which ones to evict?' Ivar was curious; at first glance the women looked no different to those who were currently scurrying about with brooms and buckets.

'Askhild. She pointed out those who don't belong here. Apparently they were brought in by Egil when he tired of the ones who were here already.'

'Ah, of course.' That made sense. Ivar looked around once more. 'What would you like me to do first?'

'Actually, since you're injured and won't be much use here for a few days, perhaps you could go with the ship to the nearest marketplace to buy the goods we need. That will speed things up. You shouldn't have to do much rowing and I trust you to haggle well for any supplies you find. I'll tell you what we are most lacking.'

A warm sensation spread through Ivar at the thought that Thorald had faith in him. It was exactly the sort of relationship he'd hoped for with his ancestor when he'd travelled back in time. He hardly dared believe that he had achieved it in such a short space of time. He nodded. 'Very well. Let me write down what to procure so I don't forget.'

The words were out of his mouth before he'd thought them through, and when he saw Thorald's puzzled expression, he cursed himself inwardly. Vikings didn't write shopping lists, for goodness' sake. They wrote rune stones and carved their name on some of their possessions, but that was all.

'You wish to do what?'

'Er, it's a strange habit of mine, writing things to aid my memory.' He figured he might as well brazen this out, as if it wasn't a big deal. 'I use bark to scratch a few runes.' Bark was the only material he could think of that would be suitable for writing on, as he couldn't very well carry around big chunks of wood or stone.

'That is . . . unusual, but if it will help, I suppose there's no harm in it. Come, let us find you some bark, then.' Thorald ushered him over to a workshop. Inside they found a man shaping pieces of wood, presumably for one of the restoration projects that had begun that morning. He had piles of bark that were to be used as underlay for the roofs, and allowed them to take a couple of pieces. Thankfully Thorald didn't tell him what they needed it for.

Ivar appropriated an iron nail as well and sat down with Thorald in the hall, scratching out a list of items to buy. He used runes, though it was tempting to write in his own alphabet, and simple lines to denote numbers. It was a good thing that most Vikings were literate to some degree, or else he would have stood out even more. His kinsman regarded him with fascination, as if he was some alien creature, but there was a small smile playing about his mouth. He seemed to be able to read what Ivar wrote, as he nodded occasionally and suggested additions.

'At least I'll know you won't forget half the things I've asked you to obtain. Now, you'd best be on your way.'

'Will do. I'll speak to the others and we'll leave as soon as possible.'

He was determined to do his best for Thorald and make him proud.

'Urgh! I'm not enjoying this part of being with child.' Askhild rinsed her mouth out with water from a cup Ellisif had proffered and spat into the grass at the edge of the forest. Moments before, she'd dashed off to be violently sick, and having seen this sort of thing many times before, Ellisif had followed.

'It will pass in a few weeks, then you'll begin to bloom.' She swallowed hard. She'd wished to experience this for herself, but despite Þjódólfr's best efforts, she'd never quickened with child. Not a single time. Yet another reason for his displeasure.

'I've fathered many a child on other women,' he'd boasted. 'So the fault lies with you. Useless wench!'

Not that she'd seen any of his reputed offspring, but knowing him, he'd probably left the poor mothers to raise them on their own. Or worse, had the babes carried out into the woods to die of exposure or be eaten by wild animals. Most likely the mothers were thralls anyway. No one would care whose infant it was, nor what became of it, least of all Þjódólfr.

'Sweet Freya, but I hope so!' Askhild sighed. 'And hopefully that will stop Thorald from fretting.'

Ellisif smiled. She'd already noticed he had a tendency to be overprotective, and she could only imagine that having a pregnant wife would make him ten times worse. 'You should be pleased that he cares.'

'Oh, I am, don't mistake me. I just wish he'd take my word for it that I'm not as fragile as I look. Anyone would think women had never borne children before.'

'I think it's sweet. He's so clearly besotted with you and wants to look after you. I'd have killed for my husband to regard me the way Thorald does you, as if you're the most precious thing in Miðgarðr.' The confession slipped out before she could take it back, but it was the truth.

'Hmm, well, it seems to me you could have that. Did you and Ivar sleep well last night?' Askhild's smile turned teasing and Ellisif felt her cheeks heat up.

'We did, and no, he didn't touch me other than to hold me close. We're not . . . that is to say, he hasn't said anything about marriage.'

He desired her, that much was clear, but she doubted he wanted anything more than her body. Whenever she'd talked about the future, he became very vague. There was something he wasn't telling her, but she couldn't figure out what that could be.

'Do you want him to? He turned up unexpectedly not long ago and we don't really know much about him, other than the fact that he is related to Thorald. Anyone can see that. He wouldn't bring much to a marriage, though, other than himself,' Askhild pointed out.

'I know.' If she was looking to marry, she wouldn't care about that, as long as she could choose a husband for herself. And Ivar was exactly the sort of man she'd want. Yet . . . she didn't think she could bear the thought of someone having that kind of power over her again. 'But no, I don't think I ever wish to marry a second time.' She couldn't help a small shudder from running through her. 'I'd like to be in charge of my own domains, and as a widow, that is my right. If only I can find a way to enforce it. I'll need men who are loyal to me without trying to wed me.' And she didn't think there was much hope of finding many such men.

'Hmm. I'm sure that can be arranged eventually.' Askhild sounded confident. 'Now, we'd best get on with the cleaning. Honestly, Egil was an absolute pig! I'm going to burn everything in his bed except for the frame, and even that will be scrubbed within an inch of its life.'

'Sounds good to me. Lead the way.'

Ulfstoft, 20 October/Gormánuðr AD *875*

As it turned out, Ivar proved to be good at haggling. He found that he enjoyed it immensely, and once he realised that he wasn't doing anyone out of a profit, he put his heart and soul into it. It helped that one of the men accompanying him was Holmstein, who was obviously an old hand at bargaining. He was also easy company and a mine of information, as he loved to talk. As a result, Ivar had a great time and learned so much his head felt like it might explode with all the new details it contained. He only hoped he'd remember everything once he was back in his own century.

He and Thorald's other men returned a few days later with the ship laden to the gunwales with provisions, including fodder for the animals. Silver gained you access to most things, and he was pleased he'd brought plenty. He hadn't had to use even half as much as he'd thought, and Thorald had sent some of his own to add to that. All in all, the journey was deemed a huge success. His kinsman beamed at him when he met them down by the jetty.

'Excellent! Perhaps I'll have to start scratching on bark myself if this is the result.' He clapped Ivar on the shoulder and smiled at him. 'Any other unusual ideas you wish to share with me?'

'Perhaps.' Ivar didn't tell him that there were quite a few things he could teach him. It was too soon to divulge all his secrets, but the time would come when he'd have to.

Sometime later, he entered the hall, which was now much improved after a thorough clean. The floor had been swept, the benches scrubbed and new bed furs laid out. The wall hangings had been washed and rehung, and there were no cobwebs in sight. Ivar barely gave the room a glance, however, as his eyes sought the one person he'd missed the most: Ellisif. He'd tried not to think about her while he was away, but his thoughts had returned to her again and again. He was well and truly captivated, and didn't know what – if anything – to do about it. Nothing would be the sensible course, but he found himself wanting to act recklessly.

At first, he didn't see her, but then he caught sight of her stunning hair as she came out of the chamber at the far end. Their eyes met across the room, and he could have sworn that time stood still. How clichéd was that? He shook himself inwardly. This wasn't some romantic film where the hero and heroine fell in love at first sight. It wasn't possible. He and Ellisif were not destined to be together. He had his life back in Stockholm, and once he'd helped her regain her domains, she'd have hers mapped out. There was no middle ground, because he couldn't stay here and he couldn't take her with him. He'd never intended to remain for any length of time; although he'd taken a sabbatical from his job at the museum, he was expected back at some point and couldn't stay away indefinitely. Besides, he didn't belong here; he was a fish out of water. Both he and Ellisif had responsibilities neither could relinquish.

If only he could remember that when she looked at him like she'd missed him too.

She walked towards him. 'Ivar, are you well? How is the wound?' She raised those luminous eyes to his. They were a very clear peridot green today in the sunshine spilling in through the open doors. He allowed himself to drown in her gaze for a moment, then pulled himself together.

'Very well, thank you. It is healing nicely. Must be all the wine you wasted on it,' he joked. He knew she'd been perplexed at his request to have it cleaned with the only alcohol he could think of, and she'd rather overdone it as a result.

She smacked him on the arm. '*Fifl!* It was you who told me to do that,' she retorted, but the smile that accompanied her words showed him that she knew he was teasing. 'Did you find everything that was needed?'

'Yes, we brought back a ship full of goods. It should hopefully see everyone through till spring. I'd best go and help unload, but I look forward to seeing you later.'

'And I you.' Her words were quietly spoken, but they sent tendrils of heat shooting through him.

'Then save me a seat beside you for *nattverðr*, please. Oh, wait, have you any idea where my travelling kist is? And where I'm supposed to sleep?' He hadn't been assigned a bench before he left to buy the supplies.

'Yes, over here. I'll show you.' Ellisif led the way to the bench closest to the dais on the left-hand side. 'Your kist is underneath and I've unpacked your bed furs and blankets.' She ducked her head to hide the blush that he saw creeping over her cheekbones.

'I . . . um, hope you don't mind, but I appropriated half for myself. Askhild offered me some, but you seemed to have enough for the both of us.'

'Of course, that's fine. You are welcome to them.' He hesitated, then couldn't help but ask, 'Where are you sleeping?'

'Here.' She pointed to the bench next to his, but wouldn't look him in the eyes. 'Askhild said I should be close to the chamber where she and Thorald sleep.' She nodded towards one of the doorways next to the dais. 'Álrik is in the other one, as is fitting.'

Ivar smiled and put his fingers under her chin so that she had to turn her face up to his. 'I'm glad,' he said. 'Then I can protect you if necessary.'

Her cheeks were still flushed, but she nodded. 'Let's hope it won't be.' She took a deep breath and turned away. 'Now I'd best get on with a few tasks.'

'And me. See you later.'

They were chasing her again. This time Ellisif turned around every so often, and she could see the face of one of the men clearly. It was Kári. His expression was one of excitement, as if he was relishing the hunt and sure of the outcome. From time to time he let out a whoop of glee, echoed by the faceless men following him, and his eyes promised that when he caught her, she'd be very sorry. She knew that they were gaining on her. The pounding of their steps echoed the thumping of her heart. She moved her legs as fast as she could, but she was flagging, and her lungs were about to burst. Sheer terror slowed her steps as well, reducing her ability to function. She couldn't go on for much longer. Then she felt it, a hand gripping her shoulder, and she screamed . . .

'Shh, *unnasta*. It's only me,' a soft voice murmured. 'You were having a nightmare. It's not real.'

She drew in a gasping breath and filled her lungs with much-needed air before turning around. Ivar was perched on the edge of her sleeping bench, his face barely discernible in the faint light from the hearth, where a few coals still glowed. 'Did . . . did I wake you? I'm sorry.' She sat up and put her face in her hands. Would she ever feel safe enough for these dreams to stop? Perhaps she ought to sleep somewhere else so she didn't wake everyone with her night frights.

'You only made a tiny noise,' Ivar reassured her, caressing her back with soothing motions. 'I was awake anyway.'

'Oh, good.' She was still embarrassed. 'I'll try not to do it again.'

'Would it help if I held you?' He'd bent to whisper in her ear, and it sent a shiver all the way down to her toes. 'These benches are wide enough for two.'

'But what will people think?' She was tempted, but they weren't in a tent any longer and everyone would see them lying entwined come morning.

'Does it matter? You're a widow and I'm an unmarried man. What we do is not their concern.' She heard a sigh. 'Actually, don't answer that. I wasn't thinking straight, sorry. Of course your reputation is important. I'm sure you'll want to remarry. You will find someone other than Kári eventually.'

'No!' Her protest came out too loudly, and she moderated her voice. 'No, I won't, and you're right, it doesn't matter.' Perhaps it was exactly what she needed in order to put others off the idea of wedding her. 'Please, hold me, then maybe I won't dream again.' In fact, she was sure of it, because he always made her feel as though she was in a safe haven.

'Very well, let me lie down behind you. I'll try to rise early, before anyone sees us.'

He dragged some of his own blankets over and arranged himself against the wall, pulling her back to his chest. It was chilly in the hall and a relief to burrow beneath the blankets once more. As on the previous occasions, she slotted into his embrace perfectly, and her limbs relaxed almost of their own accord. She sighed with satisfaction, and when he put an arm around her, she hugged it closer to her body. No one would see that, as they were covered with blankets, and she needed the connection between them.

'Thank you,' she murmured.

'You're welcome. Now sleep, sweetheart.'

She felt him press a kiss under her ear, and her eyes drifted closed. Kári couldn't hurt her now. Ivar would make sure of it.

Chapter Fourteen

Ulfstoft, 21 October/Gormánuðr AD 875

'You and Ivar looked very cosy this morning.' Askhild sent Ellisif a teasing glance. 'Changed your mind already?'

'No. No, I haven't. He was merely being kind after I had a night fright. Ever since the king's men came for me, I've had these horrible dreams . . . Well, anyway, they don't disturb me when he's next to me. Besides, you weren't supposed to see us. Were you up early?'

'Yes, I had to use the privy. You do know people will talk if they see you, don't you?'

'Yes.' Ellisif sighed. 'But hopefully you were the only one who noticed. He returned to his own bench before dawn. Anyway, we were merely sleeping next to each other, nothing more. And it might not happen again.' Although secretly she wished it would.

Askhild nodded and didn't comment further, but Ellisif was sure this wasn't the last she'd heard of it. Fortunately, no one else seemed to have noticed, or if they had, they didn't mention it to her.

'I should probably go home now,' she mused. 'If Kári is still searching for me, he will have been and gone, don't you think?'

And she'd be better off away from temptation in the shape of a tall, blond man whose embrace felt so right.

'Actually, Thorald and I were discussing that last night. He thinks you should remain here until spring. The man's son did say to stay away, did he not?'

'Kell? Yes, but . . . I thought he meant temporarily.' Ellisif bit her lip. It would be exactly like Kári to decide to spend the winter at her hall, helping himself to the supplies meant for her people. The thought made her clench her fists. The utter *niðingr*.

Askhild put a hand on her arm, as if to calm her. 'Better safe than sorry. And I would love your company through the dark months. I'm going to become large with child soon and I'd welcome your help. Truly, you'd be doing me a huge favour. Come spring, my husband and Ivar can take you back to see how matters stand at Birgirsby. After the spring planting, Thorald will be able to spare a few men.'

'That is most kind. Of both of you. I . . . thank you.' Ellisif was moved to think that these people cared about her welfare when she'd been a stranger not so long ago. The least she could do was repay them by supporting Askhild through her pregnancy. 'When is the baby due?'

'Late spring, before the Sólmánuðr, so there's a while to go yet. But at least I haven't been sick this morning. Things are improving.'

'I'm glad.' And she was pleased for her new friend, even if it was going to be painful to watch the woman's stomach grow.

But what did it matter? Since she never wanted to marry again, she wouldn't have had children in any case.

'There are some strangers down by the jetty asking for sanctuary. They claim to be related to Mistress Ellisif. Or one of them, at least. Shall I bring them up?'

One of Thorald's men had approached the dais where Ivar was

sitting with his kinsman, Askhild, Álrik and Ellisif, as well as a few others. Ivar shared a concerned glance with Ellisif, then with Thorald, but the latter nodded.

'Yes, please. Watch their every step, though, in case of treachery.'

'How would anyone know I'm here?' Ellisif hissed. Her face had turned ashen and she was literally quivering. 'Should I go and hide?'

'No.' Ivar put a hand on hers beneath the table. 'You're under Thorald's protection here. We won't let any harm come to you.'

There was no time, in any case. The doors were thrown open and a group of three people herded inside. They looked weary and dishevelled, as if from a long journey, and also wary of Thorald's men. A gasp came from Ivar's left, then Ellisif was up and running towards them.

'Hedda! Oddr and Gaukr? What are you all doing here?'

A pretty young girl, perhaps sixteen or seventeen, with hair of a very similar colour to Ellisif's, broke away from the group. Her features lit up. 'Ellisif! You *are* here. I wasn't sure if he was lying. Oh, I'm so glad. Thank the gods!'

The two women hugged, then turned towards the dais, where Thorald waited in silence for an explanation.

'This is my cousin, Hedda, kin on my mother's side. She had recently come to live with me, a few weeks before the king's men took me away. I was forced to leave her behind. And these are some of my people.' Ellisif indicated the two men, then turned back to Hedda. 'Please, tell us how you found me.'

'Well, it was Kell who told us to head for the hall of a young jarl by the name of Álrik. He said he'd met you on the way to Birgirsby and had made enquiries to find out who you were.'

Ivar heard Thorald swear under his breath, but he didn't otherwise interrupt the girl's narrative. Ellisif was frowning at her.

'Kell is at Birgirsby?'

'Yes, with his father.' Hedda's expression turned angry and disdainful. 'That pig Kári Knutsson. He arrived a few weeks ago, claiming to be your husband, and simply took over. When some of the men tried to protest, seeing as he hadn't brought you to prove this, he . . . he had them killed. And that's not all he's done since his arrival.' She ended the sentence on a sob and her eyes filled with tears.

'The complete and utter . . . Did he hurt you?'

'No, but if it wasn't for Kell, he would have done.' Hedda sniffled.

Thorald cut in. 'That does not explain your presence here. Did Kári send you to find your kinswoman? Is he following you?'

'No, absolutely not! He doesn't know where she is, and hopefully he hasn't noticed we're gone yet. He's had men out searching for Ellisif all along the coastal route, and he went with them this last time. I heard him say that if they did find her, they were to bring her back in one piece, and that he'd deal with her once and for all after her return. And then . . . then Kell told me his father was planning to kill Ellisif after their marriage and wed me instead, because she was more trouble than she was worth. As I'm her closest kin, that would give him the right to Birgirsby twice over.'

Gasps of disbelief greeted this tale, but it was Ivar's turn to frown. 'May I ask why Kári's own son would tell you such a thing? Presumably he's meant to be loyal to his father.' Although the young man certainly hadn't acted that way when they'd met at that marketplace.

Hedda's cheeks grew rosy. 'Yes, but he hates the man and doesn't agree with his methods. His older brothers are no better than their father, but Kell is different. He's been nothing but kind to me . . . er, to us. He said he couldn't stand the thought of me ending up in his father's clutches, any more than he wanted to see Ellisif in that situation. He remembered how you'd protected her and thought perhaps you could extend that courtesy to me as well. To all of us. I couldn't possibly have travelled here on my own.'

Thorald nodded. 'Of course. You are welcome here, as long as you haven't led that man to Ellisif. Is that not so, Álrik?'

'Yes, indeed. Have a seat, all of you. There should be plenty of food for everyone.'

Ivar liked the way Thorald included his young brother-in-law in decisions, deferring to him as if he was the chieftain already. The youth was learning fast, and he had to start to stand on his own feet quickly.

Ellisif shepherded Hedda towards the dais, where Ivar made room for her on the bench. If a small part of him resented the girl's presence between them, he suppressed that thought. It was only natural that she'd want to sit next to her older cousin.

'I'm so glad you were able to escape. But the thought of that man ruling my domains makes my blood boil.' Ivar could sense the barely suppressed fury in Ellisif's voice, and it was understandable. 'I wish we could go there right this moment and punish the *aumingi*. But I've promised to stay here until spring. Vengeance will have to wait.'

'It will be all the sweeter for it,' Ivar murmured, sharing a look with her over the top of Hedda's head. She nodded back, her mouth set with determination.

'I hope so.'

Ellisif had wondered what would happen that evening and whether Ivar would go back to sleeping on his own. He disappeared while most other people were preparing for bed, and only returned when the hall had fallen quiet. By then, she was curled up on her bench, dreading the dreams that would no doubt haunt her yet again.

The fire had died down and was banked for the night. Ivar was a mere shadow as he made his way past her. Disappointment flooded her, but she told herself not to be so silly. It wasn't his duty to comfort her every night; he'd only done it the once to be kind.

She heard his blankets rustling, then a large body crawled in behind hers and her pulse rate increased. 'Ivar? What are you . . . ?'

She had turned on to her back so she was half facing him, and he shushed her by putting his mouth on hers. The unexpected kiss stunned her, and she lay still until he moved his lips, caressing hers. Without thinking, she reciprocated, but it was over almost before it had begun. He pulled back and started arranging a blanket over himself.

Frustration built inside her. It was never enough, these brief kisses. She craved his touch, his mouth on hers properly, for longer. She hesitated, then blurted out in a low whisper, 'Will you kiss me again, please? Just once more?'

He stilled, and it took him a moment to respond. 'Why?'

'I . . . have never been kissed like that by anyone else. Þjódólfr didn't . . . I mean, he wasted no time on such things. I'm curious.' She felt silly admitting this, but it was the truth. Her former husband had never shown her any tenderness, and kissing was a preliminary he'd not wasted time on. Those quick meetings of mouths with Ivar promised so much more, and she wanted to know what. Yearned to find out.

'You're playing with fire, *unnasta*.' His voice was hoarse, more like a growl. 'As am I. I shouldn't have kissed you at all.'

Her heart began to beat faster at hearing the endearment, and the warning in his voice. She was asking too much. A man would want more than a mere kiss. She'd been stupid to think it was a simple thing. 'I'm sorry. Forget I said anything.'

'No.' He reached out and put a hand behind her neck, drawing her closer. 'Come here.'

The next thing she knew, his mouth was slanting across hers, touching her lips with what felt like reverence. He kissed his way from one corner to the other, nibbling slightly on her bottom lip, his tongue caressing her until she opened up for him. Then he delved inside, exploring tentatively, as if he was trying to coax a response out of her. She gave it to him, touching the tip of her tongue to his and following his lead. Despite the fact that she'd never been kissed this way before, she didn't hesitate, because it was so good, so right. It was everything she thought a kiss should be, and more.

They kissed for what seemed like ages. He took his time, as if he had infinite patience. One of his hands rested on her waist, but he didn't move it or try to touch the rest of her in any way. There was none of the rough squeezing she was used to, the painful pinching and groping. His other hand tilted her head to give him better access, while his fingers tangled in her hair. She put one palm on his firm chest where his heart jumped noticeably under the warm skin she could feel through his shirt. Their breathing became ragged, and after a while, he pulled away, resting his forehead against hers. His chest rose and fell, his lungs drawing in quick breaths as if he'd been running fast.

'Was that what you wanted?' he asked, his voice lower and huskier than usual, a whisper that no one else could hear.

'Y-yes. Thank you.'

He huffed out a laugh. 'Trust me, the pleasure was all mine. But unless you wish to be ravished in the next few moments, I'd suggest you go to sleep.'

She could tell he was reining himself in and that she had

pushed him to the limits. 'Very well. Goodnight.' Turning away from him, she tried to will her own heart to slow down. It was thumping against her ribs like a wild thing caught in a snare, and her whole body was on fire. She'd had no idea that mere kissing could have such an effect. Being out of Ivar's embrace felt wrong, though, and she decided to push her luck a tiny bit more. 'Ivar? I don't suppose . . . I mean, do you think you could simply hold me? Please?'

There was a strangled groan from behind her and a muttered curse, but in the next instant his large body curled around her back and one brawny arm snaked around her middle. 'Just don't move, or I won't be answerable for the consequences,' he hissed. He didn't really sound angry, though, and she knew she was safe.

'I won't.'

And there was no need, because she was right where she wanted to be, and sleep claimed her very soon after.

Ivar didn't sleep much but he couldn't regret making out with Ellisif. Dear Lord, those kisses had been spectacular. He couldn't remember the last time he'd been so turned on by any woman, and that was without even touching the rest of her. In a way, it was like being a teenager again, on a journey of discovery where everything was new and certain things were forbidden. Indeed, just thinking about it as 'making out', a juvenile concept if any, had him remembering his time as a young adult. It had been a period of intense emotions – overwhelming sometimes – exploration, experimentation and learning. That was what Ellisif had been doing, as it was all new to her. Perhaps that made it more exciting for him as well?

But he had a feeling it was just her. She affected him like no other. He'd had to go slowly, and teach her to trust him. Although she'd been married for a decade, she had clearly never gone through the normal stages of a physical relationship. Never been kissed properly. He guessed her husband had been of the 'wham bam thank you ma'am' variety, but minus the gratitude. She'd been hurt, both physically and mentally. It was bound to have left scars, fear and insecurities.

Again, it made him want to pound the man's skull in with his bare fists. Since that was not an option, the only thing he could do was try to undo the wrong Þjódólfr had done her. Show her that not all men were beasts. And he'd been determined not to be. He had held himself in check and only taken things as far as she was comfortable with.

It couldn't happen again, though, because he knew that next time, he might get carried away, and that wouldn't be fair to her, since he had no intention of sticking around. She deserved better. He'd satisfied her curiosity about kissing and that would have to be enough. From now on he'd go back to sleeping by himself and only hold her if she had nightmares, which hopefully wouldn't be too often.

In the meantime, there was much to do during the day. They were now in the so-called Gormánuðr, or 'slaughter month', which ran roughly from mid October to mid November in Ivar's time. It was a very busy period in general and counted as the first winter month. The first feast of the year would soon be held too – the winter *blōt*. Before that, all the produce gathered or harvested had to be processed so that it survived the winter. Ivar was fascinated by everything he saw and quite in awe of these people's ingenuity. Smoking, drying, preserving – there appeared to be endless ways of keeping food edible for long periods of time. Of course, this was essential to the settlement's survival. Most of the meat was either put into barrels of whey or smoked. Fruit and mushrooms were cut up and dried, some vegetables were pickled, while root vegetables had to be placed in cold cellars dug into the ground. There was a lot to learn and he absorbed it all, memorising the details as best he could.

Naturally, he was expected to help, not least with the annual slaughter, which he wasn't keen on.

'Ivar, do you want to come and help kill the pigs, or would you prefer to assist with the butchering?' Thorald asked him.

'I'd rather do butchering, if you don't mind.' He was relieved to be given a choice. Not that he was squeamish, but killing animals was not something he'd be comfortable with. Cutting up the meat seemed preferable; at least that way he didn't have to see any suffering, if indeed there was any. Hopefully the poor things were all dispatched swiftly.

He worked side by side with Askhild, Ellisif and some of the men and women of the settlement. They had to instruct him in what to do, as he confessed he'd never had to assist in tasks like that before.

'What, never?' Askhild couldn't hide her surprise.

'Um, no. I lived in a hall where such things were taken care of by others. Thralls.'

More lies, but he couldn't possibly tell them the truth – that ordinarily he'd go down to the supermarket and buy meat that was neatly pre-packaged and all cut up for him. It made him realise how incredibly lucky he'd been, not having to do any work in order to obtain food. He was also astonished at how every single part of each animal seemed to be used in one way or another. There was hardly any waste at all, which was admirable, even if he would personally rather go hungry than eat pig's trotters or intestines of any kind.

When it came to threshing, he was much happier to help. Once he got the hang of it, it made for a great workout, although he had to be a little bit careful, since his recent wound was still healing and slightly sore. And it had the added bonus of drawing the women's admiring glances as he and the other men shed their shirts during the sweaty work. He saw Ellisif checking him out when she came to bring them flagons of ale, and hid a smile. Hopefully she liked what she saw and he compared favourably with her former husband. Not that it should matter – he was trying to keep away from her after all – but he couldn't help but yearn for her. No harm in dreaming, as long as he didn't act on it.

Chapter Fifteen

Ulfstoft, 24 October/Gormánuðr AD *875*

Time flew by and the day of the winter *blōt* arrived. It should have been held the previous week, but because of Egil's mismanagement, they were behind with everything. Thorald declared that it didn't matter when the ceremony was held, as long as they did it when they had finished with the slaughter. No one disagreed with him.

It was cold and frosty, with the blades of grass crunching under the soles of people's shoes and the ground hard. Small puddles had a surface of ice that broke with a loud crack as you walked across them, and tree branches glistened with a coating of hoar frost. A pale sun illuminated the small grove where the settlement's inhabitants gathered to sacrifice to the gods and thank them for the harvest. In the distance, the surrounding mountaintops were white too, and covered in a layer of clouds. The fjord could be glimpsed through the trees, the waters still and dark. It was all so beautiful, it made Ellisif's lungs constrict.

She stood with the others in a large circle, watching as Álrik killed a chicken and allowed its blood to seep into a bowl. Then he took a small whisk made out of twigs and walked around, chanting an ancient incantation and flicking blood from the bowl on to each person present. She saw Thorald watching with an expression of pride. He'd obviously coached the youth and was pleased that all was progressing well. It was only right that the owner of the property should do the honours – it was his responsibility to keep the gods on their side.

She sent a quick glance Ivar's way, but he wasn't looking at her. Instead, he appeared to be concentrating fiercely on the ritual happening in front of him, as if he was trying to learn and memorise it as well. That puzzled her, until she began to wonder if he was hoping to become a landowner himself. A suspicion entered her mind. Perhaps he was planning on being the owner of *her* domains by next year. Askhild had hinted that it was a possibility, and Ivar would have to be stupid not to seize such a chance if it was afforded him.

Well, it wouldn't be. She sighed. Much as she liked him, she wouldn't marry him. If anyone was to take care of this ritual at Birgirsby next year, it would be her.

He'd been avoiding her, though, so maybe she'd misjudged him. Since the kissing session – instigated by her, it had to be said – he'd gone back to sleeping on his own bench. As she hadn't suffered any further night frights, there had been no reason for him to hold her. She was honest enough to admit that she was disappointed. Had he not enjoyed it as much as her? She'd thought he had at the time. He had indicated he wanted nothing more than to carry on, but he must have had second thoughts the morning after, as he'd been rather distant ever since.

'What are you brooding about? You're frowning as if all the cares of the world are upon your shoulders when today is a day of celebration.' Askhild walked next to her back to the hall and nudged her with her elbow.

'Hmm? Oh, you don't want to know.' Ellisif ducked her head, her cheeks heating up.

'In that case, I can guess. Ivar, am I right? Did you two quarrel? I haven't seen you talking for a while now.' The other woman took her arm in a friendly grip and Ellisif knew there was nothing malicious about the questions. Askhild simply wanted her to be happy and was concerned about her.

'No, we haven't had words. I . . . We kissed one evening, and since then he's been withdrawn.'

It was Askhild's turn to frown. 'He didn't like it? Or did you find him repulsive?'

'Sweet Freya, no, far from it! And I think he enjoyed it as much as I did.'

'Then what is the problem?'

'I honestly don't know. He, um . . . didn't take it any further, but he might have wanted to. We didn't exactly discuss it. I wouldn't know what to say. It's all very confusing. It's shameful to admit, but I think I . . . want him, but not as a husband.'

'As a man? In your bed?' Askhild gave her arm a squeeze. 'Then invite him. You told me you are unable to bear children. If you are discreet, where would be the harm? By not marrying again, you'll be denying yourself the pleasure a man can give you. Yet here is your chance to experience it.'

Ellisif sighed. 'It would be highly improper of me. And are you sure it is pleasurable? Because that has not been my experience thus far.'

The other woman laughed. 'Oh, I think I can safely say that with someone like Ivar, it would be vastly different. But you'll never know unless you try.'

'It would seem very forward of me to . . . to suggest such a thing.' It would be brazen in the extreme and not at all like her. She shivered at the thought of what could happen between them.

Was it possible it would feel even better than the kisses they'd shared? Those had sent tendrils of heat into every part of her body. It had been exciting. Exhilarating. And terrifying.

If anyone were to find out, however, it would ruin her reputation for ever.

Askhild didn't seem to be thinking that way. 'Then don't say it outright. Use your womanly wiles. Smile at him, touch him lightly on the arm or chest, stare into his eyes and brush against him as if by accident. I guarantee he'll be tempted.'

'Thank you. I'll think about it at least.'

'You do that, but don't take too long, or there are others who might snap him up.' Askhild nodded meaningfully towards Hedda, who was having a spirited discussion with Ivar as they walked a few yards ahead, judging by her wide gestures.

A sharp stab of jealousy pierced Ellisif, but she pushed it down. She had no right to feel anything of the sort. If Ivar preferred young, uncomplicated Hedda, who was she to stop him? And yet the sight of them laughing together had her insides twisted in knots. She had to at least find out if he wanted her as much as she wanted him.

If she didn't try, she'd never know.

The hall had been decorated with boughs of greenery and the enticing cooking smells hit him the moment he walked through the door. Ivar drew in a long, appreciative breath and studied the trestle tables groaning with food. This time of year there was plenty of everything, and although it would be foolish to over-indulge, as the supplies had to last a long time, a little bit of extravagance could be allowed. It was a feast, after all.

'Oh, I'm so grateful to be here and not at Birgirsby!' Hedda exclaimed, grabbing his arm in unconscious excitement.

He surreptitiously extricated her hand, as he had no wish to lead her on. He'd never told anyone here his true age, but he was technically old enough to be her father. He had no interest in her as a potential partner, and he didn't think she was romantically inclined towards him either. Every other sentence that came out of her mouth mentioned Kell. It was clear the young man had made a huge impression on her. Ivar only hoped she wasn't going to have her heart broken. Still, that wasn't his problem, and she was young enough to get over it, should it happen.

'It does smell wonderful,' he agreed. 'Now, if you'll excuse me, I must go and speak with my kinsman.'

Heading for the table on the dais where he was to sit, he glanced around for Ellisif and found her walking in through the door arm in arm with Askhild. It pleased him that the two women had formed such a great friendship. He had sensed that Thorald's wife was a lonely soul, as lost as Ellisif, and they'd needed each other. She peeked his way, then turned to whisper something to her friend. Longing surged through him, but he tamped it down. He'd have to find a proper girlfriend when he returned to his century. Here, he was merely a visitor, and he'd keep his distance.

That was easier said than done when Ellisif was seated next to him with Askhild on his other side. Space appeared to be at a premium, with some extra guests from outlying farms filling the hall, and he found himself squashed between the two women. His thighs touched theirs, but he was only aware of Ellisif's. Her skin burned him through the layers of their clothing, and he shifted uncomfortably on the bench while attempting to concentrate on his food.

'How have you been, Ivar? I've not spoken to you for a few days.'

Was that reproach he heard in her voice? He wasn't sure, and decided to take her question at face value.

'Very well, thank you. Busy, of course. Always something to

do, and Thorald is a hard taskmaster.' That was true, but he was also fair and did his share of the work. 'And you?'

'Yes, the same. I'm glad we are nearly done. If I never see whey again, it will be too soon.' She attempted a small smile, but it was stilted, as if her heart wasn't in it.

They ate in silence for a while. She had no one on her other side, as she was sitting at the end of the bench, and Askhild, as usual, only had eyes and ears for Thorald. Ivar sensed the awkwardness growing between them, until Ellisif whispered, 'I'm sorry I asked you to kiss me.'

He turned to regard her. 'Are you? I'm not.' He realised as soon as the words came out of his mouth that it was the wrong thing to say, but he couldn't take them back.

Her eyebrows came down to form a faint V. 'But . . . then why have you been avoiding me? And don't bother denying it. I'm not a fool.'

Taking a swig of ale, he weighed his answer carefully and checked around to make sure no one was listening to their conversation. 'It's for your own good, Ellisif. I can't kiss you like that and not want more. You've been married. I'm sure you understand that.'

Her cheeks turned a little rosy, but her gaze didn't waver. 'Perhaps there could be more. If . . . we wanted there to be.'

His heart jumped and excitement coursed through his veins, but he took a deep breath and tried to think with his brain rather than his nether regions. He shook his head. 'No, I'm sorry. I cannot offer you marriage and nor will I be staying indefinitely. My plans lie elsewhere. It wouldn't be honourable or fair to you for me to bed you and leave. That's not the kind of man I am.'

She bit her lip, and he closed his eyes so he didn't have to watch. He'd nibbled on that delectable mouth and she was tempting beyond reason, but he mustn't give in.

'What if it was our secret? As I've told you, I'm barren, so there would be no consequences, and no one need ever know. I'm not expecting marriage.' She looked down and twisted her fingers together in her lap. 'Sweet Freya, I can't believe I'm saying these things out loud.'

He couldn't either. He'd thought her shy and retiring, not a seductress in the making. Why was she insisting? It seemed out of character and not in keeping with the mores of Viking society. He took a moment and tried to consider the matter from her perspective. She'd been abused for years and clearly had no idea that sex could be enjoyable. Perhaps she had heard rumours that it should be and she saw her chance to find out. But why him? He had to know.

'Let's step outside for a moment. I need some fresh air. You go first, and I'll follow soon after. Best if we're not seen leaving together.'

'Um, if you wish.'

She got up and made her way out the main doors, as if she was heeding a call of nature. No one paid her any attention, nor Ivar when he followed suit after a few minutes. He found her loitering in the shadows by the corner of the hall, where the light from torches set either side of the main entrance didn't quite reach.

'Come.' He took her hand and pulled her towards the byre. As on their first night in the settlement, he encouraged her to climb up into the hayloft. Thankfully, no other couple had had the same idea as yet. Perhaps they would later on. For now, the feast was still in full flow. Moments before Ivar had left, an itinerant skald had started on an epic poem that should take him a while to recite.

'Here, let's make ourselves comfortable.' He spread his cloak over the hay and sat down. Ellisif settled next to him, their legs and shoulders touching. 'Now then, suppose you tell me why you want us to, well, take matters further. Should you not be saving that for when you next marry? As I told you, I have no intention of offering for you, although I'm aware that Thorald and Askhild both think I should.'

'That's flattering,' she muttered, leaning her forehead on her bent knees.

'No, you misunderstand me!' He cupped her cheek with one hand and turned her to face him, even though they could barely make out each other's features. 'If I'd been planning on staying in this cen— . . . er, place, I would have liked nothing better than to be your husband. But there are circumstances I cannot explain that prevent me from marrying you. Or anyone else, for that matter. It has nothing to do with your charms, which believe me are considerable. If I were less honourable, I'd be tumbling you in the hay this instant.'

'I see.' She appeared to think this over for a moment, then started to explain. 'The fact of the matter is, I have no intention of ever marrying again, but I'm still curious. When you kissed me, I had the impression there was more to come. It . . . I . . .' She shook her head. 'I want to know what everyone is talking about, and I'm not afraid of you the way I am of most men. Your touch doesn't make me cringe or want to escape. Quite the opposite. I thought . . . well, what if no one else ever makes me feel that way? Then I'll have lost my chance to find out whether I could enjoy . . . it.'

'Oh, Ellisif.' He put his arms around her and drew her against his chest. 'Of course you must marry. I know you've been hurt in the past, but do you really want to go through the rest of your life alone? That's no way to live. You're young and beautiful, with many years left to enjoy.'

Yet even as he said the words, jealousy hit him square in the chest. He didn't want to think about her married to someone else, kissing another man, letting him touch her . . . But he had no right to object. None whatsoever.

She tentatively snaked her arms round his waist and shifted closer. 'It's better than being someone's chattel. To tell you the truth, I might as well have been a thrall, because I had no more say than they do. I belonged to my husband, his to do with as he pleased. I cannot imagine ever submitting to that again.' She shuddered.

He stroked her hair, which was coming loose from the knot she'd tied it in at the nape of her neck. 'I understand. And yet I think you were merely unfortunate. This time Thorald and I can make sure you get to choose for yourself. With the right man, marriage isn't like that. Look at him and Askhild. She's not unhappy, is she? Far from it – she glows.'

'Mm, but I can't risk it. A man may seem kind and considerate at first, but once he has his hands on my possessions, who's to say he won't change? And yes, I know I could divorce him, but presumably he'd still be entitled to keep part of what I own.'

Ivar had no answer to that.

She tightened her grip on him and whispered, 'Please, Ivar, show me what it should be like between a man and a woman. It will be something to remember for the rest of my days.'

'*Unnasta* . . .' He gritted his teeth to stop himself from pouncing on her instantly, the way his traitorous body was urging him to. 'You might be wrong about being barren, and if you become with child, then what? I couldn't possibly turn my back on any offspring of mine, and yet you would want to stay here. At Birgirsby, I mean. It would be an impossible situation.'

'There won't be a child.' Her eyes became glassy with unshed tears. 'Trust me, I've wasted enough years wishing for one.'

'The fault might have been your husband's. He was elderly, didn't you say?'

'Well, six and forty winters, so yes. But he'd had children, or so he told me.'

'Hmm.' Ivar wasn't convinced. 'Did you ever see any of them?'

'No, but—'

He cut her off. 'Then the man could have been lying in order to have yet another reason to belittle you. It sounds like exactly the sort of thing he'd do, judging by what you have said. If he was incapable of fathering children, he would never have admitted it.'

Þjódólfr had obviously been a devious son-of-a-bitch and Ivar didn't trust him to have told the truth. Especially not without proof. And sure, they could be careful, but most primitive birth control methods were notoriously unreliable. Did he want to risk it? He couldn't. And yet this extraordinary woman was offering him her body – how could he possibly say no? He wanted nothing more than to touch her, to show her that she had nothing to fear.

He came to a decision.

'I'll tell you what. Just this once, I will kiss you again and give you a brief glimpse of that pleasure you've been told about, but that is all. After that, you must stop tempting me, because it isn't fair to either of us and I'm really not prepared to take matters further. Trust me on that.' When she opened her mouth as if to argue, he held up a hand to stop her. 'No, this is not up for discussion. Take it or leave it.'

He waited for a couple of heartbeats while she deliberated.

'Um, yes please, then.' She sounded hesitant, but he also heard yearning and curiosity in her voice. She raised her chin, as if gathering her courage. 'Show me.'

'Very well.'

He only hoped he could be strong enough to stick to his own decision.

* * *

Ellisif hadn't really understood what Ivar meant, but when he started kissing her, any doubts fled. If kisses like these were involved, she'd do whatever he asked of her. He used his lips, teeth and tongue. The kisses were slow, deep and sensual. It was like being under the influence of henbane smoke, something she'd experienced once. Her limbs became loose and her body tingled all over. She wanted nothing more than to float in this state of bliss for ever.

'This is only the beginning,' he murmured, trailing his lips across her cheek and down the column of her throat, biting softly into the junction between her neck and her shoulder. It stung, but at the same time her skin tingled pleasurably. He stunned her by licking the same spot and then nibbling carefully on her ear lobe.

She gasped. 'Ivar?'

'You're wearing too many clothes. If you want to enjoy this, we need to be able to touch each other's skin. Off,' he ordered, tugging at her *smokkr*.

'But we'll be cold,' she protested, even as she grappled with the two brooches holding the straps in place.

He chuckled. 'Trust me, you'll soon be very hot indeed.'

After taking off the apron dress and the woollen tunic underneath, she was left in her *serk*, a long linen undergarment. 'And this?'

'No, you can keep that on for now.' She heard more than saw him divest himself of his belt and tunic. The weapons and pouches made a slight clanging noise as he laid them to one side. 'Give me your hands,' he said. When she complied, he pulled them towards him and put her palms on the naked skin of his chest. She realised he must have tugged off his shirt at the same time as the tunic.

She drew in a hasty breath. 'Ivar! That's . . . You're so warm. What should I do?'

'Explore, Ellisif. Touch me any way you like, but not below the waistband of my trousers. I know it's dark and it would have been better if we could see each other, but for now, learn the contours of my body with your fingertips. Don't be afraid – I'll like it, whatever you do.'

She followed his instructions and began to trail her fingers across his chest, up to those broad shoulders, down powerful arms and back to his stomach. It was exciting. The velvety texture of his smooth skin added to her enjoyment of his deep kisses in a way she'd never imagined. There were hard ridges everywhere, and he was hot to the touch. His abdominal muscles jumped when she reached them, and she hesitated, wondering if she was doing this all wrong.

'No, don't stop. That was a natural reaction, not revulsion. Now, let me do some exploring of my own while you continue.'

He did, his hands stroking her back through the *serk*, moving on to gently squeeze her behind, then coming round to the front, where he cupped one breast through the thin material. As he rubbed a thumb across her nipple, she shivered and arched her back, which made him kiss her more deeply. After a while, he divested her of the *serk* and used his mouth and tongue to lavish attention on her breasts. This caused fluttery sensations to shoot through her, and she moved restlessly, silently begging for more.

They were both making little noises of appreciation, and his hands began to roam further down. Slowly he ran one of them up her leg, his fingers coming to rest on her most intimate parts. When he touched her there, she cried out in surprise. She'd expected pain, but it was the complete opposite. As he started to caress her, pleasure such as she'd never known before began to build inside her. It was breathtaking, and the pressure grew to new heights when he slid first one, then two fingers inside her to rub at a spot that felt magical. The sensations increased until they reached the crest of a wave she was helpless to stop, and she tumbled into an abyss filled with explosions and stars.

'Oh, Ivar!' She moaned and shuddered with ecstasy, and his fingers didn't let up until the ripples of pleasure died down.

For a moment, he held her close, their hearts beating frantically against each other. Then he kissed her temple. 'Did you like that?'

'Y-yes. It was beyond anything I could have imagined.' She buried her face in his warm chest, inhaling the clean scent of his skin. After a while, she became aware of something else – the fact that he was still aroused and they hadn't done anything about it. 'Um, what about you?'

'Don't worry about that. This was about you, not me. I only took my shirt off so that you wouldn't feel at a disadvantage. And so you could do a little exploring of your own.'

'Oh, I see.' Even though he'd given her immense pleasure, as he'd promised, a part of her wished that he'd allowed her to reciprocate. But she had to respect his decision, as he'd kept his word. 'Well, thank you. I . . . don't know what to say.'

Embarrassment flooded her, but he pulled her close and stroked her back with a soothing motion. 'You're very welcome. I hope that's satisfied your curiosity and you will one day contemplate marriage again without fear of your wifely duties. Rest now for a while, then we'll go back to the hall before we're missed.'

It sounded eminently sensible, and yet frustratingly disappointing, but there was nothing she could do other than murmur her assent.

Chapter Sixteen

Ulfstoft, November–January/Frermánuðr–Þorri AD *875–876*

As winter settled over the land in earnest, Ivar and Ellisif kept their relationship platonic. No more kissing, no meeting up in the hayloft, and no snuggling together because of bad dreams. He couldn't bring himself to keep away from her completely, as he enjoyed her company. They were both outsiders here, in a manner of speaking, which created a bond between them. It would have been impossible anyway in such a small settlement, where everyone congregated in the hall each evening. Instead, he settled for being her friend and spent time talking with her, paying attention to her opinions, likes and dislikes. He sensed that no one had taken an interest in her as a person for a very long time, and it was possible she needed that support more than she needed a lover.

It was exceedingly difficult not to touch her, though. Several times he found himself reaching for her, only to remember at the last moment that he shouldn't. He knew that it would only take one spark to ignite him, and he couldn't risk it. His reasons were sound and sensible, and the obstacles to them being together as insurmountable as they'd ever been. There simply was no other way than to grin and bear it. For how long, he wasn't sure. He'd never set himself a time frame for his visit to the past, but he'd have to consider it soon. He couldn't stay indefinitely, and the situation with Ellisif had brought this home to him more forcibly than anything else.

Damn it, man, he told himself. It's lust, pure and simple. Nothing more. But he wasn't sure he could convince himself of that. Still, it didn't matter, because even if it wasn't, that wouldn't change the fact that he couldn't have her.

The Yule festivities came and went, with another *blōt* to mark midwinter and ensure that the settlement was granted peace, a tolerable winter and a good harvest the following summer. As before, Ivar joined in the feasting, but he couldn't help but wonder what his foster-family back in Sweden were doing. He'd spent Christmas with them since he was fourteen. With only Storm there, he guessed the celebrations would be rather muted, if not downright awful. Perhaps Maddie might have come back, but he wasn't optimistic on that score.

Never mind, he reasoned. I'm only here this once, and next year I'll be back with Mia and Haakon. It was an experience to savour and store away in his memory. He wasn't a little kid who needed to be with his mum and dad for Christmas, and at least they knew where he was, as he'd left them that note.

There was no point thinking about home, so instead he threw himself into the festivities at Ulfstoft. He was starting to form real and lasting bonds with this group of people, not just Ellisif. He enjoyed their company, their sense of humour, and the loyalty they showed each other. A place such as this would be hell to live in if harmony was lacking, and he heard several of the inhabitants mentioning how much things had improved since the young jarl had returned to take over. He was glad for Álrik's sake that they had taken him to their hearts and didn't resent being ruled by such a young man.

Some people exchanged small gifts after the celebratory meal, and Ivar went to fetch something from his kist when the present-giving began. He sank down in his usual place next to Ellisif and held out a small package wrapped in red silk cloth.

'Here, I have a Yuletide gift for you, *unnasta*.'

'For me? Thank you.' Her green eyes met his in startled pleasure, glinting a deep moss green in the firelight. He had a feeling she hadn't expected him to give her anything, and it made him pleased that he'd thought ahead. It was easy to guess that no one had spoiled her since her father had passed away. That was one of the things he would like to rectify. She deserved to be pampered, at least a little bit, and he selfishly wanted to be the person to do that while he was here.

She took the parcel and unwrapped it with reverence. Ivar knew she'd probably treasure the silk as much as what was inside, since she could decorate one of her tunics with it. It was a luxury here, and the smallest scraps were put to good use, embellishing woollen and linen clothing.

'What is this for?' Holding up the piece of rock crystal that was revealed, she threw him a puzzled glance. 'Oh, it's a necklace?' There was a leather thong threaded through a small hole on one side.

He smiled. 'No, it is to help you see better.' He took hold of the crystal and showed her how the concave surface magnified whatever was underneath it. 'I can make a frame for you, so that if you wish to sew tiny stitches, you can just place this above the cloth. I found it when I went to buy provisions at that marketplace back when we first arrived here. One of the silversmiths was using it for filigree work, and he let me buy it from him as he had two.'

Impulsively she threw her arms around his neck. 'Oh, Ivar, thank you so much! That is the most thoughtful gift I have ever received. I wasn't aware such a thing existed.'

When she raised her eyes to his, there were tears sparkling on her lashes, and he couldn't resist – he pulled her close to give her a fierce hug. He'd never known a woman who was so easy to please and grateful for so little. And it was Christmas, after all. He could allow himself to indulge his craving to hold her this once.

'It's nothing special,' he murmured, breathing in the unique scent of her before letting her go. 'But I also want to give you this.' From his pocket he took out a gold ring etched with runes. 'I was told that it is magical and will protect the wearer from evil. I'd like you to have it, then I'll know you will always be safe.'

Her eyes opened wide. 'You don't need to give me that as well. The crystal is plenty, and I only have one gift for you.'

'Nevertheless, I want you to have it, so please give me your finger.' He placed the ring on her right hand, even though he wasn't sure whether the ring finger on the left had the same significance in Viking times. Best not to take any chances.

'If you're sure? Then I thank you.' She pulled something out from under the bench they were sitting on. 'Here, this is for you.'

Ivar unfolded a pale blue tunic edged with woven bands. 'Did you make this? For me?'

'Mm-hmm. I can see well enough to do seams, and Askhild helped me with the band-weaving. I . . . I thought it would match your eyes.' A tide of pink washed over her cheeks, as if she was embarrassed to have noted their colour.

'That's wonderful! Thank you so much. I'll wear it with pride.'

He'd never had anyone make a garment for him before, and it was truly special. She had spent many hours fashioning it, and had probably squinted over the seams, no matter what she said. He appreciated the thought that had gone into it, and she was right, it did match his eyes.

There was nothing else for it – he had to allow himself one more hug, to thank her properly, and he made the most of it, storing the feel of her in his memory. After that, he drank enough ale to drown the desire clamouring through his brain, and the little voice that whispered that she was coming to mean way too much to him. From now on, he wouldn't touch her again.

'Who wants to go skating?'

Thorald's voice rang out through the hall one morning, and a chorus of voices echoed back.

'Me!'

'Yes, please!'

'Now? Oh yes!'

Ivar looked up from folding his blankets and smiled. Everyone had been cooped up inside for days due to bad weather and heavy snowfall, but today the sun's rays were finding their way into the hall through the smoke holes high up in the gables, and the partially open front door. Thorald must have known they were all getting cabin fever and had hit on the best possible solution – making them go outside to play for a while.

'Ivar, are you coming?' Thorald called out, his blue eyes daring his kinsman across the room. 'I take it you know how to skate?'

'Of course.' Ivar accepted the challenge with a grin. Naturally he didn't mention that all the skating he'd done had been at various ice rinks in Stockholm with modern hockey skates on his feet. Nor that he'd never tried it using bones strapped to his shoes for this purpose. How hard could it be? 'I'll be with you in a moment.'

He bent to extract a few more items of clothing from his kist. It might be sunny outside, but it was still freezing. He donned just about everything he owned, including several pairs of trousers, extra socks, mittens, and the hat Ellisif had borrowed the first time they met. He was sure it had suited her better, but it would do the job of keeping his head and ears warm. Finally he wrapped a cloak around himself and fastened it securely with his bronze pin. Ellisif had helped him to add a lining of wolf fur only a few days previously, and he was very grateful for that now. It wasn't as soft as mink or squirrel, but it was thick and very cosy. He'd bought the pelts off an itinerant trader. Despite the fact that he'd always been against the wearing of fur, he had to admit there wasn't much choice in a place where thermal underwear and puffa coats didn't exist.

Outside, he found a veritable fairy-tale scene. The snow lay deep on the ground as well as on roofs and tree branches. It glittered like millions of Swarovski crystals in the sunlight and crunched underfoot. Paths had been cleared to the various outhouses, but Ivar saw that someone had also shovelled a rough track towards the small pond that lay at the back of the property. He drew in a deep breath of the exceedingly crisp air and felt it searing his lungs before emerging in a puffy cloud of condensation. It was the kind of day when you were glad to be alive and everything in the world seemed glorious.

Speaking of which . . . He caught sight of Ellisif emerging from the hall with Askhild. *Glorious indeed!* She was swathed in many layers of clothing, the same as him, but there was no mistaking the basic shape of her: soft, womanly and pleasing. Her cheeks instantly turned pink from the chill, as did the tip of her nose. Her long reddish-gold plait gleamed like polished metal in the bright light, and he longed to wrap the silky strands round his hand while kissing her senseless. As he stood spellbound by the sight of her, he couldn't help but contrast her demeanour now to when they had first met. Back then, she'd been a terrified shadow of a woman, despite her defiance and determination, whereas now she had the look of someone who was happy and carefree. Her laughter rang out and he thought it was the most wonderful sound ever.

Oh yes, I've got it bad. And there's not a thing I can do about it. He sighed, pulled himself together and started to turn away.

Before he did, though, he noticed Askhild holding up a hand as her husband opened his mouth to protest at her joining them. 'I'm only going to watch for a short while, I promise. I wouldn't jeopardise our child, you know that.'

Thorald shook his head and gave her a rueful smile. 'No, of course not. Sorry. Overreacting again, aren't I?'

She gave him a tender kiss. 'It's fine.'

Ivar hid a smile with his mitten. It was amusing to see his kinsman act the caveman where his wife was concerned. Anyone would think she was made of glass and the only woman ever to be pregnant. But at the same time, he could understand it. Life was precarious in this era, and anything could happen to Askhild or the baby. You never knew. He sent up a silent prayer to whichever gods were listening to keep them safe. He'd come to love her like a sister and wouldn't want any harm to befall her.

'Right, to the pond then!' Thorald took his wife's mittened hand in his and led the way, a sack slung over his shoulder. 'Álrik, you have the staves?'

'Yes, here.' The youth came up behind them with an armful of long poles, all with some sort of sharp iron spike at one end. Ivar knew they would use these to propel themselves across the ice; that was how you skated Viking-style.

He fell into step beside Ellisif. 'Are you good at this?' he asked.

'No, not really. I used to skate as a child, but I haven't tried it for quite some time.'

Reading between the lines, he gathered she meant since she was married. A stab of anger shot through him at the callous way she'd been treated by her dead husband. No doubt he'd forbidden her from doing anything that might be considered fun, all the while indulging his own whims. Thank the gods he couldn't stop her any longer.

'It's been a while for me too,' he confessed. 'Perhaps we can support each other.'

Her green eyes twinkled in amusement. 'If you wish, but it might be a case of the blind leading the blind.'

'I'll take my chances.'

A couple of sheepskins had been spread out by the side of the pond, and people took turns to sit down and put on their skates. These consisted of two bits of bone, seven or eight inches long and flattish on one side. Ivar knew they had been fashioned from the metatarsal bones of cattle or horses. Some of his colleagues back in the twenty-first century had experimented with reconstructed Viking skates to see if they could replicate them and understand how they were used. Excitement flooded his veins at the thought that he'd finally be able to confirm whether they'd been right.

Thorald's sack proved to contain a large quantity of them, some newly made while others showed a bit of wear and tear. He also produced four long leather thongs for each person. When Ivar was handed his skates, he saw that the bones had holes drilled through them in the sides at the front and back, precisely like the replica ones. One end was shaped into a wedge, and he figured that was the front. And the top surface was rougher than the bottom; he assumed that was to stop the smooth soles of his leather boots from slipping and sliding around on the bone.

He glanced at Ellisif, who had sunk down beside him and was busy threading her leather pieces through the holes. 'Um, I've forgotten how to tie them on,' he said. 'Can you show me, please?'

She threw him a surprised look, but nodded. 'Of course. Watch what I do. Start with the back one, like this.'

Looping the thong over the top of her foot, then behind her

leg and back to the front again, she tied it securely. Ivar followed suit, then observed as she took the front thong and crossed it over her foot before looping it round her ankle. Again it was tied in a double knot, and he did the same, then lifted his foot experimentally. It felt as if it wouldn't budge, which was good.

'Thank you,' he said, standing up and reaching for two of the poles Álrik was handing out. He gave one to Ellisif and leaned on the other while reaching down to help her up. 'Let's try this, then.'

They wobbled on to the ice of the small pond. It seemed thick enough to drive a truck on, so Ivar wasn't worried about falling through. The temperature was well below zero and the sunlight much too weak to melt anything. In fact, he needed to start moving or he'd turn into an icicle himself.

Thorald was already propelling himself along at some speed by pushing the sharp pole against the ice between his legs. He was also making a gliding motion with his feet, the way Nordic skiers did, which helped him go faster. Ivar tried to imitate him, while leaning forward slightly. One of the first rules of skating was never to lean backwards, or you were sure to end up on your backside with a painful jolt. Looking around, he noticed that some of the smaller children were using two poles, which was probably sensible. They managed to stay upright, and it made him smile.

He checked to find Ellisif next to him. 'Am I doing this right?'

'Yes.' She huffed out a breath. 'You're much stronger than me, so you'll be halfway across the pond in no time.'

'I'd rather stay with you.' He shouldn't, but it was the truth. Even if it was exhilarating to go skating the Viking way, he didn't want to leave her side. He never did.

Watching her struggling with her technique, biting her bottom lip in concentration, did something to his insides, and his heart flipped over. She was so adorable, her cheeks turning pinker by the minute and strands of her plait coming undone to wave around her face. He wished they were on normal skates so he could take her hand and pull her around. As a teenager, he'd been able to skate backwards with confidence, and he had no doubt he could have more or less ice-danced with her.

But holding her in his arms was a bad idea. That way lay danger.

He shook his head. *Concentrate. Just enjoy the moment and being with her*. It was all he would have.

Some of the youngsters were becoming boisterous, trying to outdo each other, and Thorald called out a warning. It was too late, though, as a bunch of them came barrelling into Ivar and Ellisif like little bowling balls and the whole group went down in a tangle of arms and legs. Ivar heard his kinsman bellow out a reprimand, but he himself started laughing. Looking at Ellisif, with her hat askew and her eyes shining, he could see that she wasn't angry either. She giggled and tried to find purchase on the ice to stand up. It didn't work, because one of the kids was grabbing at her skirts to steady himself, and she ended up falling on top of Ivar.

'Oof!' He lay there for a moment, winded but with an armful of lovely woman.

'I'm so sorry!' She blinked down at him, consternation in her green gaze as she scrambled to roll off him.

He wasn't having that. Keeping her there for a while longer was too tempting, and he couldn't pass up this opportunity. His arms closed round her and held on tight. 'Not so fast,' he whispered. 'I need to catch my breath and you're warming me up nicely.'

Her eyes opened wide at this blatant flirting, and he cursed himself for a fool. He shouldn't have said that.

'Ivar!' she protested, but then she smiled and he forgot about everyone around them. There was only her, the weight of her body on top of his and the sensation that all was right with the world.

Of course, the moment couldn't last for ever, much as he'd like it to.

'Ivar? Ellisif? Are you well?' Thorald's voice cut into their idyll, and Ivar swallowed a sigh. It was as well they'd been interrupted or he might have said or done something he'd regret later.

Slowly he sat up, helping Ellisif to right herself. 'We're fine. A tad winded, but no harm done.'

Thorald was scowling. 'I told them to be careful, the little varmints.'

Ivar shrugged. 'They were merely enjoying themselves. It wasn't intentional. Here, pull me up.' He held out a hand and was promptly helped to his feet. 'Thank you.' He turned to assist Ellisif, and the two of them brushed the snow off their clothing. 'Let's practise some more. I need to move, or my limbs will freeze.'

'Good point.' Thorald regarded them both for a moment, and Ivar wondered if his face was as red as hers, but he didn't think so. He wasn't embarrassed to be caught hugging her on the ice, merely frustrated with himself for his inability to keep his hands off her. It had only been a playful interlude, though, nothing serious. They were all having fun.

'How about a race to the other side of the pond?' he suggested, knowing full well that Thorald could never resist a dare. He saw the other man's eyes gleam.

'Absolutely. On the count of three . . . *ein*, *tveir*, *þrir*!'

Sometime later, they all returned to the hall, where Askhild handed out mugs of hot wine. The atmosphere was joyous, with chatter and laughter ringing out, and Ivar sank down on to a bench, relaxed and content.

Despite his frustration about the situation with Ellisif, he realised it had been a long time since he'd been this happy. He wasn't sure that was a good thing, because sooner or later he'd be leaving, which was going to be difficult enough as it was. *But do I really have to leave?* The insidious thought slithered into his brain without warning, giving voice to the doubts that had begun to assail him these last few weeks. Was there actually anything to stop him from remaining here indefinitely if he wanted to? He felt torn, as if he no longer belonged in either time period. The lines were becoming blurred, and it was confusing the hell out of him. Who was he really, and who did he want to be? Twenty-first-century museum curator or Viking kin to Thorald? His two personas were battling it out inside him.

He shook his head; he'd have to mull this over some more. For now, though, he'd live in the moment and enjoy it.

Chapter Seventeen

Ulfstoft, January–March/Þorri–Einmánuðr AD *876*

'Can I help you with that?'

Ellisif looked up to find Ivar standing in front of the bench she was sitting on. She had a tangled skein of wool in her lap and had been frowning at it.

'Er, sure. If you wouldn't mind holding it out for me?'

He sank down next to her and held out his hands horizontally, as if they were pegs on a wall. That made her smile, and she threaded the skein around his fingers as best she could.

'Did someone drop this?' he enquired mildly, his mouth quirking up on one side in amusement.

'One of the toddlers was playing with it when his mother wasn't paying attention. I have no idea how he managed to make such a mess.' She sighed and found the end of the yarn, tugging at it so that she could start winding it round her left hand. 'I need to make it into a neat ball and get rid of any knots. If you could hold it like that, I'd be very grateful, thank you.'

'Happy to.'

As always when he was near, her heart beat a little faster. They spoke most days and often sat next to each other at meals, and had developed an easy camaraderie. And yet there was always an undercurrent of something else between them, and she wanted more. Like that magical moment on the ice, when she'd longed to lie there and stare down into his azure eyes for the rest of the day. It wasn't logical and she was well aware of the fact that nothing could happen between them; he'd made that clear and she agreed. In principle. Then why was it so difficult to make her body accept this?

She'd relived that encounter in the hayloft hundreds of times in her mind. His soft kisses. The delicate caresses of his hands on her skin, his mouth on her breasts and those clever fingers giving her such incredible pleasure. There was no denying she wanted to do that again, but he'd said it was only going to happen once, and he'd refused to go further. She guessed it had taken a lot of willpower on his part, and she doubted any other man would have stopped. It was something she honoured him for, but at the same time it frustrated her no end.

I want him. All of him. But she couldn't have him.

'What are you thinking?' His question made her jump, and she couldn't stop her cheeks from heating up.

'Er, nothing. I mean . . . I'm concentrating on getting this unravelled.' She dared a glance at him and momentarily drowned in his intense gaze before bending over her work once more.

'Are you happy?' he asked. 'For now, that is. I know you want to return to your own home eventually.'

'Yes, I'm very content here. Ulfstoft is a lovely place and everyone has been kind.' She hesitated, then added, 'I think this is the first time in years I haven't been afraid or anxious all the time. It's . . . liberating.'

'I can imagine. And I'm glad. No one should have to live in constant fear.'

They sat in silence for a while, all the questions she wanted to ask him running through her mind. But she didn't dare utter them. Or did she? What did she have to lose? He was leaving anyway, perhaps as soon as he'd helped her regain Birgirsby. And then she'd never see him again. A sharp pang of pain shot through her, but she drew in a deep breath to counteract it.

In the end, she blurted out the question that was uppermost in her mind. 'Ivar, why do you not wish to marry anyone? I mean, I know my own reasons for not wanting to, but you never told me yours.' She cringed inwardly, as it was hypocritical of her to ask this when she herself didn't want to wed anyone either.

When she peeked up at him, she caught his startled expression, those blue eyes like a summer sky. 'What? Oh, well, I do, eventually, but right now, I can't. I . . . I have plans to travel and no permanent abode.'

'And there is no way you could establish a home and travel afterwards? Many men go abroad each summer and leave their wives to manage everything. It is not uncommon.' She didn't know why she was pushing him when it was fairly obvious she was making him uncomfortable. His eyelashes lowered and his mouth thinned, as if he didn't want to talk about this.

'No,' he said. 'I don't think so.' His eyes had darkened to the colour of storm clouds now. 'If there was a way of having everything I want, I wouldn't hesitate, believe me. But I'm not sure there is.'

Everything he wanted? And what was that? But she had no right to pry, and she couldn't force him to open up to her. Instead, she shrugged and pretended an indifference she didn't feel. 'I understand. I was merely curious. Now, where was I . . .'

As she continued unravelling the yarn, a silence fell between them again, and this time it was strained. He left the moment she'd finished, and as she watched him make his way to the doors, her heart clenched painfully.

She couldn't bear the thought of never seeing him again, but soon he'd be gone.

For the rest of the winter, deep snow blanketed the land and they were stuck inside most of the day. Ivar used the time to learn all he could about Viking handicrafts, and sat next to Thorald every chance he got.

'You seem to be able to turn your hand to anything,' he commented to his kinsman, who shot him a puzzled glance and shrugged.

'Doesn't everyone?'

'Not really. There are things I'm still learning, but I've yet to see you baulk at any task.'

Thorald chuckled. 'Yes, I saw that comb you attempted to carve. Tell me, how did you fare when trying to use it?'

'*Þegi þu*,' Ivar growled, and shoved the other man's shoulder in mock outrage. 'I threw it on the fire and bought one off Holmstein.'

That made Thorald laugh out loud. 'I've also noticed you helping the ladies with their wool. Is that something the men do where you come from? Or are you merely trying to stay close to one of them in particular?' The teasing smile that accompanied this statement made Ivar want to push him again. 'You do know it's women's work, right?'

'Of course, but I was curious as to how it was done.'

Thorald stopped whittling the piece of wood he'd been working on and regarded Ivar with another questioning glance. 'Why? Are you planning on doing some weaving?'

'No, but I wished to know how to in principle. Besides, Ellisif needed someone to hold the skein for her while she wound the yarn into a ball. I was being helpful.'

This was greeted with a snort of laughter. 'Of course you

were. Just like when you took your turn at weaving, right? I saw Askhild having to unpick it all afterwards.'

Ivar was fully aware that taking an interest in female pursuits put him at risk of seeming effeminate. That was something no Viking male wanted. One of the worst insults was being called *argr*, which implied sexual deviance and femininity in a man. Naturally he wanted Thorald to think well of him, and not be laughing behind his back even if his assumptions were wrong. The only way he'd be able to explain what he was doing was to confess his real identity. But dare he do that? Thorald likely wouldn't believe him, and then he'd be worse off. Perhaps told to leave.

He'd been tempted to tell Ellisif as well the other day, but what good would it do? Even assuming he could convince her he was telling the truth, it wouldn't change anything between them. He would still be leaving at some point to go back to the future, and she had obligations here.

Thorald was a different matter, though, and he came to a decision. 'Could we go for a walk, please? There is a matter I must discuss with you in private.'

'Oh, aye? Does it have aught to do with a certain red-headed woman?' Thorald smirked. 'Don't think I haven't seen you sneaking out of the byre of a morning.'

So much for being discreet. Ivar had taken to sleeping out there by himself sometimes, when the urge to crawl over to Ellisif's bench and hold her became too much. Some nights just hearing her move around made him hot and bothered, and he found it impossible to go to sleep. The only cure was to remove himself completely. He clenched his fists now and shook his head. 'No, this is something else entirely. And I'll have you know I slept alone in the hayloft. There was no one with me at any time.'

'Hmm.' Thorald looked far from convinced. 'Very well, let's go.'

They wrapped warm cloaks around their shoulders and

stepped outside. It was freezing, but the sun shone and there was only a slight breeze. Ivar turned his face towards the sun, breathing the fresh tang of frost into lungs that had been filled with smoke and stale air until a moment ago. Again he was grateful for the fur lining. He'd be frozen to the marrow without it.

'Let's go and check on the sheep,' his kinsman suggested, and they set off across the *tún* towards a nearby enclosure where the sheep were penned in awaiting the arrival of their lambs. When they were out of earshot, Thorald stopped. 'So what did you wish to speak to me about if it isn't Ellisif?'

Ivar picked up a handful of snow and shaped it into a ball, which he threw at the nearest wall. It made a satisfying *thunk*, releasing some of his nervous energy. 'I don't know where to begin, but I haven't been entirely truthful with you.'

'Mm, I suspected as much. Out with it then. Who are you really?'

'What? Oh no, it's not like that. We are most definitely related, but not in the manner I described. Let me ask you this – do you believe in *trolldomr*?'

Thorald's eyebrows rose almost to his hairline. 'Possibly. Are you trying to tell me you're a magical creature? A shapeshifter, like Loki, so that you can make yourself resemble me?'

That made Ivar laugh. 'Not at all! But I did arrive at Haukr's settlement by magic. I doubt you'll take my word for it, but actually I travelled through time.'

His kinsman stared at him with a deep scowl and a gaze so hard it could have penetrated granite. 'From whence?' he finally asked.

'A thousand years into the future.'

Leaning against the nearest wall and crossing his arms over his chest, Thorald glared at him. 'Is this a jest?'

'No, you have my oath it's the truth. Haukr knows about it, because there are others like me and he had come across them before. That was why he was so willing to accept my claim that

I'm related to you. And I am – I'm your great-great-grandson many times removed.'

'That doesn't seem possible.'

'I know, and yet here I am. There are tales I could tell you about the future that you probably wouldn't credit.'

'Hmm.' Thorald was still scowling. 'I'm not saying I believe this, but if I did, why are you here? What could you possibly gain from going backwards?'

'Knowledge. Many things have been forgotten about your time. I would like to learn everything about your way of life here, including what the women are doing. That's why I was observing them and helping them. And I had no real family left in my time, only a foster-family. Linnea, Hrafn's wife, is my foster-sister and comes from the future as well. I trust you will keep that information to yourself.'

'Aye, of course. If indeed it's true.'

Ivar smiled, relieved that his relative was taking this fairly calmly. He couldn't blame him for being sceptical. 'I know it's a lot to take in, and I don't expect you to trust me immediately, but I am telling the truth. Haukr would bear witness to that. He has seen time travellers disappear before his very eyes.'

'Am I to take it you're not staying permanently then?'

'No, I hadn't planned on it. That's why I cannot marry Ellisif. I've told her not to expect me to, and she's accepted that.' He closed his eyes for a moment, wishing things could be different.

'But what if—'

He interrupted, knowing what was coming. 'There won't be a child. We've not been together in that way, I swear. I wouldn't do that, even if she is barren as she claims. She says she never wishes to marry again, but in case she changes her mind, I wouldn't want to ruin her chances. Holding back is one of the hardest things I've ever done, but I am, I assure you.'

'I see.'

Thorald still had his arms crossed over his chest and his eyebrows lowered, but his gaze was more contemplative than angry or disbelieving. 'I suppose it explains a few things. Your strange compulsion to scratch runes on things, your insistence on cleansing wounds with odd substances, and the fact that you are good at some things yet have never tried your hand at others.'

'Exactly. Where I come from, we write everything down, hence my scratching, as you call it. I tried to learn as much as I could before coming here, but there are certain skills – like how to make a comb – that I've never attempted. That's simply not necessary in the twenty-first century.'

'Twenty-first. And this is what, then . . . the ninth or tenth, according to you?'

'Ninth, yes. We start the counting roughly from the birth of the man you call the White Christ.'

Thorald shook his head. 'This is difficult to accept. You will give me some time to ponder the matter.' It wasn't a request, and Ivar nodded acquiescence. After a moment, Thorald added, 'Have you visited other eras as well? Met ancestors besides myself?'

'No, only you. I have a device with which I time-travel, but it doesn't give me a choice as to where I go. Everyone I know who has done this seems to end up in the same period – yours. We have no idea why.'

'Hmm. I don't suppose where you come from you have more knowledge of healing and a way to stop the youngsters from being sick? A lot of them have been vomiting and shitting overmuch lately, and can't seem to keep anything down. They're wasting away and it's painful to watch.'

'Have they? I hadn't heard about that.' He'd been too wrapped up in his own concerns to pay attention to everyone around him. That would have to change.

'No, it's only been during the last few days. Askhild spoke to me this morning, as she was getting worried.'

'Unless there's some illness going around – and I don't think there is if it's only affecting the children – I would say you should check what they are eating and drinking. Make sure they drink nothing that hasn't been boiled first, and that the food isn't rancid in any way. If that doesn't work, I'll take a look at them. Oh, and perhaps you should dig a new well? Preferably as far from the midden as possible.'

He wasn't a doctor, but he knew about common symptoms of childhood illnesses and might be able to help. It sounded more like they were suffering from dysentery or something to do with germs they'd ingested, though. And he knew from archaeological digs that Viking wells had sometimes been situated much too close to where they threw their rubbish, resulting in bacteria festering.

'Very well, I'll do that. Thank you, and I'll see you later.' With a nod, Thorald walked off, and Ivar knew he had to let him mull over what he'd learned. At least the man hadn't outright laughed at him or told him to get lost. He'd even asked for his advice, as if he was coming round to the idea that time travel could exist.

It was progress.

And a few days later, when the sick children were all doing well again, Thorald nodded at Ivar as if to say, 'I believe you now.' He was content with that.

'Would you like me to comb your hair for you? It's easier for someone else to see the nits.'

'What?' Ivar jumped and sent Ellisif a startled gaze as she sank down on to the bench beside him. He'd been attempting to carve a crude toy duck out of a piece of juniper wood and had been lost in his own thoughts. And she'd been keeping her distance lately, as had he, so he was surprised to see her. This was the first time she'd spoken to him in days. '*Nits?*' He recoiled as her words registered, and blinked at her, horror creeping through his veins.

She smiled. 'Yes, you've been scratching more than usual this morning, so I thought it might be time to deal with them. No one else seems to have offered to help you.'

'Odin's ravens! Nits?'

He didn't know why he was surprised. There were bedbugs and he'd been bitten like everyone else, but for some reason he hadn't thought about head lice. It wasn't something he'd ever come across before. When some of his colleagues with children had told him tales about their tribulations when an infestation had spread through the local schools, he hadn't paid attention. He'd simply never considered the fact that he might have to confront the same thing himself.

He should have done. It made his skin crawl with revulsion.

Oh, get a grip, man! It was ridiculous to be so disgusted by tiny insects when there were far worse things to deal with in the Viking age. He'd killed a man, for Christ's sake.

Ellisif tilted her head to one side. 'Have you never had them before? If so, you're incredibly lucky.'

'*Ungh.*' An incoherent noise was all he could manage, then he tried to pull himself together. 'Please, if you wouldn't mind helping me, I'd be grateful.' An involuntary shiver juddered through him. *Nits! Yuck!* He resisted the urge to claw at his scalp. 'Can you see them?'

He bowed his head, and she leaned forward to peer at his scalp, gently running her fingers through his hair. 'Hm, no, but they could be hiding, and you know my eyesight isn't very good. Probably best to go through it with a comb just in case.'

'Good idea.' He'd prefer to be absolutely sure. 'Should I wash my hair first?'

What he'd really like to do was douse his head in something caustic to kill the little blighters stone dead, but at the same time he didn't want to end up bald. Oh, for a twenty-first-century chemist when you needed one!

Ellisif smiled and nodded. 'Yes, let's go to the bath house. It might be easier to comb when it's wet, although mine is the opposite. It gets more tangled.'

Bath house? He wasn't sure that going there with her was a good idea, but if they were only washing his hair, perhaps it would be fine. And he wanted rid of these tiny critters as soon as possible. He stood up abruptly. 'Right. Let's go.'

Like everyone else in the settlement, Ivar bathed properly once a week, and the rest of the time he washed his hands and face every morning. Hands were also washed before meals. He'd become used to the strong lye soap that was a multi-purpose cleaning product. It was rumoured that some Norsemen left the soap in their hair and beards for a long time in order to bleach them to a blonder colour, but he hadn't seen anyone here do that. Perhaps the inhabitants of Ulfstoft weren't that vain. Still, the idea of leaving the soap in for a while to kill any nits was appealing.

In the bath house, he and Ellisif set about heating water on the hearth. As soon as they had a small tub full of warm water, he shucked off his tunic and shirt. She made a strangled sound and he turned to stare at her.

'What?'

'Ivar! You can keep your shirt on, surely? You only need to rinse your hair.' Her cheeks had turned rosy and she was attempting to look anywhere but directly at him.

'No! It will get wet, and it's too cold outside to walk around with damp garments.' A devilish imp inside him had him adding, 'Why? Can you not stand the sight of me shirtless?'

That made her scowl at him. 'You know very well you're a . . . a fine specimen of a man.'

He chuckled. 'A fine specimen, eh? Well, thank you for the compliment. Now, please, pass me the soap.'

Dunking his head in the water, he added soap and rinsed. For good measure, he repeated the process several times and felt marginally better. He knew he was making a song and dance about this, but the thought of having nits was freaking him out. *Gah, what a wuss!* He hoped Thorald never found out about his reaction to something so trivial.

'Are you done?' Ellisif was standing to one side with her arms crossed, regarding him through narrowed eyes, as if she suspected him of prolonging the moment on purpose. Truly, he wasn't, but now they were here, he wasn't averse to torturing her a little bit. After all, he spent most of his time trying to rein in fantasies about her. It seemed fair for her to suffer occasionally too.

'Yes, I think so.'

'Then please, put your shirt on or I'm not combing your hair.' There was a determined set to her mouth, and he thought it best to do as she asked, after drying his hair and torso with a sheet of linen she handed him.

There was a bench on one side, close to the hearth, and he sat down there, facing away from her. 'Can you reach?'

'Yes. And I have a nit comb.' She showed him a small comb with the tines very close together. 'This should catch most of them, but if we do this again in a day or two, you'll be rid of them all until next time.'

Another shudder rippled through him. 'I hope so,' he muttered.

Ellisif laughed. 'I've never known anyone make such a fuss about nits before. They don't hurt you.'

'I know. It's just . . . disgusting.' He couldn't explain it any other way. 'Never mind.'

She began to comb his hair, using a normal comb first to untangle the tresses. It had grown quite a few inches since he'd arrived in the ninth century and was hanging down his back now. Usually he tied it into a low ponytail or twisted it into a messy bun to keep it out of the way. Soon she changed to the smaller comb, taking care to cover every inch of his scalp. It felt wonderful, soothing and relaxing. He closed his eyes and enjoyed her touch.

Was this what it would be like to have a Viking wife? She was acting like one, the moment intimate and companionable, and he was loving every second. It was so tempting to imagine a life here with her, sharing interludes like this. If he stayed in this century for ever, he was fairly sure he could persuade her to marry him, despite her reservations. She must know by now that he'd never be a domineering husband.

But what about his life back home? Could he really contemplate never returning to the twenty-first century? To his foster-family? He'd told them in his note that he was only intending to stay away for a short while, a year at most. Once he'd achieved his goals – which he had now that Thorald had accepted him fully as kin and they were getting to know one another – it would make sense to leave. And as an archaeologist, how could he refrain from going back to share all the knowledge he'd accumulated since he arrived here? Obviously he would have to present his findings in such a way that no one ever found out that he had time-travelled, but he was full to bursting with the details he'd observed, and he would find a way.

Another thorny subject was his status here. If he stayed and persuaded Ellisif to marry him, he'd be beholden to her for everything. A part of him would always be a twenty-first-century man, and it would go against the grain to be dependent on her. Everything she owned would become his if they were wed, which meant he'd basically be living off his wife. That felt wrong on so many levels, as he wanted to be the one to provide for her, or at the very least an equal partner. Birgirsby was hers and should remain so.

There were so many difficulties to overcome, and yet this woman would be worth it.

Perhaps there was a compromise to be had. An idea had been forming in his mind for a while now, potential solutions tentatively slotting into place. It could be that he'd been looking at this the wrong way. Not everything had to be black and white. He decided to test the waters.

'Have you ever wanted to travel, Ellisif?'

Her hands stilled before resuming their ministrations. 'Yes. I would like to see foreign lands, visit faraway markets, bring home exotic goods . . .' Her voice took on a dreamy timbre, as if she was seeing it all in her mind's eye. 'But that's not for most women, and I have responsibilities at home. Or I will have, hopefully.'

He let the matter drop, but there were possibilities swirling round his brain and he needed to think about it some more. Perhaps all was not lost, but first they needed to see about getting her holdings back for her.

'I was wrong,' she announced, jolting him out of his thoughts.

'What?'

'You don't have any nits. I can't find a single one.' She dried the comb off on the linen towel and put it away in her leather pouch.

'Oh, thank Odin for that!' Relief coursed through him at hearing that there were no tiny bugs making their home in his hair. It was ridiculous to be so pleased, but he couldn't help it.

Ellisif merely shook her head at him and smiled. 'You are a strange man.'

Yes, and you have no idea how *strange!* But he refrained from saying that out loud.

Chapter Eighteen

Ulfstoft, April–May/Gaukmánuðr–Eggtíð AD *876*

As soon as spring arrived and the snow thawed, Ivar and Thorald made plans to go and scout out the situation at Ellisif's domains, and she insisted on coming along.

'It's my property and I have a right to see what is happening there,' she told them.

'But it could be dangerous.' Ivar blew out a frustrated breath. 'Holmstein knows where it is and can lead us, which means there is no need for you to go. We merely need to find out what we are up against and whether that *niðingr* is still there.'

'Then if you're not going too close, there is no danger.' When he opened his mouth to argue further, she held up her hand. 'No, the matter is closed. I am ready to leave at any time.'

Shaking his head, Ivar gave up, and Thorald wisely didn't enter the discussion.

They took Holmstein and Ellisif's two retainers, Oddr and Gaukr, plus a couple more men. There was a stiff breeze, so after rowing for a short while, they were able to make use of the sail and head for the opening of the fjord. Thorald again muttered under his breath when he had to pay for passage in the

Karmtsund strait, but there was no choice but to go through it in order to reach the fjord further south where Birgirsby was situated.

'We won't take the ship all the way, but approach on foot after making a detour through the forest,' he decided. 'Like we did when we took back Ulfstoft.'

Ellisif was happy with that, and followed the men as they made their way among the trees. It was a long walk, and her legs were shaking with fatigue by the time they finally neared her property. They could smell woodsmoke and hear voices, as well as the sounds of cattle and sheep. She swallowed down conflicting emotions – happiness at finally seeing her home again, but frustration and anger that she couldn't do so openly. Thorald held up a hand to signal stealth, and they all crept forward in single file. Ivar stayed at the back and gripped her hand whenever no one was looking their way. She was grateful for his silent support as her stomach muscles contracted with fear.

As if he'd read her mind, he bent to whisper, 'Don't worry. We're here to protect you.'

When they reached a ridge that overlooked the hall and yard, they all lay down on the ground and peered over the top. Seeing her settlement again after such a long time made a wave of emotion sweep through her. Birgirsby was situated at the innermost point of the fjord, an offshoot of a larger one. There were steep mountains on three sides surrounding a fertile valley, and a bay with a river running into it from behind. The mountains formed an open V on the fourth side that framed a breathtaking view of distant hills, bright blue sky and puffs of white cloud. The still waters of the bay reflected everything, doubling the impact of nature's beauty. The buildings were spread out around the main hall, which had been rebuilt by her father. She longed to go inside, but this wasn't the time.

'Let us observe,' Thorald whispered. 'Count the men and make note of anyone you recognise.'

Ellisif's spirits sank when Kári himself came into view, striding out of the hall with his perpetual scowl. Even at a distance, there was no mistaking him.

'That's him, Kári, in the yellow tunic,' she whispered.

He bellowed something at a couple of men lounging in the spring sunshine, and they sprang to attention, rushing off to do his bidding. She spotted several of his sons too, but not Kell. Just as she'd started to wonder where he could be, he came walking through the trees not far from where they were hiding. Ivar swore under his breath.

'What?' Thorald fixed his kinsman with a piercing gaze. 'You know that man?'

'Yes, that's Kell, the one who helped Hedda. Should we have a talk with him?'

'No, I don't think—' Ellisif started to say, but the others took no notice. Gaukr had already hissed an emphatic yes.

As Kell headed deeper into the forest, they all got up to follow him. Once they were far enough from the settlement not to be overheard, they rushed out from behind the trees and surrounded him. He froze, his gaze flitting from one man to another, his right hand coming to rest on the hilt of his knife. Then his eyes settled on Ellisif. Seeing her instantly relaxed him, and he held up his hands while looking her straight in the face as he addressed her.

'Mistress Ellisif. You shouldn't have come here. It is too dangerous.'

'I know, but we needed some answers.' She motioned for the others to stop their belligerent posturing. It was clear that Kell wasn't a threat to her. She could see nothing in his demeanour that indicated he meant her harm.

'I understand.' He turned towards Ivar. 'Did Hedda and the others find you?'

'Yes, they are safe.' Ivar motioned for Oddr and Gaukr to step forward. The two of them nodded at Kell. 'Here are her two escorts. You may remember them.'

'Ah, yes, good.' He swept his gaze around the circle. 'If you wish to take back this place, you'll need more men. My father is prepared.'

Ivar crossed his arms over his chest and stared at Kell. 'Why are you on Ellisif's side? Why should we trust you?'

The young man shrugged. 'I hate him,' he said simply. 'Everything he does sickens me. I had to watch what he did to my mother before she mercifully passed away, and I wouldn't wish any woman to fall into his clutches. I want to make my own way in the world, as far from him as possible, but for now, I'm stuck.'

Thorald and Ivar exchanged a glance, then both nodded. 'Very well. We'll return after the spring sowing with more men. Be ready to escape if things go badly and you've shown your true colours. You'll be welcome to come with us if you wish. Don't so much as think of betraying us, though, or we'll hunt you down.'

'I won't. Thank you.' Kell smiled, and Ellisif could see why Hedda was so smitten with him. He was a nice-looking young man with an innate kindness that shone through. Even a father such as Kári hadn't been able to beat that out of him.

'We'll see you anon. Let us go.' Thorald turned on his heel and headed off the way they'd come, and Ellisif followed.

Ivar hung back and whispered something to Kell, but soon he was back walking next to her.

'What did you say to him?' She was curious, as she'd had the impression he wasn't convinced about trusting the young man.

'I gave him a piece of advice. Something that might help him in case we never see him again.'

He refused to say more than that, and she let it go. She'd find out in due course.

Ivar had decided Kell was genuine, and he sympathised with him. The young man was in an impossible situation. It reminded him of his own experiences with an evil and domineering father. His had had a tendency towards neo-Nazism and some strange ideas about white supremacy, which Ivar hadn't understood as a youth. It was only later that he'd been told exactly what his father had stood for, and it sickened him, as Kell's father's actions clearly disgusted his son. Ivar could definitely empathise with that, and something had occurred to him before they left.

He'd whispered to Kell, 'I have it on good authority that King Haraldr will win the upcoming battles. If you wish to get out from under your father's thumb, you should join that king rather than the one who tried to force Ellisif into marriage. When you're on the winning side, you'll be rewarded, I'm sure.'

Kell had sent him a startled look. 'You are sure?'

'Yes, absolutely. I thought you should know, in case we don't succeed in taking back these domains and you are still stuck come autumn.'

'Thank you. I'll plot accordingly.'

Ivar was glad he'd given the man a way out. He'd been listening to rumours about the coming clash between King Haraldr and King Hjorr. It seemed that Haraldr and his allies would face a coalition of petty kings, jarls and chieftains from the eastern part of the country, including Hjorr and men from Denmark. Traditionally, the Danish royals had been in control of the Viken area for a long time, but apparently there had recently been lots of internal strife in their ranks, and therefore their influence was not as great as it had once been. Still, they couldn't ignore the threat that Haraldr posed, and would have to act.

Either way, if he was correct in thinking King Haraldr was the one who was usually referred to as 'Fairhair' in the twenty-first century, the man would win, and Kell would do well to change sides.

'It's so frustrating to have to wait even longer,' Ellisif grumbled at his side as they trekked back towards their ship. 'Every moment I'm away from Birgirsby, my people are suffering under Kári's yoke.'

He took her hand and gave it a squeeze. 'I know, but Thorald can't afford to take men away from the spring ploughing and sowing, else everyone at Ulfstoft will starve this year. You'll have to be patient. He's given you his word he will help, then all will be well.'

She sighed, but there was nothing either of them could do other than wait.

As the time of year known as Eggtíð began, Askhild's baby was due. One night Ellisif was woken by an old woman, who shook her roughly.

'Mistress Askhild needs you. She's asking for you. Come quickly, please.'

Rubbing the sleep from her eyes, Ellisif stumbled into the chamber Askhild shared with her husband and took in the scene. Thorald sat next to his wife holding her hand as she lay on the bed, her face pale and screwed up in pain. An older woman, who was acting as midwife, directed thrall women who were bringing in hot water and linen towels, as well as trays of food and drink.

She pointed at her master, frowning. 'You shouldn't be here. This is women's work.'

'She's my wife. I'll stay if I please,' he snarled, his anxious gaze fixed on Askhild.

'Really, *ást mín*, I'm not sure I want you to watch this. I'm not exactly at my best,' she protested weakly.

He leaned over to kiss her with fierce possessiveness. 'I'm not leaving your side until this is finished. I need to see for myself that you are well and to make sure all is done as it should be.'

The midwife harrumphed, but nothing she could say would make him budge, so in the end she ignored him and concentrated on the woman giving birth.

'Ellisif, I'm glad you're here. Come, distract me, please.' Askhild held out her other hand and beckoned her forward.

'You seem to be well taken care of already.' Ellisif smiled at her and perched on the edge of the bed. 'I'm not sure you need me.'

'Oh, but I do. There's no one else I'd rather have by my side, other than Thorald, of course. The two of you will give me strength, won't you?'

'You can count on it.' What she could do if things went wrong, Ellisif had no idea. Still, she'd do her best to be supportive.

Hours passed, and the hand Askhild gripped became numb as her hold tightened every time a contraction hit. Thorald kept calm, but Ellisif could see the worry in his eyes. He continued to soothe his wife and murmur endearments and encouragement. The only time he raised his voice was when giving orders to the midwife.

'You are to scrub your hands with lye before touching Askhild, do you hear?' he barked. 'And make sure anything you use has been boiled.'

'What does that mean?' Askhild wheezed out the question, her face bathed in perspiration from her exertions.

'It's what Ivar told me. He has experience of these things and I trust him.'

That made both women stare at him. 'Ivar?'

'Yes. Don't ask me to explain; just take my word for it. His instructions may save your life.'

Ellisif was puzzled, but also pleased that the two men were getting on so well. If Thorald trusted his kinsman in a matter of life and death that concerned his beloved wife, Ivar had made progress indeed. She was happy for him. It was what he wanted.

She swallowed hard, trying not to think about what else he had said. He'd told her he wasn't staying, and she assumed that meant he might leave soon now that winter was over. How would she bear it? Although she was still loath to marry anyone, she was beginning to wonder if she'd make an exception for him. Not that he wanted her, but still . . . Either way, she simply wasn't ready to say goodbye yet.

'Push! You are very nearly there.' The midwife was encouraging Askhild, and Ellisif clutched her friend's hand for dear life. 'That's it. Once more. Harder!'

With a scream of pure agony, Askhild finally managed to expel a small, slippery shape, and the midwife – with newly scrubbed hands as per Thorald's instructions – caught it. She looked up with a smile. 'You have a fine son. Let me just clean him up and you can hold him.'

'A son! We have a son?' Thorald and Askhild exchanged misty-eyed glances, and Ellisif let go of the hand that was now limp with fatigue.

'Congratulations,' she said. 'What will you name him?'

Askhild turned to her husband. 'It is for you to choose,' she said softly, her voice hoarse from screaming.

'Thorulf,' he murmured, and watched as the midwife brought the little one to them, all wrapped up in linen. 'I've always liked that name and it's close to my own. Welcome to the world, my son.'

Ellisif blinked away tears of joy and pushed down the tendrils of jealousy that threatened to come to the fore. Whether or not she would ever experience this happiness for herself, she knew she'd love Askhild's little boy.

She left them to it and returned to her sleeping bench. Though she wasn't the one who'd given birth, she was exhausted. She found Ivar pacing the hall. He rushed over to her as soon as he caught sight of her.

'How is she? Is all well? I heard screaming.' He sounded almost as worried as if he was the father himself.

She smiled at him and put a hand on his arm. 'Everything is fine. They have a son. I'm sure they'll show you soon. For now, I need some rest.'

'That's wonderful news! You look like you've been through battle.' He smiled back. 'Lie down. I'll wait here for Thorald.'

With a yawn, she curled up under her blankets and within moments she was asleep.

Chapter Nineteen

Ulfstoft, May/Eggtíð AD *876*

A week later, a large ship glided into place next to the jetty and everyone paused what they were doing to see who the newcomers were. Shading his eyes with one hand, Ivar dropped the axe he'd been wielding to split logs and sprinted down to the shore. He recognised the man who was the first to jump out.

'Hrafn, what are you doing here?' He came to a halt in front of his sister Linnea's husband, whom he'd met several times before. This was the last place he'd expected to find him, though, especially as he hadn't gone to see the couple when he'd first arrived in this century.

'Ivar! So you *are* here. I thought Haukr was jesting. It is good to see you.' Hrafn beamed at him, then changed his expression to a mock scowl. 'Though I'm not sure your sister will forgive you for not coming to see us first.'

'I know, I know. I'm sorry. I had things to accomplish before I could visit, but I fully intend to, I promise.'

'Hmph, well, I'll leave you to her wrath.' His eyes twinkled.

Thorald had by now joined them, and smiled a greeting. 'To what do we owe this honour? And why didn't you bring Haukr?'

'He was needed at home, he said, but he told me where to find you. I'm on a trading journey to Ísland. As I had to pass near here anyway, I thought I'd stop by to see how you have fared. I take it all is well and Álrik has regained his domains?'

'Indeed. His uncle is dead and order has been restored. We're in the process of rebuilding and strengthening the place. Come up to the hall and we will talk more.' Thorald gestured for everyone to go up the hill.

'Why are you going to Ísland?' Ivar was curious. Usually Hrafn went on trading ventures to the east Baltic and what he called Garðaríki – roughly Russia in modern terms. He'd never headed west before, or at least not this far.

'To see if Geir has survived his first winter there.' Hrafn's expression was slightly sheepish, and he shrugged. 'I know, I know, he's a grown man and I shouldn't interfere, but I need to assure myself that he's well. After that, I'll leave him alone.'

That made sense. Hrafn and his brothers were close and had always looked out for each other. Since Geir was the youngest, the other two were extra protective of him. Ivar had been told by Linnea that Geir had left for Iceland the previous year, determined to strike out on his own. He could see why that would worry his family. It was a long way to go, and Iceland was a harsh place to settle in.

'Can I come with you?' he blurted out. Seeing Viking-age Iceland and the first ever settlements there seemed like an opportunity he couldn't miss. Then he glanced at Thorald. 'That is, if you can spare me? I don't suppose we'll be gone for long. A few weeks at most?'

'No, that's fine. Go! If I didn't have responsibilities here, I'd want to come with you as well.'

'Thank you.' Ivar turned to explain to Hrafn. 'You may congratulate him. He's recently become a father to a fine son.'

'Really? How wonderful – my felicitations!'

They celebrated with ale and had an evening of catching up. At one point when it was only the three of them, Thorald made sure they couldn't be overheard, then cleared his throat.

'So, Hrafn, Ivar tells me your wife has a somewhat unusual background and that she is his foster-sister from another age.'

Hrafn's eyebrows rose and he stared at Ivar. 'You told him?'

'Yes. He had the right to know and I didn't like to deceive him. He's my kin, even if the relationship is somewhat strange.'

'It is true then?' Thorald regarded Hrafn intently. 'It's not that I don't want to believe it, but you must admit, travelling through time sounds impossible.'

'Indeed. It took me a while to trust Linnea when she told me, but now I have experienced it for myself. Ivar and I have only ever met in a different time, never here. You have my oath that he's telling the truth.'

'Good. I'm glad. I have come to regard him as a brother, and I very much want complete honesty between us.' Thorald clapped Ivar on the shoulder and smiled at him. It gave the latter a mushy sensation in his stomach, which he tried to suppress. This was not the time to go all emotional, but he appreciated his kinsman's support and friendship more than the man would ever know.

'Thank you. I feel the same.'

'Let's drink to that.' Hrafn held up his mug. 'That means we're all kin now, right? Excellent!'

'You're leaving? Today?' Ellisif stared at Ivar in the faint light from the glowing embers of the hearth. She had to take a deep breath to stop herself from shouting the word 'No!' out loud.

The time had come. He'd be gone from her life and he would never return. There was nothing for him here. She knew it was irrational to want him to stay longer, but she didn't want to let him go. Not yet.

'Only for a few weeks, but I wanted to say goodbye without an audience.' To her surprise, he'd crawled in behind her on the sleeping bench and slung an arm around her waist. He placed a gentle kiss on her lips. 'From what I hear, it doesn't take long to reach Ísland, and Hrafn has promised to drop me off here before he goes home to Eskilsnes.'

'But you'll have to cross the sea. It's dangerous.' She'd heard tell that many of those who did so never returned. The thought of him in a watery grave made her want to shudder.

'It will be fine. I have every faith in Hrafn's skills. He has sailed from his home to Garðaríki more times than I can count. That can be treacherous too. Don't fret, *unnasta*. I'll soon be back, and when I return, there's something I wish to discuss with you.'

'Oh? And what is that?' Had he changed his mind about leaving for good? But if so, why couldn't he tell her now?

'Patience,' he murmured, and bent to kiss her again. This time there was more passion, and fire licked through her veins, but she sensed he was still holding back.

'If you drown, I'll seek you out in the afterlife and beat you,' she murmured between kisses. His answering chuckle reverberated through her entire body, but she didn't think he understood how serious she was.

'If I drown, I'll welcome the company,' he joked. 'Now, I'd better return to my own bench.' He sat up. 'Oh, before I forget, I wanted to give you something.' She heard him rummage in his pouch. 'Here.'

She felt him place a cool metal object in the palm of her hand. Squinting at it in the glow from the banked hearth, she frowned. 'Is it a charm for luck? If so, you should be the one carrying it.'

'Not exactly. It is a swan's-foot amulet and may have belonged to a *võlva*. You might not believe me, but I found this before meeting you, and sometimes when I touched it, I had strange visions. They showed me a woman with red-gold hair – you – and the fact that you needed my help.'

'That is . . .'

'Strange. Unbelievable. I know, but I am telling the truth. I saw you being taken from your home by the king's men, and some of what happened to you afterwards. When we first met, I had no doubt I'd seen you before. As if we were destined to meet. Do not ask how it works, as it is clearly *trolldomr* of some sort. But perhaps if you touch it while I'm gone, it will show you that I am well.'

Ellisif gripped the little amulet tighter. 'Thank you. If nothing else, I will keep it safe for you until your return.' He'd have to come back in order to regain possession of the charm, and that made her happy.

'Very well. Wish me good fortune for the journey, please.'

'I do. I shall pray to the gods for your journey to be smooth.'

And if he didn't come back, she'd never forgive him.

'He's done well, don't you think? It seems like a prosperous settlement, if a little makeshift as yet.'

'Yes, it's a beautiful place. Truly stunning. I mean, look at that view!'

Ivar stood in the bow of the ship with Hrafn as they neared Geir's homestead in Iceland. It had the appearance of a fairy-tale settlement. Houses entirely built out of turf, with smoke seeping from the roofs, were surrounded by the most incredible landscape. Mist-wreathed mountains and several shimmering waterfalls formed a dramatic backdrop to wide open plains. There were fields and pasture, a flock of sheep and some cattle grazing nearby, and the sounds of hammering came from one of the smaller huts. All seemed peaceful and picture-perfect.

The journey across the sea had been uneventful and had only

taken them five days. They'd sailed north first along the coast of Norway, then struck out due west. They'd sighted the Shetland Islands – at least that was what Ivar guessed they were, although Hrafn called them Hjaltland – then changed their direction to a more north-westerly one. After passing the Faroe Islands – the Færeyjar, according to Hrafn – there had been nothing but open sea until they reached the southern part of Iceland. There an abundance of seabirds indicated that they were getting close, and the spectacular coastline hove into view not long afterwards.

'Where is he most likely to have gone?' Hrafn had asked Ivar at that point. 'I assume you know from your time which areas were settled first?'

'Yes, we should sail west and north. The area around Reykjavik – a large settlement in my era – must have been the best place. At least, that's my guess.'

'Good, let's do that then.' After many years of being married to Linnea, Hrafn had learned to have faith in modern knowledge.

They'd stopped at a settlement called Vik, where they had been directed further north by its owner, and now here they were. A cow horn blared out a warning. As the ship made contact with the small beach, people came running down the slope and in from the nearby fields. The first to reach them was Geir. Or at least, Ivar assumed it was him, as he looked a lot like his brother. He'd never actually met him, since only Hrafn and Rurik, the middle brother, had visited the twenty-first century.

'*Hrafn!* By all the gods, I don't believe it!' The man had a huge grin on his face as the brothers gave each other a bear hug. 'Odin's ravens, what are you doing here?'

Ivar was vaguely aware of the conversation that followed, and the fact that a big black dog came running and leapt at Hrafn with barks of joy. But this all faded into the background when he caught sight of a woman with wild red curls, who shrieked as she ran past the others and threw herself into his arms. He barely had time to catch her, and staggered back a step from the impact.

'*Ivar!* What on earth are you doing here?'

'Maddie?' He blinked in surprise and crushed his little foster-sister to his chest. Shock reverberated through him, and he blinked again, hardly able to believe his eyes. Although he and Storm had suspected she'd ended up in the ninth century, he'd never have expected to find her here, of all places. He tightened his arms around her, emotion clogging his throat. Now that he had found her, he could acknowledge just how worried he'd been. But she was alive and well, and she was in his arms. *Thank the gods!*

She seemed to be struggling with the same thoughts. 'I just can't believe it! What are you doing here? And in this time? Did you go and visit Linnea?' The questions poured out of her in a torrent of English mixed with Swedish. Luckily that meant no one around them would understand their conversation, which was a very good thing.

He held her hands as they caught up on how they had both ended up here, and he told her how worried they'd all been. He needed the connection between them to show him that this was real. She was really here, and she was safe and sound. *Thank heavens for that!* It seemed like a miracle, but he'd learned by now that magic was probably involved. He wouldn't question it, but simply be grateful to the gods or whoever had made them find each other.

She led the way up to the largest of the turf buildings. Along the way, Ivar learned that Maddie and Geir had been married since the previous autumn. Something seemed to be troubling her about that, but he decided to wait until later to ask her about it. Hrafn planned to stay for at least a week, so there would be plenty of time. For now, he focused on her husband, who greeted him with a smile.

'Welcome to Stormavík. I'm Geir, Maddie's husband.'

'Thank you. I'm Ivar, her foster-brother. Glad to meet you.'

After teasing Maddie about being a married woman, despite the fact that he thought of her as the baby of the family, everyone settled down to some of the ale Hrafn had brought. Ivar was still in a daze as he took in his surroundings and chatted to Maddie, but at the same time, happiness sparked in his veins. He hadn't allowed himself to think about her for a long time, and now it was as though a huge weight had dropped off his shoulders.

One less thing to worry about.

It soon turned out that things were not that simple. Hrafn had brought a woman along on the journey by the name of Vigdis, as well as her three-year-old daughter, Hilda. Vigdis was a pretty young widow, blonde and curvaceous, and Ivar suspected Hrafn had been hoping to make a match between her and Geir, since they apparently had history. That went down like a lead balloon.

Not only did his brother's meddling infuriate Geir – and rightly so, in Ivar's opinion, although he kept that to himself – but Vigdis's presence exacerbated misgivings that Maddie had been harbouring about her marriage. He didn't completely understand her reasoning when she told him she was convinced she'd never be able to have children, but he wasn't able to talk her out of her doubts. He couldn't help but compare her situation to that of Ellisif, but since Geir was young and healthy, he felt certain Maddie had a much greater chance of becoming pregnant in time. And unlike Þjódólfr, Geir wasn't blaming his wife for not conceiving.

'No. Don't you see? I'm doing Geir a disservice by staying married to him. If I left, he could marry Vigdis instead, as the woman is clearly fertile.' Maddie glanced at little Hilda, the proof of this, with a longing in her eyes that made Ivar's gut clench with sympathy.

'I'm sure you're wrong.' They hadn't been married very long, after all. 'You need to be patient. These things don't always happen at once, you know.'

'But what if it never happens? He's a Viking, the owner of all this.' She gestured at their surroundings. 'He needs children. Sons. And if I can't give them to him, surely he'll tire of me.'

Ivar highly doubted that. Geir was a man deeply in love, anyone could see that. Except Maddie, apparently. Something had her convinced that Geir would soon become disillusioned with the situation. That it would be wrong of her to stand in the way of him marrying Vigdis, who was a woman of his own time and therefore better suited to being a Viking's wife. She wanted to spare them both years of misery.

Ivar remembered how Maddie had been bullied at school because of her height and her red hair. Her confidence had never been high, and although things had improved when she'd started learning various self-defence techniques, the doubts must have remained in the background. More so than he'd realised. The present situation had clearly brought them to the surface again, and he wasn't sure how to counteract this.

He attempted to give her a pep talk. 'Come on, this isn't my fierce little sister talking. Where's the girl who survived the bullies at school? The one who got herself a black belt in karate? At least give it some more thought. Don't be hasty.'

He enveloped her in a big hug and tried to imbue her with his own strength. Obviously no outsider could be privy to everything that went on inside a marriage, and Ivar guessed there might be things Maddie wasn't telling him. He tried to soothe away her fears and worries as best he could, but it would seem her mind was already made up. No matter what he said, she wouldn't see reason. In the end, he decided the only thing he could do was support her in whatever decision she made.

* * *

Ellisif had resisted the temptation of the swan's-foot amulet for the first week, but ten days after Ivar's departure, she could no longer ignore it. Leaving the hall after the evening meal, she went outside to find a quiet place where no one would disturb her. There was a spot high up on the hill behind the buildings where you could sit and look out across the fjord. It was peaceful and the views were stunning, but she barely spared them a glance. Instead, she sank down on the grass and took out the silver item from her pouch.

'Are you really magical?' she whispered.

She hadn't been sure whether to believe Ivar, but he had seemed sincere when he'd told her of the visions he'd had. The thought that he had seen her long before they'd even met made her shiver. It was as though it was preordained, their meeting decided by the Norns. What did that mean? That they were destined to be together, or that this all had some other purpose?

She swallowed hard and stared at the amulet. It lay on the palm of her hand, glinting in the early-evening light. Closing her fingers around it, she took a deep breath and concentrated on the feel of it on her skin. The air around her became suddenly charged, almost humming, and the hairs on the back of her neck stood up. Her eyes drifted shut and dizziness assailed her, but at the same time a vision rose up inside her mind.

Ivar. He was standing behind a strange-looking building made entirely out of turf. She could see the layers of it, with tufts of grass still growing at intervals. But he wasn't alone. A tall woman with the most beautiful dark red curls Ellisif had ever seen was in his arms. She saw him leaning his cheek on the top of her head, his arms tight around her as if he never wanted to let go. The woman wore a sad expression and burrowed closer into his embrace, clearly comfortable there. This was no stranger. It was someone he knew intimately.

Someone he loved.

She let out a moan of despair, which brought the vision to an abrupt halt.

'*Skítr!*' Jealousy clawed at her insides, making her feel physically ill. She was finally ready to acknowledge just how much she wanted him, but it was too late. Or rather, she'd never stood a chance, because his heart was already engaged elsewhere. Even if she told him she'd changed her mind about remarrying, he wouldn't want her.

'Fool,' she muttered. He had tried to tell her. Had warned her he'd never stay with her, no matter what. She should have listened. It might have saved her from a broken heart.

Now it was too late for that as well.

The final straw came when Maddie caught Vigdis throwing herself at Geir in the byre, kissing him as if she had every right to. Although he pushed her away and swore it was all the conniving woman's doing, something seemed to break inside Maddie. When she told Ivar about this incident, all the fight had gone out of her. She'd become convinced Vigdis would stop at nothing until she had what she wanted, so she decided to go back to the twenty-first century.

Against his better judgement, Ivar agreed to help her. They snuck away from Stormavík and time-travelled together. Back in their own era, they managed to return to Reykjavik, where he saw her off at the airport on her way home to her parents in Sweden.

'I'm sorry I can't come with you, but I have unfinished business in the ninth century.'

He hadn't told her about Ellisif, but he'd promised to return to Ulfstoft, and he was determined to keep his word. Nor did he divulge the fact that he planned to tell Geir where Maddie had gone. He'd seen the deep love the man had for his little sister, and was truly convinced that she was making a mistake. No one could persuade her of that except her husband, however, so Ivar would do what he could to help. It was just a shame he couldn't have told Geir *before* Maddie left, but he'd never been a snitch and he wasn't planning on starting now.

He proved to be right about Geir's emotions.

The man had clearly been going out of his mind since Maddie disappeared. Ivar had only been gone for just over twenty-four hours, but it must have felt like a lifetime to his brother-in-law. Geir grabbed the front of his tunic when he returned to the settlement, his eyes threatening violence. 'Where is she? What have you done with her? Tell me, or I swear I'll—'

'Whoa, calm down and I'll tell you whatever you wish to know.'

It took him a while to explain, but once Geir understood that Ivar was on his side, he relaxed slightly. He was ready to do anything to get his wife back, and therefore opted to return with Hrafn to Svíaríki, from where he would attempt to follow Maddie to the future. The meddlesome Vigdis was dropped off at the settlement of Vik along the way, where she would hopefully find someone else to marry. There was a distinct shortage of suitable women of marriageable age in Iceland, and Hrafn and Geir had every confidence she would catch herself a fine husband. Although Geir wasn't feeling particularly well disposed towards her, he appeared sincere when he wished her well. And once she'd accepted that her fate didn't lie with him, she went off quite happily.

Ivar breathed a secret sigh of relief. At least Maddie wouldn't have to see the woman again if she did return with Geir.

Chapter Twenty

Ulfstoft, June/Sólmánuðr AD 876

Ellisif had tried to keep busy while Ivar was gone. She couldn't stop thinking about the dangers he faced, and every time she pictured him out on the vast sea, her insides clenched. Since she'd had the vision, there were other worries as well, but she tried her best not to think about them. There was no point. He might never be hers, but that didn't mean she'd want any harm to come to him. She prayed to the gods he'd return safely.

'I think someone is missing her man,' Askhild teased. She was sitting on a bench feeding little Thorulf, and Ellisif had been keeping her company. She was using the crystal Ivar had given her to sew tiny stitches on a minuscule tunic for the baby, but that only brought her thoughts back to him yet again.

She sighed. 'He's not my man. I merely worry about him. The sea can be dangerous.'

'Mm-hmm. And why is that? Admit it, you're smitten.'

'So what if I am? You know I don't wish to marry.' This wasn't true, but it was now irrelevant.

'What if Ivar asked you?'

'He won't.' Ellisif closed her eyes and blew out a frustrated breath. 'He's made it clear he doesn't want to stay here. Even if I regained my property, he wouldn't want me.' And now she knew why, but she didn't want to tell Askhild about it. Not yet. Her emotions were too raw.

'I'm sure you could find a solution, but you need to talk to him. I mean, really talk.'

'Maybe. I'll think about it,' she replied vaguely.

'Very well.' Askhild tactfully turned the conversation to other matters.

Summer had arrived at last, and Ellisif delighted in being outdoors after all the months cooped up in the hall. She often went for walks into the forest to gather the herbs and plants needed for potions and tisanes. Making them was a task she'd always enjoyed. It was peaceful among the trees, and she savoured the scents of pine and moss all around her.

Ivar was expected back soon, by Thorald's reckoning, and she couldn't resist pulling the swan's-foot amulet out of her pouch. Would she see him on board the ship? She clenched her fist around it and briefly closed her eyes, but this time nothing occurred. Perhaps the gods had already shown her what she'd needed to see. That had to be it. Before she'd had that vision, she'd been so excited to see him again. He had said he had something to tell her, and a small flicker of hope had burned in her heart, hoping he'd changed his mind about staying. Perhaps even proposing to her. But she knew now that wasn't going to happen. It must be merely a business proposition of some sort, and—

Her daydreams were cut short by a hard arm snaking round her throat from behind and a callused hand being placed over her mouth. She dropped her basket and the amulet out of sheer fright as she struggled to free herself from the harsh grip.

'Don't utter a sound, or I'll hurt you. Badly.' The voice

that hissed in her ear was eerily familiar, and Ellisif stiffened. Her entire body went as cold as if she'd jumped into a frozen lake.

Kári. How on earth had he found her?

As if he'd read her thoughts, he murmured, 'Didn't think I'd come for you, eh? Well, your hair caught the attention of some men who visited here recently, and I heard them talking. Knew it had to be you. Now come with me without a fuss, or I'll make sure your new friends suffer. I could snap that baby's neck in an instant, understand? Newborns are so fragile.'

She hadn't thought she could feel any colder, but his words made the blood in her veins freeze, and bile rose in her throat. The fact that he'd been watching the settlement and seen little Thorulf was terrifying. Nodding to show she'd do as he said, she stood mute while one of his men came over with rope to tie her hands and a gag for her mouth.

'Now walk,' Kári hissed. 'And fast.'

There was no choice but to follow him if she wanted to keep Askhild and her son safe. No one in the settlement was expecting an attack, so she didn't doubt that Kári could make good on his threat.

Far better she died than that precious child.

After another five-day journey across the North Atlantic, the ship was nearing Ulfstoft, sailing up the fjord with a strong following breeze to propel it. During the final part of the journey, Ivar stood at the front, clinging to the figurehead so he wouldn't fall overboard. He was eagerly awaiting the first glimpse of the settlement and his heart was beating fast. Soon, very soon, he'd be reunited with Ellisif, and this time he was going to tell her of his plans for the two of them. It wouldn't have been right to do so before the journey, in case anything happened to him, but now there was nothing to stop him. He only hoped she'd approve of his ideas. If not, he'd have to persuade her.

He jumped out as soon as the ship hove to by the jetty. Hrafn and Geir hopped off as well in order to say goodbye. They weren't staying, as Hrafn was itching to get home to Linnea and Geir was even more impatient to go after his wife. Ivar hugged the older brother first. 'Thank you for letting me come along. I'm so glad I did, as finding Maddie has taken a weight off my mind.'

'You're very welcome. Don't forget to come and see us when you're back in Svíaríki or I won't answer for the consequences. Linnea will no doubt give you a piece of her mind, but I know she'd love to see you.'

'I will, I promise.'

He turned to Geir and gave him a hug as well. 'I wish you the best of luck. Don't take no for an answer. Maddie can be stubborn, but she belongs with you, anyone can see that.'

'Thank you, brother. I'll do my best.' Geir was subdued, but there was a determined expression on his face. Ivar didn't think his little sister stood a chance of holding out on this man.

He smiled at the word 'brother'. He hadn't thought about the fact that he'd gained another brother-in-law, even if he and Maddie were only foster-siblings. Here, that counted as kin, and it would seem his family was growing by the day. It made him realise that the loneliness he'd been suffering had faded into nothing. He wasn't alone, either here or in the twenty-first century. Family didn't have to consist of blood ties, he knew that now. And his were the best.

He headed up the hill towards the settlement and was met by bad news.

'What do you mean, she's gone? Gone where?' He stared at Thorald, not wanting to believe what he was hearing.

'I don't know, but my guess would be that Kári has something to do with it.' His kinsman sighed. 'Askhild tells me Ellisif had taken to walking in the forest and she didn't return this morning. I've had men out searching and calling, in case she's fallen down a ravine or hurt herself, but there's no trace of her except for her basket and this.' He proffered the silver amulet Ivar had given her before he left. 'We found them discarded next to one of the paths.'

'*Fan också! Helvetes jävlar . . . Bloody hell!*' Ivar hissed out swear words in Swedish and English while pacing the width of the hall. He'd been so looking forward to seeing her, and now they had no idea if she was even alive. Then something occurred to him. 'Hold on. Let me have that, please. I think I know of a way to confirm her whereabouts.' He held out his hand for the little charm.

'What? How?' Thorald stared at him, but handed it over. 'More *trolldomr*?'

'Yes. Wait here. I'll be back shortly.'

He set off for the byre and climbed the ladder into the hayloft as fast as he could. Once there, he settled down on the few remaining wisps of hay and gripped the amulet. He hoped it would still work. Would the connection between them remain? Only one way to find out.

Taking a deep breath, he closed his eyes and squeezed the silver item in his fist. 'Show me where she is, please!' he murmured, but his words were superfluous as the dizziness hit him instantly. Images flooded his brain . . .

Ellisif, being dragged out of a ship and led up a slight incline to a hall. Her hands were bound, her mouth gagged, and her gleaming tresses hung in disarray down her back and around her face. She was taken into the hall, but soon the vision changed and she was coming out again, her chin raised in defiance. She didn't cower as she was led off towards one of the outbuildings. The man holding her arm in a firm grip was Kell, no doubt about it, his expression stony. Without a backward glance, she walked into her prison and the door was slammed shut . . .

As abruptly as it had come, the vision vanished. Ivar blinked, but now he knew. He still had a bond with Ellisif via the swan's foot, and if he kept checking, he could make sure she was alive. He'd recognised the hall, its surroundings and her captor all too well. She was at Birgirsby.

Returning to Thorald, he told him what he'd seen, and how.

'You are sure this magic is to be trusted?'

'Yes. It's always been right before. What I don't understand is how on earth Kári found out she was here. Kell?' He shook his head. 'No, I won't believe it. I trust him.' And the man hadn't been gloating as he led Ellisif towards the hut.

Thorald shrugged. 'Who knows? Either way, it's happened and we have to do something about it.'

'Right. Well, I'm going after her. May I borrow your ship, please?'

Hrafn had already left, or Ivar would have begged a ride with him. It was a shame in more ways than one, as Hrafn was handy in a fight too.

'Of course, and I'll come with you. It's time to take back her domain and kill that *niðingr*. Let me just gather my men.'

Ivar held up a hand. 'No, wait. I have a better idea. There is still so much to do here, and I can't wait. I'm going to rescue Ellisif with magic. I will take her to the future briefly, then we can return here. Later, when you're ready and can spare more men, we can attack Birgirsby properly. Besides, it would take too long to get word to all Álrik's tenant farmers. You'd need most of them, and time is of the essence.'

They'd already discussed how many men would be necessary in order to defeat Kári, and Ivar knew the ones here in the main settlement wouldn't be enough. Stealth and magic would have to see him through for now.

'But . . . the future? Are you sure that will work?' Thorald regarded him with scepticism.

'Yes.' Ivar tried to imbue his reply with sincerity, even though he wasn't at all certain he could pull this off. What if the magic didn't work for Ellisif? But it seemed like the best chance they had for now, and he'd put his faith in the Norse gods. He had to. 'All will be well as long as I can reach her and that *argr* hasn't forced her into marriage already. I must hurry.'

Thorald nodded. 'Very well. Take the smaller boat. Oddr and Gaukr can go with you in case you don't remember the way.'

'Thank you.' Ivar gave the man a bear hug, inordinately pleased that Thorald trusted him. 'It may take some time, but I'll bring her back as soon as I can.'

He only hoped the gods were on his side.

Ellisif walked into her own hall with her head held high. She ignored the expressions of consternation and pity on the faces of people she'd known since birth. Out of the corner of her eye she caught a glimpse of Kell. She thought it best not to look at him. He'd tried to help her before, and she didn't want to get him into trouble.

'Sit.' Kári shoved her on to a bench next to the carved chair Þjódólfr had previously occupied on the dais. It was as though she was stuck in a horrible dream where the only thing that had changed was the face of her tormentor. Everything else was eerily familiar, down to the sneer on Kári's face. It exactly mirrored that of her dead husband whenever he'd looked at her.

If only I hadn't been so stubborn! I could have been married to someone else by now. Anyone would have been better than Kári, surely. But there was no use repining.

Someone cut the ropes binding her wrists and gently removed the gag, disentangling it from her mussed-up hair. She glanced over her shoulder to find that it was Kell. His expression was carefully blank, and she pretended to glare at him. It was better for his sake if everyone believed she hated him as much as the rest of his family.

'My intended bride has finally deigned to join us,' Kári called out. 'We'll be married tomorrow and I want a feast to end all feasts, understood?' He clapped his hands. 'Start preparing now! What are you waiting for?'

As people scurried off to do his bidding, Ellisif felt the stares of every person present like needle pricks on her skin. Some were gloating, others sympathetic. It didn't matter, though. All was lost, and even if Thorald somehow managed to come to her rescue, it would be too late. Unless she could find some way of killing this swine herself . . .

She was served a cup of ale and a bowl of stew with flatbread to dunk in it. The knot in her stomach meant she wasn't hungry, but she was no fool. She knew she needed to keep her strength up, and in any case, her mouth was parched and tasted bad from that disgusting gag. Without a word, she began to eat and drink.

'Glad to see you have an appetite, wife. You'll need your stamina on the morrow.' Kári guffawed. When she didn't so much as look his way, he grabbed her arm and pulled her around to face him. 'Cat got your tongue? That's as well, I suppose. I never could abide a woman who talked too much. But when I address you, you will pay attention, yes?'

His fingers came up to take her chin in a vice-like grip, squeezing until she gave a small nod.

'Good.' He let go of her and turned to Kell, who was sitting quietly on her other side. 'When she's finished, lock her in the hut.'

'Yes, Father.'

Ellisif had eaten as much as she could manage and nodded at the younger man. 'I'm ready.'

Too late, she realised that he hadn't finished his own food, but he stood up immediately and took hold of her upper arm. 'Come then.'

Neither said a word until they were outside the hall and well out of earshot. 'I'm sorry,' Kell muttered. 'I wasn't able to help this time. He didn't tell me where he was going or I would have tried to get word to you.'

'It's not your fault. I'm grateful for what you did for Hedda and the others. Perhaps this was always my fate and I have to accept that.' She swallowed down the tears that burned the back of her throat. 'Know this, though – Thorald and his men will come after me. You'd better be prepared to hide or show your father your true colours.'

She didn't mention Ivar, because she had no idea whether he was back yet.

'I will.'

He led her into a small hut that appeared to be used for storage, and she sank down on to a makeshift pallet of straw with one blanket on top.

Tomorrow she would have to marry Kári, and she'd never see Ivar again.

'Are you out of your mind? Where are the rest of the men?' Kell hissed out the question. He was staring at Ivar as if he couldn't believe what he was seeing.

'Not here yet.'

After Oddr and Gaukr had reluctantly left him in the forest near Birgirsby, Ivar had watched the settlement and waited to see if he could spot Ellisif. He hadn't seen her yet, but a serving woman had brought food to the small hut on one side of the yard that he'd seen in his vision. She'd been accompanied by a burly man, who'd barred the door afterwards. He guessed that meant she was still being held there, unless Kári had already installed her in his bed.

That thought made him almost snarl out loud, but either way, he'd rescue her somehow. She'd survived one brutal husband, so he knew she was strong enough to cope with whatever fate had thrown at her.

Luck was with him, and not long afterwards he'd seen Kell on his way into the forest. The man seemed to make a habit of going walkabout, or perhaps he just wanted to get away from the toxic environment of his father's household. Ivar had managed to attract his attention, and they were now standing behind a large oak tree.

'Has your father married her yet?' He clenched his jaw as he waited for the answer to his question and prayed to all the gods that he wasn't too late.

'No, but he plans to do it today. A feast is being prepared and will be ready shortly.'

'Thank the gods!'

The relief at Kell's words made Ivar light-headed, but he told himself not to celebrate prematurely. The bastard could have already raped her, but either way, he had to concentrate on the here and now. 'Listen, I have a plan, but I'll need your help. You have to pretend to have caught me skulking around the settlement. Beat me up a little if you wish so that anyone watching thinks you've incapacitated me. Then lock me in the hut with Ellisif before you go and tell your father. Make sure someone sees you do that, else you'll be under suspicion later. And try not to hurry, please. I'll need some time alone with her.'

Kell frowned. 'How will that help you? You can't free her if you are a captive yourself.'

'Ah, but I can. I won't tell you how, but trust me, when you return for us, we'll be gone.' At least, he hoped so. If his plan didn't work, they were both dead, or as good as.

'Very well.'

The young man was regarding him as if he had taken leave of his senses, but he must have been paying attention, because the next thing Ivar knew, Kell had punched him in the face. The blow landed to the side of his left eye and one of the young man's rings inadvertently tore the skin. Blood poured down and Ivar swiped at it, smearing some across his cheek. 'Good, thank you,' he muttered. His face throbbed, but it was a small price to pay if he was to pull off this ruse.

'You've lost your wits,' Kell muttered, but he didn't say anything else or try to reason with Ivar.

Together they disordered their clothing to give the appearance that they'd been fighting, then Kell pulled Ivar's arms behind his back and tied them loosely with a piece of leather cord. 'There, that should do for now. Ellisif's hands are not bound, so she can free you. Let's go.'

As he marched his supposed captive into the yard, several people stopped what they were doing to gawk. Kell pushed Ivar ahead of him and made him stumble, a move the latter exaggerated so that it would seem as though he was dizzy and disorientated.

'In here,' he growled, slamming Ivar into the wall next to the door to the hut while he lifted the heavy bar that secured it from outside. 'I'm going to get my father, *niðingr*, and he can deal with you.'

As Ivar stumbled into the dim interior, the door slammed shut behind him with an ominous bang. It took him a moment before his eyes adjusted, but he heard Ellisif's gasp.

'Ivar? *Oh no!* No, no, no . . .'

She rushed forward and grabbed his upper arms to assist him, but he straightened of his own accord and whispered, 'Are you well? Has he hurt you?'

'M-me? I'm fine, but you—'

He cut her off. 'There's nothing wrong with me and no time for explanations right now. We must act quickly, before Kári comes. Do you trust me?'

'Yes, of course.' She was staring at him with wide eyes, but he read the truth in their depths.

'Good. Then please open the smaller of my pouches and take out the sewing shears you'll find there to cut my bindings.' He nodded towards his belt. 'As fast as you can.'

She quickly extracted the item and sliced through the leather cord. As soon as she'd finished, he grabbed the shears and took hold of her hand.

'Now I'm going to make a small cut in your finger and mine, and at the same time we have to say the words "*Með blōð skaltu ferðast*". And please hold on to my hand. Don't let go, promise?'

'Very well, but why?'

He could hear voices approaching. 'I'll explain later. We must do this now or it will be too late. Are you ready?'

She nodded.

'On the count of three, say it with me. One, two, three . . . *með blōð skaltu ferðast*.'

He used the sharp edge of the little shears to slice at their fingers at the same time as the words rang out from them both. As the familiar dizziness swirled him into darkness, he gripped her hand as hard as he could and prayed to Odin and all the gods that they'd allow him to take her with him.

If not, all was lost.

Chapter Twenty-One

Birgirsby, June 2023

'Ugh! What happened?' Ellisif sat up and regretted it immediately. She raised her hands to clutch her head, which was swimming. The nausea was receding somewhat, but she still had to swallow several times to make it go away.

'It worked!' Ivar was sitting next to her under a tree not far from the fjord, and his beaming smile made warmth spread inside her. 'Welcome to the twenty-first century.'

'The what?' She blinked at him and wondered if he'd taken leave of his senses. Had Kell hit him that hard? There was still blood on his face and his cheek was swollen, while a bruise was forming under his left eye. 'And where is the hut? My settlement?'

'Long gone. Kári won't find you here. Thank Odin I reached you in time!'

Without warning, Ivar pulled her into his arms and gave her a searing kiss. It might have been meant as a quick celebratory one, but the instant their lips met, it turned into something deeper. Neither of them ended it until they had to come up for air. By that time, they were lying on the springy moss with Ivar half on top of her, and he was still smiling broadly.

Ellisif suddenly recalled the stunning redhead he'd been holding in Iceland and pushed at his chest. The happiness that had been surging through her veins was rapidly fading. What had she been thinking, kissing him like that when he was promised to another? He let her sit up again, but his smile dimmed when she glared at him and demanded, 'Explain, please. I don't understand what just occurred. And what did you mean by the twenty-first century?'

He took her hand and plaited their fingers together. She allowed it only because his next words stunned her. 'You've experienced magic – *trolldomr*,' he said. 'The shears I used to cut our fingers are very special and quite possibly forged by the gods. They allow their owner to travel through time, which is what we just did. I've not spoken to you about this before because I didn't think you'd believe me, but it seemed the only way to save you from Kári. We are now a thousand years into the future. This is where I am from. It's also the reason I told you I couldn't stay with you indefinitely. I was always planning to return to my time.'

Lost for words, Ellisif could do nothing but stare at him. It was too much to take in. She couldn't help but wonder if the blow to his head had disordered his mind, but he appeared lucid and sincere. She saw nothing but honesty in his blue gaze. And yet, how could what he claimed possibly be true?

'You are serious?'

'Never more so. And I will prove it to you. There is much to show you here, as soon as we find our way to the nearest settlement. I know everything you will see is going to seem very strange, but I swear there is no danger to you. We'll no doubt be stared at because the people of my time don't wear this type of clothing, but I have an explanation for that, so all will be well. You did say you trust me, did you not?'

'Well, yes, but . . .' That was when she'd still considered him to be sane and rational, but she thought it best to keep that to herself.

If she was dealing with a madman, it behoved her to tread carefully.

He leaned over to give her another kiss, but she turned her head and it landed on her cheek. Fortunately, he didn't appear to notice. 'Listen, it's going to take a while for you to accept this, but follow my lead for now, please. Can you do that?'

She nodded, too overwhelmed to reply properly.

'Then let's go. No, wait, I need to extract something from the seam of my tunic.' He used the shears to pick at the stitching on the bottom hem, and soon dislodged a small shiny blue square that had some kind of writing on it, picked out in gold. Not runes, but similar.

'What's that?'

'Something that is used as payment here.' He tucked it into his leather pouch, and stowed the shears as well.

'Is silver not good enough, then? You have plenty of that.' Ellisif was confused. How could that little square possibly be better than all the arm rings he wore? He carried a small fortune about his person.

He laughed. 'Sometimes, but usually we have other ways. You'll see.'

They set off along the edge of the fjord and soon glimpsed houses. Ellisif frowned as she noticed how many there were, as if lots of small settlements had been placed right next to each other and were encroaching on their neighbours' land. The buildings were strange too, and some were painted in vivid colours. They had large openings with what looked to be sheets of glass in them – more glass than she'd ever seen in her life. She'd never come across anything like it. And there shouldn't be any settlements so close to Birgirsby. At least, there never had been in the past.

Ivar held her hand and she didn't protest. It was comforting and the only thing anchoring her to reality, as otherwise she would have believed herself to be in some sort of dream world. As they entered a long, smooth track with buildings either side, they met a strangely dressed man leading a dog by a long leather cord. Ivar stopped him and asked something in a language Ellisif didn't understand. A few of the words sounded familiar, yet foreign. She frowned and kept her gaze on the ground.

'The man told me of a place where we can buy some food and spend the night,' Ivar said as they walked on. 'It's not too far.'

He tugged her along and she followed without question. What else could she do? If he was telling the truth, she'd be completely lost without him.

Ivar could tell that Ellisif was shell-shocked, and no wonder. He'd rather sprung it on her that they were in his century and that time travel was possible. Perhaps he ought to have talked to her about it before, the way he had with Thorald, but until recently, he'd never thought she needed to know. Originally he had planned to leave as if he was going back to Svíaríki, and then disappear from there when the time came. But after thinking matters over all through the winter, he'd come to the conclusion that he had to find another solution. They needed to discuss things thoroughly. He'd acknowledged to himself that without her, his life would have no meaning. Simply being with her made him happy. There was no way he wanted to give that up now.

Before he'd had a chance, however, she'd been kidnapped. And now they were here, in his time.

He wanted to laugh out loud at the thought of how surprised Kári must have been to find the hut empty. No blame could be attached to Kell, as there had been several witnesses when he'd pushed Ivar into the building. The bar would still be firmly in place on the outside of the door. Hopefully it would give the older man something to think about. Thwarting his evil schemes was certainly extremely satisfying.

The little town or village they were walking through didn't boast much more than a mini supermarket and petrol station, by the looks of it, but the man walking his dog had told him there was a motel, and that was where they were headed. They'd need somewhere to spend the night before making their way up the coast so that they could return to the ninth century much closer to Ulfstoft.

'Here we are.' He led Ellisif towards a low building with doors along a covered walkway. A sign pointed to the reception, and a middle-aged woman greeted them from behind a tall counter. Her name tag said *Marit*, and as her startled gaze took in their clothing, Ivar hastened to explain.

'Good afternoon. My wife and I have been to a Viking re-enactment meeting, but we got a bit lost. I think we'll need a place to stay before continuing in the morning. Would you happen to have any rooms for tonight, please?'

'Er, sure. One moment.' Marit tapped the keys of her computer and Ivar felt Ellisif stiffen beside him as she took in their surroundings. He could only imagine how weird this must be for her, but he couldn't explain anything right now. 'Yes, room seven is available. It's a small double with en suite. Will that do?'

'Perfect, thank you.' He handed over his credit card, which he'd kept sewn into the broad hem of his tunic for precisely such an emergency. To his relief, it worked, and he remembered his pin number.

'Excellent. Here's your key. Breakfast is served between seven and nine and is included in the room rate. If you require dinner, the bar staff can rustle up a few things. There aren't really any restaurants around here. You'd have to go to the nearest big town.'

'No worries, that's fine. Thanks again.'

He took the key with a key ring in the shape of a Viking helmet with horns, which made him smile and cringe at the same time. It was a modern construct, as no Viking ever fought wearing anything of the sort – it would be incredibly impractical. The name of the motel was Asgard – as in the home of the Norse gods – another cause for amusement, but he didn't comment on it. Instead he took Ellisif's hand and tugged her outside again, looking for room seven.

'Ah, here we are.' He unlocked the door and allowed her to precede him. As Marit had said, the space was small, but it had a double bed with an invitingly soft duvet and four plump pillows. To the left of the entrance door was a bathroom with a shower, an extremely welcome sight as he suddenly felt very grubby compared to everyone in this century. And on the opposite side of the room a large window faced the forest behind the building. 'Let me show you a few things.'

He gave her a tour of the facilities, demonstrating how to turn the lights on and off, how to use the toilet and sink, and finally how the wall-mounted TV worked. She was silent the entire time and only nodded. He could tell she was teetering on the brink of overload and needed to simply process everything she was seeing and learning.

'Listen, why don't you sit down for a moment while I go and buy us something to eat and drink.' He'd decided to go to the supermarket rather than take her to the bar, as eating in a place like that would no doubt be too much for her at present. Plus everyone would stare at their outlandish clothing. 'Can you promise me that you'll stay right here and not go wandering off? I won't be long, I promise.'

'Very well.' She sank down into the room's only armchair and leaned her head back, closing her eyes. 'I'll rest for a moment.'

'Good. I'll try to hurry, but don't worry, nothing can hurt you here, you have my oath.'

Rushing down the road to the supermarket, he set a speed record for fastest shopping spree ever, buying everything he thought they might need. In order not to freak Ellisif out completely, he grabbed the simplest things he could find – plain white bread, cheese, bottled water and a couple of beers. He also added soap and shampoo, a comb, toothbrushes and toothpaste, and at the last minute, some condoms. They were in his time now, and he wasn't going to miss this opportunity to finally finish what they'd been skirting around for months. As long as she was willing, of course. Finally, he couldn't resist a couple of chocolate bars. He wanted to see what she'd make of those. He knew Hrafn and Rurik went crazy for them every time they visited the twenty-first century.

When he got back to the motel, he found Ellisif asleep in the chair, looking lost and rather vulnerable. The sight tugged at his heartstrings, and he finally allowed himself to acknowledge the truth that had been staring him in the face all winter – he was fathoms-deep in love with her. One way or another, he wanted them to be together. There were obstacles, yes; she had her life in the Viking era, with responsibilities she needed to shoulder, while his was here. In principle, he could have left his life behind – and he would, if there was no other way – but they should be able to work out some kind of compromise. A discussion was necessary, but it could wait. For now, he fully intended to enjoy the moment.

He put away the groceries in the room's mini fridge, then knelt before her, leaning forward to kiss her cheek.

'*Unnasta*,' he whispered. 'Want to come and bathe with me?'

'Hmm? What?' Her stunning peridot eyes blinked open. As she tried to focus on him, he made a mental note to take her to the supermarket in the morning to buy her a pair of glasses. He'd seen a stand with cheap ones. All she'd need to do was try different lenses until they found some that were perfect for her. She frowned at him. 'Did you say bathe? Isn't the fjord a bit cold still this time of year?'

He smiled. 'Probably, but we're not going there. We have our own bathing hut. Come, let me show you.'

Taking her hand, he pulled her up and over to the bathroom. There wasn't a lot of space after he'd closed the door, but enough for him to remove his belt and tug his tunic over his head, swiftly followed by his shirt. Ellisif gasped and stared at his naked chest.

'Ivar? What . . . ?'

'Trust me. You're going to love this. Please, undress. No need to be bashful. I've seen every part of you before, remember.' Although he'd only caught glimpses of her body that time in the hayloft as it had been so dark, it wasn't a sight he'd ever forget. Images from that evening had tormented him over and over again. The thought of being able to feast his eyes on all of her properly at last sent darts of lust arrowing through him, heading straight for his nether regions.

To his surprise, she shook her head. 'No, Ivar. It wouldn't be right.'

He stopped with his hands on the drawstring of his trousers. 'What? Why not? I thought . . .' He swallowed hard. Had he been presumptuous? Misread the situation? He'd been so sure she wanted him as much as he craved her. He put a hand on her cheek, stroking it softly. 'I'm sorry, *unnasta*. I didn't mean to rush you. If you're not ready for this, of course I'll abide by your wishes.'

A tear formed at the corner of her eye and made its way downwards as she took a step back. 'It's not that I don't want you,' she whispered, anguish making her voice crack. 'I do. I mean, I did. But I saw you. With her. The amulet showed me . . . the beautiful woman with red curls. You cannot dishonour her this way. I won't let you.'

'What woman?' Ivar scowled. Had the little charm played a trick on them?

Ellisif sighed. 'Tall, almost as tall as you. You were standing behind a turf house, holding her as if you never wanted to let go.'

'You mean Maddie!' he exclaimed, then started to laugh as he realised he hadn't had time to mention what – or rather whom – he'd found in Iceland. 'Sweeting, that was my sister, not my lover. She's been living there for the past year with her husband, but I had no idea. I was so relieved to find her. And I was comforting her, as she'd been having some problems, that is all.'

'Your sister?' She blinked at him. 'You're not enamoured of someone else?'

'Foster-sister, but still . . . And no, of course not. The only woman I want is you. Desperately!'

'Oh, thank the gods!' She moved forward and slumped against him, pressing her cheek to his bare chest. 'I'm sorry, I thought . . .'

He hugged her tight and kissed the top of her head. 'No need for apologies. It was understandable that you would jump to conclusions. But all is well, yes?' He pulled back a little to look her in the eyes.

She nodded. 'Yes. Yes, never better.'

Without further hesitation, she began to remove her garments, and he was left speechless as he took in the view before him. '*Wow!*' he breathed. The English word was the only thing that sprang to mind as he gazed at her gorgeous breasts, small waist and gently rounded hips. She was sheer perfection. He hurried to take off his shoes and trousers, and Ellisif seemed too busy staring at him to be self-conscious about her own naked state.

'You . . . you really want me.' Her gaze headed south, and a chuckle escaped him.

'That's rather obvious, I'm afraid.'

'But I thought you said we couldn't. You didn't want to take matters that far . . .' Confusion clouded her gaze yet again.

'We can in my time, without consequences. If you want to, that is? I'll explain it later.'

He stepped forward and put his arms around her, drawing her close. It was the first time they'd held each other this way, skin on skin, in full daylight – or electric light, as the case was right now. Every nerve ending was on high alert as her nipples pressed against his chest and his arousal nudged her stomach. They both shivered simultaneously, despite the warmth of her silky skin against his.

'Let's wash, and then I'm going to show you something wonderful. No, wait, first I'm going to teach you how to brush your teeth.'

'Brush . . . my teeth?'

He plopped toothpaste on to one of the new brushes and demonstrated the technique. She grimaced at the taste of peppermint at first, but seemed to get the hang of it. After she'd finished rinsing, she grinned at him in the mirror that took up the entire wall above the sink. 'That was very fresh. Cold almost, against my tongue.'

'Mm-hmm. And it makes kissing taste delicious.' He pulled her close again and tested this theory. There were no complaints.

Grabbing the soap and shampoo he'd bought, he guided her into the shower stall. Then he turned on the water and watched her eyes light up with wonder as the hot spray landed on her chest and shoulders. It was the best sight he'd seen for a long while, and it made him grin.

This was going to be such fun.

Ellisif was by now convinced that she'd died and gone to some unknown afterlife where everything was magical and wonderful. Her mouth still tingled from the strange white cream Ivar had made her wash her teeth with, not to mention his kisses afterwards. Now the hot water pouring down on to her tired body was quite simply amazing. When he began to soap her skin with gentle strokes, she closed her eyes and gave herself up to the sheer pleasure of it all. Every part of her quivered in the wake of his caresses, but he kept his movements fairly impersonal until they were both clean, with their hair washed and smelling like a meadow in full bloom.

Only then did he use the soap to deliberately touch her most sensitive parts.

She moaned as he rubbed her nipples, before rinsing them with water and replacing his fingers with his mouth and tongue. His hands travelled down across her stomach and around to cup her behind, stroking all the way. When he finally reached the juncture between her thighs, a sigh of contentment escaped her, and she heard him chuckle again. He seemed to be enjoying this as much as she was, even though he'd only allowed her to soap him a little bit.

His questing fingers brought her to an explosive release, her legs shaking and barely keeping her upright, but he wasn't done. As soon as she'd returned to earth, he hustled her out of the enclosed space, turning off the water and enveloping her in a fluffy piece of cloth. She'd never touched anything so soft, and revelled in its comforting embrace.

'This is like the finest goose down,' she murmured, stroking the material.

'You can admire it later. Dry off, *ást mín*,' Ivar urged, while doing the same to himself. When she took her time, he became impatient and helped her to finish the task more quickly. 'Come. I can't wait any longer,' he whispered, his voice deep with desire.

He lifted her up and placed her in the middle of the bed. It was so squishy she felt as if she was lying on top of a cloud. Stretching out beside her, he reached for a box on the table next to the bed and took out a small shiny parcel. 'This is something that will protect you from becoming with child,' he told her as he extracted a round item. 'Will you allow me to make love to you, Ellisif? Properly?'

It was what she'd wanted for months now, so she nodded and watched in fascination as he rolled the thing on to his member. The protection appeared to be see-through, and she had no idea how it worked, but she trusted him on this. He'd been so adamant about not getting her pregnant. If he said this would prevent that, she believed him. And she was not afraid he'd hurt her, the way Þjóðólfr always had. With Ivar, things would be vastly different, of that she was certain. He'd given her nothing but pleasure so far, and she was no longer afraid of the marital act. Not with him, at any rate.

He took her in his arms and kissed her, long and deep, his hands working their magic as they roamed her body and brought her close to another release.

'You are so beautiful. I feel as though I've wanted you for ever,' he whispered, his voice a husky growl.

As she hovered on the brink, at last he positioned himself above her and gazed into her eyes as he slid inside her. Ellisif felt as if she too had waited a lifetime for this moment. She could only stare back, seeing her own emotions reflected in his blue irises. He moved slowly at first, as if savouring the sensation, but soon he picked up the pace and she followed his rhythm instinctively. They stared at each other, their intense emotional connection adding something special to the occasion. It was glorious, and quite possibly the most incredible thing that had ever happened to her.

They climaxed together, crying out each other's names, and then he collapsed next to her and just held her tight. She never wanted to leave his embrace or this bed. Ever.

Chapter Twenty-Two

Birgirsby/Stavanger/Ulfstoft, June 2023/Sólmánuðr AD *876*

'This is unbelievable! I can see everything in such detail. How is this possible?'

Ivar had been watching Ellisif as she tried on glasses, searching for the pair that worked best for her. These appeared to be it. 'It's merely crystals, honed to the right thickness to help your particular problem.' He gestured to the others on the stand. 'As you see, there are various types, as everyone's eyes are different. Do you want those, then?'

'Yes, please!'

Her eyes were huge behind the lenses. He allowed himself to drown in their green depths for a moment, before recalling that they were in the middle of a supermarket and he couldn't very well push her against the nearest shelf and have his way with her. The mere thought of it made him want her again, but they'd already spent the better part of the previous night making up for lost time and were both a little sore now. Quite apart from the fact that they needed to get going.

'You will have to hide them when we return to Ulfstoft, though. It will be our secret.' He held out his hand for the glasses, and reluctantly she removed them and gave them to him.

'Can I confide in Askhild? That way, if I'm sewing with her in her private chamber, I could wear them. You did say you'd already told Thorald about where you came from, did you not?'

'Yes. As long as you swear her to secrecy. I wouldn't want any rumours about me to spread or a taint of *trolldomr* to fall on the settlement. People can be so suspicious.'

He didn't know for sure what the average Viking's attitude towards magic or unexplained phenomena was, but he didn't want to take any chances. And he couldn't risk someone trying to steal his magical shears, or he'd never be able to return home.

Not that he was in any hurry. Now that he was in his own century, he found himself longing to go back to the Viking era. Everything here was alien and somehow brash and too bright. He definitely wasn't ready to return to normal life quite yet.

'I will make sure Askhild keeps your secret, I promise.' Ellisif threw her arms around his neck and kissed him, making him stumble back. He had to put his arms around her to steady them both. Not a hardship at all and for a moment he hugged her closer. 'Thank you so much. You have no idea what this means to me,' she added.

He shook his head with a rueful smile. 'You're so easy to please. Most women would ask for gold and silver, but all you want are two polished crystals.'

'*Fifl.*' She punched him on the arm, grinning at him. With a flirtatious glance, she added, 'I'd never say no to gold and silver as well, I'll have you know.'

Ivar laughed. 'I didn't think so. Very well, how about I give you this?' He pulled off a thick silver ring and slid it on to her middle finger, which was the only one big enough for the ring not to fall off.

'Oh, I didn't mean . . .' Her cheeks turned rosy, tempting him to give her another kiss, which cut her off.

'I know. But I want you to have it to remember your time in the twenty-first century by. It's yours.'

'Thank you. I'll never forget.'

He was certain he wouldn't either.

He paid for the glasses and headed for a bus stop where he'd been told they'd find a bus service to Stavanger. From there, he'd look for another one heading north. The closer they could get to the fjord where Ulfstoft was situated, the better, as they wouldn't have so far to walk once they returned to the ninth century.

A bus was approaching, and he turned to Ellisif, watching her reaction to what she'd termed a large metallic beast when they'd seen one pass earlier, together with quite a few cars. 'Now remember what I told you – this wagon is not dangerous in any way and it will take us one step closer to our destination. Are you happy to trust me and ride in it?'

'Yes. I trust you in every way, Ivar.'

That made warmth spread through him, and he forgot his surroundings for a moment as he looked into her eyes. The truth of her words hit him in the gut. This amazing woman was prepared to take his word for anything. It was both a gift and a responsibility, and he hoped he'd never let her down. For now, they had a journey to make.

'Come then, let us be on our way.'

Ellisif flinched when the huge, shiny beast let out a loud hiss as if there were snakes or dragons hidden inside. Gamely, she followed Ivar up the steps and into a comfortable seat after he'd used his blue payment item once more. There were handles to grip as the wagon started moving, but she was too curious about it all to be truly afraid.

Large sheets of glass divided them from the outside, and as the beast gained momentum, forests and fields began to fly by. She watched in fascination, while the sensation of rapid movement tickled her stomach. With a grin, she turned to Ivar.

'This is amazing! I can't believe how fast we are travelling.'

He grinned back and squeezed her hand, which she hadn't realised he was holding. 'It is quite something, is it not? I'm glad you're enjoying it and taking it all in your stride.'

Eventually the novelty wore off and she relaxed enough to sleep for a while, her head leaning against Ivar's broad shoulder. When she woke again, they had reached an even larger settlement, bustling with people, wagons and all manner of strange sights. She sat up straight and tried to take it all in.

'Where are we?'

'This place is called Stavanger in my time. It is not too far from Avaldsnes and the Karmtsund strait. We'll need to journey north from here and I have to make enquiries as to how best to do that. There's no rush, though. Would you like to spend the night here if I can find a room?'

The twinkle in his eyes told her she'd be in for another night with not much sleep, but that was absolutely fine with her. She nodded. 'Yes, please. One ride in a beast each day is more than enough.'

That made him laugh and give her a tender kiss. Her insides twisted at the thought of how comfortable they were together. Like an old married couple who genuinely enjoyed each other's company. But they weren't a couple and there was no possibility of that ever being the case. This was his world and he'd always been honest with her, telling her he wasn't staying in hers. Having seen where he came from, she could understand it. Who would want to leave all these comforts for the hard work that awaited in her century? No one.

These thoughts made her breath hitch in her throat. Their time together would come to an end soon. No manner of wishful thinking would make it otherwise. She swallowed a sigh and followed him off the bus. At least they had some time together now. They'd have to make the most of it.

'Peets-aah? Sweet Freya, that smells good! Oh! Mmm . . .'

Ivar laughed at Ellisif's exaggerated pronunciation, and the expression of intense bliss on her face as she chewed her first bite of pizza Margherita. He'd figured it was best for her to start with the basic variety, then she could try his mushroom and pepperoni one with onions, peppers and extra cheese if she wanted. They were having takeaway in their hotel room, since he still wasn't sure she was ready for the full experience of a twenty-first-century restaurant. Besides, he wanted her all to himself.

'Here, let me.' He reached over and caught a piece of mozzarella that was dripping down her chin, licking it off his finger.

Her eyes opened wider, and she stilled for a moment as she followed his movements. She swallowed hard, then closed her eyes without saying anything. He gathered she'd found it sensual but didn't know how to express that. Her lack of experience in such matters was immensely endearing, but at the same time, she was learning fast, and he wanted to be the one teaching her. Always.

He wanted to spend the rest of his life with her.

So far, she had taken everything in her stride. Once she'd accepted that time travel was real, and that they really were in another century, she'd bombarded him with questions and was drinking it all in. He was proud of the way she coped with every new experience and embraced it. She'd made him join her for several more showers, so she could stand under the running water. She'd also spent ages inspecting the various electrical gadgets and light fittings. Whenever they were outside, she held on tightly to his hand, but looked around with fascination, absorbing all she saw. Nothing seemed to faze her unduly, although it was inevitable that sudden noises like car horns would make her jump. Only the first few times, though; after that, she relaxed.

Perhaps she was also ready to listen to his suggestions for their future now the reality of his origins had sunk in? He decided to risk it. They didn't have much time left here and he wanted matters to be settled between them before they returned.

'Tomorrow we should be able to travel north to a place near Ulfstoft and return to your time,' he told her.

'Mm-hmm.' She ducked her head and concentrated on picking up another pizza slice, having more or less inhaled the first one.

'Ellisif, when we get back there, will you please marry me?'

She choked on the bite she'd just taken, and he cursed himself for an impatient fool. He should have waited until they'd finished eating, but the words were waiting to tumble out of him. Now that he'd decided on a course of action, he didn't want to wait any longer.

'What . . . did you say?' She coughed, and Ivar handed her a soft drink, which also proved to be a mistake, as the bubbles went up her nose and made her wheeze.

He shook his head and chuckled. 'I'm sorry. I shouldn't have sprung it on you like that. Especially not right now. Forgive me. I'm an oaf.'

She clutched his arm. 'No, say it again,' she demanded. 'I didn't think I heard you right.'

He took both her hands in his and regarded her earnestly. 'I was asking you to marry me. After what we shared last night, I think it's clear that we are extremely compatible, and I can't bear the thought of losing you. Of not having you in my life. I know you are afraid of marriage, but I will swear an oath in front of witnesses not to interfere with the running of your domains. To always be a kind and considerate husband. I would never beat you. Never demean you or belittle you, I promise. Will you take a chance on me? Please?'

Moisture shimmered in her eyes, and she nodded. 'I would like that above all things, Ivar, but . . . what about all this?' She gestured to the room and the city outside their windows. 'This is your world. How could you bear to leave it and stay in mine?'

'Well, I've been thinking about that. It should be possible to find a trustworthy man – or woman – to oversee your property for a few months every year. Perhaps as much as half the year. Then you could come with me to spend time in my era while I do the work I'm trained to do. What do you think? Could you envisage yourself here for any length of time?'

'I . . . don't know. I hadn't thought of that.'

'If you can't, I'll understand. It's a lot to ask and I will content myself with the odd visit alone to see my family, if that's how it has to be. Before you make up your mind, though, you might want to see my home back in Svíaríki. It's a lovely place and I think you'd like it.'

'That sounds like a good idea. But . . . you want to marry me either way?'

'Yes, if you'll have me and you are certain you can trust me.' He guessed she was nearly there, if she wasn't already, and he didn't want to pressure her in any way. It had to be her decision. The last thing he wanted after what she'd been through was to coerce her.

'I do,' she whispered, stroking his cheek and smiling at him. 'You have rather surprised me, but in the best possible way. To tell you the truth, I'm a little overwhelmed.'

He leaned forward to kiss her. 'I know. There's no need to make up your mind this instant, but think about it, yes? I'll give you some time to mull it over.'

'Thank you.' She shivered and shook her head. 'I thought for sure . . .'

'What, *unnasta*?' Pulling her close, he hugged her to his chest.

'That I was going to lose you once we returned. Perhaps not straight away, but soon. And I . . . I didn't want to.' She nestled into him. 'I was so afraid.'

Her confession made him overcome with emotion, and he had to clear his throat. 'I'm here now and I'm not leaving you. We can talk about it some more in a week or two. I'm content to wait, now I know you're not totally opposed to the idea.'

And meanwhile, he would take full advantage of the night stretching before them because once they were back in the Viking age, he wouldn't sleep with her again until they were married.

'Odin's ravens! I don't think I'll ever get used to that whirling sensation.' Ivar sat up and tried to control his breathing so as to keep the nausea at bay.

Through a combination of bus journeys and hitchhiking, they'd reached a place not too far from where he reckoned Ulfstoft was situated. Then they'd used the magical shears to return to Ellisif's time. He looked around and could no longer see the village that had been visible before they performed the magic. That must mean they'd succeeded, or at least he hoped so.

'*Unnasta*, are you all right?'

She was lying next to him on a bed of moss, and groaned as she pushed herself into a sitting position. 'That is vile,' she muttered. 'I hope we don't have to do that again any time soon.'

He didn't remind her that she would need to repeat the process twice a year if she agreed to his proposal. This was not the time to discuss the matter further, so he concentrated on the here and now.

'Are you ready? Let's go and see if we can find the settlement. It shouldn't be too far.'

That proved to be correct, and as they walked into the yard, they were greeted with hugs, smiles and cries of joy.

Thorald pulled Ivar in for a man-hug, extremely pleased to see them judging by the huge grin on his face. 'You succeeded! That's a relief. We were starting to worry, especially as Oddr and Gaukr returned ages ago.'

'I told you to have faith in me,' Ivar teased. 'Did you think I'd fail?' He hadn't been sure himself, so this was pure bravado, but his kinsman growled and punched him lightly on the shoulder.

'*Fífl!* Of course I knew you wouldn't fail. Just wondering what took you so long.' Thorald glanced at Ellisif, who was fairly glowing. 'Although I think I can guess.'

'*Þegi þu!*' muttered Ivar, but he didn't deny it, and Thorald chuckled.

In the meantime, Ellisif had been reunited with Askhild, and the two women headed indoors, chatting and laughing. He stared after them, pushing away the wistfulness and tenderness that welled up inside him. Their days and nights together had been perfect, and he wished they could have had longer. But he knew they had to straighten matters out properly before that could happen, and he would be patient.

'Let's go for a walk.' Thorald gestured towards the forest. 'I want to hear what happened and what we are up against if we decide to attack Kári.'

With a last glance at the women walking into the hall, Ivar followed his kinsman. He would give Ellisif all the time she needed to make a final decision. It was the least he could do.

Chapter Twenty-Three

Ulfstoft, June–July/Sólmánuðr–Heyannir AD *876*

As it turned out, there were no opportunities for attacking Kári and reclaiming Birgirsby during the next few weeks, as events overtook their plans. At first, there was the midsummer celebration to prepare for. That required everyone to pitch in and help with hunting and fishing to replenish food stocks. Ivar hardly saw Ellisif, except at night, when he snuck on to her sleeping bench and allowed himself to hold her.

She hadn't given him a definite reply yet, but the way she welcomed him so eagerly made him certain that all would be well. He didn't want to pressure her, especially as he'd rather sprung his proposal on her when they were in Stavanger. She was probably still processing the fact that he came from the future. Deciding whether to join him there for part of every year was a huge decision. One only she could make.

Then there were rumours flying round about a huge clash being imminent between King Haraldr and his allies on the one side, and his enemies from Vestfold and Denmark on the other. Messengers arrived at the settlement from both parties, trying to gauge where Thorald and Álrik's loyalties lay, and whether they could count on their support in a possible battle.

'Make no mistake, King Haraldr is ruthless, and should you be on the losing side, he will not forgive or forget,' one messenger warned, while others pointed out that the kings of Denmark had no intention of losing to this 'upstart'. It would seem this king was making quite a name for himself, but not everyone appreciated his methods.

Talking it over in private with Thorald, Ivar echoed the messenger's sentiments, adding, 'I know for a fact that Haraldr will win, so it would behove you to be on his side in this conflict.'

'You are sure about that?'

'Yes. Even in my time, the coming battle is still talked about. It will take place at Hafrsfjordr, which is somewhere south of here, is it not? Didn't we pass it on the way to Birgirsby?' It was close to Stavanger, but he couldn't say that, as he wasn't sure that town existed in Viking times.

'Yes, I believe so. And I'll take your word for it that Haraldr will prevail,' Thorald declared, and soon sent the messenger on his way with promises of their support for him.

Personally, Ivar was unsure what to do. He'd come to the past in order to get to know his kinsman if possible, something he'd now achieved. His other goal had been to study everything in the Viking age and learn as much as he could about the time and the people. That too he had done, although it could be argued that he would never be completely finished. There were probably an infinite number of additional things to find out about. He hadn't decided on a time frame beforehand and could, in principle, have left at any time when he decided he had enough information.

In fact, he could leave now and avoid the upcoming battle, but that felt wrong. Cowardly.

Without even realising how much, he had become an intrinsic part of this little community, and Thorald was his kin. As much of a brother as Storm had ever been. He cared about the man and everyone else at Ulfstoft. There was no doubt in his mind that if they'd been together in the twenty-first century and threatened by war, neither would have hesitated to help the other by any means necessary. Was it any different here?

And then there was the added complication of Ellisif. If she agreed to marry him – and he was fairly certain she would – he wouldn't merely be a visitor in this century. He'd be a part of it for at least half of every year, and have obligations to the people in her settlement. Presumably that included fighting on their behalf, but he hadn't counted on having to take part in actual battles. To put his life on the line for a cause that wasn't really his. Yes, he was trained for warfare, but he wasn't a naturally violent man and had no wish to kill anyone. Well, anyone else, since he'd already taken a life, albeit not on purpose.

I could die! But so could the others if he didn't help them. A cold sliver of dread snaked down his spine. He owed them his allegiance.

He was still mulling things over when someone else arrived at the settlement. Ivar was busy chopping wood one morning when a small rowing boat hove to down by the jetty and a young man jumped out. After tying the boat to a mooring post, the newcomer strode up the hill. Ivar went to greet him while surreptitiously scanning the perimeters of the settlement for movement.

'Kell, what are you doing here?' The man had arrived alone, but others could be hiding in the forests all around.

'I'm following your advice.' Kell came to a halt in front of him as Thorald and a few others rushed to join them. They stopped behind Ivar, allowing him to take the lead in this situation, for which he was grateful, as it showed their trust in him.

'And what would that be?'

'To ally myself with those who'll be fighting on King Haraldr's side. My father is firmly in the other camp, but I found myself believing more in your words than his blind faith in King Hjorr.' Kell spread his hands and shrugged. 'So here I am, hoping you'll allow me to join you. I'm willing to work hard until the time comes for the battle, and I will swear an oath of fealty to whoever owns this settlement.'

'You definitely came alone?' Ivar couldn't see anyone lurking nearby, but he needed to be sure.

'Yes. I left at night, after everyone else had gone to sleep.' Kell snorted. 'I doubt they noticed until they needed someone to run errands the next day.' He sounded sincere, and as he'd already proved to be an ally, Ivar decided to trust him.

'Very well.' He turned to Thorald. 'What say you – shall we welcome him to Ulfstoft?' He communicated with his eyes that he considered it safe to do so.

'Yes. Welcome, Kell Kárisson. You are just in time to help with shearing.'

Kell smiled. 'One of my favourite tasks. Lead on.'

Ellisif was very pleased to see Kell, since Ivar had told her how Kári's youngest son had helped him to free her by going along with his plan. He'd proved himself to be trustworthy and she was glad Thorald accepted him too.

Someone else who seemed extremely happy was Hedda. The girl was obviously head over heels in love, and turned beet red when she caught sight of Kell. She was still very young and impressionable, and Ellisif hoped she wouldn't have her heart broken. Hopefully Kell felt the same way, but it was early days. She said as much to Ivar when they met up in the hayloft a few days after the young man's arrival. He'd asked to speak to her in private, and as it was raining, this place was better than a walk in the forest.

'I'm glad he listened to you and came here,' she added. 'I would hate to think of him being under Kári's thumb for the rest of his life. Hopefully he'll survive the upcoming battle and perhaps receive a reward for his services.'

'Mm, maybe.' Ivar seemed subdued, and so far he hadn't taken her in his arms either. They were merely sitting side by side in the hay as they chatted.

A knot of anxiety formed in her stomach. 'What's the matter? What are you thinking about?'

He sighed and looked away. 'The battle. You do know I'll have to fight, don't you? And there is a very real possibility that I won't live to see the next day. I . . . I think it best if we wait to consider marriage until we see how it goes.'

'You don't want to marry me any longer?' Dread settled like a quern stone in her stomach, because she'd been about to tell him she was certain she wished to wed him now. She held her breath, waiting for his reply. She'd tried to hide the hurt in her voice, but he must have noticed it, as he turned to face her, cupping her cheek with one hand.

'*Unnasta*, no, that's not what I meant. I want you, more than I could ever say, but there's no point marrying now if I'll be dead in a few weeks' time. I know that King Haraldr will be victorious. This battle is going to be so big and important that even the people of my time have heard about it. But the fighting will be fierce and brutal. An awful lot of men will die. I have to be realistic – one of them could be me.' He turned his anguished gaze on her. 'And what if you're already pregnant at that point? *Ást mín*, I can't bear the thought of leaving you behind to cope with all that on your own. Of leaving both you *and* a child. You would probably recover and perhaps marry again one day, but our baby would never know its father.'

'I can't have children, I've told you. And I wouldn't have to cope on my own. I'm sure I can stay here. Askhild would never throw me out. I'll be fine.'

'We cannot be certain, and I'm simply not prepared to risk it. Please, Ellisif, let us take things one step at a time. I need to concentrate on readying myself for battle. If we were to wed now, I'd be distracted, and that could lead to me making mistakes.'

He didn't use the word 'fatal', but it hung in the air between them.

Ellisif had come to the hayloft prepared to tell him yes. Yes to marriage. Yes to spending half of every year in the future. Yes to anything he wanted, basically, because she couldn't imagine a future without him. But she understood his reasoning and had no choice but to agree with it, because it made sense, even if it was very far from what she would wish.

She nodded. 'Very well. We will wait. Just promise me one thing.'

'Anything.'

'Do your utmost to stay alive, and don't take any stupid risks.'

His blue eyes were solemn as he bent to give her a tender kiss. 'I promise.'

She would pray to all the gods to keep him unharmed.

Ivar's days were taken up with chores around the settlement, interspersed with a lot of training for the upcoming battle. He joined in with the sparring and weapons practice. It was good to keep in shape, and he was learning techniques he'd never been taught before. He found it fascinating, and tried to push thoughts of how real it all was to the back of his mind. If he allowed himself to think about the fact that he was training for actual bloodshed, he'd lose his focus. That would never do, and he'd promised Ellisif to try and stay alive. In order to do that, he needed to be as prepared as possible.

There were times he didn't succeed, however, and Thorald noticed.

'What ails you, man?' His kinsman scowled at him. He'd just taken Ivar by surprise and wrestled him to the ground without any problems. 'You need to keep your mind on what you're doing or you'll be dead within the first moments of the battle.'

'I know, I know. Forgive me. I'll do better, I promise.'

'Make sure of it.' Thorald fixed him with a glare. 'If we're to come through the conflict alive, I need you by my side with your focus firmly on everything going on around you. Want to talk later?'

Ivar shook his head. 'No, thanks. It's something I have to figure out by myself.' How to turn off the worry about Ellisif, and the regret that their perfect future might not come to pass.

Oh, stop being such a glass-half-empty kind of guy, he admonished himself. Why was he thinking the worst when it hadn't happened yet? What was the point? That wasn't how a Viking saw things, and he needed to adopt their mindset if he was to survive.

A part of him had secretly been hoping for some other solution to present itself, but Thorald's words made him realise one thing – his kinsman expected him to fight with him, and there was no other choice. He would need every available man if they were to come through this alive and victorious. If Ivar left now, he'd be letting the other man down. The relationship he'd fought so hard to build between them would be gone, because Thorald would see it as a betrayal at best, and cowardice at worst.

Swallowing hard, he faced the indisputable fact that he, a twenty-first-century archaeologist, would be taking part in the Battle of Hafrsfjordr. To all intents and purposes, he was a Viking.

* * *

'Excellent shot, Ellisif! You've improved no end. And you too, Hedda and Askhild.'

Hedda's cheeks turned pink with pleasure at the compliment from Kell, who strode over to the target to retrieve their arrows. He'd taken to teaching the women archery, as the king's messenger had said that all archers would be needed in the upcoming battle, male or female. To Ellisif's surprise, she'd proven good at it, and enjoyed learning a new skill. Being around Kell was no hardship either, as he was happy and easy-going most of the time, and a great teacher. But as for developing feelings for him or seeing him as a possible husband, as Ivar had suggested so long ago, there was no way. Try as she might, she could never imagine him as anything but a friend, and for his part, he treated her more like an older sister.

Hedda was a different matter. The girl was keen to do anything that involved Kell, and the two of them were together more often than not, making eyes at each other. In the unlikely event that Ellisif had ever contemplated marriage with the young man, she couldn't have done that to her cousin. She wasn't that cruel.

Besides, she didn't want him. She wanted the stubborn time traveller who was avoiding her since their exchange in the hayloft.

A part of her understood that it was self-preservation on his part. That he needed to concentrate on his battle preparations without being distracted by her. And yet she longed for him to merely spend time with her, talking and holding hands. Yearned to be able to tell the world that she was his wife. Because she wanted to be, desperately.

She'd come to acknowledge that he'd been right about one thing – she was no longer afraid of the wedded state. Or at least she wouldn't be if he was the man she was married to. To stay unwed for the rest of her life because of what Þjódólfr had done to her made no sense now that she knew what conjugal bliss was like. The only problem was how to persuade Ivar that marrying her wouldn't make him worry about her more. In fact, should the worst happen, she'd be safer as his widow than as an unwed heiress, of that she was certain.

Making her way back to the hall, she contemplated her options. Was there any way of changing his mind? She wasn't hopeful, but she'd do her utmost to try.

Chapter Twenty-Four

Hafrsfjordr, July/Heyannir AD *876*

'Are you sure it's a good idea to bring the women?'

Ivar glanced around the two crowded ships that were to transport half of Ulfstoft's inhabitants down to Hafrsfjordr, and frowned when his gaze snagged on Ellisif. She sat with Askhild and Hedda, the three of them wearing identical expressions of determination and stubbornness. He'd seen them practising their archery skills and knew that they could hold their own. They also wouldn't be in the front line of any battle, but the mere thought of them – of her – being present and so close to danger made his insides turn to ice.

He wanted her safe and well at home, not in the middle of mayhem and destruction. It had never occurred to him that she wouldn't be staying behind where he wouldn't have to worry about her.

'They'll be fine.' Thorald appeared calm as he steered his ship away from the jetty. 'Do you really think I'd bring my wife and son if I thought they'd be at risk? We'll make camp inland, far from the battle site. And as far as I understand, the archers will be positioned high up on a ridge and not in harm's way. Stop fretting.'

'Who says I'm fretting?' Ivar asked with a scowl, but that merely made his kinsman laugh.

'I don't suppose your discontent has anything to do with the amount of time they've spent in Kell's company recently?'

'No, not at all.' But they both knew it was a lie.

Ivar was jealous of the younger man, pure and simple. He'd resented every moment Kell and Ellisif practised together, even though he had no right to any such emotion. He should be happy that they got on well. He should be pleased if she changed her mind and married Kell instead of him. That would kill two birds with one stone – Kell would gain property and status and be able to oust his father from Birgirsby, and Ellisif would have a husband young enough to give her children. One, moreover, who was a thoroughly nice man.

The fact that Kell was kind and considerate should also have pleased Ivar, but instead it made him resent the younger man more. It was madness, and definitely not logical, but who said love was logical?

And he was most certainly in love. What he felt for Ellisif was different to anything he'd ever experienced before. A deep, visceral knowledge that she was the woman for him. That they belonged together and he'd do anything for her. Anything at all. And that he couldn't bear to see her hurt.

In need of distraction, once the sail had been hoisted Ivar went to sit next to Thorald. 'Please tell me more about King Haraldr. What do you know about him?'

'Well, he's the son of Hálfdan Svarti – the Black – of Hringaríki, who died when his son had only seen ten winters. A drowning accident, or so I've been informed. The boy was apparently raised by his maternal grandfather, Haraldr Gullskeggi – Goldbeard – of Sogn. I believe Haraldr inherited his father's domains, as well as those of his grandfather eventually, which gave him the means to entice warriors to his side. He began to fight while still a mere youth and managed to beat those who were scheming to take what was his. He's still young and hungry for power now. I'm told he has a reputation for ruthlessness and strategy; he's a force to be reckoned with. And violence. I wouldn't want to get on his bad side, that's for certain, as he can be brutal in the extreme.'

'That tallies with what I've heard too.' Ivar nodded. Or rather what he'd read in his time, but he didn't mention that. 'And now he's made alliances with other powerful men in order to do battle with the kings and chieftains from the east, as well as the Danes.'

'Indeed. He has Hákon Grjotgardsson, the jarl of Trøndelag, on his side, as well as the great chieftain Rögnvaldr of Møre. Not to mention countless others. You did say he'll be victorious in this conflict, did you not? It stands to reason that he has many allies.'

'Yes, I'm sure he has enough.' Ivar crossed his fingers, hoping that travelling back in time didn't mean he'd changed the course of history. What if he was wrong and Haraldr lost? Then he would have given Thorald and everyone else bad advice. He had to hope that wasn't the case.

'We're up against some formidable foes, though,' Thorald mused. 'Not only King Hjorr, but all the Agder and Vestfold chieftains, as well as a Danish contingent. There are rumours that men are coming from as far away as Írland, Ísland and the Suðureyar.'

'Hmm, we'll have to hope they are tired from their journeys then,' Ivar commented.

It was no wonder this battle had resonated through the ages. With such huge forces taking part, it would have enormous consequences. He couldn't tell Thorald, but if all went as he expected it to and Haraldr proved victorious, it would go down in history as the beginning of Norway as a unified nation. To think that he would be a part of this was mind-boggling in so many ways. Perhaps even an honour.

It took them all day to find their way to Hafrsfjordr. The entrance was protected by a small, narrow sound, which would probably be easy to defend or cut off if necessary. It couldn't be more than four or five metres wide at low tide, and Ivar caught himself holding his breath as they sailed through. They continued into the fjord, past some islands and islets, then turned left into a huge, round bay, like a basin or pool, where literally hundreds of ships were moored. Along the shore were boathouses too, twenty to forty metres long. They were similar in shape to upside-down ships made of planks. From inside came sounds of hammering and other carpentry work, as if more vessels were being readied. There was no doubt that there was a whole lot of nautical power concentrated in this one place.

As soon as they entered the bay, the wind died down and the seas calmed. In the shelter of the surrounding hills there was a settlement of maybe twenty to thirty houses, one large enough to be the king's residence. Around the perimeter of the basin, they also spied several forts. Ivar counted five, and someone on board named a few of them.

'That's Haga to the west, Reynibjarg and Ytribjarg to the east, and up there to the north is Ullarlandshaugr mountain.'

The whole place was seriously impressive. Ivar's breath caught in his throat as he thought about the fact that he was about to experience one of the turning points in Norway's history. If only he lived to tell the tale, he'd be a very lucky man. But that was a big if.

'How many ships do you think are here?' he asked Thorald.

'Don't know. Upwards of a hundred, if not more. The messenger mentioned that the king was hoping to gather at least five thousand men. No doubt his opponents will do the same.'

Ivar digested that. Five thousand was a huge number for this time period. Twice that equalled ten thousand. He doubted anyone had ever seen that many people gathered in one place before, except perhaps in Anglo-Saxon Britain, where the Great Heathen Army was rampaging at the moment, if he remembered correctly. He'd never heard of a fleet of this size, though. It was exceptional.

With that much power, he'd have to hope that King Haraldr really did win. Anything else didn't bear thinking about.

They carried their tents and supplies a good way inland on the northern side of the bay to where others had set up camp to the left of Ullarlandshaugr mountain. Thorald figured there was safety in numbers.

'Also on this side it's possible to head north to reach the coast, if that should become necessary. We wouldn't want to be trapped, and we can moor the smaller ship north of here, as we won't need it for the battle. I'll leave two of my men behind with orders to get the women and Thorulf to safety if anything should happen to the rest of us. I'm not taking any chances.'

Ellisif knew he was concerned about Askhild and their son. He'd insisted on bringing them because he was afraid Ulfstoft could be attacked while he was away and he'd rather have them with him. A few trusted men had been left in charge of the settlement, but there was no way Thorald would leave his little family behind. Álrik had insisted on coming along to fight too. The boy had now seen seventeen winters, and had filled out considerably, but he was still way too young for warfare in Ellisif's opinion. Still, that wasn't for her to decide, and the other men saw nothing wrong with him taking part.

'Do you want help with that?'

She looked up to find Ivar pointing at the pieces of tent she was attempting to assemble. It was the first time he'd spoken to her since they'd left Ulfstoft, and the sound of his voice made her stomach flutter, while her heart did a somersault. She ought to ignore him, as he'd been doing to her, but he was trying to be helpful, so it would be churlish to refuse.

'Yes, please.'

They worked together in silence, constructing the tent the way they'd done on the way from Skiringssal. Thinking about those first weeks of their acquaintance brought a lump to her throat. She'd been terrified, but at the same time life had seemed full of possibilities and excitement. All because of the man next to her.

'You will be careful, won't you?' he said gruffly once the tent was finished.

'I was about to say the same to you.' She stared into his blue eyes, so familiar and dear to her now. The thought that she might lose him in the next few days sent a shaft of pain knifing through her innards, even though he wasn't truly hers yet. 'This isn't really your fight.'

He shrugged. 'It is now. I can't let Thorald do this on his own. He has no one else . . . and neither do I.'

She wanted to shout, 'You have me!' but held her tongue. 'Ivar, I . . .'

He closed his eyes and came over to embrace her. His strong arms closed around her and she burrowed into his chest, breathing in the familiar scent of him. 'Don't, Ellisif. Just promise me you'll be happy, whatever the outcome. That's all I ask. Take care of yourself and live life to the full. Please?'

She only nodded, because she didn't trust herself to speak.

'I'll see you later at the *blōt*.' With that, he crushed her to him one last time, then turned and strode off, presumably to share a tent with some of the other men.

Ellisif stared after him, her fists clenched. She didn't want things to end this way between them, but what else could she do?

The king made his way personally around the various campsites, and greeted each and every one of the chieftains who had come to fight on his behalf. Ivar didn't speak to the man, but he watched him and was impressed by his confident manner and aura of invincibility. It was clear to see that this was a leader of men – and women – and one to be reckoned with. He didn't need the trappings of fine clothing and jewellery to show that he was in charge. He was the epitome of steely determination wrapped inside a kid glove. Tall and muscular, with a tangle of blond tresses that looked to have grown wild for some time, he wasn't merely handsome, but charismatic as well. He had the qualities needed to make others obey him, and at the same time he could charm people into doing his will. A lethal combination.

Later that evening, a huge crowd congregated at the top of Ullarlandshaugr, the tallest mountain around the fjord, albeit at some distance from the water. The sun was going down, staining the sky in vivid pinks, lilacs and purples, but the light was still good and the air incredibly pure and fresh. Up here, there were extensive views in every direction, and the bay was clearly visible, with the islands further out. Any approaching ships could be seen long before they passed through the narrow sound. Ivar guessed it would take quite a while for the enemy to enter and rally inside the fjord. No doubt that had been Haraldr's intention, as it gave him a distinct advantage. Anyone coming in that way would immediately begin to feel trapped – he knew he would.

'Why are we here again?' he whispered to Thorald, who was holding tight to Askhild's hand so as not to lose her and their son in the throng. Ivar wished he could do the same with Ellisif, but he didn't have that right yet. Instead he kept an eye on her as best he could.

'The king is going to make a sacrifice to the god Ullr to ask for help with the coming battle. You invoke him for luck. He is also the god of archery, so it behoves our womenfolk to beg for his assistance as well.'

Ivar assumed the mountain was named for this god, so it made sense to pray to him here.

Several animals were slaughtered, and Ivar heard chanting and incantations. Then Haraldr's voice rang out, loud and clear. He asked for help from the gods, for strength and courage, and above all for victory against his enemies. Others joined in, their shouts echoing over the mountaintop. As he wasn't standing close to the king, Ivar couldn't see exactly what was going on, but he preferred it that way. To him, the killing of some poor beast seemed pointless, and he'd rather not be splashed during the ritual. He might believe in magic, and suspect that the Norse gods had had a hand in his time travelling, but he didn't think they needed to be appeased with blood. Not to this extent, at any rate.

Still, it wasn't up to him.

After the ceremony, a sense of excitement rippled through the crowd as everyone returned to their campfires. Ale casks were brought out, tales were told and laughter rang out.

'You'd never think these people were on the verge of something as serious as a battle,' Ivar muttered. He was nursing a single mug of ale, since he'd prefer to have a clear head the following day.

'Oh, they know, make no mistake, but this could be their last night in this life, so they're going to make the most of it,' Thorald replied, swallowing the last of his own ale. 'As am I. We'll see you on the morrow.'

He stood up, grabbed Askhild's hand and pulled her towards their tent, ignoring the teasing remarks being aimed their way.

Ivar glanced over towards Ellisif, who was sitting on the other side of the fire, and found her staring at him with an expression of pure anguish. Kell was nowhere to be seen, and neither was Hedda. He hadn't noticed them slipping away, but he could guess that they'd gone together. The two youngsters only had eyes for each other. Ivar had to acknowledge that he'd never really had any cause for jealousy where Kell was concerned.

Studying the beautiful woman across the flames, his heart ached. What if he never saw her again? They could both be killed tomorrow, although the likelihood of it being him was much higher, since he'd be in the front line. She wanted to marry him. Hadn't been fazed by the thought of being left pregnant. And thinking about it, a child might be the only thing left of him if he fell in battle. It would be a consolation. Something for her to focus on. Could he really deny her the possibility of that? Deny himself the chance of leaving some part of him behind?

She stood up abruptly and sent him a glance over her shoulder, as if inviting him to follow her. He waited a few beats before obeying her siren call. There was no way he could resist her. Not now. Not ever. It had been futile to try.

When she crawled into her tent a few moments later, he was hot on her heels. As she turned around, he took her in his arms and pulled her towards his chest. She came willingly.

'Ivar . . . ?'

'*Ást mín*, I need you,' he breathed. 'I love you. Give me this night, please.'

'Yes! I love you too, and I want that. So much.' She knelt before him and put her mouth on his. It was the only invitation he needed.

All sense flew out the window. He was a man possibly living out his final hours, and he wanted to spend them with her. Kissing her, caressing her, making love to her. He wanted her like no other, and he knew he always would. It would seem she felt the same. *Thank the gods!*

'Give me all of you, Ivar. Now!' she urged, and he didn't hold back. He would make it the best night of her life.

When Ivar woke the following morning, he had a strong sense of déjà vu. He was curled around a soft woman, her back to his front, and her red-gold hair glinted in the sunlight that made its way in through the tent fabric. This was how it had all started, but was it also how it would end? The thought made him swallow hard. Best not to think about that now, because there was no turning back. He'd chosen his path and had to stick to it if he was to keep his honour intact.

He placed a soft kiss on her neck, underneath her ear, and she sighed and snuggled closer. 'Ivar,' she whispered, her voice husky with sleep. 'I love waking up next to you.'

'Mm, me too.' He'd like nothing better than to wake with her in his arms every day for the rest of his life. But would that be his fate? He had no idea, and there was no point debating the issue now.

It was almost time to leave, and he'd be a fool not to make the most of the time they did have. They'd made love several times during the night, but his body wasn't quite sated yet. *Just one more time . . .* She was only wearing her *serk*, and when his fingers stroked a path up her thigh underneath it, she didn't resist. He whispered, '*Ást mín*, I have to go in a moment, but—'

She cut him off with a tender kiss that quickly turned more passionate. He was shirtless, as it had been a warm summer night, and her questing fingers soon pushed his linen trousers off, while he got rid of her shift. There was no time for finesse. It was all urgent caresses, tongues and lips, moans and whispered endearments. They made love fiercely, as if their lives depended on it, and he tried not to think about the fact that it might be the last time he ever touched her. The sounds she made, the sensation of supple curves underneath his hands, the intoxicating scent of her – it was all imprinted on his brain, stored away in case this was the only chance they would ever have.

Breathing heavily, he clasped her to him afterwards and buried his face in her glorious hair. '*Unnasta*, if there is a child, I want us to be married. You were right, it was foolish to wait. I won't be any less worried about you either way.'

She stroked the back of his head and tugged on his hair until he hovered above her, looking into her eyes. 'Ivar, if there is a child and you're not with me, I won't care.'

'But I do. I wouldn't want your reputation tarnished because of me, and I'd like the child to carry my name. A tiny Ivarsson or Ivarsdóttir. Please, come outside. Quickly. There is still time.'

'Very well.'

They dressed in a hurry, and he tugged her out of the tent and over to the burnt-out fire, where Thorald stood with some of the other men, preparing to leave.

'Listen, everyone,' Ivar began. 'I wish you all to witness mine and Ellisif's marriage. We want to pledge ourselves to each other as man and wife right now, in this moment, and for as long as we both shall live. Does that make it legal and binding?'

Thorald nodded. 'If I tie your wrists together and you both swear an oath, then that is so.' Someone handed him a piece of leather cord and he wound it round their arms several times. 'Now say it again.'

'I, Ivar Thoresson, take Ellisif Birgirsdóttír to be my wife from this day forward, and pledge to love and honour her always.' He had no idea if that was the correct wording for a wedding ceremony, but it sounded about right and came from the heart.

Ellisif smiled, but there were tears hovering on her lashes as she made her own vow, echoing his words, and added, 'I am yours, Ivar. For ever.'

'We all bear witness to this union,' Thorald pronounced, unwinding the cord from their wrists, and the others present murmured their agreement. 'May the gods be with you and your marriage be one of happiness and good fortune.'

'Thank you.' Ivar nodded to them all, then pulled Ellisif slightly out of the way. He caressed her cheek and gazed deep into her peridot eyes, storing the memory of their exact colour in his mind. 'Look after yourself, my love, and hopefully I will see you after the battle. Oh, and take these, please.' He pulled off most of his arm rings and handed them to her. 'You can keep them safe for me until I return.'

They both knew that might not be the case, and that he wanted her to be provided for in any eventuality, but she didn't voice her fears on that score, merely nodded. 'Good fortune, and may the gods be with you.'

With one last kiss, he walked away. If he'd stayed even one more second, he would never have been able to leave, but he was at peace in a way he hadn't been for weeks. Whatever happened, he was Ellisif's husband. Nothing could change that.

Chapter Twenty-Five

Hafrsfjordr, July/Heyannir AD 876

'This is an incredible sight!'

Ivar put up a hand to shield his eyes against the glare of the sun as he took in the impressive rows of Viking ships lined up in the bay of Hafrsfjordr. There were literally hundreds, stretched out across the widest part of the fjord. He'd never seen anything like it. Huge warships, their sterns decorated with snarling beasts or dragon's heads, were placed in the centre of the two opposing lines. King Haraldr's was in the middle, its back to the shore.

Ivar had been told that the king's *hirð* consisted mostly of berserkers and so-called *ulfhednar*. Both were special warriors, bare-chested but swathed in bear- and wolfskins respectively, who apparently fought like men possessed. Next to the king, on one side, was Rögnvaldr of Møre in his dragon ship, and on the other Hákon Grjotgardsson. Surrounding them were smaller ships and vessels of every size and shape, all filled with men armed to the teeth. Thorald's ship was one of the medium-sized ones, positioned halfway towards one flank.

'Our task is to board enemy ships that get too close to the larger ones and fight them off,' Thorald told his men.

'Who are Haraldr's main opponents, there in the middle?' Ivar pointed at three massive warships facing the king's.

'I'm told that is a Danish chieftain by the name of Thorir Haklång, and flanking him two men called Önundr and Trond. I'm not sure where they are from exactly. There's also Kjotve the Rich, who hails from Agder, and I'm guessing that man over there is King Hjorr. There's a rumour going round that Olaf the White is here somewhere as well.'

'Who?' The name rang a bell, but Ivar couldn't immediately place it.

'He's the king of the Írska, or so I understand.'

'Oh, *that* Olaf.' According to legend, he was an Irish Viking king who'd fought together with Ivar the Boneless and ruled Dublin for many years. Ivar knew he was a real historical figure but hadn't expected him to show up here. Despite the gravity of the situation, a thrill ran up his spine at the thought that he was part of this pivotal moment in history, together with men who'd be talked about through the ages. It was hard to fathom.

'You know of him?' Thorald's eyebrows rose.

'Yes, but don't ask me how.'

That made Thorald's mouth twitch with amusement, but he refrained from pushing for answers.

The enemy fleet had been trickling into the fjord all morning, the manoeuvre taking hours because of the tiny entrance passage that only let in one ship at a time. In theory, the king could have simply picked them off there one by one, but that was not how things were done. It was more honourable to allow the opponents free entry without being harassed. They were still arriving, and Ivar could see that most of them had white shields. Presumably they'd painted them that colour so that they could recognise friend and foe during the battle.

The ships were filled with battle-hungry men bristling with

sharply honed weapons that gleamed in the sunlight bouncing off the tiny waves. It was a chilling sight. He gripped his own sword and made sure his battleaxe hung securely from his belt. One hand gripped a shield lent to him by Thorald. He knew it could mean the difference between life and death during a fight, so he was grateful to have it.

This is it. I'm going to fight in a Viking battle. Jesus! It hadn't really sunk in until now.

He must be mad, but what choice did he have? Having chosen to come here, he couldn't abandon his new relatives and friends at the first sign of danger. If he really wanted to feel the kinship, he had to act accordingly. These people had taken him in, accepted him and befriended him. They were family, in every sense of the word, and he owed them his allegiance. To the death. Forget twenty-first-century thinking. Forget where he'd come from. This was his reality. This was where he belonged for the moment.

As if he'd read Ivar's thoughts and understood some of his conflicting emotions, Thorald asked, 'Are you ready for this?'

'As ready as I'll ever be.'

That was an honest answer, because he didn't think it was possible to be totally prepared for what was coming. But the small nod his kinsman gave him helped. He wasn't alone in this. They would have each other's backs.

Swallowing down the fear that threatened to paralyse him, he concentrated on memorising the sights and sounds of the amassing fleets. There was a chilling silence as the opponents weighed each other up. A staring contest of epic proportions between chieftains and petty kings all with one goal – to be victorious. Ivar detected no terror on anyone else's face, merely a sort of restless energy, as if they were all raring to go. He knew these men weren't afraid of death, not the way his modern compatriots would have been. To them, death was just another dimension, a continuation of their life here. And there was no more glorious way to go from one to the other than through death in battle.

He had to try and think like them. Adopt their mindset. Believe that there was something more than nothingness awaiting him. Would he end up in Valhalla? That thought almost made him smile. It had never been his ambition, so that would be exceedingly weird.

Concentrate on the here and now. Speculation was fruitless. He was here to help keep Thorald and his men alive, to fight for Ellisif, Askhild and the others. That was all. He had to block everything else out of his mind.

'I think we're about to begin,' Thorald muttered, then added in a louder voice, 'Be ready, men!'

The sound of horns suddenly echoed across the water, loud and insistent. Men started banging on their shields with axes and swords, creating an almighty din. They called out war cries and egged each other on. The trumpeting had barely finished when arrows began to rain down from the neighbouring hilltops. It was a deadly hailstorm that temporarily blotted out the sunlight. Ivar heard the eerie swooshing sound as they sped past and embedded themselves in wood and flesh. Cries of pain and loud curses rang out, while men on the enemy ships crumpled or fell head-first overboard. He hadn't realised the arrows would be quite so accurate or lethal, but there was no time to mull that over.

'*For King Haraldr!*' Thorald roared. Ivar and the others took up the cry, repeating the king's name over and over again while slamming their weapons on to the surface of their shields in accompaniment. The rhythmical pounding was soothing and calmed Ivar's mind, helping him to focus.

Meanwhile, the berserkers and *ulfhednar* howled like animals and worked themselves into a frenzy. Ivar had considered this a possible myth, but apparently not. He wished he'd had more time to watch them, as it was a fascinating spectacle, but they were already heading for their first opponents. The king's *hirð* were throwing spears and stones at their opposing crew and preparing for hand-to-hand combat as the ships drew close.

After attaching their own ship to one of the enemy's with hooks, Thorald's men swarmed aboard the vessel.

'Watch out, behind you!' Ivar jumped out of the way as something swished past his head, then turned to fight with a man whose eyes shone with bloodlust.

This was it, the moment he'd been training for all those years, and it was all too real.

The next half an hour or so passed in a blur. Ivar attacked, parried, ducked and generally did everything in his power to stay alive. After the first few moments, there was no time for fear; not a second to so much as think about it. His senses were on high alert, blocking out the sights and sounds of bloodshed while at the same time keeping him from getting killed. Around him, men were being butchered and maimed, but he didn't allow his gaze to linger on any of the gruesome sights.

He stuck close to Thorald and Álrik. As if by silent agreement, he and Thorald shielded the younger man as much as they could without making it too obvious. There was no doubting Álrik's courage, but he had no fighting experience and wasn't as big as some of their opponents. Kell stayed close by as well, and proved his worth time and time again. Ivar guessed he'd been trained hard by his evil father, but it was standing him in good stead now.

'We make a good partnership, kinsman,' Thorald called out at one point, when together they'd beaten back a group of enemy fighters until they'd had no recourse but to jump into the sea. He flashed a smile, which Ivar returned. Warmth spread through him at the acceptance and camaraderie he saw in the other man's eyes. This was why he was here, risking everything. Family. Brotherhood.

'Yes, you're not too bad for an old man,' he shot back teasingly, even though he'd confessed by now that he was seven years the elder of the two.

Thorald laughed and lunged at yet another fighter. 'I'll show you old!'

With one ship's crew dispatched either into the afterlife or the depths of the bay, they rowed towards their next target. Ivar glanced around and saw that King Haraldr was doing well. His main rivals appeared to be either dead or in retreat. In fact, the whole enemy fleet was in disarray, with men throwing themselves overboard and trying to swim to shore. Ivar winced at the sight of warriors in chain mail being dragged under the waves, their clothing too heavy for them to keep afloat. They didn't stand a chance. Others, who had pulled themselves on to dry land, were met by Haraldr's forces there and had to fight for their lives while dripping wet. It was a recipe for disaster.

Some ships disgorged their men on to the shore or to one or other of the islands to take a stand there. But Haraldr's men were soon with them, blocking any attempts at escape or survival. A few made for the entrance to the fjord, but this time their passage was cut off. Others sank after having been rammed by larger vessels. It was complete and utter pandemonium.

A loud noise and a jolt brought another ship alongside theirs, and Ivar heard Kell cry out, 'Father!'

He turned to see Kári preparing to board them, and shouted out a warning to Thorald. Their opponents swarmed over the railing, and there was no time to think after that. Ivar was becoming weary, every muscle in his body screaming in protest at the extreme workout. He was also bleeding in several places and felt bruised all over. But it wasn't finished yet.

'So you thought you could escape me, did you, you little runt? Traitor! You're no son of mine henceforth.' Kári's angry words were bellowed at full volume, but Kell didn't so much as flinch.

'I don't want to be. Why do you think I left, you disgusting old *argr*!' he shouted back.

Ivar admired the young man's spirit and realised it must have taken a lot of courage to stand up to someone like Kári. He flanked Kell on one side, while Thorald took up position on the other. The father's gaze flickered from one to the other.

'And you're the ones who took my wife away from me, aren't you. But never fear, I'll get her back as soon as I've killed you.'

'We'll see about that,' Thorald muttered.

There was fierce fighting going on all around them, with Thorald's men battling Kell's brothers and the rest of Kári's crew. Ivar didn't have time to check how they were faring, however, as he knew their most dangerous opponent was the one before them. There was a crazed expression in the older man's eyes that he mistrusted. The loathing when he regarded his youngest son was spine-chilling.

It soon became clear that Kári's hatred fuelled his strength. Despite being much older, he held his own against the three of them, and two of his other sons soon joined him. Ivar fought one of them and eventually succeeded in disarming the man. He decided that was a good time to use alternative methods, and with a few martial-arts moves he knocked him out and heaved him overboard.

'You'll pay for that!' Kári roared, but Kell and Thorald kept the man fully occupied and left Ivar to fight yet another of Kári's sons.

A vicious curse came from Thorald's direction, and Ivar turned briefly to see him gazing at his left hand in wide-eyed disbelief. Where there should have been five fingers, there were now only two, the thumb and index, and blood flowed freely.

'*Skítr!*' Ivar dispatched his own opponent and pushed Thorald out of the way. 'Bind it with something. Quickly!'

'There's no time. Later.'

Together, Ivar and Kell attacked the enraged Kári with renewed vigour. With another of his martial-arts moves, Ivar managed to sweep the man's feet from under him. He was large and fell heavily, but he was also quick and got to his knees, continuing to fight despite Kell slashing him across one hand.

'You little *niðingr*! I'll make you pay for this.' Kári jumped to his feet, but his grip on his sword was slippery now that blood ran down his fingers. Ivar took that opportunity to swing his shield at the man, connecting with the side of his head. It made Kári lose his balance again, and this time when he stumbled backwards, he tripped and toppled over the railing.

'Father? *Father!*' Another of his sons leaned over the side to scan the water.

Kell didn't hesitate, but ran his sword right through him. 'You can join him in Ran's hall. You're cut from the same cloth, *aumingi*.' Ignoring the stunned expression on his brother's face, he shoved him into the sea, where he sank surrounded by a stain of red.

Glancing at Ivar, Kell muttered, 'You have no idea how he tormented me when I was a child. Said it was to make me strong, but I know he just enjoyed being cruel.' He spat into the water. 'Good riddance.'

The decks were now free of enemy fighters, apart from one final brother, who must have known he was beaten and jumped overboard, weapons and all. Thorald's face was ashen, and he had tucked his maimed hand into his armpit, out of sight. Ivar hoped he hadn't lost too much blood but there was a stain on his tunic that was growing with every moment. Losing a few fingers wasn't life-threatening as such, but they would need to clean the wound and staunch the blood as soon as possible or it could be.

'*Nooo!* He's getting away!' The anguished cry from Kell made Ivar swing around and stare in the direction he was pointing.

Kári was swimming towards the shore, helped by the son who'd jumped in a moment ago, and the one Ivar had heaved overboard, who must have rallied. They were making good progress and would no doubt soon reach land. Unease shimmered down Ivar's spine. That man wouldn't stop until he had what he wanted, and that included Ellisif. What if he went to find her immediately?

'No, this ends now,' he ground out. 'Thorald, we have to row after them.'

His kinsman nodded. 'Everyone, to the oars!'

'What is happening down there? I can't make it out.'

Ellisif and Hedda stood on top of Ullarlandshaugr, squinting into the afternoon sun as they tried to follow the battle that raged in the bay below them. Once they'd fired off all their arrows, they'd been sent away to safety, while the male archers swarmed down towards the sea to help fight any enemy warriors who tried to come ashore. Askhild and her child had been taken back to the camp by one of Thorald's men who'd been left behind to guard her, but the other two women hadn't wanted to leave yet.

'I need to know that they are safe,' Hedda had said, and Ellisif couldn't argue with that, because she felt the same. Her eyes were glued to the violent spectacle before them and she couldn't look away.

Once they'd reached their vantage point, however, it soon became clear that it wasn't easy to see what was going on. There were so many ships, all in a tangle, that it was difficult to make out who was who. They were also quite far away, making it even harder to spot which side was winning.

'I can't see our men,' Ellisif muttered. Thorald's vessel didn't stand out in any way, and she wished he'd had a distinctive figurehead or something. At the moment, she couldn't spot him or his crew. They must be on the far side of the bay.

'Me neither. Oh, I can't bear it!' Hedda moaned. 'I don't want to lose him now. He promised to marry me if he survived. Please, sweet Freya, keep Kell alive for me.'

Ellisif added her own request to the goddess, but silently. She was already Ivar's wife, but one night in that role would never be enough. She wanted to spend the rest of her life with him. Live and laugh with him. Grow old with him. Odin's ravens, but she loved him so much it hurt, and the thought of losing him now was simply unbearable.

They stood there for what seemed like hours, and watched as the enemy was slowly but surely routed. King Haraldr's ship was easy to keep track of, and he never wavered. All around him other vessels sank or were boarded, but his stayed afloat and carved a path through those of his opponents. Enemy warriors were becoming desperate, fleeing in every direction, but they weren't having much luck.

'I think we've won,' Ellisif ventured to comment. 'But where is Thorald and his crew?'

She scanned the bay again, but couldn't see them anywhere. Had his ship sunk? Fear gouged at her insides, and she wrapped her arms around herself to contain the pain. No, she wouldn't believe it. Surely they'd be coming back?

Other ships were being rowed to the nearest shore. Men swarmed on to dry land, shouting for joy, their fists held high in victory. But no matter where she looked, Ellisif saw no sign of anyone she knew.

'I can't s-see them.' Hedda's voice broke on a sob.

'We'd better go back to the camp. I'm sure they'll be along shortly. They might still be on one of the islands.' Ellisif tried to make her voice sound as if she really believed that, but hope was dying fast. She had to be strong for her cousin and friend, though. Now was not the time to fall apart. Grief could wait. 'Come, let's find Askhild.'

Chapter Twenty-Six

Hafrsfjordr, July/Heyannir AD *876*

By some miracle, two thirds of Thorald's crew were still in one piece, and they soon had the oars fitted. In grim silence, they set off after the fleeing men. A couple of times, desperate enemy warriors tried to cling to their vessel and climb aboard – anything rather than drown – but it didn't slow them down much. The ship's keel hissed on to the shore not long after Kári and his sons had dragged themselves on to dry land.

The older man was sopping wet, but despite panting from the swim, his eyes still blazed with hatred and determination. He pointed at one of Kell's brothers. 'Knut, deal with them. I have a wife to find, then I'll swear an oath to the upstart king so I can keep my new domains. You know where to find me.' With a loping gait, he took off in a northerly direction, obviously certain that at least one of his sons would obey him.

Ivar's insides turned to stone. He'd been right: the man was going after Ellisif. How had he known she was here? He must have a spy somewhere. '*Bastard!*' he hissed in English.

To Kell, he whispered, 'Leave me and Thorald here, then take the ship and go and find the women. You must keep them safe.

Now! Hide them if necessary. Or take them to the king and tell them Ellisif and I are married, which means Birgirsby is ours. That way he can't gift it to your father, no matter what he claims. We'll deal with him and your brothers, I swear.'

'But . . .' There was indecision on the young man's face. He'd wanted to be the one to kill his sire. Ivar could understand that, but he was also certain that patricide would haunt Kell for the rest of his life, no matter how justified it was. It would be better not to have that on his conscience.

'If you don't save them, he'll have won. He'll take both Ellisif and Hedda. Is that what you want? It will take him a while to find them, while you know exactly where to go. Rowing across the bay is faster, but hurry!' They were all the way on the other side of the fjord, miles from the camp where they'd left Ellisif and the others, but with any luck, Kell could reach them first.

A muscle jumped in Kell's jaw, but he was far from stupid and saw the sense in Ivar's reasoning. 'Very well. Kill him for me, please. He's scum.' With that, he turned back to the ship and pushed off into the water, shouting orders at the other men.

Knut, meanwhile, had thrown himself at Thorald. Ivar could see that his kinsman was flagging fast. His face was ashen and he was having trouble holding on to his shield with his injured hand. The large bloodstain on his tunic showed that the wound was still bleeding, and having to exert himself wasn't helping. Ivar knew time was of the essence, so he threw his sword and shield to the ground and bounced on the balls of his feet. Turning to the other brother, he executed a perfect roundhouse kick and caught him behind one ear, sending the man flying. Hampered by soggy garments, he'd been too slow to move out of the way.

'Thorald, deal with this one!' Ivar ordered, and his kinsman didn't hesitate, but lunged forward and pierced the man with his sword.

Meanwhile, Ivar had turned his attention to Knut, and they fought in grim silence for a few moments. There was no time for either finesse or chivalry, though, and again he used his modern fighting techniques to deal with the man. A couple of rapid kicks had Knut stumbling backwards, straight into Thorald's waiting sword. One well-placed thrust and it was all over. Almost too easy, really.

Ivar was about to say, 'Well done,' when Thorald himself sank to the ground.

'*Shit!* Don't die on me now. *Come on!*'

He knelt next to his kinsman and saw that he was still breathing. Tearing off a piece of material from the bottom of his shirt with his teeth, he made quick work of tying the linen round Thorald's hand in a makeshift torniquet. Hopefully he had only passed out from lack of blood, and that could be remedied.

Thorald stirred and opened his eyes. 'Go!' he rasped. 'I'll be fine. Wait for you here.'

As if he was in any state to do anything else, but Ivar didn't say that out loud. 'Very well. I'll be back as soon as I can.'

He stood up and sprinted off in the direction Kári had gone. Having done a lot of jogging, he was a fast runner, with good stamina. Adrenaline kicked in. Although he was exhausted from the fighting, he dug deep and found the last of his strength. With a bit of luck, he ought to stand a chance of catching the older man.

'Odin, Thor, Ullr – help me, please!' he called out, hoping that the gods might be listening.

The path through the trees snaked round the bay to the left and would end up near the campsite. Ivar had no intention of letting the man get that far. This was where all those hours of sparring and exercise should pay off. He was younger and fitter than Kári, and he wasn't weighed down by soaking-wet clothing.

Soon he caught sight of a glimpse of red material visible through the trees.

'Excellent,' he muttered. He was gaining on his quarry. Raising his voice, he called out, 'Kári, I'm coming to get you! There's no escape.'

The older man's steps faltered as he glanced over his shoulder, but at first he didn't stop. When he became aware of Ivar closing in on him, however, he came to a halt and turned to face him, battleaxe in hand.

'She's mine, and so is Birgirsby. You can't take either from me,' he growled, but his chest was heaving and it was clear he was tiring fast.

Ivar was out of breath himself, but not as badly. He shook his head as if he pitied the man. 'Oh, but I already have. We were married this morning. And you're about to pay for all your misdeeds.'

He was still carrying his shield, which gave him an advantage, but instead of unsheathing his sword, he pulled his own axe out of his belt. Better to fight with the same type of weapon, he reckoned.

Kári charged forward like an enraged bear, but he was clumsy from being wet and his hand was still bleeding. The running had taken it out of him as well. 'The trolls take you!' he panted.

'I'm fairly sure they're about to take *you*,' Ivar muttered, but he didn't waste time arguing with the man. Instead, he attacked relentlessly, using the shield to defend himself against Kári's increasingly erratic blows. Finally an opening presented itself. Kári's wet shoes slipped on a patch of grass, leaving his left side wide open. Ivar didn't hesitate, but aimed his axe straight at the man's head.

Game over.

This time, he had no regrets. Kári deserved to die, and Ivar had promised Kell he'd do the deed.

'Thank the gods he's gone,' he muttered. He was breathing hard from the exertion and bent forward, resting his hands on his knees.

But there was no time to gloat. He had to return to Thorald. He only hoped he wasn't too late.

'Hedda! Ellisif! You must come with us now, this instant!'

'*Kell!* You're alive!' Hedda, who had been half-heartedly helping Ellisif to dismantle the last of the tents, shrieked and shot across the ground to throw herself into the young man's arms. He hugged her close, but only briefly, before turning to the others.

'Sorry, *unnasta*, but there is no time to lose. My father is coming for Ellisif. Somehow he knew you are here. We must leave, quickly!'

'Kári? What? Why?' Ellisif blinked at him.

'We were fighting with him and his crew, and chased him on to the shore. Instead of staying to fight us, he ran off, saying he was going to find you. If he catches you, he'll take you straight to the king, claim you as his wife and swear an oath of fealty so he can keep Birgirsby. Ivar said we must prevent that at all costs.' He shrugged. 'Obviously it would be a lie, since you were married this morning, but I don't think my father knows that. Still, you'd have to prove it and the king might not take your word for it.'

Ellisif's cheeks heated up as Hedda turned to blink at her. 'You're married? You never said.'

'You're Ivar's wife? When did this happen?' Askhild added, looking just as astonished.

Hedda and Askhild hadn't been around at the time, and for some reason Ellisif hadn't wanted to mention it. She'd hugged the knowledge to herself, like a talisman, planning on telling them later.

Waving the question away, she prevaricated. 'It's complicated. But . . . Ivar is alive?' She hardly dared ask.

'He was when I left them, but he was going after my father. Thorald is injured, though. Never mind that now, there's no time. Grab your possessions and let's go!'

Askhild, who had been hugging her brother with one arm, obviously relieved that he was unharmed, grew pale at the news about her husband. 'How bad is he?' she whispered, her eyes fixed on Kell as she clasped her baby son tightly to her chest.

'I'm not sure, but he was standing and fighting last I saw.'

This seemed to reassure her somewhat, and she nodded and picked up her bundle. She'd been stoically pretending that everything was fine ever since the other women returned without news. Ellisif knew her friend was sensible enough to do as they were told right now. There would be time to question Kell later.

With the help of the man who'd been left behind and some of the crew members who had arrived with Kell and Álrik, they grabbed all their belongings and set off for the shore.

'If we board the ship and head out into the fjord, my father won't be able to reach us,' Kell said. 'We'll stay out there until we're sure he's been dealt with. Ivar gave me his word he'd kill him, and I trust him.'

That made sense, although Ellisif wondered how Ivar was to find them if they were out on the water. But that was a problem for later.

'Thorald? *Thorald!* Can you hear me?' Ivar shook his kinsman, whose face was now the colour of ash bark. He'd been lying in the exact same spot where Ivar had left him, and for a horrible moment he'd thought the man was dead.

Putting a couple of fingers on his throat confirmed that there was still a faint pulse. Lifting Thorald's maimed hand, he could see that the bleeding was no longer as profuse, but that could simply be because his body was already drained dry. The remaining stumps were dirty and had been lying on the ground. God knew what bacteria had already taken hold. It was a terrifying thought.

There was only one thing that could save him – modern medicine.

He'd listened to the tale of how his sister's friend Sara had saved her Viking husband's life when he'd been knifed in the stomach. She had transported him to a twenty-first-century hospital in York, where he'd been treated for life-threatening wounds. Ivar would have to do the same; there was nothing else for it. Only one problem, though – he needed Thorald conscious enough to say the magic words with him.

'The *jōtnar* take it, man, wake up! Please!' He slapped Thorald's cheeks and saw his eyelids flutter. '*Hei!* I know you can hear me, you stubborn *fifl*. I need your help. Open your eyes!'

They were running out of time. As a last resort, Ivar rushed down to the shore and filled his cupped hands with cold water. Hurrying back, he dashed it into Thorald's face. That made the man open his eyes and glare at him with an angry splutter.

'What are you doing? Have you gone mad?' His voice was hoarse and came out as a breathy whisper, but it was strong enough to give Ivar hope.

'I need you to say something with me. On the count of three, you have to say "*Með blōð skaltu ferðast*".' He could see that Thorald was about to protest, so he held up a hand. 'Don't argue. Just trust me and say it. Hold on.'

He extracted the magical shears from his pouch and took hold of Thorald's hand. 'Are you ready? *Ein, tveir, þrir* . . .'

He cut his own finger, mingling his blood with that of his kinsman, then said the magic words, pleased that Thorald repeated them with him. Then, grabbing the man's hand in a steady grip, he closed his eyes and prayed the gods would help them.

'It must be safe to go back now. I can see scores of people milling around the king's hall. And we need to find out if Kári has already petitioned him for my hand and Birgirsby.'

Ellisif was sitting next to Kell, who heaved a sigh and capitulated. She'd been trying to make him return to shore for ages now, but he'd been resisting. It was close to dusk, though, and they needed to know where they stood before night fell.

'Very well. Men, let's row.'

Once on shore, they made their way towards the crowds while keeping an eye out for Kári.

'Make sure you stay together,' Kell urged, and no one argued. He nudged a stranger in front of them and asked, 'What is happening here, please?'

'Oath-swearing, and the king is rewarding everyone who helped him. If you wait your turn, I'm sure there'll be something left for you.'

'Very well. Thank you.'

They decided between them that Kell and Álrik would do the talking when it was their turn, in case Haraldr was not favourably disposed towards females who spoke for themselves. It proved to be a long wait. Little Thorulf was grizzling by the time they finally stood before the king, but the monarch was in good spirits. The battle and the long day seemed not to have taken their toll on him, or else he was buoyed up by his victory.

'Welcome to my hall, and thank you for your assistance this day. Who might you be?'

'Álrik Ásbjornsson of Ulfstoft, here to swear fealty on behalf of myself and my settlement.' The young man looked the king in the eye and Ellisif was sure his sister must be very proud of him. He had certainly matured a lot during the previous year, and he'd come through the battle more or less unscathed. How much of that was due to Ivar and Thorald protecting him, she didn't know, but it was immaterial. The main thing was that he was here and glowing with confidence.

'I accept your fealty and thank you.' There was some complicated ritual involving the king's sword, but as soon as that was done, Kell stepped forward with Ellisif beside him.

'I am Kell Kárisson, and this is Ellisif Birgirsdóttír of Birgirsby. Will you allow her to speak on behalf of her husband, Ivar Thoresson, who has not yet returned?'

The king's gaze sharpened for a moment, as if he understood what Kell was saying – that Ivar might not come back at all. Since there was still some confusion and chaos outside, the possibility remained, and they all knew it.

'I will,' Haraldr said. 'Welcome, Ellisif Birgirsdóttír.'

'Thank you. I hereby swear fealty to you on behalf of my husband Ivar, myself and our settlement, Birgirsby. Please accept my oath until my husband can give it himself.' The king nodded, and she went through the same ritual Álrik had already done.

'Now, please take these tokens of my appreciation.' Haraldr beckoned someone forward with a couple of silver brooches. 'May the gods watch over you, and thank you again for your assistance. I shall not forget.'

'Thank you.' Ellisif hesitated. 'If you can spare one more moment, please, there is something I need to tell you.'

'Yes?'

'I was promised in marriage by King Hjorr to a man named Kári Knutsson, but I was not willing. Instead I married Ivar

Thoresson, against that king's wishes. It may be that Kári will come to try and claim me and my domains from you, but he is not to be trusted. Even if he swears an oath to you, he may not keep it.'

The king frowned at her and glanced at the others in her group. 'And why should I believe you over him? Do you all concur?'

Kell spoke up. 'Aye. I am his son but he disowned me for fighting on your behalf. And since we do not acknowledge Hjorr as our king, we are all of the opinion that Ellisif acted honourably in marrying Ivar instead.'

That seemed to do the trick. 'Very well. I thank you for the warning.'

Standing outside the stuffy hall some moments later, Ellisif felt as if a huge weight had left her shoulders. Whatever Kári did now, he had lost.

Chapter Twenty-Seven

Hafrsfjordr and Stavanger, July/Heyannir AD *876*

The time from waking up in the twenty-first century to when Thorald was finally admitted to a hospital in Stavanger seemed to pass in a blur. The whole experience was surreal, as if everything moved in slow motion and yet at the same time really fast. Ivar told so many lies, he was sure he was going to trip himself up, but fortunately no one caught him out. They were too busy trying to save Thorald's life.

They'd woken up on a side street in an area he later found out was called Grannes, south-west of the city, and he had flagged down a young man in a beat-up old Volvo. He'd explained that his friend was badly injured and needed medical attention as soon as possible. One glance at Thorald's maimed hand had the guy leaping out of his car and helping them into the back seat. He threw an old blanket at them – 'Here, try not to let him bleed all over the upholstery, please' – then floored it to the nearest hospital, where Ivar started on the long line of untruths.

'We're re-enactors. I found him on my way back to the B&B I'm staying at. I don't know what happened to him, but he's lost so much blood. You've got to do something, please!'

Remembering what Sara had told him about the time she took her husband to A&E, he'd added that he thought Thorald was Icelandic. 'I can help with translation if necessary,' he'd said. Then he dug out his credit card and offered to pay for all expenses until such time as they could find out whether Thorald could cover the costs himself.

'He had no wallet or anything, as far as I could see, so perhaps he was mugged?'

Two hours later, he found himself sitting on an uncomfortable plastic chair next to Thorald's bed. It was one of six in a quiet ward, and everyone was sleeping except for Ivar. His kinsman was dressed in one of those ridiculous hospital gowns, but still managed to appear intimidating. His injured hand lay across his stomach, covered in pristine bandages, and with his arm in a sling to keep it still. The other arm had tubes snaking out of it, giving him essential fluids and antibiotics. He'd already had a blood transfusion, so his face was less pale than earlier, even if it was not quite back to normal yet.

'Thank Odin for that,' Ivar muttered, then smiled at himself. Invoking a heathen god among all the modern machinery that bleeped and blinked around him seemed strange, but he didn't take it back. The Norse gods *had* been on their side, otherwise Thorald wouldn't be alive now.

He woke some hours later, with a crick in his neck and a stiff back. '*Bloody hell*,' he hissed. He must have fallen asleep. When he opened his eyes, he found his kinsman's gaze on him, his eyebrows forming a fierce V of a scowl.

'Where am I?' Thorald whispered. 'What have you done?'

'You are in a place of healing in my time,' Ivar told him, keeping his voice down as much as he could. 'I will explain later, but for now, please do whatever you are told to. You won't understand the speech of those who are caring for you, but I'll be here to translate. I'm not leaving you, I promise.'

'Hmph.' Thorald's scowl didn't let up, but his posture grew less tense. 'I thought I'd died and ended up in a new Valhalla, only I didn't know which god it belonged to.'

That made Ivar smile. 'If this is the afterlife, I'm not sure I want to be here with you.' He shook his head. 'No, you're not dead, but you came very close. I'm sorry I had to bring you here, but it was your only chance. I couldn't face having to tell Askhild I'd lost you.'

Thorald's expression turned sombre, and he reached out his good hand to clasp Ivar's. 'Thank you. I am in your debt.'

'Not at all. I acted in my own best interest too. If you hadn't survived, you might not produce any more sons and your line could have died out. That would mean I'd never exist.'

This statement was greeted with a low chuckle. 'I suppose that makes sense, but still . . . you have my thanks.'

'Try to sleep now. The sooner you heal, the faster we can go back to our women.'

'Our women?' Thorald smirked. 'I like the sound of that. Thank the gods you married Ellisif at last! I thought I was going to have to bash you over the head before you saw sense and made her yours.'

Ivar shook his head and grinned. 'Perhaps you should have. I do love her and I could never leave her behind. It just took me a while to figure out a way for us to be together. We worked out a compromise, but I'll explain it to you later. That is, if she hasn't changed her mind, of course. Now rest, please.'

'I don't think there's any doubt she'll want to be wherever you are. Goodnight.'

Hafrsfjordr and Ulfstoft, July/Heyannir AD *876*

'I think we should go back to Ulfstoft and wait there,' Álrik said the following morning. 'There are too many men here for my liking. I've caught at least three leering at my sister already. Thorald and Ivar will make their own way back.'

Or not, as the case may be. Ellisif couldn't keep the dark thoughts at bay, and her stomach was churning. There still hadn't been any news of the two men, but Kári hadn't arrived either. Did that mean they'd all killed each other? Or were Thorald and Ivar pursuing Kári as he fled inland like others of the enemy? There was no way of knowing.

'I agree.' Kell nodded, as did most of the other men in their group.

Ellisif was pleased that they all looked to Álrik for directions, as if they had finally accepted him fully as their chieftain. The young man had definitely grown into his role, and with the experience of battle behind him, he appeared more self-assured. He had proved he was no weakling or coward and was ready to shoulder his birthright. That was excellent, as they would need leadership if Thorald didn't return.

'Very well.' Askhild stood up, holding her son to one shoulder. Her expression was bleak, but she was keeping her emotions in check. 'Let us leave now and we might be home before nightfall.'

Ellisif didn't protest. A part of her wanted to go straight home to Birgirsby, but until she found out whether Ivar had bested Kári, that wasn't a safe option. She knew that Kell, Hedda and the men from her settlement would go with her, but better not to risk it yet.

The journey back took a bit longer than expected due to some contrary winds, but soon after dusk their ship came to rest next to the jetty below Ulfstoft. Men and women rushed out of the hall, uniform expressions of relief on their faces when they saw that most of their loved ones were back in one piece. There were a few cries of anguish from those who'd lost someone, but on the whole, it was a joyful, if slightly subdued, homecoming.

'I feel like I could sleep for a week,' Askhild murmured as the women made their way up the hill.

'I doubt little Thorulf will allow that.' Ellisif smiled. 'He's always hungry, and growing apace.'

'That he is.' The pride in her friend's eyes made up for the fatigue and sadness that also lurked in their depths. 'Let us hope he sleeps at least through the night.'

Ellisif too was happy to curl up on her sleeping bench, but she was acutely aware of the empty space on one side of her. She swallowed down the tears that threatened. They didn't know for certain that Ivar was dead. No point grieving yet, but it was hard not to. If he was alive, why hadn't he come to find her? He'd sworn an oath. Only the direst of circumstances should have prevented him from returning to her.

She didn't want to imagine what those might be.

Stavanger, July/Heyannir AD 876

'The Fenrisúlfr take it, I'm as weak as a newborn kitten,' Thorald grumbled as Ivar helped him out through the hospital doors. He had jumped when they'd swished to the sides automatically, but hopefully no one other than Ivar had noticed.

'Some food and rest, not to mention ale, will have you right as rain again soon. And the healing potions they gave you to take with you.' He meant antibiotics, but didn't know what to call that in Old Norse. 'You need to be patient. It's not every day you cheat the Valkyries and come back from the brink of death.'

'True. Odin's ravens, what is *that*?' Thorald had stopped on the pavement and stared at the cars zooming past on the street. 'Where are the horses and oxen?'

'I'll explain later. Come.' Ivar led his friend over to a waiting taxi and gave the address of the hotel where he'd secured a twin room for a couple of nights. He had purposely avoided the one he'd stayed at with Ellisif. There was no way he could explain why he was turning up in re-enactment clothing yet again so soon.

Thorald stayed quiet all through the ride, but his eyes were wide and trying to gaze everywhere at once. Ivar tried to imagine what this experience must be like for him, but failed. A lesser man might have freaked out, but Vikings weren't made that way. They seemed to take everything in their stride. He was sure there would be lots of questions once they were on their own, but for now, Thorald kept them to himself.

'This is incredible! I don't understand why you'd ever wish to leave a place like this to come and stay with us,' he said as they lounged in their room later that evening.

They'd gorged themselves on takeaway hamburgers and chips, washed down with a couple of beers. There were no complaints about the fare. Thorald had dipped his food in ketchup and mustard as directed, making appreciative noises and wolfing down every last crumb. Once he'd had a chance to digest his meal and rest for a while, Ivar had given him a tour of their room. Just like Ellisif, he was fascinated by the light switches, the taps and the toilet, as well as the furniture and bedding. Now they were sitting in a pair of very comfortable armchairs next to a window with a view of the harbour.

'Perhaps it's not the surroundings that matter but those you share them with,' Ivar mused, taking another sip of beer. Now that they were away from the hospital at last, and the worst was over, he could relax.

'Hmm, yes, but still . . . I'd be loath to live without all this if I were you,' Thorald insisted. 'You said you had a foster-family in this time, did you not? Will they not wonder where you are?'

'They know. My sister, the one I found in Ísland, was returning to them and I asked her to explain.' Ivar had told him about Maddie and Geir, so Thorald knew he didn't mean Linnea. He shrugged. 'They'll miss me, but I'm sure they will understand if I stay away a while longer. All they've ever wanted was for me to be happy, and I am.' He regarded the man sitting opposite in a chair that was a hundred times more comfortable than any he'd likely been in before. Contentment and warmth washed through him. 'You are my kin too, and I'm very glad I found you. Now that we have met, I am at peace in a way I never was before, even though I realise that kinship by blood is not everything. The gods have been exceedingly good to me.'

'*Hei*, do not forget Askhild and Thorulf. And hopefully there will be more children.' Thorald grinned. 'You might even have some of your own.'

Ivar smiled back. 'You're right. My family is definitely growing, and I couldn't be more pleased. Hrafn pointed out that he and his brothers are also my kin, through marriage. Soon I'll have so many relatives I won't know what to do with them all.' He laughed.

'You said you and Ellisif had agreed on a compromise. What did you mean?'

'Well, I gave her a few options. We decided we'd try and find someone trustworthy to oversee her domains for a few months every year. During that time, she'll come with me to my time, and the rest of the year we'll spend at Birgirsby. I want to go back to my old life from time to time. I feel I owe it to my foster-family not to disappear altogether.'

'That sounds sensible. As long as you come up with a plausible excuse for why you're leaving. Domains in Svíaríki that also need your attention, perhaps?' Thorald stood up and clapped him on the shoulder. 'Now how about you show me that magical rain shower again? I wouldn't mind enjoying that for a good long while.'

Ulfstoft, July/Heyannir AD 876

A week passed. The mood at Ulfstoft was tense and sombre, but no one wanted to say outright that Thorald and Ivar were not coming back. With every day that went by, however, the likelihood decreased. If they'd survived the battle, they should have been home by now, unless they were lying wounded somewhere, unable to travel.

Ellisif spent all her time with Askhild, the two of them sitting together in the latter's private bedchamber with the door closed. They played with little Thorulf, worked on a weaving project together, or sat and sewed. With the rest of the household excluded, she was able to use the eyeglasses Ivar had bought for her, and her stitches improved no end. It was a joy, but at the same time it made grief gnaw at her, because he'd made this possible and now she might never see him again.

'Some of Thorald's men are talking about returning to Birkiþorp in Svíaríki,' Askhild said. 'It's where they grew up, and without him here, I think they'd rather go back to Haukr.'

'That is understandable. Will that leave Álrik with enough men of his own?'

'Yes, we'll be fine.'

'So you're staying as well?'

Askhild shrugged. 'There is nothing for me to go back to. Thorald was going to build us a home next to Haukr's domains, but I don't see the point in starting on anything now. Thorulf and I can just as well remain here. My brother will take care of us, and

I have the silver we brought with us as well. It means I can pay for our keep.'

It made sense. Askhild had grown up here and had no kin in Svíaríki other than Haukr, who was only distantly related to her. Besides, her brother still needed her to manage his household for him.

'Well, if I may be selfish, I am glad, because that means I can see you from time to time. Birgirsby is not too far from here, as you know. We can visit each other.'

Askhild looked up. 'Oh, you'll be going home soon then?'

'Yes, but not quite yet. I'll stay here for as long as you need me.' Judging by the way her friend dragged herself through each day, that would be a while yet. And hopefully Birgirsby was safe. Ellisif had sent Oddr and Gaukr back there to make sure everyone knew the settlement was in her possession once again. As long as Kári hadn't returned, all would be well. The two men had promised to be careful and ascertain his whereabouts first.

She was about to say something else when shouting came from the hall. Sharing a look of consternation, the women rose as one and headed for the door. As Ellisif opened it, Hedda came barrelling towards them. They would have collided if the girl hadn't managed to stop in time.

'Hedda? What's the matter? Are we under attack?'

'No, but come quickly!' Without further explanation, she turned on her heel and ran towards the entrance doors.

Askhild picked up a sleeping Thorulf, and she and Ellisif followed at a smart pace, reaching the opening a few moments later. As they stepped outside, Ellisif thought at first she was having a vision, because two golden-haired men were striding up the hill. They were bathed in sunlight, which gave them a dreamlike aura, but they were no figments of her imagination. They were real.

She shouted, '*Ivar!*' at the same time as Askhild yelled, '*Thorald!*' and the two of them took off down the path. Ellisif arrived first, unencumbered as she was by a baby, and threw herself into Ivar's waiting arms. He crushed her to his chest and she wrapped her arms around his torso, hugging him close.

'Ellisif, *ást mín*,' he murmured. Then his lips found hers and he kissed her as if he'd been starving for her and she was the only thing in the world that could keep him alive. He was tender and fierce at the same time, alternating between the two while raising his hands to cup her cheeks. 'Gods, but I have missed you,' he whispered.

'And I you. I thought you were . . . that you'd never . . . Oh, Ivar!' She blinked away the tears that spilled over. 'You are well? What happened? Where have you been?'

He grinned and slung an arm across her shoulders, steering her up the hill. 'I will tell you everything, but first let us go somewhere we can be alone.' His eyes twinkling, he added, 'Hayloft?'

She smiled back and snuggled into his side. 'Yes, please.'

As they walked through the door to the byre, she glanced back at Thorald and Askhild, who were walking towards the hall. They only had eyes for each other, and their expressions of joy made her want to cry happy tears again. She noticed he was wearing a bandage on one hand, and his face was paler than usual, but other than that, he was in one piece.

'What happened to Thorald?' she asked, winding her arm around Ivar's waist.

'Lost a few fingers, but he's fine now.'

'That's a relief.'

Askhild wouldn't care about a few missing digits as long as she had the rest of her man back. And as for little Thorulf, he had learned to smile in the last few days. He'd woken up during their mad dash outside, and was busy unleashing all his charm on his doting father.

It was the most wonderful sight Ellisif had seen in a long time, apart from the man at her side. Her husband.

At first, they wasted no time on words but let their bodies do the talking. Afterwards, Ivar lay in the hay with Ellisif draped across his chest. He dropped kisses on her cheek every so often and toyed absently with her silken hair. It shone in a beam of sunlight that had found its way inside the byre, and he thought it stunning. He could hardly take in the fact that they were together at last and that she was his now, for real. It had been a stroke of luck that she'd still been at Ulfstoft and not back at her own settlement.

'Does this mean you are going to marry me in front of our friends and family now?' he murmured. 'It might be best to do it again properly if I'm to stay here with you.'

She lifted her face to smile at him, her moss-green eyes shining. 'That would be lovely, and I'm sure Álrik wouldn't mind hosting a feast in our honour.'

Ivar felt his eyebrows shoot up. 'Álrik? Don't you mean Thorald and Askhild?'

'No, he's really come into his own these last few weeks and grown into his role as chieftain. I think he'll soon be ready to be left to his own devices.'

'That is good news. Thorald will be pleased. Well then, let us ask him.' He caressed her back. 'After that, we had better go and reclaim your domains. The gods only know who is in charge at the moment.'

'Gaukr is. I sent him home with Oddr to let everyone know what had happened. I spoke to the king and swore an oath on your behalf, and even if you hadn't killed Kári, he wouldn't have given him the lands. The only reason I'm still at Ulfstoft is because

I couldn't leave Askhild to grieve on her own. She's been distraught but trying to hold herself together for her son.'

Ivar pulled her closer. 'And you? How did you cope with my absence?'

She leaned up to give him a lingering kiss. 'I was as distressed as Askhild, but I tried not to show it. The thought of you not returning . . .' A shudder racked her, and she shook her head. 'I simply didn't want to contemplate a future without you.'

'Good.' He'd been afraid she might have changed her mind when the threat of battle no longer hung over them, but he could see he'd been worrying for nothing. 'I love you, you know, and I'm not letting you go. Ever.'

'I love you too, which is why I've been thinking . . .'

'Yes?' He read determination in her eyes and wondered what she was about to say. Even so, he wasn't prepared for her answer, which flummoxed him.

'I want to come and live in the future with you all year round.'

'You what?' He blinked at her, wondering if he'd misheard.

'I don't think you'd be happy here in the long term. You need to be in Svíaríki, close to your foster-family. Thorald and Askhild will be there too, as they are planning to build a hall of their own. Perhaps we can live with them when we visit. I liked everything you showed me in your world, and there would be many exciting things for me to learn.'

Ivar was still having trouble catching up. 'You are serious? But what about everything you'll give up here? Your settlement, your friends and family. They are every bit as important as mine.'

'I don't really have any friends at Birgirsby, and my only family is Hedda. I will give the settlement to her and Kell as their wedding present. I know they'll take good care of it and the people who live there. If you don't mind? I know that through our marriage you are its true owner now.'

'No, no, it's yours to do with as you wish. I never wanted you for your possessions.'

'Then that is settled. With the help of your magical shears, I'm sure we can visit them, can't we? Everyone else we care about will be in Svíaríki. Askhild is my closest friend and Thorald is like a brother to you. It makes sense, don't you think?'

He pulled her face up for a lingering kiss. 'What I think is that you are an amazing woman and I'm the luckiest man in Miðgarðr.' He stared into her eyes, turning serious. 'But I want you to be absolutely certain before you decide. Thanks to my shears, we could certainly make it work, and you could see Askhild often. Birgirsby is yours by right and I wouldn't wish you to regret giving it away.'

'I won't, I promise. To tell you the truth, the place holds too many awful memories for me. We'll make new ones, of course, but I'd rather start afresh somewhere else. As long as I'm with you, it doesn't matter where that is.'

'Well, mull it over for a while longer, then we can make a decision. In the meantime, let's ask our friends if they will throw us a wedding feast.'

Chapter Twenty-Eight

Ulfstoft, July/Heyannir AD *876*

Álrik was more than happy to host a feast in their honour, as well as to celebrate Thorald's safe return to his sister and nephew. In fact, it turned into a triple feast, because Kell and Hedda didn't want to wait any longer for their nuptials either. There was an atmosphere of joy that permeated the entire settlement as everyone joined in the preparations, wreathed in smiles. It was a far cry from the miserable place they'd all arrived at the previous autumn, and it made Ivar want to shout with joy. The fact that he'd be marrying the love of his life – again – was the icing on the cake.

'I don't think I've ever seen two such beautiful brides in my life,' he whispered to Ellisif as they sat together on the dais, next to the other couple and their hosts. 'But you outshine your cousin by far, my love.'

She shook her head and smiled at him. 'Methinks you are a tad biased, but I thank you for the compliment.'

'I am but telling the truth. To me you will always be the most beautiful woman in the world.' He couldn't resist stealing another kiss, but had to stop when Thorald cleared his throat and banged on a pewter mug with his eating knife.

'Good people,' he called out, 'it is my very great pleasure to raise a toast to the two happy couples today. We wish them every joy and a long and prosperous life together. To Ivar and Ellisif, and Kell and Hedda!'

'And thanks be to the gods for bringing my brother-in-law back to us!' Álrik added with a grin.

Everyone joined in the toast, their voices echoing to the rafters. Thorald raised a hand to stop them from breaking into excited chatter afterwards. 'Wait! I believe Ellisif has something she wishes to say. Sister?'

She swallowed down the lump in her throat at hearing that word. It meant a lot to her that Thorald and Askhild saw her as kin, and she knew it would mean even more to Ivar that he was considered a brother by this man. Standing up, she glanced at all the smiling faces around her and gave silent thanks to the gods for having ended up among them.

'I want to thank you all for making us so welcome, and for your good wishes today. It means more to us than we can ever say and we hope to come back and visit you often. It won't be quite as regularly as I thought, however, as Ivar and I will be travelling back to Svíaríki with Thorald and Askhild.' She gripped the hand Ivar offered her in silent support and smiled. 'We have decided to make our home close to them.' No need to tell everyone they'd be a thousand years into the future. 'Therefore, I hereby gift all my domains at Birgirsby to my kinswoman Hedda and her husband Kell, to own from this day forward. I know I leave them in good hands and trust you to look after my people as your own. Ivar and I will travel there with you at first, to make sure there is no misunderstanding of my intentions. And we will also inform the king. May you and your children thrive there!'

Kell's and Hedda's mouths had fallen open, and they stared at her with wide-eyed wonder. 'You are giving Birgirsby to us? Are you sure?' Kell got out in a strangled voice. 'We could simply manage it for you.'

Ellisif shook her head. 'No, Kell. From the moment we first met, you have acted kindly and honourably towards me, and I owe you a huge debt of gratitude. There is no one I'd trust more with my former possessions. You have earned them, so please accept with my best wishes.'

Kell glanced at Ivar, as if unsure what he was making of it all, but her husband merely smiled and told him, 'This is entirely up to Ellisif. I am happy with her decision.'

'Then thank you, from the bottom of our hearts.'

'Yes, thank you, that is more than generous,' Hedda added, as they both rose to hug her.

'You're very welcome.'

Ellisif knew she'd done the right thing, and now she was excited to begin her new life with Ivar.

Thorsholm, November 2023/Gormánuðr AD 877

'Your hall is magnificent, Ivar! I cannot believe how many separate chambers there are.'

Ivar had just shown his wife round Thorsholm, his twenty-first-century home by Lake Mälaren. Walking through the house with her, he'd seen it with new eyes and an appreciation he'd never felt for it before. He was incredibly lucky to own such a beautiful home, and now he had someone to share it with as well. Things couldn't possibly get any better.

'I'm sure you'll get used to it, *unnasta*. And any time you are homesick for your time, we'll go and stay with Thorald and Askhild.'

After sorting out the official ownership of Birgirsby, they'd spent the autumn there easing Kell and Hedda into their new roles. This was interspersed with frequent visits to Ulfstoft, where Thorald continued to prepare Álrik for his duties. The young chieftain and Kell had formed a firm friendship, which would hopefully help them both in future. Ivar had promised Thorald he'd take him to visit in secret a couple of times a year. Flying to Norway for short weekend breaks shouldn't be a problem if they were in the twenty-first century.

Once spring arrived, they'd travelled back to Svíaríki, where they'd been welcomed by Haukr and his family. By that time, Thorald and Ivar had made plans to build a hall together. They called it Thorsholm, since Ivar had told his kinsman about the home he owned in the same spot in the future, and spent the summer working on it. Now it was autumn once again, and Ivar had known it was time to return to his world, at least for a while.

'Are you ready to meet my parents?' he asked, wrapping his arms around Ellisif from behind as they gazed out over the lake through the large windows at the back of the house. 'They're on their way.'

It felt right to call Mia and Haakon his parents now. No blood relatives could have looked after him better or cared more, and he had come to realise that family was made up of more than DNA. It was love and consideration for others. That was what those two had always given him – support, encouragement and complete acceptance of the person he was.

The doorbell rang and he went to open it, a smile on his face that widened the moment Mia threw herself into his arms. 'Ivar! Oh, thank goodness at least one of our children has had the decency to return to us!'

He laughed out loud as he was enveloped in a bear hug from Haakon, then ushered them into the living room, where Ellisif waited. She was nervous, judging by the small frown on her forehead, but she didn't need to be, of that he was sure.

'You have to thank my wife for that. I can't take any credit, because I was prepared to stay with her in ninth-century Norway. Luckily for you, she's a courageous and curious woman who wanted to try something new. Ellisif, these are my parents, Mia and Haakon.'

He saw Mia's eyes widen at this introduction. He'd never openly called them that in the past, but she took it in her stride and merely went to give Ellisif a massive hug. 'Welcome, my dear,' she said in her best Old Norse. 'I hope you will be very happy here and that we shall become great friends.'

Ellisif blinked, as if tears threatened, but she managed to keep her composure and hugged Mia back. 'Thank you. I should like that very much.'

Haakon gave her a more restrained hug, perhaps sensing that anything else would be too overwhelming. 'Welcome. We are very grateful you brought Ivar back to us. As you've probably gathered, the rest of our children have abandoned us.'

His words were uttered with a smile, though, and Ivar knew he didn't hold it against any of them.

'No word from Storm, then?' When speaking to them on the phone earlier, Ivar had been told that his brother had been missing since the previous year as well. They could all guess where he'd gone, but the gods only knew if or when he'd be back.

'Not yet, but we have to be patient. He was never great at communicating even when he was in the same century as us,' Mia said. 'On the plus side, at least we know that Linnea and Maddie are happy, and we'll be seeing Linnea soon. She's promised a visit with our latest grandchild.'

As if the word stirred something up, Ellisif suddenly turned extremely pale and murmured, 'Excuse me,' before rushing out of the room. Ivar stared after her for a moment, then followed her.

'*Unnasta*, what is the matter?' She'd dashed to the nearest bathroom and he could hear her retching. A wave of worry washed through him. Had Mia made her uncomfortable with her talk of grandchildren? It hadn't happened for them yet, but he'd planned to take Ellisif to a fertility clinic to see if anything could be done. That was part of the reason he had agreed to return now, despite the fact that Thorald's hall was barely finished.

He waited outside the bathroom while his parents occupied themselves in the kitchen, wisely keeping out of the way. The scent of coffee wafted through to the hall where he stood. Finally Ellisif came out, her cheeks slightly less ashen, and walked right into his open arms.

'I'm so sorry, my love. Mia didn't mean to upset you. She doesn't know,' he said. 'I've not had a chance to speak to her yet.'

But Ellisif shook her head and, to his surprise, lifted her face to his with a huge smile. 'It's not that. I . . . I think I *am* with child at last. I've been nauseous for days now, and this is exactly what Askhild was doing before we left. I didn't dare hope, but I honestly don't know what else could ail me.'

'With child?' Ivar echoed, dumbfounded. Happiness spread through him and he laughed out loud. 'That's wonderful! Oh, thank the gods! I was so worried you were hurt by Mia's talk about grandchildren, but now you'll be adding to her brood. Sweetheart, that's incredible news. I'll go and buy a *test kit* later on so we can be sure.' He didn't know how to say pregnancy test in Old Norse, but he'd explain it later. At her questioning look, he just said, 'It's a way of confirming your suspicion immediately.'

'Oh, good. Thank you. We'd, um, better return to your parents and explain.'

'Yes, indeed. Let's see if you can stomach some coffee. Actually, no! No caffeine for you. You'd better stick to water or juice.'

Leading the way back to the kitchen, he was walking on clouds. This would mean the world to Ellisif, so he hoped she was right.

* * *

'I cannot fathom how a little blue line can tell you there is a child!'

It was a couple of hours later and they were sitting curled together on Ivar's big double bed, staring at a plastic stick.

He laughed. 'It is rather extraordinary, isn't it? You're going to learn that humans have progressed so much during the thousand years since you were born. A lot of things are amazing; some are less so. It will probably be a relief to both of us to spend time with Thorald and Askhild in the past. I'm afraid I've changed quite a bit since I decided to time-travel as well, and I don't like a lot of what I see in my time. Still, I'm looking forward to showing you the good parts.'

She turned in his arms and snuggled closer. 'Are you certain this means I am with child?'

'Yes, there is no doubt whatsoever. I will take you to see a *doctor* – a man of healing – or a midwife soon, and they'll be able to confirm it in a way you're more used to. For now, you'll have to take my word for it.'

'I do.' Everything in Ivar's world was overwhelming and strange, but the one thing she did have faith in was him. He would never lie to her and he would always take care of her, of that there was no doubt. It was what he'd been doing since the moment they met. 'I can't believe it has finally happened for me. For us. I know you always told me the fault didn't lie with me, but it was hard to let go of those thoughts.'

He'd told her to just relax and enjoy their lovemaking, then it would be up to the gods whether they were rewarded with a child or not. Although he had hinted there might be something that could be done in his time to increase the odds. She was glad that hadn't been necessary. The fact that her body worked fine on its own was a huge relief. Now she'd be able to experience the joy of motherhood with the best possible father for her child.

'I shall give thanks to Freyr and Freya,' she murmured. 'Will you buy me a chicken, please?'

'A what?' He leaned back to stare down at her. 'You're going to cook for the gods?'

That made her laugh. 'No, *fifl*. I'm going to sacrifice it, of course.'

'Ah, you meant a live one. No, sorry, but that's not going to happen here. No killing anything. How about we leave them an offering of something else? Silver, perhaps? There is a sacred grove not far from here. We can put an arm ring or two there.'

'Very well.'

There were clearly a lot of new rules she'd have to become accustomed to, but with Ivar as her teacher, she'd manage.

'How will this affect our plans, though?' she asked, remembering the many conversations they'd had about their future.

They had decided that Ivar would take on temporary assignments from the Historical Museum whenever they needed him. Perhaps also join archaeological digs from time to time, if there were any places going. Meanwhile, Ellisif was to learn Swedish, and then they could offer private lessons to re-enactors – a concept he'd tried to explain to her, but which she still found odd – in various Viking skills. Ivar could teach sword-fighting, how to handle an axe and things like carpentry and comb-making, while Ellisif would teach people weaving, spinning and dyeing. Apparently, Ivar had enough silver for them to live on indefinitely, and all these pursuits were only meant to give them something fulfilling to do. It sounded exciting, and she couldn't wait to get started.

'Don't worry about that,' Ivar replied. 'In my time, there is childcare available to help mothers who work, if they want it. I would also bet my last piece of silver that Mia will want to be involved as much as possible. We'll manage, one way or another.'

'Oh, good.' She relaxed again, incredibly grateful for the strange turn her life had taken.

He kissed her cheek and moved on down the column of her throat, making her whole body tingle. 'Do you think our child would mind if I made love to their mother? I'd like to enjoy our time alone together as much as possible before the little one makes an appearance.'

She turned and burrowed into his arms. 'I don't think they will mind at all. And even if they do, I decide and it's what I want.' She stroked Ivar's cheek. 'I will always want you and I love you more than I can say. Thank you for rescuing me, in every sense of the word.'

'I love you too, so much, and trust me, the pleasure was all mine.'

Author's Note

I just wanted to let you know that I used a little bit of artistic licence when it came to the Battle of Hafrsfjordr. No one knows exactly what year it took place – it could have been any time from AD 868 onwards. Most historians seem to agree on 872, but that didn't quite fit with my story, so I made it happen in 876. I also chose to set it in July, before the harvest, although it's more likely to have been late August, when harvesting was done.

As I mention in the text, Haraldr Hálfdanarsson has gone down in history as Harald Fairhair, but there is no real evidence for this nickname. Everything about him was written many centuries after his death. Some historians believe he was more likely called Haraldr Luva – meaning he either had very long messy hair (some warriors let it grow until they attained a specific goal) or was born with the amniotic sac still over his head (in Swedish, this is called *segerhuva* – 'victory hat' – and is meant to signify good fortune to the child, so might be more appropriate in this case). The nickname could simply be made up and based on Germanic myths in which long hair on a man was seen as a symbol of strength.

There is another Haraldr who is also called Fairhair in the *Anglo-Saxon Chronicle* – he is the one we normally call Harald

Hardrada (his real name was Haraldr Sigurðarsson). The name Fairhair would seem to fit him very well, as he was said to be handsome and blond. Perhaps he had several nicknames. We will probably never know for sure.

Some of the other participants in the battle mentioned in this story were real historical characters, but there are few details as to what happened to most of them other than in the sagas, which are not entirely reliable and could be fictitious. I've included them anyway and hope that no one minds.

Acknowledgements

I can't believe this is the fifth instalment of the Viking Runes series and I want to thank my amazing editor Kate Byrne and her team at Headline very much for allowing me to continue with it. I never imagined I would get to write the stories of all the family members and it is a great privilege to do so. A special thank you to the cover designers Caroline Young, Sarah Whittaker and Emily Courdelle for the gorgeous covers – I love them all – and to the fabulous narrator of all my books, Eilidh Beaton, who does such a great job! And thank you also to Lina Langlee, my wonderful agent, for your encouragement and support. As always, it is a huge pleasure to work with you all!

When I first outlined the series, I knew I wanted to set each book in a different location in order to make things more interesting, both for myself and for the readers. As the Vikings travelled far and wide, that wasn't difficult, and it has meant that I've had the pleasure of travelling to quite a few new places for research purposes. For this particular story, I headed to Norway, a country I'd never visited before. It was, quite simply, stunning! My daughter Josceline very kindly came with me on this Norwegian adventure and we had a fabulous time, driving 1,260 km in four days – a record for me. So thank you, Joss, it wouldn't have been even half as much fun without you! And thank you for being so patient with all my Viking research and helping to keep me calm when driving through all the tunnels in the mountains.

Two lovely Norwegian friends, Natalie Normann and Anne-Marie Ugland, were on hand with help and advice regarding travel in Norway. Thank you both so much and for meeting up at such short notice! And special thanks also to Natalie for beta reading to check my Norwegian facts – much appreciated! I really wanted to do your country justice.

One of the places we stayed at was Gudvangen, the most picture-perfect Norwegian valley ever, and home of a reconstructed Viking village, Njardarheim. Fjalar Olofsson, one of the guides there, was incredibly kind, patient and funny. He let us try our hand at shooting with a bow and arrow, then throw a Viking axe at a target – a truly awesome experience and great for research purposes! So a big thank you to him for making our visit extra special.

As ever, thank you to my lovely friends – Henriette Gyland, Gill Stewart, Sue Moorcroft, Myra Kersner, Tina Brown, Carol Dahlén, Nicola Cornick and the other Word Wenches: Anne Gracie, Andrea Penrose, Patricia Rice, Mary Jo Putney and Susan Fraser King. You all keep me sane and I couldn't do this without you!

And thank you to Dr Joanne Shortt-Butler for help with Old Norse words, phrases and pronunciation, your help was invaluable as always.

To Richard and Jessamy – much love and thanks for being there!

And last but not least, a massive thank you to all the readers, reviewers and book bloggers without whom my books would get nowhere! I'm so grateful for your support and really hope you'll enjoy Ivar's story!

Christina x

PS. If you want to keep up with news, behind-the-scenes information and special deals, please sign up for my newsletter – you'll find the details here: https://tinyurl.com/mr3fu9ch

Promises *of the* Runes

Bonus Material

Hrefna's Choice

Eskilsnes/Birkiþorp AD 896

'I don't *want* to marry Cadoc! If you force me, I'll run away to Grandmother and Grandfather in Mother's time. They'll take me in, I know they will. Women there decide for themselves. You said that's what you would let me do as well. You promised!'

Hrefna watched her older sister Estrid pacing in front of their parents, and protesting vehemently as they tried to persuade her to marry the son and heir of her father Hrafn's best friend, Haukr. The whole family were gathered together in a private sitting room, the *stufa*, where no one could overhear. They always met in here to discuss matters of import to the whole family, a custom their mother Linnea had instituted. Hrafn allowed her an equal say in running their domains, and usually listened to her advice and suggestions. But right now, they were both stumped in the face of their oldest daughter's defiance.

'Well, it's not as though you've found anyone else, and you have already seen four-and-twenty winters,' Hrafn said, clearly displeased with how the conversation was going.

'No!' Estrid stopped her perambulations and fixed them both with a glare. 'He's a grumpy, boorish man, and still grieving for his first wife who's only been dead a couple of years. I'd be miserable. He's never given the slightest indication he'd want to marry me either, otherwise he would have done so years ago. I'm sorry, Father – I know you and Haukr have always had the dream of uniting our families this way, but it won't work. Trust me.'

Cadoc had made an alliance with another great neighbouring family three years ago, but his wife had died in childbirth a year later and the baby with her. Although he'd been quiet and withdrawn ever since, Hrefna wouldn't say he was grumpy or boorish, just sad presumably. Surely that was understandable? He needed a new wife to make him smile again.

'I'd have him in a heartbeat,' she blurted out, then felt her cheeks heat up as she realised she'd given herself away. For years, she'd been in love with Cadoc, even though he was older than her by six winters. But she'd always known he wasn't for her. He was destined for Estrid or someone's heiress. Marriage was a game of alliances, as much as anything else, and a younger daughter with a smaller dowry wasn't normally wedded to the heir of a huge property like Haukr's.

'What did you say?' Her father turned his ice-blue eyes on her and blinked. She'd inherited those from him, as well as his dirty-blond hair, while Estrid had her mother's white-blonde tresses and cornflower blue eyes.

'Nothing,' Hrefna muttered, bending over the sewing in her lap to hide her flaming cheeks.

When she finally looked up, her parents seemed to be having some sort of silent conversation, staring at each other. Finally, Hrafn turned back to her and said, 'It might do. There's no harm in asking.'

'What?' She almost dropped her handiwork.

'If Estrid doesn't want the boy, and Haukr wants the alliance as much as I do, I can suggest Cadoc takes you instead. I'd have to increase your dowry, but I can do that. Are you sure you're willing? I'll not have you backing out once we've agreed terms.'

'I am. Definitely, but . . .'

He nodded. 'It's decided then.' He stood up. 'Time we all left. The ship is waiting.'

Hrefna thought perhaps she was dreaming. Everyone was looking at her as if waiting for her to nod as well, but she was too stunned. This couldn't be happening. She'd fantasised about marrying Cadoc for so long, she couldn't believe it might be in her grasp. Swallowing hard, she stood up and put her sewing away in a basket, her stomach fluttering. As the whole family filed out of the room, her mother put an arm round her shoulders and whispered, 'Thank you. You've saved Estrid from having to run away.'

Hrefna wasn't so sure as her sister was volatile, headstrong, and likely to do things like that in any case, but she held her tongue. That was a problem for another day.

They all trooped down to the shore and boarded Hrafn's trading ship which was already packed with everything they would need. It was a few days before the midsummer *blōt* and the two families were going to celebrate together before holding a wedding ceremony. They'd been invited to stay for a week at Birkiþorp, Haukr's domains, as one of his younger sons, Bryn, was getting married to Hrefna's cousin Gytha. The latter's family would also be there and she was looking forward to seeing everyone.

It wasn't a long journey along the shores of Lake Mälaren, and they arrived late afternoon. Haukr and his wife Ceri greeted them down by the jetty, closely followed by Hrefna's uncles Geir and Rurik, and their wives, aunts Maddie and Sara. Children of these couples swarmed the place too, but Hrefna couldn't see Cadoc anywhere. Presumably he was out on the farm seeing to something.

After the initial greetings, everyone headed for the longhouse chattering loudly. It was some time before Hrefna found herself seated next to her mother and Ceri – Cadoc's mother, a lady she'd known since birth and whom she liked immensely. She didn't take much part in the conversation around her, as she'd noticed her father and Haukr repair to a smaller chamber adjoining the great hall, where everyone else sat. Her uncles Geir and Rurik had joined them, and soon after, Cadoc came striding in from outside, heading for the same place. He didn't stop to greet anyone, just nodded to his mother on the way. It was clear he'd been summoned, and the slight frown he wore showed he wasn't best pleased about it.

Linnea whispered something to Ceri, who watched her son as he seemed to take a deep breath before going through the doorway. He didn't shut the door behind him. Hrefna wondered if that was on purpose because he didn't want to discuss anything in secret. Her spirits sank. Everyone admired her sister, as Estrid was reckoned to be a great beauty, and at the age of four-and-twenty winters she should have been married already. She'd had offers aplenty, but stubbornly held out for a love match. Hrefna had no illusions that she herself was as good a catch, and her looks could not compete. She had passed nineteen winters though and it was high time she was wed.

'Let's go and join them, dear,' Ceri suddenly said, standing up. She picked up a plate of oatcakes and a jug of ale. 'We can bring them these and your father can introduce you to Cadoc.'

'Introduce me?' Hrefna stared at her hostess. They'd known each other forever, even if he'd never deigned to talk to someone so much younger than himself.

'You know what I mean. He hasn't seen you for a while. You were away visiting your grandparents the year before last, and last year he was still grieving for his wife and didn't take part in the festivities. I doubt he'd recognise you now you're all grown up. It'll be a nice surprise.' Ceri smiled at her kindly. 'Come along.'

Hrefna did as she was told, mostly because she couldn't stand the suspense any longer. She entered the small chamber behind Ceri, just in time to hear Cadoc snarling angrily.

'So because your daughter doesn't consider me good enough to marry, I'm to accept second best. Is that it? Well, thank you very much, but I think I'll decline.'

His fists were clenched, and he looked as though he was about to stalk out of the room, but the widening of his father's eyes, and the loud gasp from his mother, had him turning around to stare at her and Hrefna instead. The latter felt her insides turn to stone as she watched his face go pale. Then something snapped inside her and fury coursed through her veins.

Taking a few steps forward, she slammed the plate of oatcakes down onto the table and headed for the door, sending Cadoc an icy glare over her shoulder. 'Don't worry. You needn't bother, because I wouldn't marry you now if you were the last man in Miðgarðr.'

Unlike him, she slammed the door shut on her way out and then she ran all the way down to the shore, where she curled up in the stern of her father's ship and cried while her heart broke into a thousand pieces.

'Well done, son,' Haukr muttered sarcastically, before sighing and turning to his friend Hrafn. 'I'm sorry. I guess we'll have to look to your elder son and one of my daughters if we want an alliance between our families. Perhaps we'll have more luck with them.'

Cadoc stood frozen in place, feeling like the lowest of the low. That his father was taking this so calmly only added to his misery. He deserved a tongue-lashing and he knew it. He'd behaved abominably. All because he had felt cornered, even though he knew his father wanted him to be happy, and would never have coerced him.

His mother wasn't quite as forgiving. She smacked him over the back of the head even though she had to stand on tiptoes to reach. '*Fifl!*' she hissed. 'I thought I'd brought you up better than that. I'm very disappointed in you. *Very!*' With that, she followed Hrefna out the door without so much as looking at Cadoc again.

He sighed and closed his eyes, swallowing hard. What had he done?

The woman who'd just told everyone she'd never marry him now had been exquisite, and quite unlike the Hrefna he remembered from when they were younger. Tall and beautiful, like her sister, with a figure any man would kill for, but with a gravity Estrid had always lacked. He'd just listened to her father telling him that Hrefna would make a much better wife because she was hard-working and intelligent, and fully capable of running a place like Birkiþorp. That she wasn't as flighty as her sister and would be respectful of his mother, not headstrong and demanding in any way. It had sounded boring and just like his first marriage, one of duty.

And yet, the only thing Cadoc could think about now was the deep hurt in those incredible ice-blue eyes, so like her father's, and the stunning features that had captivated him instantly.

There was clearly fire and passion in Hrefna, but unlike Estrid, she knew how to control it most of the time. Today her fierceness had been warranted. Cadoc wanted that passion, but he'd ruined his chances of having it without thinking. He sighed again and spoke up, addressing not only his father, but Hrafn and his brothers too.

'I apologise. I acted without thought. If you will allow it, I would like to reconsider and my answer would be yes.'

Hrafn snorted and shook his head. 'I doubt it matters what you want now. Hrefna will never have you after this. I know my daughter and I told you, she's no fool. I wish you luck trying to persuade her.'

'But if I can, you'll allow the marriage to go ahead?' Cadoc pressed.

'That depends on why you've changed your mind.' Hrafn pinned him with a piercing look. 'If you're just doing this out of guilt, she'll see through you and so would I.' He turned to his brothers. 'Rurik, Geir, a word, if you please. Haukr, we'll see you later.'

The three men left the room and Cadoc was about to follow them when his father stopped him. 'Wait. We need to talk too.'

Swallowing another sigh, Cadoc went over to sink down onto the bench next to Haukr. 'Go ahead, berate me. I know I deserve it.'

His father chuckled. 'Yes, you do, but I just want to say that if you're not ready for marriage yet, I won't push you. I was about to mention that but your little outburst didn't give me a chance. I know you're still grieving for Birthe and the babe, so perhaps it was too soon to spring this on you.'

'No, it's past time and you're wrong. I don't grieve for Birthe overmuch because I never cared for her, and only married her to please you and Mother. In truth, I feel extremely guilty about that. The child is another matter, but that was decided by the gods. This . . . it was just my pride talking. The fact that Estrid didn't consider me good enough to be her husband riled me, but I've known her since forever and I should have realised it wasn't personal. She's simply not willing to settle for anything other than a love match. She's said so enough times, and neither of us have ever felt drawn to each other in that way. She's like a sister to me. We played together as children.'

Haukr clapped him on the shoulder. 'And you now think Hrefna would be better?'

He shrugged. 'At least she was willing, and for my part, the moment I actually saw her . . . well, let's just say she changed my mind in an instant.'

An image of her long silver-blonde braid swishing as she stormed angrily out of the room made him draw in a hasty breath. He would bet anything her hair looked magnificent loose. He'd get to see it soon as the girls wore their hair with just a circlet of flowers for the midsummer celebrations.

His father laughed. 'Well, it seems to me you have some grovelling to do, son. Go to it!'

That evening, at supper time, Hrefna sat with her siblings at right angles to the high table where her parents, uncles and aunts, and the host and hostess sat. Cadoc was supposed to sit opposite. She'd made sure there was no room on either side of her, just in case, and her brothers Eskil and Eysteinn flanked her. She was fairly sure he'd been told to apologise, and she was prepared for that, but no more.

As expected, when he came into the hall, he walked straight up to where she was seated and stopped in front of the trestle table. She glanced at him briefly, then stared pointedly at her plate.

'Hrefna, I owe you an apology. I spoke out of turn and I didn't mean to hurt you. Please, will you forgive me?' He sounded sincere, and no doubt he'd be giving her puppy eyes, but she wasn't interested in seeing them.

'Apology accepted,' she mumbled, then waited for him to leave.

'Are you sure?' His voice was slightly gravelly, as if he was nervous.

She sent him another quick glance and nodded. 'Yes.' She

raised her chin, deciding perhaps it was better to look him in the eye. 'You've done your duty. Now you may go and enjoy your supper.' With a regal nod, she indicated that he was dismissed.

His eyes widened, and he opened his mouth as if to say something else, but she turned to Eskil and made a comment about the food. After a moment, she heard Cadoc's footsteps leaving and breathed a sigh of relief. She hadn't broken down and she hadn't cried. That had to count as a win.

Now all she had to do was stay out of his way until the visit was over.

That proved more difficult than she'd thought. Wherever she went, Cadoc seemed to follow, apparently intent on speaking to her. She couldn't imagine why, unless he was still feeling guilty about his cruel words. He didn't need to; she was used to coming second in everything to Estrid. It was just unfortunate that she had heard him. No doubt her father would have smoothed over his refusal and softened the blow, but he hadn't been given a chance.

Well, Cadoc need not bother now.

Somehow, she managed to evade him until the night of the midsummer *blōt*. There was a big bonfire, food and dancing. She'd spent the afternoon collecting flowers and making a wreath for her hair. Then she'd gone to the lake with the other girls and scrubbed herself and her hair clean with sweet-scented lye soap. They'd all left their hair loose, and once it was dry, combed it out to hang in shining curtains down their backs. Hrefna knew hers wasn't as pretty as Estrid's, but it was still lovelier than most, thick and so long she could sit on it.

Take that, Cadoc!

As she danced around the fire with the others, she noticed him standing in the shadows, watching but not taking part. Perhaps her father was right and he still grieved his first wife too much. He may not want to marry at all. But his words had sounded more specific, as if it was Hrefna he didn't want. She hardened her heart and stopped looking for him.

After a visit to the privy, however, a shape materialised out of the shadows and took hold of her wrist. Her heart flipped painfully, and she gasped until she saw who it was. Cadoc.

'Hrefna, please, I need to speak with you. Won't you grant me a few moments?'

'Why? You've already apologised. What more is there to say?'

He shook his head. 'Trust me, there is a lot more. Come, let's go somewhere private.'

She didn't know why, but she allowed him to tug her along past some of the outbuildings until they were standing near the door to the byre. Everyone else was down by the lakeshore, which seemed far away as the sounds of revelry were muted. Here it was quiet, but not dark as it was the longest night of the year, and the light was still only muted.

She pulled her hand out of his grasp, and leaned her back against the wall for support. 'So what did you want to say?'

Instead of speaking immediately, he sighed and pushed his fingers through his hair. He wore it loose this evening, and she couldn't help but notice how wonderful it was. Long, thick and curly, the same colour auburn as his mother's tresses. Hrefna had often longed to push her own fingers into that unruly mass. He looked at her with green eyes, also like his mother's, but currently pools of despair. She must have been right; he was a very sad man and she'd been wrong to hope he could love another woman so soon after Birthe died.

'Hrefna, I want you to know that I made a huge mistake and spoke without thinking yesterday. I meant no disrespect to you. To tell you the truth, I wouldn't have known you unless you'd been pointed out to me. You have changed since I saw you last. For the better, I hasten to add. Much better. You are a very beautiful and desirable woman now. Before, you were merely a child.'

He seemed sincere, and she supposed it wasn't his fault if she wasn't to his liking. She held up a hand to stop him saying anything else.

'Very well. I accept your apology properly this time. I'll admit I was hurt, but only because all my life I have been compared unfavourably to my sister, and I am tired of being "second best", as you said. It was not what I wanted to hear from a prospective husband, and I will never settle for marrying anyone who prefers Estrid to me. Please, let us forget this and put it behind us. Our fathers are best friends so we will need to see each other from time to time. It's better if it isn't too awkward.' She was proud of the way she managed to stop her voice from wobbling. There was no way she wanted him to know how much it had cost her to say that.

'No, I wasn't finished!' He stepped closer and she became aware of just how big he was, towering over her with broad shoulders and powerful arms. Although she was tall for a woman, she still only reached to his chin and had to look up at him. She could smell him too – his scent enveloped her, a blend of pine soap and man that made her shiver.

'Wh-what do you mean?' she stammered, wanting to get away from him, but at the same time needing to be closer. This man turned her brain to mashed turnips.

'I mean, I don't prefer Estrid. Not at all. I want to marry *you*, if you'll have me. I never should have been so hasty, rejecting you without even talking to you. Seeing the woman you have become. One look at you yesterday and you had me ensnared in an instant. Right this moment, I can't even remember what Estrid looks like. I see only you. And I want you. Badly.'

'Me? You want me?' She couldn't believe it. Dared not believe it. She shook her head. 'No, you're just trying to make amends. What did your father say? That you were a fool and had to make things right? Well, it won't work. I'm not falling for it.'

She pushed at his chest with all her strength, but he didn't budge. Instead, he gripped both her hands in his and leaned his forehead against hers. 'Hrefna, please. I'm serious. This has nothing to do with our fathers. Forgive me for being crude, but feel this. They can't influence my reactions to you.'

He pushed his body flush against hers, and she felt the evidence of his desire against her stomach through the layers of their clothing. Her cheeks burned with sudden embarrassment, and she closed her eyes for a moment, blocking out his intense stare. She knew what happened between men and women, and how. Her mother had seen to that. There seemed no doubt he wanted her desperately, but she still wasn't convinced it was her in particular he wished to have.

'Perhaps you just haven't been this close to a woman for a while,' she countered.

He huffed out a reluctant chuckle. 'Ah, you're not naïve then and you know what I'm talking about. That's good. But I can promise you this is all your doing. I've not wanted a woman since Birthe died and that's the truth. I . . . the thought that I killed her by getting her with child was enough to dampen my ardour, believe me.'

She raised her eyebrows at him. 'You can't really be blamed for that.' These things happened, and Birthe had known the risks when she agreed to the marriage. But Hrefna didn't say that out loud, instead studying him intently. 'And now you wish to kill me?'

She knew that wasn't what he was saying, but she was interested to see his reaction to her words.

'No! Absolutely not, but you are not a tiny weakling like she was. I have no doubt you'll bear children as competently as your father tells me you do everything else. And I don't fear making a child with you, quite the opposite. I want to, desperately.'

Hrefna took a deep breath. 'This is a strange conversation. I don't know what to think.' She gazed into his eyes. 'I . . . I dare not believe you. You have always been clever with words. I've heard others say so.'

'Then believe this, *unnasta*.' He bent to place his mouth on hers in a gentle kiss, moving his lips to softly caress hers, over and over again.

She stood still, hardly daring to move. Cadoc was kissing her. *Her!* She'd dreamed of this for years. Yearned for him, and now it was happening she didn't know whether to trust him or not. He raised a hand to push her hair behind her ear, and then stroked her cheek with his thumb while licking the seam of her lips. She opened for him and his tongue explored, pushing against hers, urging her to play with him. There was no way she could resist. If this was the only time she'd ever get to experience this, she was going to do it properly.

Hrefna lost herself in the kiss, and Cadoc seemed to do the same. He pushed her against the wall, caging her in with his big body, but not in a threatening way. She enjoyed the weight of him, the heat of him, and the feel of his hands caressing her slowly, gently. Wherever his fingers touched, they left a trail of fire, and she wanted more. Much more. But he was holding back, she could tell, as if he was afraid of spooking her.

He broke the kiss, his breaths shallow and fast. 'Hrefna, please, say you'll marry me so I can make you mine. I want you so badly. I swear, I'll never desire another woman as long as I live. Only you.'

She looked up to find his mossy green eyes gazing at her as if she was the only woman in the world, and still she hesitated. 'This is just lust,' she murmured. Not that she wasn't tempted too. She wanted nothing more than to beg him to carry on where they'd left off, but she couldn't.

'No! No, I give you my oath. You are not second best, not to me, and you never will be. I swear to all the gods and may they strike me dead if I'm lying. Please, be my wife. Be mine.'

It was what she'd wanted for so long – how could she resist? Even if he was lying, she hadn't expected undying love. She'd been ready to enter into a marriage of convenience, hopefully based on liking and respect. The fact that he desired her, at least, was good. She could live with that. Most men had concubines and although her mother hated the idea and would never have tolerated it – not that she had to, as Hrafn adored her – Hrefna was much more pragmatic and prepared to turn a blind eye. She'd still be his wife, in charge of this household one day, the most important woman in Cadoc's life. And she had to face the fact that no other man would ever live up to him in her eyes – he was the only one she wanted.

'Yes,' she whispered. 'Take me to the forest, now.'

It was where lots of other couples were sneaking off to, she knew. The night of the midsummer *blōt* was made for love-making. The fertility gods demanded it. And she was so ready to experience this for the first time.

A huge smile spread across his features and he kissed her deeply. 'I have a better idea,' he said. 'Come.' He took her hand and dragged her into the byre and over to a ladder. 'The hayloft will be much more comfortable.'

She nodded and climbed up before him. As soon as he had ascended, he put his arms around her from behind and kissed her neck. 'You won't regret this, I promise.'

* * *

'Hrefna? *Hrefna!*'

Cadoc sat up and blinked, swearing softly as he saw daylight seeping in through the open byre door. The tousled woman next to him shot up too, running her fingers through her mussed hair. Her wreath of flowers was long gone and she looked sleepy and content. And beautiful. So lovely it took his breath away.

'*Skítr.* They're looking for you,' he whispered. 'I guess we must have fallen asleep. I meant to return you to the hall, but . . .'

Hrefna glanced at him, slightly wary and blushing profusely. 'I can tell them I fell asleep here by myself. If you've changed your mind, I'll—'

He grabbed her face and kissed her hard, claiming her mouth, plundering it. Then he looked her in the eyes. 'I have not changed my mind and I never will. We'll marry this afternoon. If you're still willing, that is?'

She gave him a small smile. 'I don't think I have much choice now.' When she noticed his frown, she added, 'And of course I'm still willing, you dolt. I've wanted to marry you for years!'

Before he had time to reply to that, she leaned forward to kiss him this time, and he felt a grin spreading across his features while happiness fizzed inside him. He was convinced he didn't deserve this, but if the gods were willing to give him this amazing gift, who was he to argue?

'Good. Then let's go down together. They'll never believe you slept alone, my love.' He smirked as he took in the state of her rumpled clothing, hay everywhere and lips that were swollen from his kisses. If he'd had time, he would have liked to ravish her again, this instant, but he'd have to be patient.

'Oh.' With pink cheeks she attempted to straighten her skirts but it was a futile effort.

'HREFNA!' The shouts outside were growing more frantic and propelled the two of them down the ladder.

'I'm here, Father!' she shouted, walking out of the byre first, while Cadoc stopped to pull his tunic over his head and buckle his belt.

'What on earth . . . ? Hrefna!' Her father sounded scandalised.

'I'm sorry, I fell asleep in here. I didn't mean to. But all is well.'

Cadoc walked out to stand beside her, putting his arm around her waist. 'We both did,' he confirmed, watching with amusement as Hrafn's eyes widened, then narrowed as he took in the implications of what he was seeing.

Haukr had come round the corner just as Cadoc spoke, and he studied the two of them, clearly noting Cadoc's possessive grip on his woman, and the way she unconsciously leaned into him for support. He loved the feel of her against his side, and wasn't planning on letting her go any time soon.

'That wasn't quite the kind of persuasion I had in mind, son.' Haukr chuckled. 'But it appears to have worked.'

Hrafn wasn't quite as amused. 'Do I take it the two of you are now willing to marry? You'd better be,' he added, sending an icy glare Cadoc's way.

'Yes,' he replied. 'We wish to be wed this afternoon.' He turned to his father. 'Do you think Bryn and Gytha will mind sharing the ceremony with us? It saves Mother from having to arrange two feasts.'

'You'll have to ask them yourself and sort it out with your mother.' Haukr clapped Hrafn on the shoulder. 'Looks like you and I have some negotiating to do. Come, my friend. What was that bride-price you demanded? Daylight robbery, if you ask me.'

Hrafn didn't immediately comply. Instead, he studied his daughter, presumably looking for signs of coercion. 'Hrefna, are you sure this is what you want?'

'It is, Father. Most certainly.'

Her radiant smile when she replied must have pacified him as he nodded. With one last glare at Cadoc, Hrafn allowed himself to be led away, and as soon as they were out of sight Hrefna burst out laughing. 'Sweet Freya, did you see Father's face?'

Cadoc joined in the laughter, feeling lighter than he had in ages. 'I'm not sure it's a laughing matter. I was moments away from being killed, I think.' He wrapped his arms around her. 'I shouldn't have seduced you. That was badly done, but I just couldn't help myself.' He kissed her again and it soon turned passionate.

They were interrupted by someone clearing their throat and Cadoc reluctantly looked up.

'Ah, Bryn, just the man I was hoping to see,' he said.

His brother smirked. 'Although perhaps not quite so soon.'

Cadoc sighed. 'No, but you're here now. Let's talk.'

The marriage oaths were sworn in front of everyone in the hall that afternoon, and Hrefna felt as though she was floating through a dream. She was marrying the man she loved, and he'd shown her last night how much he desired her. It was enough and almost everything she'd wanted. As they were, in effect, usurping Bryn and Gytha's big day, they allowed them to be married first, but it didn't matter. As her wrists were bound to Cadoc's, and she heard him utter the words that made her his wife, she was so filled with joy she could burst.

All through the meal that followed, Cadoc was attentive to her every need, feeding her choice morsels of food and sharing a cup of mead with her. He didn't leave her side and kept one hand either on her leg or around her waist the entire time, as if he couldn't bear to be parted from her.

'Oh, you two are nauseatingly sweet.' Hrefna looked up to find Estrid standing in front of them on the other side of the table. A niggle of doubt shot through her and she glanced at Cadoc, but he was merely smiling, and not looking at Estrid with the sort of heated glances she usually garnered wherever she went. Estrid winked at Hrefna. 'You can thank me later. I'm glad my little ruse worked.'

'What ruse?' Hrefna blinked in confusion.

'Telling Father I didn't want to marry Cadoc.' Her sister glanced at him. 'No offence, my friend. I'm sure we would have dealt well together, but there's never been any passion between us and I knew Hrefna wanted you. I couldn't be so cruel as to crush her dreams without giving her a chance. I'm glad you saw sense, *fifl*.'

'You . . . what?' Hrefna stared at Estrid. 'That whole temper tantrum was for my benefit?'

'Of course. Like I said, you're my little sister. I will always do everything in my power to make you happy. Now I'll leave you love birds to it. Congratulations! I'm so pleased for you.'

Cadoc and Hrefna looked at each other, then he grinned. 'Well, I'm glad that was cleared up. Now I understand. Estrid is cleverer than I gave her credit for and she's so right. She and I would have rubbed along well enough, but I would never have had with her what we share.'

'And what is that?' she dared to ask.

'Passion and desire, *unnasta*, and a wish to always be together. I can't bear to let you out of my sight, and whenever any of the other men so much as look at you, I want to growl at them and go berserk. I've never been possessive of anything before in my life, but I swear, if they touch you, they're dead.'

She leaned over to kiss him. 'No need. I will never so much as look at another man while I have you.'

'Good.' He kissed her back, a long and lingering kiss that had her father glaring in their direction yet again. 'Does that mean you love me too?'

'Too?' Hrefna jolted.

'Yes. I love you! Have done from the moment you swore you'd never marry me. I'm so glad you changed your mind, and I feel like the luckiest man in all the realms.'

'You love me? Truly?' Joy burst through her veins and she saw the truth of it in his eyes. 'Of course I love you. I told you, I have done for years. And I always will.'

'Excellent, because I'm never letting you go.'

Later, he carried her into his parents' private sleeping chamber, which they were borrowing for the night, and put her down, pulling her close. 'Now, let me show you just how much I love you. Without clothes, this will be so much better, trust me.'

'I do.' She would trust him till the end of time.

Separated by time.
Brought together by fate.

'Seals Christina Courtenay's crown as the Queen of Viking Romance'
Catherine Miller

Available now from